PRAISE FOR SU[illegible]

“This th[illegible] into the ac[illegible] kground on them, or on the situation they fi[illegible] mselves in. We are told they need to flee, now, and we follow.”

Science Fiction & Fantasy Book Corner

“This is a well-paced, enjoyable read with characters that feel rounded and real… The writing shines.”

SFX Magazine

“*The Waterborne Blade* is an intriguing and compelling fantasy woven from a fascinating story set in a vibrant world inhabited by vivid characters. Susan Murray is a consummate storyteller who fulfills everything you could desire of a book and leaves you wanting more.”

Graeme K Talboys, author of Stealing into Winter

“This is a wonderful thing, a sweeping fantasy which somehow manages to pull off the trick of being intimate and very human at the same time. It begins with a realm in peril, and then puts its shoulders back and strides confidently towards a horizon packed with magic and love and abandoned palaces and a huge and very real evil. Susan Murray has written a debut novel of great skill and depth, and I loved it.”

Dave Hutchinson, author of Europe in Autumn

“The plot moves at just the right pace, keeping it exciting while also allowing some time to develop Alwenna and Weaver as characters. This makes it really easy to become invested in the outcome since you actually know them well. I never felt like it was dragging and it was difficult for me to put it down. I almost missed my MAX stop on my way home because of this book. It's totally engrossing, which makes this book go by pretty quickly, and leaves you wanting more.”

Roberta's Literary Ramblings

ALSO BY SUSAN MURRAY

The Waterborne Blade

SUSAN MURRAY

Waterborne Exile

ANGRY ROBOT
An imprint of Watkins Media Ltd

Lace Market House,
54-56 High Pavement,
Nottingham,
NG1 1HW
UK

angryrobotbooks.com
twitter.com/angryrobotbooks
A deeper cut

An Angry Robot paperback original 2015
1

A catalogue record for this book is available from the British Library.

ISBN 978 0 85766 438 9
EBook ISBN 978 0 85766 440 2

Set in Meridien by Epub Services.
Printed by 4edge Limited.

To my grandmother and great aunt,
who epitomised strength without ever needing to define it

PART I

CHAPTER ONE

He was going to burn. And he deserved it. Until then, Weaver knew only one thing: he must hold the attackers back to cover the Lady Alwenna's escape. Flames crackled behind him, heat snagging at the back of his neck. His padded jacket was drenched with sweat, so heavy it hampered his movements and dragged against his arms. He was tiring, yet the dead-eyed priest before him thrust and parried with his staff, fighting on without any loss of pace. Sweat stung Weaver's eyes and his defence faltered as he wiped his brow. The priest somehow failed to capitalise on Weaver's distraction, fighting like one whose thoughts were elsewhere, completely absent from the moment. There was an air of placidity about the man that was unnatural: his dead stare made Weaver's flesh crawl. He tried to damp down the sense that his opponent would never stop, ever. Had he drawn some curse upon himself for his part in the death of his liege lord? That was nonsensical – Weaver had not killed him. But he had failed to protect his king – or the husk that had once been Tresilian.

The priest's staff connected with Weaver's temple as, concentration fading, he parried the blow a fraction too late. Damn the priest's reach, damn his unflagging determination. Weaver glanced over his shoulder to where the king's form lay slumped on the floor. Was Tresilian really dead this time? Or was the priest trying to press him back towards his fallen king?

Smoke eddied towards Weaver as a draught caused the air in the room to shift and the king was lost from his sight. Had he glimpsed the movement of a hand there, just before the smoke shrouded Tresilian's body?

Impossible. But how many impossible things had he already witnessed since returning to the Marches? Weaver shivered, even as the heat of the flames behind him seared the back of his neck. Mustering all his strength, Weaver launched a committed stroke at the priest, slicing through the man's neck. Blood spurted, but it was heavy and dark, unnatural. The man toppled like a felled tree, legs kicking, grey robes stained with blood that was more brown than crimson, as if it had been dry when it left his veins. Yet that was impossible.

The other priests in the doorway fell back one at a time and Weaver paused to draw breath, dimly aware the action brought little relief to his tortured lungs. The last priest to leave flung up his arm to shield his face with his voluminous sleeve as he fumbled for the door handle.

Too late, Weaver realised the man intended to shut him in with the fire. He watched with bovine torpor as the door swung shut. Smoke billowed across the room in the draught caused by the motion, curling and thickening, sending cloying tendrils into Weaver's nostrils and throat, probing the depths of his lungs. From somewhere Weaver found enough sense to drop to the ground, his thoughts as thick and leaden as the blood from the priest's veins. From behind him came a crash as the tall window collapsed into the room, swiftly followed by a rush of air as smoke billowed out through the new opening, permitting the ingress of fresher air. For a moment of blessed relief he gulped in air that filled his lungs instead of searing them. But only for a moment. The fire welcomed it too, drawing it in with a roar and a surge of heat. The roof timbers above Weaver creaked ominously and he knew – with the reason brought by that moment of unpolluted air – that he must escape that room or lie there forever next to his fallen king. And above all he knew he didn't want to enter eternity at the side of the king he'd betrayed in every way possible – by thought and by flesh and finally by steel. Weaver scrabbled across the floor, heading for the door through which the priests had escaped.

When Weaver dragged on the handle the latch twisted and the door swung ajar. The last priest had not locked it; if he escaped this coil he would offer fervent thanks to the Goddess at the first opportunity. At that moment he noticed he was clutching a handle fashioned in the form of three snakes, not the entwined leaves more commonly used as a motif at the summer palace. But he had no time to ponder this mystery, even as it seemed to take hold of his mind and the snake heads reared up between his fingers, hissing, tongues flicking in and out as they fixed the gaze from their empty eyes upon him. Weaver tugged at the iron ring and the snakes vanished. It was just the ordinary leaf motif after all. He dragged the door open and crawled through, suddenly weary.

It would be so easy to simply lie down and stop. Right there. Only the thought of his dead king's vengeance pushed him on to crawl across the flagstone floor of the anteroom that led to the private quarters Tresilian had occupied. The stone was so cool beneath his fingertips. He might rest there, only for a moment, just to draw breath and gather his wits.

Only a moment.

CHAPTER TWO

She pushed her way through the crowd, unheeding of who she bumped into, who she shoved out of her path. The priests should have let her follow them instead of turning her away. Had she not been chosen by the Goddess for special favour? A broad-backed man was blocking her path. A bucket dangled from his hand, forgotten as he gazed up at the flames. She tried to duck past him. His coarse woollen tunic was damp and stank of sweat. In exasperation she shoved against him with both hands, willing him to move out of her way.

He held out a solidly muscled arm, barring her progress as effectively as any wall. "Steady on, lass. You can't go in there." His tone was not unkind; it spoke of regret, laced with resignation. "The roof's like to collapse any minute."

He was trapped in there, her lord, their king. Why would no one help? "You can't give up. Your king is in there." She side-stepped round the man, but he closed his fist about the fabric of her tunic and tugged her back. "It's not safe, I tell you. Enough have died today without adding your young flesh to the tally."

How to make him understand? He was kindly enough. Perhaps…

He released her garment, giving her a gentle push away from the building. "It's too late to help any in there, help yourself now. Stand clear."

She stumbled away, losing her footing for an instant on the slick cobbles, biting her lip as she lurched against another of the onlookers. The taste of blood sprang hot and alien to her tongue. Wrong. Everything here was wrong. She should be in there, with her lord.

She fought back tears. She never cried.

She stumbled away to the edge of the yard, losing her footing altogether as something in the burning building caught fire with explosive force.

The sound of the explosion from the king's chambers brought everyone to a halt, water buckets forgotten in their hands as a great plume of ash and black smoke burst from the roof of the palace. Shouts sounded from within the burning building. Someone screamed. Another burst of smoke through the roof was followed by billowing sparks. Those closest to the fire stumbled back in disarray, shielding their faces from the sudden burst of heat.

Tad gaped, open-mouthed, feeling the heat of the fire against his face even at that distance. Glowing fragments drifted down around them. One settled on his forearm, stinging the flesh before he could brush it away. It left a smear of soot where it had landed.

"The bucket, lad. Quickly."

The big man next to him reached over and tugged at the bucket handle, forgotten in Tad's grasp. Tad struggled to lift and simultaneously hand over the bucket, slopping water into his loose-fitting boots before the man took it from him. He turned his attention back to the water chain, doing his best to ignore the bite of the blisters on his right hand. Bucket after bucket went along the line, but the fire grew ever higher and all their efforts seemed to be for nothing. Finally the priests called a halt. Across the yard men were pulling down part of the stables in an effort to prevent the fire spreading further along the range. All was shouts and crashes and confusion. Tad withdrew from the commotion, flexing his fingers. One of the blisters had burst, leaving a raw, sore patch of skin. Dirt from the rope handle of the bucket was embedded in the tender flesh. He retreated to a corner of the yard, hunkering down at the base of the wall, huddled over his knees.

His sister found him there.

"Have you seen him?" There was a wild look in her eyes.

Who did she mean? Their father? Who else could she mean right now? Tad swallowed. "No."

"He's in there. I just know it."

Tad drew in a breath, but he couldn't speak. Miserably, he nodded. He'd watched them enter the palace earlier that day. They'd not been among those who had left the building again before the fire overwhelmed it.

She sat down on the ground next to him. Tad shifted uneasily. He was never sure of his sister's moods.

"They won't let me in there. You could try. We need to search the building. Before it's too late." This time, her voice was cajoling.

"If they won't let you in, they for sure won't let me by."

"Of course they will – you're not important to them."

As if he needed that reminder. Tad picked at the torn flesh around the edge of the blister.

"Go on. Try. I already have." She nudged him with a sharp elbow. "They wouldn't let me near."

Tad glanced at her. Were those tears in her eyes? Goddess. She really did care about someone other than herself.

"Where... where do you think he could be?" He eased himself up on his haunches, flexing his arms, which were impossibly tired after all the heaving of buckets.

"Where?" She glared at him. "In the throne room, of course. Where else would the king be?"

The king? He stilled.

"Why? Who did you think I meant?" The glare intensified.

"I... I thought you meant our father."

"Him? How can you be so stupid?" Her lip curled. "That was just a story."

"But you said... You swore..."

She laughed. A hollow, mirthless sound. "Oh, you are such a fool. I made that up. It was just a story to pass the time."

Tad pushed away from the wall. "You lied to me."

"Did you really believe our father would have left us if he was rich enough to live in the palace?"

"But he had to. The King's Men have to swear an oath."

"Ma told me once. We don't even have the same father. Mine was a drunk who didn't come home one night. Yours was some soldier, too poor to pay her the full rate. That's why you're not the full shilling now."

"I'm still good enough to do your dirty work though."

Tad spun away and left her there, his eyes stinging. He was sick of being her dupe, sick of doing what she told him, sick of the taunts that he was nothing but her stupid little brother – and all for what? He clenched his fists and his blistered hand stung. He would show her. One day, he would. He'd be properly useful to her, and she'd have to thank him. And when she did he'd curl his lip and say, "I was going to do it anyway – it wasn't for you – none of it."

The smoke from the fire had penetrated all along the range of buildings, even the basement storerooms. It scratched at Tad's throat as he crept through the disused rooms but he fought the urge to cough, even though there could be no one to hear him. The storerooms were all black with it. It was as well most of them were empty. If they'd been full so much foodstuff would have been wasted.

As he progressed the smoke grew thicker, carrying with it a cloying smell, one he'd not encountered before. It took him a few moments to realise the pungent odour was singed flesh. His eyes began to water and he hesitated. His plan wasn't going to work. The heat may not be so intense this way, but with every breath his lungs burned. He couldn't reach the throne room after all. But had he heard a movement? He listened, nerves on edge, the fine hairs on the back of his neck bristling. He was not alone in that room.

Somewhere nearby he heard scuffling and a pained exhalation, then a fit of coughing, rapid bursts that the cougher could not suppress any longer. Tad scanned the room. A few barrels, abandoned in the corner, and behind them... a foot? Someone lay prone on the floor behind the slight cover. His first instinct was to run. Except... He inched closer, ready to spring away, head swimming from the smoke he'd inhaled so far, stooping so he didn't breathe in more of it as he approached the figure. The compulsion was too strong.

The coughing had stopped. It could be anyone lying there, dying or even dead. But Tad was convinced even in the poor light he recognised the brigandine. It was him: the man he'd believed was their father for a few precious days.

CHAPTER THREE

The stench of smoke clung to everything in the infirmary. It prickled her nostrils and abraded her throat. The priestess suppressed the cough that tried to fight its way free of her lungs. She mustn't draw attention to herself.

Another soldier had died in the night. Only three of those rescued from the conflagration clung to life. Two priests lifted the body of the dead man. She stepped out of the way as they carried him past her to the door. No one paid any attention as she carried a jug of water over to the patients. She replenished the beakers set by their beds, pausing to study each face. One was ruined beyond recognition, his face terribly blistered. He would not see the day out – the Goddess had already marked him for her own. But he was too slight. The next had black hair. He was not burned, but had bloody bandages wrapped about his shoulder. He must have a grievous wound. The third was too young, she guessed him to be not much older than herself, eighteen at best. His face reddened and soot-marked, he lay uneasily on his bed, hand twitching, blistered fingers clenching and unclenching. His injuries were not so grave. With the right care he would live. But Tresilian was not there.

As she turned away from the bed she found herself face to face with prelate Durstan. She hastily sidestepped, but too late. The frown told her she had incurred the prelate's displeasure.

She folded her hands and lowered her head in an assumption of pious obedience.

"Did I not order you to remain in seclusion?"

"Forgive me, sire. I was concerned for those injured in the fire." She risked a glance up at the prelate.

Durstan studied her with a severe expression. "My orders to you were very clear. Until we know if you have been Goddess-blessed you remain in seclusion."

Dare she? The prelate had been well enough pleased with her visions while Tresilian lived. "I... I had a troubling dream, sire. One of the patients in the infirmary – as he slept, an evil force reached towards him. I... I feared for his wellbeing."

Durstan's brows snapped together, his lips curling. "Indeed?" He took half a step away then paused, looking back at her. "Which patient?"

Which patient, indeed. "The young one, sire."

Durstan's lips twisted. "It was ever thus. The proper thing would have been to inform your confessor and he would ensure prayers were offered up for the young man. You will not walk among the brethren again, unless you are proved free of taint. Return now to your chapter house. If you are seen within the bounds of the palace again you will be punished."

She lowered her head. "Forgive me, sire."

Durstan walked away without a backward glance. The slight unevenness in his gait was more apparent than usual and he carried his weight awkwardly on his right leg. He carried his right shoulder infinitesimally higher than his left. She willed the broken creature to trip, to fall. To see him spreadeagled over the flagstones in ignominy... He stumbled, and her heart leapt with glee, but he recovered his balance and, muttering a curse, continued to the black-haired soldier's bed.

The soldier roused and sat up, clutching his injured shoulder.

"I have been told you witnessed a number of riders escape during the fire."

"Yes, sire, that is right. Three riders, two of them women. I did my best to stop them–"

"Well, girl. Do as the prelate ordered you." One of the hospital orderlies waited in the doorway, arms folded as he watched her. His expression was not unkind, but she knew him of old. He'd heard the prelate's command and this would be the last time she could sneak unseen into the infirmary. She'd need to find someone else to keep an eye on things. There were times when it was useful to have a brother so much younger than herself.

CHAPTER FOUR

Weaver woke to darkness. Something dug hard into his hip and his ribs. When he breathed in, pain seared his lungs. He drew a deeper breath and was lost in a paroxysm of coughing. There was no air... He pushed his shoulders up from the hard surface he lay upon, discovering worn stone slabs beneath his fingertips, polished smooth by the passage of countless feet over the years. Disoriented, he tried to work out how he had come to be in the dungeon at Highkell once more. But these stone slabs were clean. A different sort of decay filled the air here: that of dry emptiness, of doors never opened or closed, and of air unchanged. This was a space unused, not overfilled. And the stink of smoke overlaid it all.

He sensed he was alone in the darkness here. His eyes were adjusting to the gloom and he could make out the outlines of barrels stacked nearby. This was no dungeon: this was a storeroom. Some cellar, perhaps, although it was not as dank as he might have expected of a room dug out beneath ground level. It took him a moment to realise the odd rasping sound was his own breathing. Now he began to think about it, the pain with each inward breath seemed to grow stronger. He slumped forward as another burst of coughs racked him. When he was finally able to straighten up he discovered the room was lighter than before. And a slight figure was standing over him, watching, something held carefully between his hands. The lad looked vaguely familiar – Weaver could recall seeing him about the summer palace over the past few days.

With a hesitant smile the boy crouched down. "I brought you water. It's fresh, I drew it just now."

Weaver tried to draw a breath but could summon no air and no words – either for thanks or for questions.

"Drink. It will help." The lad held out the cup with that same hesitant half-smile. Weaver raised one hand and pain tore through his lungs. It took longer before the coughing passed off that time. When he was done the boy still waited there, anxiously clutching the water. He offered it again, raising it to Weaver's lips and he was able to drink at last. It tasted sweet, laced with something Weaver couldn't identify, but the moisture was welcome and he had to fight the urge to gulp it all down. The boy lowered the cup for a moment. "Good?" he asked, hesitantly.

Weaver could only nod. His head began to swim. The boy raised the cup to his lips and he swallowed more liquid down. After another pause the boy repeated the action, tilting the cup so Weaver could drain the last from it. The pain in his lungs was easing, but he felt a cold sweat break out across the top of his shoulders and his forehead. The room slid out of focus, wavering as if seen through a heat haze, then Weaver knew no more.

CHAPTER FIVE

Wine goblet in hand, Drelena took up a stance in a quiet corner of the room. The Outer Isles nobility certainly knew how to celebrate. A sweatier, rowdier bunch of revellers she had rarely encountered. She'd seen a few wedding gatherings in recent years, and it was true, all the good ones were taken – had been for quite some time. Her second cousin Edric sat at a nearby table, engrossed in conversation with his wife. It wasn't entirely obvious until she shifted in her seat that her belly was swelling with their eagerly anticipated first child. Drelena sipped her wine, watching Edric lean close and murmur something in his wife's ear. She blushed, visibly, quite a feat in the already overheated room. Yes, the good ones had been taken for quite some time.

Drelena ran her eyes over the gathering. Her parents had been dropping heavy hints of late. There was another cousin, Lassig, from The Sisters, one of their most recent suggestions. He'd had a deal too much to drink and subsided groggily onto one of the benches lining the edge of the great hall, resting his elbows on his thighs, his head lowered. Quite the catch for some lucky girl. Her father's family was as extensive as her mother's was not. Between them they must have achieved some kind of balance. It was not that she had any deeply ingrained dislike for matrimony – her parents' marriage was a happy one, after all – it was rather that she had met no one with whom she could imagine emulating their success. Lassig gave up the unequal battle to contain his drink and vomited copiously on the floor. No, Lassig was not a promising candidate.

It was time. Her veins buzzed with the certainty of what she was about to do. The matriarchs were busy fussing over – or castigating, it was hard to tell at this distance – Lassig. Drelena reached out to set her goblet down among several other discards, but fumbled as she did so, slopping red wine over her sleeve and the bodice of her gown. "Oh, no. How vexing." She made an ineffectual attempt to wipe the wine off, succeeding in spreading it even further. She suppressed a giggle. One or two of the elders sitting nearby had noticed. She made a play of indecision, then mouthed to the nearest matriarch. "I had better go and change." The woman nodded, returning her attention to the activity centred on the hapless Lassig.

Cursing herself aloud for her clumsiness in case anyone happened to be within earshot, Drelena slipped from the room. Butterflies danced in the pit of her stomach as she made her way out past the garderobes.

She was halfway across the old, smaller hall when the door opened at the far end and a man stepped through. The laughter died in her throat before she recognised Bleaklow, her father's steward. How like him to avoid the feast. Probably working late again over her father's ledgers. He had no use for lively occasions like tonight's gathering.

"Good evening, my lady." He spoke with precision and bowed, correct as ever.

"Good evening. Do you not care to join the others at the wedding feast?"

He straightened up and studied her. The light from the torchères along the walls flickered, making shadows leap across his face, accentuating the height of his cheekbones. "My lady, if you are not there to adorn the gathering, what could induce me to join them now?" He spoke carefully again, almost too carefully.

Goddess, was he drunk? Gallantry from Bleaklow. This was unexpected. For a moment the urgency of her mission was forgotten. This was intriguing.

Bleaklow studied her. "You appear to have spilled wine down your gown."

He looked so sombre. She would love to shake him out of it, if only for a moment. "Why yes, I have. So clumsy of me."

"A great deal of wine."

She smiled. "Yes, it was a great deal of wine. Expensive wine, at that."

"You should change before you catch a chill." He studied her a moment more then took a step away, as if to continue his interrupted journey. On an impulse she reached out to take hold of his arm.

"Wait. If you're going to the feast now... will you wait while I change? I'll be quick."

His eye twitched visibly and did she imagine his mouth pressed tighter into a disapproving line?

"My lady... I would not presume."

"It's a wedding feast. We're supposed to be happy, Bleaky. Do cheer up."

He stared at her, eyes widening in... what? Panic? Or was that something else she read in his expression? Something he tried to keep hidden?

She was intrigued now. "Really, do try. Wait here for me while I change. I'll be only a couple of minutes. Then we'll rejoin the feast and dance the night away. I would like that."

Panic. Definitely panic in his eyes now. The muscles of his forearm tensed beneath her fingers. "My lady, it would not be seemly – not for one of my station."

"Oh, that's nonsense. I never met anyone named so well as you: bleak by name and bleak by nature."

"My lady, I've told you before, it's pronounced 'Blecklow'."

Drelena smiled. She knew she had a winning smile, she'd been told so often enough. "Nonsense. You'll always be Bleaky to me. Unless… Unless you care to prove me wrong?" She leaned closer, her plan forgotten, her discontent, decorum, everything forgotten. She closed her fingers about his forearm. For a moment he tensed more than she thought was possible, then with a muttered oath he wrapped his free arm about her and pulled her close, kissing her hungrily. And what a kiss. It ignited her body so she melted against him, pressing every inch of her body up against his. And suddenly nothing else mattered, none of it, but this delicious sensation as their breath and tongues mingled, the taste of brandy on his lips. Then a door clattered open at the far end of the hall and Bleaklow released her as laughing voices entered the room. They sprang apart guiltily, only to see the merrymakers vanish through a door at the far corner of the hall. Their lapse in decorum hadn't been noticed at all.

She couldn't stifle the bubble of laughter, but Bleaklow looked horrified.

"My apologies, my lady. I ought never have presumed."

"Oh, but Bleaky, you almost had me convinced."

"I am sorry, my lady. It was wrong of me. I swear it won't happen again."

This time her winning smile didn't work. Bleaklow hurried away towards the great hall, as if he feared she'd chase after him. She even considered it for a moment. But that was a moment of madness, and she chided herself for such weakness. It was his loss, not hers. Damn him. She wouldn't be rebuffed a second time. And she wouldn't risk being turned from her purpose again.

She hurried to her chamber in the tower, casting off the soiled gown. As she'd anticipated, most of the servants were enjoying the festivities, as was only right and proper. This was the perfect opportunity. She stuffed the clothes she'd selected earlier into a bag she'd hidden in the depths of her cupboard – she hadn't dared pack the bag beforehand in case one of the servants spotted it. They were a diligent bunch – excellent servants, of course, but too observant to risk it. She extracted two purses from beneath the mattress where she'd hidden them. The slimmer one she fastened about her waist. The fatter one she likewise fastened about her waist, but tucked it inside the waistband of the heavy skirt she'd chosen. The weight of the purse pressed against her thigh, beyond the ken of cutpurses. To complete the outfit she added a heavy jacket and hooded cloak, all garments she'd discreetly acquired on trips to the local market.

She was almost ready. One last thing remained. There she met a slight hitch – the shears she'd appropriated for the task were no longer in her workbasket. After a quick search she gave up and took her eating knife from its sheath. It would have to do. She couldn't hope to pass for a commoner if she wore her hair in the long tresses of a noblewoman. It took a few minutes to hack her hair to shoulder length, not so unevenly, she hoped. She tied it back with a leather lace and took a cool look at her reflection in the mirror above the side table in her chamber. It might be a long time before she had the luxury of studying her own reflection again. The difference without her long hair was already startling; the shapeless woollen garments, just a bit too big for her, completed the transformation. She already felt as if a stranger looked back at her from the mirror. A stranger who was about to embark on the adventure of a lifetime.

Drelena pulled up the hood, took up her bag and opened the door, peering out to check her way was clear. The butterflies intensified. She didn't have to do this. She could step back inside, change her clothes and return to the party in a fresh gown, ready to dance until dawn with the string of eligible nobles her parents had invited. And Bleaklow might be waiting for her after all. He might have had second thoughts.

Her stomach did a tiny flip-flop. To turn back now would be craven. She stepped over the threshold, pulled the door gently shut behind her and made her way out through deserted halls, the sounds of merriment fading behind her.

Even the guards at the gatehouse had been partaking of a little festive spirit to toast the happy couple on their way.

"Leaving so soon?" the guard asked jovially as he moved over to the gate.

Drelena nodded, hefting the bag slung over her shoulder and muttering a word that might have been "laundry".

"Aye, there'll be plenty more of that made before the night's over, I'll warrant. Can't beat a fine wedding for making work for honest folks."

She nodded again, mumbling an approximation of his rather more guttural "Aye."

The guard eyed her, thoughtfully. "Not seen you before. You new?"

"Aye. In from Norport."

"Norport, is it?" The guard drew out a pipe and tobacco pouch, leaning back against the gate. "I've a cousin from there. Jed, Jed Thatcher. You might know of him? Strapping big blond feller."

"Not to talk to. Might have seen him in town." She was warming to her deception. "There's a few that could be in Norport."

He fussed with the pipe, lighting it at last. "Aye, that's right enough. But you don't have the accent."

"I was a lady's maid. The missus liked us to talk proper." This wasn't going to plan. She was used to approaching the gates and having the guards spring forward and open them up so her horse didn't even need to break stride. That was one of the benefits of moving about with an armed escort at all times. She ought to have anticipated this.

"Lady's maid, is it? Job for life, that. What happened? You get to talking improper with the master?"

"I did no such thing! Why don't you open the gate and let me get home?"

The guard drew on his pipe, inhaling a slow lungful of smoke before exhaling it in a cloud that hung heavy and aromatic on the night air. "Jus' being friendly. No harm in that." He grinned, studying her up and down. "Night like this there's no harm at all in it."

"No harm at all if you open that gate now. If you don't I'll be having words with your commander." She straightened up, glaring down her nose at him.

"No harm in it and even less fun." He cleared his throat and spat on the cobbles at his feet. "I won't be holding you up any longer, hoity toity lady's maid who has to take in laundry these days." He hitched up the bar that held the gate shut, pulling open the small pedestrian gate.

"Thank you. Good evening." She stepped over the wooden bar across the base of the opening, hitching her skirts up just far enough so they didn't snag on her boots.

"Aye. It's a very good evening indeed." The guard slapped a hand on her rump, squeezing for good measure. "And a very fine arse you have on you."

She hopped through the doorway with precious little dignity, failing to suppress her squawk of outrage. She spun round to remonstrate with him, but the door slammed shut. On the other side the guard bellowed with laughter. She heard the wooden bar drop into place, then retreating footsteps as he returned to his guardroom.

Curse his insolence. If she'd been of a mind to turn back now it was too late. She turned her back on the gatehouse. The cobbled street stretched down the hill before her, lit at intervals by large torchères brought in especially for the wedding celebrations. The street was quiet now. In a few hours it would be bustling with life again. The tide would turn in a couple of hours and she would be on the first eastbound ship to leave the harbour.

She stepped forward. She would leave the guard's insolence behind her along with everything she'd ever known since she'd been old enough to remember anything.

CHAPTER SIX

Brett peered over the edge of the rocky promontory. The plain was hidden from view as the morning haze hadn't quite burned off yet, but already the day was oppressively sticky. Nothing moved on the plain below. There'd be no travellers now before nightfall. Another day with his father away. Rina wasn't so bad, but... well, his father had been gone too long this time. He was about to turn away when something stirred in the distance. Dust eddying in a stray breeze? But no, the air was too still for that. He studied the ground below until his eyes began to prickle. There it was again, another swirl of dust. And the hint of shapes moving through the haze, drawing closer to the entrance to the valley. He blinked and rubbed his eyes and this time he was sure, even though their outlines were indistinct: horses and riders. They moved across the plain with the certainty of those who knew where they were heading.

He should go and raise the alarm, but he studied them a moment longer, heart in his mouth. The horse in front was grey, he reckoned. Behind that followed a – chestnut? And then a bay appeared from the haze at the back. But even at this distance he was sure. It was not his father's tall bay – this animal was too short.

Brett wriggled back from the edge before jumping to his feet and running. His boots slithered in the dust as he sprinted across the valley floor, then began the short climb to the dwellings. "Horses! There are horses coming!"

Rina appeared at the door of her cave as he hurried up the slope, a cloth in her hands. "Is it your father?"

"I don't know. I don't recognise the horses, but they're heading straight for us. Three riders."

Rina's eyebrows snapped together as she frowned. "Three? Are you sure? Tell Rogen – he'll need to go and look."

Did she think he couldn't count? Always the same – his word was never good enough.

"Quickly, now. Tell Rogen."

When Brett burst in on Rogen still at his breakfast the old man's reaction to the news was more gratifying. He took up his bow – he adhered to the tradition that freemerchants should not carry edged blades – and followed him outside, questioning him for more detail.

"Heading straight for Scarrow's Deep from the south, you say? It could be your father. Or Nicholl. But you say you didn't know the horses?"

"No. There was one bay, but it was a short, cobby animal."

"Could be he met trouble on the road. He has a knack for finding it, your father."

They hadn't long to wait before the horses could be heard climbing the slope towards Scarrow's Deep. From the cover of a pile of boulders, Rogen nocked an arrow and shouted out a challenge to the approaching riders.

"Halt and state your business."

"My business? Putting food on freemerchant plates, as it ever has been."

With a flush of relief Brett recognised his father's voice. Rogen eased his bowstring and returned the arrow to his quiver, before pushing himself to his feet. Brett followed him out from behind the cover of the rocks. Close to he had no difficulty recognising his father's taller figure, riding a grey horse without the benefit of saddle or bridle, only a meagre halter. Behind him, the other two riders were women, both mounted the same way as his father, without saddle or bridle. Both women slumped on their horses. They must have been riding half the night. Their heads were wrapped in scarves to protect them from the heat of the sun and the dust. They rode side by side, until the track they followed narrowed and the slighter-built one reined in her horse, dropping to the rear. She had tanned skin and freckles. Wisps of hair escaped from beneath her scarf; her forearms were wiry, strong.

Brett moved his attention to the woman who rode behind his father, eyeing her with curiosity. She had fair skin, ill-suited to the desert heat. There was something ethereal about her, something he couldn't quite name, some sense of – what, he wasn't sure. As if aware of his scrutiny she looked up and her eyes met his. Brett caught his breath. For a moment it was as if she could read his innermost thoughts. But that was silly. No one could do such a thing. There was a slight twist of her mouth that might have been a smile then she nodded and he found he could turn his eyes away at last, aware of a sudden sense of great grief. Such a sorrow as he'd never known before. He felt strangely guilty, as if he'd intruded somehow.

He fell in behind their horses as they picked their way up the valley. This was something important here, something momentous.

CHAPTER SEVEN

Tad had to balance on a block of wood to reach the sink properly to scrub the pans. The other kitchen apprentices were pleased to shove him off it for their own amusement. Since the fire, part of the summer palace had been abandoned and there were fewer cleaning tasks to keep Tad's persecutors occupied. Mostly he kept his head down and tried not to attract their notice. Sometimes it worked. Other times it didn't. He picked himself up off the floor, nursing a grazed elbow as the two lads hurried away, suppressing their laughter as the cook in the next room growled a warning to them. Tad winced as he heaved the last of the heavy pots out of the stone sink and set it to dry on the sloping shelf beside it.

Other times this had happened he'd promised himself he'd run away, but it wasn't that easy now. He had responsibilities. He hugged the secret to himself: he had a reason to stay.

Tad recognised the familiar rush of air through the muggy room: the cook had stepped outside to smoke. This was his chance. He stepped down from the block of wood with elaborate care and tiptoed to the kitchen door, peering through. The room was empty. Tad spun away on his heel and hurried over to the pantry. He tugged a rough-woven bag from the waistband of his leggings and stuffed it with food – taking some fruit from here, some vegetables from there. Reluctantly he left the grain as he had nowhere to cook it. He risked taking a single bread bun from the latest batch, rearranging the others on the tray so there was no obvious gap. He slipped out of the pantry, gently closing the door behind him then hurried down the corridor. He stowed the bag carefully out of sight beneath a stone sconce in one of the disused rooms before scurrying back to his perch on the wooden block. He was just in time to hear the outer door slam as the cook returned to the kitchen, bellowing for Tad to bring the stockpot through.

It was dark before Tad had the chance to take the food to his patient. One of the servants had noticed a water carafe had gone missing. There had been an awkward moment when all eyes turned to him and he thought they'd guessed his guilty secret, but, no, he'd been accused of breaking it and hiding the pieces. He didn't deny it, hanging his head in apparent shame while he kept his lips pressed tight together, fighting the relief that made him want to grin.

Josh, the ringleader of his tormentors, rounded on him afterwards. "You're a liar, Tad No-name."

Tad shrugged one shoulder, keeping his eyes fixed on his work.

"You're a stupid no-good liar with no family, that's what." Josh shoved him and Tad had to flail to keep his balance, half stepping and half falling from his perch.

"I'm here in the same place as you. Your family couldn't wait to be rid of you, could they?"

That riposte earned him a few more grazes, a black eye, and a sharp reprimand from the cook. But Josh fared little better and when Tad had done cleaning the rest of the pots and pans that evening, Josh wasn't lurking outside the scullery waiting to resume battle. That suited Tad just fine.

He made sure no one was around to see before he ducked down the corridor to the unused storerooms.

The soldier was lying on the makeshift bed, propped up

against the corner of the room, chin sunk in a half doze. He raised his head when Tad entered the room. The soldier's breathing was heavy, sluggish. His chest heaved as he drew in each breath.

"Oh. It's you." The soldier was listless. Even these words seemed to be too much effort for him.

"I brought you fruit. It's good. It will help you fight the infection." Tad noticed the bandages he'd carefully applied to the man's arm had fallen loose again. The skin beneath was raw, red, angry still. He'd cleaned it as best he could, but he worried his best was not enough. How could the soldier be getting worse now, when he'd survived the fire? He'd seemed so much better the first couple of days, but now…? The man slumped in the corner with an air of defeat. A rank smell hung about him. A smell of impending death. Tad shuddered. He knew that smell well enough, having tended the grey brethren before their rites. Of course he'd never seen the ritual itself performed, but he had helped prepare the altars.

The man's chest rattled as he drew in a laboured breath. Tad winced. He needed to get a proper healer to the man, and quickly. But any healer would have awkward questions to ask – and like as not hand him over to Prelate Durstan for questioning anyway, even if they didn't recognise the former King's Man. And Tad would get into so much trouble… But he couldn't abandon his patient now. There had to be a way.

It dawned on him slowly that his sister had been trained in healing arts by the cult. He'd hoped to keep the injured soldier a secret from her. That had been the game, at first: to defy her. Pure and simple. To prove to her that he existed for reasons other than to do her bidding. And perhaps, deep down, he still wanted to believe the story she'd told him about the man being their father. Here, hidden in this room, he could pretend it was true. The shadows were sympathetic to his daydreams. Once she knew, then her scorn would peel away the layers of illusion that he found so comforting.

Tad peeled and sliced a peach for his patient, who offered him a hoarse word of thanks in return. Even by the poor light in the storeroom Tad could see the man's pallor was increasing. And there could be no ignoring the disturbing sound that issued from the man's lungs each time he drew breath or exhaled. The fruit sat forgotten in the soldier's hands.

"Here, you need to eat if you're going to recover." Tad hesitated before taking a slice of peach from the man's lax grip and holding it up to his mouth. "Taste it. It's good. It's the best, brought in for the prelate's table." He tried to prevent his hands shaking. This didn't look good, not at all.

The soldier opened his mouth and chewed the fruit painfully slowly. Tad repeated the process with the next, and the next, until the peach was gone. He tried the same with the bread but the man's strength was spent. "Have some wine, at least. It'll strengthen your blood." He'd heard the healers say that often enough, it had to be true. Surely this would help, if only the man would drink it. He held the beaker up to his lips and the man gulped. As much wine dribbled down his chin as he managed to swallow, but half the beaker was consumed that way, until the man shook his head.

"No more." His voice was painfully hoarse, and the effort of speaking set off a rasping deep within his chest.

"Good?" Tad asked. There was a little more colour in his patient's cheeks.

The man nodded, summoning a tight smile, and he stirred himself enough to raise a hand to wipe the spilt wine from his chin. "The prelate's, too?"

Tad grinned with relief, and nodded. "Yes. I'll leave the rest here for you. In case you're thirsty later."

Tad set the beaker down on the stone floor, within reach, but not so close he might knock it over by accident. "I'll be back at first light. Mind you rest." He left his patient picking at a chunk of bread and made his way back to the kitchens, pausing to wipe his eyes on the back of his hand. Surely the Goddess would spare the soldier now, after all he'd been through? She could not be so cruel. Tad offered up a guilty prayer, hoping the Goddess hadn't heard him doubting her, but he didn't think she'd heard anything at all. And, worse, he didn't think she cared to make the soldier live.

He had to act. There was no doubt his patient's condition was worsening. And he could think of only one thing to do.

CHAPTER EIGHT

The meeting had been going on all evening. Drew flung his book to one side. He was in no mood for foolish stories. Not when something of such importance was happening in Jervin's office at the far end of the hall. The one room in the house Drew had never been permitted to enter.

Not for the first time he wished he had the nerve to just barge in there. How could he help Jervin with the business if he didn't know the half of it? He'd heard enough snippets of conversation – only that day he'd been on the point of returning a book to the library. For some reason – Goddess knew what – he'd hesitated before pushing open the door which he'd found ajar. Perhaps some instinct had warned him there were people in the room already.

Then came a man's voice, raised. "This wasn't part of our deal. News, you said. I should let you know if anything important came up." Rekhart, Drew guessed.

"And so you have, most reliably. I don't see what your problem is. I pay you generously, do I not?"

"Of course. But I must be careful." It was definitely Rekhart's voice. "Carrying word to you is one thing. Tampering with records... Well. The chances of getting caught are severe. I daren't–"

Behind Drew a door handle rattled and he jumped back from

the library door. He hurried on to the stairs and began to climb them, hoping it was not apparent he'd just been eavesdropping.

He risked a glance back from the half-landing. It was only a servant, shuffling along the hall with an empty log basket. The man never so much as glanced in Drew's direction. Wasn't that the way of it: Drew's fate was to be always invisible. With a grimace he continued up the stairs.

Drew had spoken with Rekhart a few times and found the leader of the city watch to be pleasant natured, easy to talk to. He knew he had known Weaver for many years, and had remained on good terms with him despite the price on Weaver's head in Highground. But hearing Rekhart question Jervin like that troubled him. This wasn't an isolated incident. This wasn't the first time he'd had reason to doubt Jervin's... He hesitated to use the word "honesty", but he could not deny Jervin had displayed a certain lax attitude towards the law at times. He knew Jervin had a past – he'd worked his way up to this grand house from nothing. A childhood in the slums of the biggest port in the Peninsula was bound to have left indelible marks on Jervin. Of course, he had to be driven to have achieved so much. But now he had, Drew reasoned, he might be expected to focus on the more positive aspects of his life, to pause long enough to enjoy the fruits of his labours. He might step away from the less savoury business that had brought him to this point, surely? How could a man of his urbane tastes and sophistication not wish to do so?

Yet Rekhart must have had good reason to take issue with the terms of his agreement with Jervin. Drew was not so naive he expected the commander of the city watch to have no dealings at all with local businessmen – after all, information could flow in both directions, wittingly or otherwise. Certain associations were only prudent. But for Rekhart to remonstrate with Jervin – the hitherto mild-mannered Rekhart – for him to risk alienating Jervin, who was famed for his short temper. Well, that troubled Drew.

Jervin had a reputation to uphold, Drew understood that. Jervin's dealings with Drew had always been considerate, affectionate when the two of them were alone. As Jervin's live-in lover, Drew knew a side of his character few would have seen and certainly not his business associates. And yet...

There had been that time, on his way to run an errand of some kind, Drew had passed the parlour door which stood open and seen Jervin in conversation with a number of strangers. Jervin had glanced up as Drew hesitated, nodded curtly to him and gestured to someone unseen who closed the door firmly, leaving Drew alone in the hallway, excluded. That had been the early days of course, while he had still been a relative stranger and Jervin had been cautious with him, but time had passed since then. Drew felt as natural and familiar with his lover as if he'd been family – more so even than that. He helped with many matters of Jervin's business, keeping accounts for his shops in the town. But here he was again, shut out of an important meeting in that room he'd never caught so much as a glimpse of.

Downstairs, a door thudded. Voices in the hallway told him the meeting was over. As ever, they left the house by the back door. Drew eased his curtain aside with a fingertip. The night was still clear, no fog yet, and he could make out the figures as they crossed to the back gate. Two were tall men he didn't recognise. The third was a short, stout man he'd taken a dislike to early on – from the snide remarks he'd made, Drew surmised the man to be a jilted lover of Jervin's. The other was indeed Rekhart, who paused long enough by the lamp over the gate for Drew to be sure. Rekhart looked back at the door he'd only just left, as if he'd return to the house, but then with a gesture of frustration he spun on his heel and strode away, his shoulders hunched. Drew could picture the frown he most surely carried on his face. A footstep on the landing prompted Drew to drop the curtain and move away from the window, feeling as if he'd been caught out in some wrongdoing. This was becoming a habit.

The door opened and Jervin stepped in. His face was not the usual unreadable mask, tonight there was a scarce-suppressed smile lighting his features.

"Your meeting is over, then?" The words sounded more petulant than Drew had intended. But in truth they mirrored how he felt.

"What's the matter? Have I been gone too long for your liking?" Jervin was in a playful mood. His smile was assured as he approached Drew and raised one hand, sliding his fingertip down the front of Drew's shirt, over his sternum, down to his stomach.

Drew snatched in his breath, almost involuntarily, but stepped back. "Don't tease. I'm not some child to be turned from my purpose so easily."

"You have a purpose, do you?" Jervin grinned, unbuttoning his own shirt. "So have I. But tell me about yours first. I like purpose in a man."

"Of course I have purpose. Why wouldn't I? You always assume the least of me."

Jervin dropped his silk shirt on the floor. "If your purpose is to bore me you're going the right way about it. Come now, we have better things to do than argue about nothing."

All Drew needed to do was summon a rational argument. But it always went like this. Jervin had a way of leaving his thoughts in disorder, just when he most wanted to express something he'd barely become aware of. And the sight of Jervin's naked torso was too tempting a distraction. And he was right. Of late they'd had little enough time together, without spending it arguing – over what, in the end? A moment's pique, that's all it was. When Jervin reached out again for Drew he didn't step away. Instead he leaned closer, closing his eyes as Jervin's fingers moved deftly over the buttons of the shirt Drew wore. Life was too short for petty squabbles.

CHAPTER NINE

It was night before the priestess was able to sneak into the kitchen building, long after the evening meal was done. There was no sign of her tiresome little brother in the kitchens. Typical, when she needed him to tell her what was going on in the infirmary. She crept into the scullery in case he was still working, but the place was empty, heavy pots clean and draining by the sink. He might come back to set things square for the night, so she hunkered down behind the door to wait. And wait she did, growing increasingly vexed as he failed to turn up. She was nodding off in a half doze when the door from the storage cellars creaked open. She started awake, startled to find the room was almost dark now as the sun was setting outside. Whoever was making their way in from the cellars was doing their best to be quiet. She didn't speak up, alert for any sound from the intruder – for such it must be. No one else would be sneaking around the stores after the day's work was done. The intruder ghosted over to the sink and she saw his silhouette against the remaining echo of light at the window and realised with another start the intruder was every bit as slight as her brother, Tad. In fact, it was Tad. Creeping around the scullery as if he had no right or duty to be there.

She stayed crouched behind the door, hoping the stone

sconce would shield her from his sight if he should happen to glance her way. He stowed something on the shelf beneath the huge stone sink, then he reached up and hefted the big pan from the draining board and, wiping it dry with a towel, heaved it up onto the shelf where it belonged. He repeated the procedure with the other two pans, wiping each finally dry before setting it in place on the shelf with an odd deliberation. Then he draped the cloth over a rail to dry and moved noiselessly from the scullery, closing the door softly behind himself.

Why was he sneaking around the one place he had every right to be found? She eased herself up from the floor, stretching her limbs. He'd come from the storeroom. Maybe he'd just been doing the sort of things most teenage boys did in unattended places.

Maybe.

That didn't sound like her dutiful brother. He was the sort who was gullible enough to believe all the dire warnings it would drop off. What had he hidden under the sink? She crept over and felt around the shelf. Her fingers encountered nothing but an empty sack, neatly folded and tucked away at the back, out of sight unless someone bent down to inspect the shelf closely. She unfolded the sack, and opened it, sniffing the inside. It smelt of old bread. And perhaps apples. She felt inside with her hands and found a few breadcrumbs at the bottom. She dusted her fingers off on her gown, shaking the stray crumbs to the floor, and shoved the bag back under the sink, not bothering to fold it. It made no sense for Tad to steal food and carry it away – he worked in the kitchens and could help himself whenever he had the opportunity. She frowned. Had that been some sound? She crossed the room to the door and put her ear against it, listening intently. All was quiet. After a moment's hesitation, she eased up the latch and drew the door open, tiptoeing through and drawing it softly shut behind her.

She had to wait an uncomfortable amount of time before

her eyes adjusted to the dark. Only a hint of the day's dying light found its way beneath the cellar door, barely enough to illuminate the uneven floor of the corridor leading to the storerooms. She would be wise to return with some kind of light to assist her. But if she did that, she'd be more easily seen herself. She began to make her way slowly along the corridor, keeping one hand on the wall, testing the uneven ground under her feet as she crept along. She was about halfway to the first storeroom when she heard the sound again, muffled as if some distance away and oddly distorted by the hard walls of the corridor so that it echoed and rebounded. She froze. All was silent once more. She pushed along further, reaching the first storeroom, alert for any intruder, her nerves on edge.

That sound again. She jumped, took a step back, when the sound repeated, and this time she recognised it: a cough. Or rather a series of coughs, half stifled, weak... There was someone in the very next room.

CHAPTER TEN

"This'll have to do." The older woman's voice was parched, as if the desert heat had baked and desiccated her until she was one with the arid landscape. "It's dry, at least."

As if anywhere in this Goddess-forsaken place wasn't dry, Alwenna thought. The woman stepped back, gesturing Alwenna towards a squared-off opening in the cliff face.

Alwenna ducked inside the low doorway. 'This' was an uneven chamber, part natural, part enlarged by previous inhabitants. Sand had drifted across the floor, banking up in a line where the draught through the uncovered doorway had dropped it. 'This' was to be home for the foreseeable future. A bed frame made up of rough-hewn wood stood in one corner, an ancient mattress sagging over the ropes supporting it. It reminded her of the room she had entered at Vorrahan, what seemed like several lifetimes ago. Where those lodgings had been grey and cold and cheerless, this place was harsh and alien, all red sand and desert heat. Weaver had reprimanded her then for being ungrateful. Weaver, who... Abandoned back there at the summer palace, left to Goddess knew what fate. She could not afford to let her thoughts dwell there.

Alwenna returned to the door, ducking outside once more. The desert sun was still low and caught her in the eyes, stinging them. She summoned a smile for Marten's wife, but it was too bright, too brittle. "Thank you. Your generosity…" What? Overwhelms me? Hardly. "I am most grateful."

The woman pursed her lips. "It's little enough. This is Brett. He will bring you what you need." The woman turned away from the doorway.

"Once again I thank you." Alwenna touched her hand to her shoulder in the freemerchant gesture of greeting and leaving. "Your generosity will be remembered."

The woman echoed the gesture, and said what was proper, but scarcely broke stride as she picked her way back down the slope to the dwelling she shared with Marten. Alwenna hadn't been able to count all the doorways they passed, but there must have been a dozen at least: doorways of varying degrees of sophistication cut from the rock. Some were rectangular with regular frames and wooden doors. Others were little more than rudimentary gashes in the rock with once-colourful blankets draped over them in place of actual doors. The cliff was of reddish rock, sandstone, in some places fashioned into elaborate fluting by long-departed water. In other places it formed bellying slabs, criss-crossed by lines of crystal, scintillating in the morning sunlight. Occasional veins of ochre rock ran through it, glowing in the low sunlight. This landscape was as rich and colourful as Vorrahan had been grey and cold, but somehow she found it even more desolate. The red stone was unlike that of Highkell – this stone was softer, more friable. A fingertip rubbed against it would come away gritty with grains of sand, detached from the rock.

"My lady? Tell me what you need and I will find it for you."

Alwenna turned her attention to the youth who had spoken. Brett, had Marten's wife said? She dusted the sand from her fingers, trying to drag her attention to the here and now. The youth watched her intently, as if they were all taking part in something momentous. Maybe fifteen or sixteen, his hair was fastened back in oiled braids but not yet faded to the russet hue she was used to seeing. The line of his nose and chin bore an unmistakable resemblance to Marten. His eagerness was heartening. But where to begin answering his question – they had nothing but the clothes on their backs. They needed... everything... But she dared not suppose the everything she might have expected at Highkell would be available here in this remote spot. "Erin, tell me, where do we begin?"

The girl emerged from the doorway where she'd been inspecting the cavern with a doubtful expression. "A broom, my lady. We should begin with a broom." She appeared no more delighted with their new lodgings than Alwenna.

"Can you secure us the loan of a broom?"

"Yes, my lady." Brett nodded, his braids bobbing forward. "Is that all, my lady?"

"We'll need water, of course. And something to carry it in." Their recent journey over near-desert terrain had brought that need into sharp focus. "Something to cover the doorway, perhaps?" And a change of clothing, and bathing water, and food, and a table to sit at, and... "Erin, go with him, see how much might be done." She felt oddly dizzy.

She watched as the two of them set off down the hill, the lad responding eagerly to Erin's questions. The sun was climbing in the sky and already the day grew hotter. Alwenna stepped into the shade of the small chamber. She set one hand on the rock. It was cool to the touch, reminding her of the day she'd been taken back to Highkell as prisoner. And she'd discovered Weaver lived. Without thinking further about what she was doing, barely able to hope, she planted both hands on the rock wall, fingers spread so she could contact as much of it as possible. But she was an alien thing here. The rock was ancient, laid down aeons ago. It carried few echoes of human doings, barely even a trace of the effort it had taken to sculpt the natural cave into a more serviceable form. She concentrated until the blood hammered in her ears, willed the ground to yield up its secrets, to tell her where Weaver now lay, but its refusal was absolute. She dropped her hands, defeated, and slumped down on the bed. Was this not a freemerchant place, and did not freemerchant blood run in her veins, brought here by the foremost freemerchant of them all?

Perhaps that wasn't how these things worked. She had forged no connection with this place. At Highkell, well, that place had taken her kin from her. Perhaps the secrets it had yielded up were only what she had been due. Or had she earned it through the offering of blood, sweat and tears over the years?

How did any of this madness work?

She must hope the freemerchant elders would know.

CHAPTER ELEVEN

It drew nearer and nearer. Drew twisted and turned, determined to outrun the brooding presence, but it was as if his arms and legs were bound by leaden chains and they would not respond to his commands. Whatever it was, he didn't want to be there when it rounded the corner. He was in a vaulted chamber, not unlike the dungeon at Highkell. That thought alone was enough to fetch bile upwards to bite at his throat. He fought his fear: he needed to be calm and rational to work out the best way to escape. But the dread presence was coming closer and closer. He could hear neither footsteps nor breath, see neither shadow nor form in the flickering torchlight, but he knew it was almost at the corner of the corridor. Any moment now...

He twisted and fought against his shackles, but they still hampered him, all his efforts producing only a leaden clunk. And still it drew nearer. Sweat broke out on his brow. Goddess, the thing would smell him if it hadn't already heard his struggles. So many times it had gone on past, but he knew tonight it was going to uncover his hiding place at last. He pressed his eyes shut, tried so hard not to gasp his horror. Then he opened his eyes, sensing he was being watched.

It took a moment for his eyesight to pull into focus, he was in such a state. It stood there, and for the first time he saw the brooding presence that had been stalking him through his nightmares. Shorter than a fully grown man, of slight build, the creature of his nightmares resembled – indeed, appeared to be – nothing more than a young woman, probably no older than himself. She stepped forward into the dim light that surrounded him, raising a hand to shield her eyes–

And then she was gone.

Drew woke with a start in the pitch dark. His heart was racing and he was tangled in sweaty sheets. The shadow of some menace lingered over him from a dream – or nightmare – that was already slipping from memory. Just some night fear. He stretched, then reached out for Jervin. That was one sure way to chase away the remnants of the horror. He found only warmth where Jervin had been lying, surely only minutes before. Disappointed, Drew sat up. Had Jervin gone through to the next room to make water? All was quiet.

Drew got up and shuffled through. Sure enough the room was empty. Drew availed himself of the facilities then wandered back to the bedroom. The bedcovers were tumbled half off the bed and he stooped to straighten them. Moonlight glanced off something on the floor. On closer inspection, he found it was a coin. He picked it up – it was good luck, after all. He absentmindedly hefted the weight of it in his hand. It was thicker than the coins he was used to handling, but deliciously cool to the touch. He set it down on the storage chest, passing close to the window. It was then he heard voices from outside. He moved to the curtain and peered out. Rekhart again, this time arguing with whoever stood on the doorstep. Drew recognised Jervin's bass voice, kept low so no one would overhear. But not so low Drew couldn't sense Jervin's cold anger towards the commander of the city watch.

Rekhart stepped back, then bowed his head. "Very well. It will be done as you wish." Rekhart walked away, moving uncertainly, with the air of a defeated man. The sight troubled Drew. He slipped back between the sheets, tugging them up off the floor. When Jervin returned to bed a few minutes later, Drew pretended to be asleep.

Jervin climbed into bed and lay down next to him. "Are you awake?"

Drew made no reply. The bed frame creaked and the mattress shifted as Jervin turned over.

CHAPTER TWELVE

The priestess waited on the hard bench outside the room where Durstan worked, her hands folded in her lap. She was taking a risk, demanding his attention like this, but, with a little luck, it would be worth it. The past hour spent sitting there with the hard bench digging into her slender backside might yet prove not to be a waste of effort. She must appear humble and obedient. Maybe, in truth, she was more obedient than she had ever realised. That thought gave her little joy – she didn't want to be obedient to the grey brethren any more than she wanted to be obedient to Durstan. But she couldn't seem to think her way into a world where she wasn't dependent on them for her wellbeing. Maybe that was her true problem, not her fall from favour since the death of Tresilian. She'd had a glimpse of a different world then: one where she was valued; where her needs were met with plenty to spare; where she enjoyed something akin to comfort. And it had all been taken from her. Taken by that woman from Highground, traitor to her own people in the Marches. And with her, that soldier, the one who'd dared to turn against his king and side with the traitor queen. Oh, yes, she knew all about them – or at least, as much as she needed to know. The rest she could guess. And now her brother had handed the traitor queen's lapdog to her. Her foolish little brother, of all people. She'd never expected that of him – nor had she expected he'd defy her enough to keep it a secret from her. He was full of surprises, her little brother. All because of that idle lie she'd told him.

She was pulled from her reverie by the scuff of approaching footsteps. She straightened up where she sat, composing her features into the meek expression that seemed most effective when dealing with the dignitaries of the order. There was no mistaking Durstan's uneven stride, one heel scuffing on the ground every other step.

The permanent frown creasing his brow deepened when he saw her, but he straightened up and the unevenness of his gait became less apparent. That was worthy of note – something she might perhaps turn to her own advantage one day. She pushed herself to her feet and bobbed a curtsey, keeping her head lowered. If he ignored her now, all her efforts would be for nothing.

"You should be in your chapter house."

"Yes, sire, I should." She kept her head bowed. "But I have important news." She risked an upward glance. His expression was forbidding.

"I very much doubt that."

"I will not intrude upon your time any longer than necessary." She hurried on before the prelate could dismiss her. Already he had reached for the door handle to step past her into his office. "My brother works in the kitchens and he found an injured soldier in the storerooms after the fire. He is still there now, terribly ill. But, sire, I knew the man straight away: he was King's Man to my late lord, the same who was in the queen's confidence."

Durstan's frown cleared. "The former King's Man? Are you sure of it?"

"Yes, sire. I am sure. My brother made up a story that the soldier was our father – he is prone to such imaginings – so I knew the man's face immediately. I pray you don't think too harshly of my brother for his disobedience. He has formed an attachment to the soldier, I think, but I fear the man is close to death and in need of the most skilled healers."

"And this man is to be found where?"

"He is lying in the deepest storeroom off the sculleries."

The prelate nodded. "Very well. This information is valuable. Find Curwen and send him to attend me at once, with two priests to assist."

"Yes, my lord." She curtsied as low as she could without overbalancing, then hurried to do the prelate's bidding. For the first time since Tresilian's death something promised to be going right for her.

CHAPTER THIRTEEN

Vasic made no attempt to conceal his impatience as he watched Marwick approach along the length of the throne room. The old man had taken the death of his nephew and heir badly. But it had at least stirred him into action at court – and he was a more astute creature than his nephew ever had been. Stanton had traded a great deal too much on his looks. Old Marwick was made of sharper stuff, but the trouble was just that – he was old. Some of the younger nobles had distanced themselves from Vasic's court since that disastrous wedding. Their excuses were fluent and florid: there was unrest on the borders of their estates; their proximity to the Marches meant they needed to keep a high profile at home; they were all as predictable as they were apologetic. And he had all their names on a list. He would not forget. And when he had overcome recent setbacks either they would step into line, or he would deal with them much as he had dealt with his own cousin. In the end they would be happy to comply with his wishes. Once the first example had been made, there would be little doubt as to the outcome. In the meantime he was watching their activities more closely than they realised. Oh yes, Vasic had been made for kingship. Tresilian hadn't understood the half of it, with all his prosing on about the love of the people. Just like his fool father before him – and only look where that had ended: cut down quelling some minor rebellion in the east.

"Sire, pray forgive my tardiness." Old Marwick's voice was wheezy. He'd lost a deal of the excess weight he'd carried when he returned to court after his nephew's death, but it had already taken its toll on his health. "I was unable to return immediately as the quarter-sessions were not complete. There has been some difficulty over tax collection, as I am sure you are already aware, and I felt it incumbent on me to ensure order was maintained and to make an example of the worst offenders."

The old man's voice caught every few words, and Vasic felt a growing urge to clear his own throat. Greater still was the urge to throttle the old fool, but, damn him, he needed every loyal man right now. Rumours about the Lady Alwenna's death flew about the kingdom. Some said she had ascended to the Goddess's side to receive her blessing and would return to free her people from the yoke of southern rule. Some said she had not died at all, that she was merely biding her time in the wilderness and waiting for the right moment to strike.

Whichever was the truth of it, Vasic was heartily sick of hearing her name. He doubted she could have survived the collapse of the tower. If she had survived, then there could be no accounting for the way her curse upon him had lifted. It was the only thing that made sense. She must have been trapped in the rubble for days before the end. Such a waste.

He realised Marwick had finally ended his monologue. He needed to keep these northerners sweet, and Marwick's family was one of the oldest and most highly regarded. If they'd been a bit more fecund it might have made Vasic's job rather easier. One old man could only stretch his influence so far. It remained to be seen how court loyalty would shift now Stanton was gone – the younger man's sword arm would have been a more useful deterrent for malcontents than any amount of the old man's prosing. But Vasic had to work with the materials he had to hand.

"And is that an end of it?" Vasic studied the old man; for a moment he appeared confused.

"An end of what, sire?"

An end to your endless prating, Vasic thought. But he kept his vexation in check. "Your difficulties in collecting our dues."

"Time will tell, sire. I believe my response to have been adequate."

"Northerners are legendary for their dislike of parting with taxes." It was one of the reasons for the importance of the stronghold at Highkell. A stronghold that was in sorry state right now, thanks to the collapse of the tower and the road bridge with it.

"I cannot deny it, sire. But I have a suggestion to make, if I may be so bold?"

Vasic steepled his fingers and surveyed the old man just long enough to put him out of countenance. "I appointed you to my privy council so you might offer counsel. What is this suggestion?"

"Why, sire, if you will forgive my presumption. You may recall my youngest sister went in marriage to the lord convenor of the Outer Isles?"

Now there was something to catch his attention: the Outer Isles boasted a wealthy ruling family. Fishing fleets and merchant vessels that paid their way and more. "Can't say I do recall. Your sister, you say?"

"My youngest sister. She was blessed late in life by the Goddess, but her daughter – my niece, and their only child – will be of marriageable age now. When last I saw her she was a fair child, very fair indeed. By all accounts she's a beauty now."

"Marriageable age and never yet been presented at court, Marwick? That's lax. Or she's not as fair as you'd have me believe – I have a memory for fair faces."

"Sire, I am convinced you would not find her lacking. She was, I believe, unwell last year when they might have brought her to the mainland. I can assure you there was no slight intended."

"And none taken, unless she turns out to be as ugly as a bucket of rusty nails."

"Of course, sire, as her uncle I am far from impartial, but I can assure you she favours her mother's side of the family for looks."

And her father's as far as wealth might be concerned? Such a paragon would be too good to be true. "Then she should without doubt be presented at court without delay."

"I shall write to my sister immediately, sire." Marwick hesitated, rubbing his hands together. "They are keen now, I understand, to make an eligible match for their daughter."

Vasic steepled his fingers again and surveyed Marwick. It didn't do to seem too eager. It helped a great deal that his last venture into matrimony – one which he'd anticipated all too keenly – had culminated in disaster. A man did not endure calamities like that without acquiring a certain amount of caution. "If they are keen as you say, then they will let the girl be seen at court that we may judge her worthiness."

"Then I shall write to my sister, sire."

"Write by all means. We will discuss her future as we find most fitting."

"I thank you, sire." Marwick bowed, his effort less than elegant thanks to lumbago, and backed away from the throne in suitably subservient position before Vasic waved him away.

Marriage. Vasic had developed a certain distaste for that particular institution. Perhaps a fresh-faced innocent from the furthest corner of the Peninsular Kingdoms might cure a jaded palate. And perhaps not. If the girl were unsuitable he would doubtless find other uses for her.

He watched Marwick's retreating back thoughtfully. The fellow wasn't so decrepit, acted older than his years. He might be glad of a young bride to lighten his twilight years. With his heir dead, he might be ready to reconsider his unmarried state. Vasic was acutely aware of the need to recover lost ground. A rash of marriages throughout the court might be just the thing to cement his new peace. And to secure funds for rebuilding the damaged bridge, at the very least.

CHAPTER FOURTEEN

Brett didn't feel good about following his father like this, but sometimes it was the only way to find out what was happening. From the room he shared with his brothers, deep at the back of the cave, he'd heard his parents talking, long into the night. What with the snuffling of his younger brother and the snores of his older one, he'd not been able to catch many words, but he knew they hadn't been in agreement over something. And he guessed that something was the Lady Alwenna.

She was the most exotic creature to have been seen at Scarrow's Deep. He'd been thrilled beyond measure to learn she was an actual royal queen – and true heir to the throne of the Marches, too. His father would set her back on her throne and he, Brett, would become a knight of her court. She would smile upon him for his bravery...

He was pretty sure his stepmother didn't agree with his father's plans, and wouldn't agree with his own plans if he told them to her. But for many years he'd simply elected not to tell her what was in his head, that way his dreams couldn't be trampled under her proficient feet. Yet she wouldn't have him travelling about the country with his father, learning the trade, either. He was old enough, and then some – plenty of his friends had been on the road with the caravans since they were twelve. Here he was, nearly sixteen and knew nothing of what it truly meant to be a freemerchant. He knew his father went to places other freemerchants wouldn't venture, and handled business other freemerchants saw no value in. That was why he'd brought the deposed queen here, after all. And Brett was burning to find out everything he could. About her, about his father's world, about... Well, everything. Everything beyond the arid confines of Scarrow's Deep.

Brett peered out from behind the pile of boulders. His father stood by their mother's grave, his head bowed. Brett wondered if he was actually talking to her. His heart sank – it looked as if his father was not after all engaged on some mysterious business. He felt a twinge of guilt for eavesdropping on a private moment, but it was not long lived as he heard the footfalls of someone approaching along the path from the settlement. Hastily he checked over his shoulder to be sure his hiding place was secure, and breathed a sigh of relief. One of the elders was making his way along the path, leaning on a wooden staff to keep the weight off an ageing hip.

The grizzled beard marked him out as old Brennan. Brett's father raised his head and turned away from the grave.

"Ah, Brennan, I should have known you'd be the first." Smiling, he walked over to meet Brennan on the path, and accompany him to the area where various stones had been set out as rudimentary seats. Marten helped him settle on a boulder, but remained standing himself, pacing restlessly. There was no sign of anyone else on the path. Were they waiting for more?

"Jenna said she would join us if she could, but Virrin's time is close and she's far from well."

"I'm sorry, I did not know. May the Hunter and the Goddess together protect her."

"Your good wishes are welcome, Marten, but your apology is unnecessary."

"No, I should have known. I've been away too long. I've

returned to find my children grown into full men I scarce recognise. And all for what, Brennan? Was it worth it?"

Brennan tilted his head. "The lady queen is safe, is she not? You hold an important card, however the gods deal the next hands."

"But Brennan, was it worth it?" Marten turned about again, moving closer to the boulder where Brett crouched in hiding. "I took her into such a nest of vipers at the summer palace. I could not have lived with myself had I left her there. And even at the end I was fool enough to believe Tresilian might be persuaded to honour his word. No, I will admit to you things there went from bad to worse so swiftly I was caught badly unprepared. I count myself fortunate to have escaped with my life."

"You know there are many who will say it is what you deserve for treating with the landbound."

"But they still have all the advantages, Brennan. We cannot fight them by traditional means, so we must persuade them by other methods."

"Again, there are those who will say we need neither fight nor persuade them, but simply carry on as we have been."

"What, have they talked you round to their way of thinking in my absence?"

Brennan laughed. "I'm not such an old relic, Marten, as well you know. If we do not embrace change, the freemerchant ways will be as nothing in another generation. We will be swept away like sand from the rock face here, leaving no trace but the dust of our passing."

Marten paused in his pacing to and fro. "Some would say that would be better than changing."

"I never shall. And nor will you. Plenty agree change is necessary."

"And have any agreed to have their children taught to wield an edged weapon?"

The old man shook his head. "You might have led them by example there."

"Rina wasn't keen. I would have taken the boys to Highkell to be fostered there a while, but… she wasn't keen on that, either. I confess as things worked out it is as well they were safe here. My friend, it's such a mess."

"Rina will come round eventually. She always does – her bark's worse than her bite."

"Not this time. She thinks a broken queen is a poor gift to bring her after such a long absence. I cannot help but see her side of things."

Brett had never heard his father sound defeated before. He was used to hearing laughter, larger-than-life plans and ambition to match. But he had a bit more insight into what his parents had been talking over in the night – and the tense time before his father had left the year before. There had been much talk about travelling to Highkell and seeing how the landbound lived there. He'd been bitterly disappointed when the time came for the caravan to depart and he and Malcolm were not part of it. Hearing that may have been Rina's doing… No, he didn't want to dwell on that.

His father and Brennan continued to speak in low voices, but a slight breeze picked up, sending sand across the ground and making just enough noise to prevent him hearing what they were saying.

Not long after that the two men made their way back up the slope towards the settlement together. Brett remained behind his boulder, brooding over what he had heard. If things had been different, he might have been at Highkell now. He might have been caught in the collapse of the tower. Or he might have been squire to some knight by now, and safe away from all that. So many 'might have beens'. Instead, here he was, hiding behind a boulder at Scarrow's Deep in order to get some hint of what was really going on. Almost sixteen years old and still treated like a child. He'd done everything that was required of him, proved himself responsible in every way he'd been given the opportunity, yet... Surely he was old enough to be told something of the adults' concerns? And how would he prove himself worthy if he was never given the opportunity?

Maybe it was for him to make his own opportunity.

CHAPTER FIFTEEN

Lord Convenor Etrus of the Outer Isles gestured to the serving boys to bring him more wine.

"And for our esteemed guest."

His esteemed guest tilted his head politely. "You are too kind, Lord Convenor."

Both men were still the safe side of drunk, after several courses of food, several hours of drinking and a few meagre minutes spent discussing the real object of the dignitary's visit.

Bleaklow, seated further down the table, watched in fascination. The Lord Convenor Etrus, of course, was a well-built – if not outright bulky – man and his frame could absorb prodigious amounts of alcohol. But the dignitary from Vasic's court was best described as skinny, tall with it, to be fair, but he hardly seemed to have the bulk to absorb the half of what he'd put away that day. Bleaklow watched in admiration as the pair of them danced in delicate conversation around the issue at hand. His admiration for his liege lord increased – even though he had not thought such a thing possible in peacetime – with every carefully calculated sentence. And given the matter foremost in both the men's minds, he could only admire his lord's forbearance the more. No one looking on could guess at the weighty matters preying on his mind at present.

Bleaklow could only admire the sheer stubbornness of the

two engaged in diplomatic wrangling over the table, as they negotiated peace terms in the most roundabout of ways. Long may that peace last: it was imperative that these talks with King Vasic's representative went well. Vasic had a reputation for being too easily offended and since his reach had extended to include Highkell and all of Highground around it, it behove Lord Etrus to keep on his good side. Even if it meant offering up his beloved daughter as marriage material.

"I look forward to meeting your daughter, my lord. It is a great disappointment that she is unable to join us this evening, for her looks are already spoken of with great favour in Lynesreach."

"We are as disappointed as you, Sir Kaith. It is unfortunate she should become indisposed."

"It is often the way after a large gathering such as your nephew's recent wedding. People meeting from all corners of the land, after all, bring new illnesses in their wake."

Did Kaith know? Bleaklow listened intently as his lord calmly deflected the gambit.

"Indeed. We can travel so far, so fast, yet we cannot outstrip contagion. Would you care for more wine, Sir Kaith?"

Sir Kaith accepted graciously. Bleaklow began to suspect he was pouring half of it down his sleeve, but could see no evidence of it. There was even less evidence of Kaith having consumed all that wine in the first place. Was he one of those who drank so much he never sobered up? A strange choice on Vasic's part to handle such delicate business, if that were the case, for all the man had polished manners and breeding.

"Will I have the opportunity to speak to your daughter tomorrow, perhaps? I heard many compliments on her good looks from the wedding guests who had already returned to the mainland. She was quite the topic of conversation, as I'm sure you can imagine."

Goddess, he knew. He must know. Or why hint so bluntly?

Bleaklow held his breath as Etrus considered his answer.

"She favours her mother for looks – except, as I'm sure you would agree had you been able to meet her – she exceeds her mother's beauty at that age."

"I await our introduction even more eagerly than ever. It is a great shame her illness prevents her travelling to court on this occasion."

"A great shame," Etrus replied smoothly. "Fortunately the portrait artist has almost finished her likeness and you will be able to take that to King Vasic, so he may judge for himself whether or not reports of her good looks have been exaggerated."

Kaith bowed and nodded, and pursued the matter no further, but there had been some sharpness about his eyes that led Bleaklow to suspect he knew rather more about the Lady Drelena than he chose to admit. He would require careful watching for the remainder of his stay at the palace. Bleaklow had already caught him poking around a wing of the palace where he had no business being. Lost, he had claimed.

Shortly after that Kaith claimed tiredness and withdrew from the feasting hall. Bleaklow watched him make his way down the length of the room, his steps perfectly measured and even. Consummate courtier and consummate drinker. Bleaklow nodded to a manservant who waited near the door. The manservant indicated acknowledgment with the slightest tilt of his head and followed Kaith out, keeping a discreet distance. The fellow wouldn't be poking his diplomatic nose anywhere it wasn't wanted tonight, that much was sure.

Bleaklow was taken aback to hear himself addressed in a low voice by the lord convenor. "I beg your pardon, sire?"

"I take it you have no further news for me?" Etrus turned piercing brown eyes upon him – startlingly like his daughter's. He was staring at Bleaklow as intently as she had stared the night of her cousin's wedding, when he'd come to his senses after exceeding the bounds of propriety.

Bleaklow blinked and lowered his eyes. "I fear not, sire. I continue to make discreet enquiries, but can find no word of her whereabouts."

"Then be more forthright, Bleaklow. This charade has gone on long enough. We need to find her now."

CHAPTER SIXTEEN

Tad couldn't find his sister in any of the usual places. He'd even tried the infirmary, in case she'd been released from her seclusion and not thought to tell him. It was when he'd given up and was crossing the quadrangle on his way back to the kitchen wing that he caught sight of her, on the far side of the cloister, hurrying in the opposite direction.

"Hey, wait!" He turned and ran across the yard. He would have called out her name, but their old names had been set aside when they joined the order, a symbol of their rebirth in purer, chaste forms. In truth, he was no longer sure what hers had even been. He had sometimes wondered if she'd even had one. She had all the memories of their childhood home before the order, and she'd never mentioned their old names at all. As for himself, he was well enough suited with Tad. She'd often spoken about the name she might take upon becoming blessed by the Goddess; most of her choices had been long and complicated until she'd settled on the name Ilsa. He'd not bothered to point out to her that in the end it wouldn't be her choice at all, but a name would be bestowed upon her by the order.

Even after he shouted out her chosen name she hurried on her way without giving any sign of having heard him, so he had to sprint to catch up with her.

"Wait up!" It took him a moment to catch his breath.

She watched him gasping, with a frown creasing her forehead. "I haven't any time to waste, Tad. I'm in a hurry."

"I– I just wanted to..."

The frown deepened.

"I... need to ask a favour. I need your help."

She folded her arms, her mouth tightening in a straight line. "And what idiotic thing have you done this time?"

Tad hesitated. "You know when you wanted me to search the fire?"

"You mean when you refused to help me?" Her lip curled. "And now you want me to help you?"

"It's not the same. This is different. I wouldn't ask if it wasn't really important."

"Really important? Oh, you fool. I already know." She smiled, that humourless smile Tad knew so well. His stomach sank down to his tattered boots. "You've got that soldier hidden away in the cellars."

She spun away from him, laughing. "What did you imagine you could do for him? What do you even know about healing? I know more about it than you could ever hope to learn. If you'd come to me in the first place I might have been able to save him. But it's too late and he's dying. He might already be dead." She turned to face him again, face composed in a holier-than-thou expression. "But of course you didn't, because you're a fool. And now he's bound to die because of you."

She spun away again and hurried off along the cloister. Tad realised with a sinking heart she was heading straight for the prelate's offices. How had she even found out? Had she used that sight the order guarded so jealously?

And worse still, was she right? Was the soldier really at death's door? Goddess, let it not be so.

Tad turned back to his original destination. If she refused to help... She already had... But... Was she going to report him to the prelate? He trailed reluctantly back to the kitchen wing.

The cook looked up as soon as he stepped inside the door. "Lad, there's pans need scouring. Where do you think you've been all this time? Your break was over long ago. You'll do extra tonight when we're finished and scrub the floors right through."

Tad bowed his head. "Yes, sir." He trailed through to the scullery, disconsolate, calculating how soon he could slip through to check on his patient. A great pile of pans waited by the sink – he might almost believe the cook had dirtied extra ones on purpose to hold him back.

As it was, Tad had only started on the second pan when the prelate arrived, accompanied by the head cook, with three of his subordinates in his wake and following behind them, hands clasped demurely before her, his sister. Perched on the wooden block that raised him up to reach the sink, Tad could only turn and watch as they opened the door to the storerooms. The cook glanced a warning his way, making a sharp gesture with his head towards the sink and Tad turned back to the pans in his care, risking the odd surreptitious glance over his shoulder.

Several uneasy minutes went by before the party returned, two brethren half-carrying the inert soldier between them, supporting his shoulders and upper body while his feet dragged: he appeared unable to coordinate sufficiently to walk between them. In the light of the scullery his face was pale and drawn. He did indeed look close to death's door. The two brethren dragged him to the outer door, which was opened and closed again by the third brother. The prelate stepped through the door next and his eyes turned to Tad, with not a hint of a smile on his face. The blood in Tad's veins turned to ice.

The cook stepped through the door behind the prelate, and after him his sister, her features arranged in her best pious expression.

The cook moved over to the sink. "Leave those pots now, lad.

The prelate wants a word with you." He wiped his hands on the cloth he habitually carried, and turned to the prelate. "He's a good lad, sire. Always obedient. Willing and a hard worker."

The prelate inhaled, raising one eyebrow. "An obedient worker would not conceal known criminals in his employer's premises."

The cook turned back to Tad. "Step down now, Tad. Best not to keep the prelate waiting."

Tad obeyed, stumbling slightly as he reached the uneven floor. Behind him he could hear gleeful whispers from the other kitchen boys who must be watching at the door. He felt his skin flushing deep red under the scrutiny of the prelate.

"Brother Joran, take the boy and prepare him for questioning." The prelate seemed almost bored by this turn of events as he gave the order.

The priest took Tad by the shoulder, not ungently, and steered him to the outer door.

The cook spoke up once more. "As I said, sire, I can vouch for the boy's character."

The prelate made no reply that Tad could hear. Tad felt a sudden glow of affection for the gruff cook. If he was prepared to speak up for him like that, everything would be all right, wouldn't it?

CHAPTER SEVENTEEN

Drew woke with a fuzzy head. He'd not felt this rough in a long time. It reminded him of how he'd sometimes felt at Vorrahan, after lessons with Gwydion: tired, while every bone in his body ached and a sharp pain had settled behind his forehead. Beside him, Jervin slept on. Drew pushed himself up from the mattress and swung his feet to the floor, setting them down on luxurious carpet. Jervin had imported it from some distant place overseas. It was woven with rich colours, an abstract design of such complexity he never ceased to marvel at the ingenuity of its creators. Elaborate swirls and spirals and stylised mythical beasts entwined in a never-ending dance around the border. The centre was filled with self-contained panels made up of similar motifs, although the stylised creatures could only be identified in the border, as if they patrolled the perimeter to contain the energy of the pattern. He trod carefully over the carpet, and reached for the ewer to fill the small basin. The floorboards at the edge of the room were cool beneath his feet. Jervin slept on. Drew splashed his face with water. It eased the ache in his forehead, even though it was not as cool as freshly drawn water.

Behind him, Jervin stirred and sat up, rubbing his eyes. "You're up early."

"Sorry, I didn't mean to wake you." The daylight streaming

in around the edges of the curtains told him it was not so terribly early anyway. It was rare for Jervin to sleep in. "You were late last night."

"Not that late. Come back to bed awhile." Jervin turned back the covers, smiling lazily. It was a smile that could melt greater resolve than Drew had ever had.

"I– I have a headache. I need some fresh air, I think." Drew didn't want to turn him down – in fact he couldn't think of a time when he had before. "Really. I'm feeling quite off-colour this morning."

Jervin's mouth twisted in – Drew hoped – disappointment. But it looked a lot like disapproval from where Drew stood. Goddess knew he'd seen enough of it in his short lifetime to be able to recognise it.

"Maybe later, when I've cleared my head?" Drew felt he should make amends somehow.

"Goddess, no. If you're hatching some dire illness I don't want it." Jervin threw the covers back and stood up, stretching luxuriously, displaying every lean, muscled inch of his body. Drew couldn't help staring: that was one sight he might never get enough of. Jervin picked up his robe which he'd left on the floor the night before and pulled it on, knotting the belt carelessly. He grinned at Drew. "Your loss. I'll be busy later – I've a lot to get through today. I'll be back late."

Again. Drew nodded, wincing as his head throbbed at the movement.

"I'll need to go through the accounts tomorrow. You'll have the books ready, of course."

"Of course."

"I always knew you were more than just a pretty face." Grinning, Jervin strode out of the door, leaving Drew to his headache and a sense of having been ill used. He splashed his face once more with water from the ewer. As he reached for the towel something fell to the floor with a clatter. He stooped and picked it up. The coin he'd noticed yesterday. He'd forgotten all about it. By the daylight getting into the room around the curtains he could see it was not some local coin, as he'd assumed last night. In fact it was utterly unfamiliar. He'd grown used to handling various coins from the Marches as well as those from Highground, since he'd been working for – he couldn't say "with" – Jervin, but this was different again. Thicker, made from a different metal, but too worn for him to make out the lettering around the face of it. He'd ask Gurney in the counting house, he'd know it.

Drew forgot all about the indifferent start to the day as he became absorbed in the bookkeeping. Whatever bad memories he might have about his time at Vorrahan, he would be eternally grateful for the skills he had been taught there. Without the librarian's patient tuition he'd never have mastered this work with numbers so readily. He'd completed the accounts up to date, all ready for Jervin's inspection tomorrow. He straightened up and stretched, stifling a yawn. He'd worked through most of the day, even though it seemed little time had passed since lunch. Gurney was standing up, setting his desk straight when Drew remembered the strange coin.

"Oh, before you go, I wanted to ask you about this." He fished in his scrip for the coin, and held it out for Gurney's inspection. The old man peered at it.

"Now, you don't see many of those in these parts. It's a southern guinea. No use here at all, unless you know someone who's bound for Highkell or the sea ports. Worth some then, of course. But if you don't, then you've been cheated."

"Really? How so?"

"Traders are supposed to surrender them for local coin when they land from seagoing vessels, or cross through Highkell from the south. So's the administration can take their cut in tax. They're not legal to use otherwise – stops traders dodging taxes. Not even freemerchants are meant to carry them."

"I see." Drew studied the coin in his hand.

"Of course, making the rules and enforcing them's another matter. But if the powers that be find you trying to spend one of those in the north, there's the import tax and a hefty surcharge to pay on top."

"I won't be trying to spend it then."

"Might be worth waiting to see what our new king does. It was one of the peace terms the late king's father – Goddess grant them both rest – agreed. I've heard it was pretty unpopular with southern folk. Could well be King Vasic has plans to do away with it – and draw the north's teeth at the same time, I've no doubt."

Drew tucked the coin away in his scrip. "You think that's likely? I doubt I'll be venturing near Highkell any time soon."

Gurney pulled on his cloak. "Likely? Oh, yes. We'll be seeing some changes before Vasic's done, you mark my words."

CHAPTER EIGHTEEN

Goddess, what had they fed him? Weaver's head spun. His eyes were closed, but still the dizziness raced through his skull, rushed through his ears with every beat of his heart. And Goddess, the pain. His chest burned with every inward breath. Was this the price he must pay for betraying his own king? Should he have burned back there in the palace, instead of crawling to safety like the craven coward he was? Was he finally being brought to account?

He cracked his eyes open. The room spun about him. It was light enough to see that, at least. Where was he? There wasn't much light – did that mean it was night, and the room was lit by candles? No, for all his dizziness the light was constant, he could sense it, the steady glow of early daylight, but Goddess, would it not stay still? He pressed his eyes shut, then eased them open a fraction. Better this time. He was looking up at a ceiling. Plain, flat, whitewashed a long time ago. A layer of grime and dust and cobwebs adhered to the surface above him. He could be anywhere. Had the storeroom had a vaulted ceiling or flat? He couldn't recall. This place was lighter though, for sure. He thought he heard a movement nearby and twisted his head. Was that a door? Everything pitched dizzyingly from the unguarded motion. He pressed his eyes shut again.

"Does it hurt?" The voice was a young woman's, sweet,

perhaps too sweet to be true. A Marches accent. She may even have been from the same small town as his wife...

Where was the crazy boy? How had he come here? He opened his mouth to speak, but no sounds emerged beyond a harsh croak. He closed his mouth again, opening his eyes a slit to see if he could see the speaker. The room pitched less violently now, but it was still enough to turn his stomach. He closed his eyes again.

A hand pressed on his shoulder, oddly insistent. Sharp, prodding at him. "It does hurt, doesn't it? Are you even awake?" Not so sweet now.

He eased his eyelids open once more and could see a figure moving around. Too close to focus, nothing but a blur. Then his other senses stirred, bringing him a familiar flowery scent. Soap? His... wife? She had used soap with that scent.

"Erian?" He forced the syllables between parched lips.

The hand pinched the flesh of his shoulder. "No, you fool. I have no name here."

This made no sense. Weaver took another inward breath, more hasty, and his chest rattled. A cough escaped. And having coughed once, he had to cough again and again, each more painful and gut-rending than the last. Finally, exhausted, the coughing stopped. It was silent in the room again. The daylight remained steady, as before. The young woman, whoever she was, seemed to have gone. Good. He hadn't liked her.

This time the dizziness had faded, but the pain in his chest weighed down on him like a boulder. He could remember now, being dragged along between two priests, face down, feet trailing. The one on the right had stunk of sweat. They'd brought him here, dropped him on this – bed? – without ceremony. Then they'd forced liquid of some kind between his lips. That was it. They had fed him something. He could recall much more clearly. But Goddess, the pain...

"You're awake." The young woman's voice. The rustling

of skirts as she crossed over to his side. She must have been watching him this whole time – he had no idea how long, but guessed it might have been as much as an hour. "Does it hurt again?"

Weaver nodded minutely, a tiny gesture, wary of setting the room spinning once more. For now the room held its peace.

"It'll hurt worse by the end." Her tone was indifferent. "But they want you alive, so until then I've to physic you." When she bent over him, holding out a deep-sided spoon, her eyes were cold as a shadow on winter snow – the palest grey. He'd seen those eyes before, somewhere. She pressed the spoon against his lips, pouring syrupy fluid over them. Some ran down his chin, before he twisted his head away and the rest spilled over his neck. He wanted nothing from this creature.

"Don't be stupid. Or would you rather die in agony?"

He might, before he accepted anything from her.

There was a rustle of skirts as she turned away, the clink of a glass stopper. She was refilling the spoon.

"This will make you feel better." The saccharine note had returned to her voice. A hand clamped over his nose, thumb and forefinger digging into his jaw muscles. He tried to struggle, but he hadn't the strength to shake off her grip. The instant he parted his lips to draw breath, she jammed the spoon between his teeth and he had to swallow the fluid or choke on it.

She leaned close to him. "That wasn't so bad, was it? Next time, don't be so difficult." Her words were all sweet reason, but her smile chilled him.

The room about Weaver seemed to fade, taking with it the pain. He could no longer focus on those cold eyes, which was a blessing. He could imagine himself alone, disturbed only by the clammy trickle of poppy syrup creeping down his neck.

CHAPTER NINETEEN

At the lower end of the desert valley stood a gnarled old tree. Twisted by countless years spent in the arid environment, its growth stunted by lack of rainfall, it nevertheless spread a generous canopy beneath which the freemerchants were wont to sit. All business of the community took place there. Children would play there, laughing and singing, or as often squabbling, in the shade of the canopy. But today the children had been chivvied away and they were playing among the boulders that had long ago slid down from a loose section of the escarpment from which their homes had been carved. Laughs and shrieks punctuated the still air from further up the valley as they played some elaborate game of tag.

The elders were assembled under the shade of the tree, waiting as Alwenna and Marten walked down the slope. As they approached the group Alwenna had an overwhelming premonition of hostility. She had enemies here today, no question about it. Grit crunched beneath her feet – everything at Scarrow's Deep was coated in a fine layer of sand or dust. Everything. How desperate did one have to be to call this arid place home? She wasn't that desperate, not yet, despite the trail of death that she'd left in her wake. She'd sooner climb those mountains that lay beyond the escarpment and live out her days there, lost in the mists, where the air turned not just chill, but cold. Every night. Where streams gushed in spate down steep, narrow channels, water tumbling over the rocks and plunging into deep pools at every twist and turn...

"My lady, are you unwell?" At her side Marten frowned.

"I beg your pardon. I seem to be always tired these days. Always distracted."

"Are you suffering visions again?"

"No. Not like before."

"I see."

If he noticed her evasion he didn't comment upon on it. Of course he didn't – this was Marten. He played so many games of his own, adding one of hers to his list was the merest– No, perhaps she was being unfair. Perhaps he simply knew this was not the time to push the issue. She turned her full attention to the elders, trying to divine the source of hostility. There were several men and a few women, some appearing no more than middle-aged while others were clearly very old indeed. Alwenna would have guessed them to be elders, simply because of the preponderance of grey hair and wrinkled faces. Not to mention a certain air of weighty self-importance that hung about them. But she ought not prejudge them, even if they did remind her of every group of royal advisors she'd been obliged to mouth polite acquiescence to in the past.

The canopy of the stunted tree grew mainly off to one side of the trunk, shaped by unrelenting winds at some time in the past. Beneath this side were boulders on which the elders now sat, arranged in two arcs facing the tree itself. At the foot of the tree was a bench, fashioned of stone, and it was there that Marten indicated Alwenna should sit. It reminded her very much of the courtroom at Highkell. Did this assembly presume to put her on trial?

Marten cleared his throat, glancing uneasily at Alwenna. "I am sure you are all by now aware this is the Lady Alwenna, rightful ruler of the Peninsular Kingdoms and beloved of the Goddess."

Quite what he hoped to achieve by that, Alwenna wasn't sure. Perhaps half the assembled elders regarded her with thinly veiled suspicion. One woman, with a deeply wrinkled and tanned face, watched her with alert curiosity. Alwenna was reminded of a small bird that had once frequented the palace gardens, always following her about when she and Wynne had worked there, gathering herbs or thinning and replanting plants. It felt like a lifetime ago. A faint movement in her abdomen reminded her that in some cases it was literally a lifetime ago. Beloved of the Goddess...

Marten had continued speaking and she had no idea what he'd been saying.

"– And the circumstances of our departure from the summer palace meant I have sought this meeting at the earliest opportunity, for the Lady Alwenna is in great need of your wisdom and advice."

A skinny old man stood up. "It is incumbent on me as leader of the council to offer the Lady Alwenna our greetings, and our condolences on the death of her husband. King Tresilian was ever a friend to the freemerchants." He fixed Alwenna with a steady gaze.

Here was the source of the hostility. How much had he heard of Tresilian's death already? Alwenna drew on her years of training to remain outwardly cool. "I must thank you and your people for your hospitality in my hour of need, sir."

The old man did not smile. Instead he cleared his throat and addressed Marten. "Before we take this discussion any further it is the wish of this council that you first give us a full account of recent events. It was our understanding you were to reunite the lady with her husband. It was never part of your plans to bring her here. We must consider the full implications of her presence among us now."

Marten smiled. There was little to betray his displeasure at the line the elder had taken, but Alwenna knew the displeasure was there, nonetheless. "Sire, we have already discussed this, have we not? I made all the facts known to the elders last–"

"But some were not present, for the meeting was called at short notice. And it is imperative that we put certain questions to the lady herself, in the circumstances."

Marten spread his hands wide. "I hope you do not doubt my veracity, Rogen?"

"I daresay all is as you said, Marten, but I doubt you've told us the full of it. In which case I must assume you have withheld certain knowledge for your own purposes. And your purposes, I confess, I find as impenetrable as they are frequently outrageous."

There were one or two murmurs of agreement from those seated behind him. There appeared to be two distinct factions within the elders, as well as a number of people who as yet adhered to the views of neither group. Alwenna's champion was not the most popular in freemerchant circles, it would seem. Marten certainly appeared to have his fair share of opponents. Whether he had a similar or greater number of supporters remained to be seen.

Marten waited for the murmuring to die down before he spoke. "My purposes remain to ensure the wellbeing of the freemerchant people. This is as they ever have been."

"And pray tell me how it promotes our wellbeing when you flout our time-honoured codes? It is well known you were carrying a sword on your travels through the Marches. With as little shame as any landbound peasant."

"Had I not been carrying that sword I would not be standing before you today, sire. And neither would the Lady Alwenna."

"In which case we might all have been a great deal better off!" Rogen responded, spittle flying from his mouth and catching in his beard.

"Come now, Rogen. Our meetings would be dull indeed without Marten here to stir us from our complacency." The bright-eyed old lady had spoken up. "At least listen to his report. He has spent more time out in the world than we have of late. Need I remind you a freemerchant who no longer travels the roads is no longer true? Marten is truer to our kin than you or I now." Again there were murmurs of assent, but also one or two voices, seated behind Rogen, who muttered disagreement.

Rogen sniffed. "He's forgotten too many of the old ways, I tell you. It is not for us to meddle in the affairs of the Peninsular kings."

"And what happens when those same kings close the bridges to us? What then, Rogen? You know, do you not, that the usurper Vasic intends to charge a toll for everyone crossing the new bridge at Highkell? For everyone, without exception?"

The forbidding Rogen turned his attention to the woman, whose demeanour didn't alter in the slightest. "These are nothing more than rumours and idle gossip. The bridge is not yet even begun – better, perhaps, to ask yourself who tore it down in the first place."

He swung to face Alwenna. "Or do you attempt to deny that, Lady Alwenna?" He spat the name as if it were a curse.

Once Alwenna might have been shamed – flustered, even – by his accusation, but his hostility stirred a similar response deep inside her. She sensed the curl of anger with a strange detachment. Oh, she knew resentment of old, a petty, fleeting, moody thing. But this was... Something harder, unyielding. As if a sleeping demon stirred inside her, stretching and close to the brink of awareness, but not quite waking. Even as she thought it an odd fancy, she knew she must respond to Rogen.

"Your ways are not the ways I was raised to at Highkell, sire Rogen. But our blood is the same. I was named sister by Nicholl on the road from Highkell months ago, and that, I understand, is according to the old ways. Or would you sooner set aside some of the old ways yourself, when it suits your purpose?" At her side she heard Marten murmur agreement.

Rogen's face worked before he recovered his composure.

"That is not the issue here. I spoke of the bridge at Highkell. What have you to say about that?"

"The bridge was torn down when the tower collapsed. I was given to understand the collapse of the tower was the will of the Goddess." She saw again Garrad's face, the moment he realised, the moment before he turned the blade upon himself. Was it the truth? It was her version of it, to be sure.

"Do you dare deny you caused the collapse of the tower at Highkell?" Rogen rounded on her triumphantly.

"I did not will it." Not wittingly, anyway. She would not admit her doubts to this audience.

Rogen turned to face the other elders. "You see how she twists everything? We cannot make such a one welcome among our people."

Another old man stood, tall, his features vaguely familiar. "If my son named her sister – and I have no reason to doubt he would have done – then she is by right welcome among us."

"She will bring disaster down upon us. It is well known she was predicted to destroy Highkell."

Nicholl's father shrugged expansively. "This is what happens if you put all your faith in the word of landbound seers. Is that our way?"

Rogen turned away from Nicholl's father. "She will bring danger to our people. Heed my warning now, before it is too late. She's already led Marten away from his true path."

"Come now, Rogen. You see demons behind every tree." The bird-woman, as Alwenna thought of her, spoke up again. "All I see here is a fellow traveller who has met trouble on the road. This young woman is in great need of our compassion. We must do everything we can to set her on her way again – I am sure she has no more wish to remain immured here with us than we would care to hold her back from her path."

"Dam Jenna, I would gladly set her on her way, if that path were not one beset with death and destruction. Now she is here among us I believe our duty is to stop her entirely. Marten has told us of the dread knife she wielded. We should turn it upon her while she is still too weak to prevent it." Rogen glared at Alwenna, and she felt that sleeping demon stir again. If all he could show her was hatred, she was more than happy to reflect that back at him. She'd met such hatred before, less overt, to be sure, but she knew it of old. It was as familiar to her as the lines that criss-crossed the palm of her hand. She knew the blood-rich taste of it in her mind, knew the final death-squeal of it and the dreadful loss of it and the awfulness of its final flutterings to be free–

Goddess, what was she thinking? Her fingers had closed around the front edge of the stone bench on which she sat. She was acutely aware of every grain of sand within the ancient slab, every tiny crystal of quartz glinting inside its hidden depths, every tiny, tiny space between each of the grains. The slab on which she sat had once sheared from the cliff above them, and now she knew it, knew every grain of it, knew the place it had sheared from, the rain that had dislodged it, so slowly, year after year until it fell. From... That spot right there, that spot where its siblings still rested, so ancient. And the hairsbreadth fracture line between that slab and the cliff that was gradually, almost imperceptibly, widening. She could sense it: the rock cried out to join its sibling there on the valley floor, beneath the tree among the loose grains that had given up the uneven struggle against gravity so long ago. And it was tired, so tired. Alwenna understood it – she too was tired... It was no longer worth the effort of holding on... Easier to let go... To give up the struggle... To fall free... She scarcely heard the cracking sound as the block of stone sheared oh so slowly from the cliff face above, scarcely felt the ground shudder with the impact as it landed and began to slide on the loose sand beneath the cliff, tilting and twisting as the banks steepened and a cascade of smaller stones scattered around it. So easy now, just to let go...

CHAPTER TWENTY

Tad was dragged from his cell in the darkness. They stripped him of his clothes and doused him in a water trough. No one told him why. As they dragged him out, coughing and spluttering, he caught a glimpse of the glow of sunlight appearing on the eastern horizon. It was not long before dawn. Again without explanation they threw a linen tunic over his nakedness. He shivered there in the predawn light, trying to fathom what was going on, but whenever he met a soldier's eye, the man would turn away.

Tad hunkered down on the cobbles by the trough, his teeth chattering, clutching his arms about his knees in an attempt to get warm. The soldiers ignored him and he crouched there for ten miserable minutes before the brethren came for him.

Durstan himself stood before the boy and ordered him to stand. Tad tried to comply, but his frozen limbs were slow to respond. Durstan watched with impatience as Tad pushed himself up to a standing position and stood there as best he could, knees knocking.

"You'll have to do, I suppose." He turned away, casting an order over his shoulder. "Bring him to the altar room. We have no time to waste."

The air in the altar room was warm and filled with incense. The heat hit Tad like a wall – it should have been welcome, yet still he shivered and broke out into a sweat.

"Kneel in the presence of the Goddess." The priest's voice was indifferent.

Tad complied, trying desperately to control the shaking of his limbs by clutching his hands together. His bladder suddenly felt overfull. He could not face the shame if he were to lose control here before the assembled people.

He realised someone was speaking to him in a low voice. "Here, drink this. It will help." Hands held out a small, silver bowl to him. In the bottom was a milky liquid, viscous and syrupy.

"It will help." This time he recognised his sister's voice. He hadn't known it without that edge of scorn he was so used to hearing. This was the voice she saved for important people, for people who mattered. That thought strengthened him.

He reached in gratitude for the bowl, but his hands shook so much he risked dropping it. She bent down, and wrapped her fingers over his, holding the bowl so he could sip the syrup from it, tilting it carefully until he had taken every drop. The trembling of his fingers ceased, and the rest of his body somehow unknotted.

"May the blessing of the Goddess be upon you." His sister's voice seemed far away now. She must have taken the bowl from his hands, for he no longer held it. He knelt there, facing the table where other, larger bowls were sitting. There were ornate patterns etched into the metal and he gazed at them in wonder. Never had he seen such beauty.

He was vexed when a priest stepped in front of him so he could no longer marvel at the intricate patterns. He tried to voice a protest, but he could make no sound issue from his mouth, could form no words. Instead he gaped up at the priest, open-mouthed. Durstan looked down at him and set a hand on his forehead, intoning verses in a language Tad could not understand, but he could feel the blessing of the Goddess flow through him. He smiled up at Durstan. This was the most beautiful thing that had ever happened to him.

One moment seemed to drift into another. He scarcely realised when the priests lifted him and placed him on a stone bench with such care as he'd never known before. He gazed up at the ceiling for a moment or two, while voices around him began to chant. Somehow the ecstasy left him as the voices rose up in unison and the chill of the stone struck through the thin tunic and into his bones. The stone slab was unyielding, digging into his tailbone and his shoulders where he had too little flesh to cushion his body. He tried to raise his arm to shift his weight and ease the discomfort, but he could not. He tried the other arm and it was the same. That was odd. The chanting had grown in volume and he began to feel he was being watched. The feeling was so overwhelming... He twisted his head to one side, but there was nothing there but stone wall. It was almost too much effort to look the other way, but he summoned all his strength and twisted his head round once more. He was so drowsy now, he wanted to sleep. But he was being watched. He opened his eyes, but all was a blur. Then he blinked and his vision cleared. There was the soldier, the man his sister had told him was their father. He was lying on a stone slab, his hands lashed down to a bar of wood that ran beneath the slab, feet tied, trussed up like a goose ready for roasting.

His father. He might have been, after all. His sister didn't know everything. He was watching Tad now, as the priests chanted around them. Tad could see concern for him in the soldier's eyes: he'd never felt more valued in his life.

CHAPTER TWENTY-ONE

A single, high scream pierced the air and the chanting ceased. At the last the boy had fixed his gaze on Weaver who, hardened soldier though he was, had to close his eyes to escape the pain he saw there. When he reopened them the boy's body lay limp and still on the stone slab. The air was redolent with the boy's blood. The priest, carrying the bloodied misericord dagger, stepped around the end of the stone altar and out of Weaver's sight.

He heard the footsteps cross the stone floor of the altar chamber, one foot shuffling slightly with each step yet still somehow deliberate and measured, each footfall in time with Weaver's own rasping breaths. He could picture the unevenness of the man's gait, could picture his face, the grey eyes and heavy brows. The priest had made his way past Weaver's head now and moved round to his left side, still out of vision. Weaver recognised his face, he was sure of it. But recalling where was too much of a fight and he was so blissfully tired. Too tired to puzzle over it. Too tired to think about anything at all. So tired.

The chanting began again, with renewed vigour, cutting through the haze that clouded his mind. Something prompted Weaver to twist his head round. A familiar face in the ring of worshippers surrounding the stone altar caught his eye. Tresilian's priestess watched with fierce interest. Gone was the cool disregard; now her eyes were fixed on Weaver – the eyes of a feral creature, starved and desperate for its next meal, her lips parted as she watched with supreme confidence that her hunger would soon be sated. Somehow Weaver couldn't tear his eyes away. She closed her lips then, the corners turning up in a feral smile, the rise and fall of her chest accelerated. And he knew what was coming next. He had a split second of full awareness – barely time to tense up – before his world folded in on itself with intense, all-consuming pain as the misericord pierced his heart.

PART II

CHAPTER ONE

Peveril sat in the darkest corner of the taproom. He'd formed the habit long ago and it had never yet served him ill. He liked the *Miners' Tavern* best of all the inns in Highkell because the darkest corner also happened to be close to the back door. He could be long gone before trouble had even had a chance to focus on the occupants of the dimly lit room. And Captain Art Peveril liked to avoid trouble. He wasn't averse to causing it when the odds were stacked in his favour, but he wasn't fond of taking unnecessary risks in pursuit of either his dubious pleasures, or financial gain. In troubled times such as Highkell was going through at present, a man prepared to sit quiet for long enough could learn many things to his advantage. Often from such questionable sources as meant they were probably untrue, but he'd long ago formed the opinion that there was indeed no smoke without fire, and even the tallest tale would contain a grain of truth that might be turned to his advantage.

And the group of lads arguing in the corner nearby? They were the source of one of the tallest tales he'd heard in a while. It promised to be very lucrative indeed.

The lads were clad in smocks and baggy trousers, typical of labourers and probably of an age to be apprentices. It must be their payday. They looked – and sounded – as if they'd been in the tavern for the better part of the day.

"It's true, I tell you," the shortest one insisted. He pounded his fist on the table, determined to be heard. It always was the short ones, of course. Always the keenest to prove themselves, the first to step out of line, the hardest to fell in battle. "I tell you. A fine lady was rescued from the rubble there. My mate Barney was fetching water and arrows for the archers on the walls. An' when everything had gone quiet – like it did, you remember, after the tower collapsed and the stone stopped falling? Well, then." He picked up his drink and swallowed some down, secure in his audience's attention. "Like I said–" He wiped his mouth on his shabby linen sleeve. If the colour of the garment was anything to go by this was far from the first time he'd done that. "When it all went quiet the archers went back up on the walls like they'd been ordered, and Barney had to fetch 'em water. An' he did. While he was up on the wall carrying water skins a group of riders appeared on the far side of the gorge. Like they'd been passin' by and just noticed what had happened and were takin' a good look. Anyway, they rode on an' Barney fetched more arrows. Then he saw, as he was goin' back down, that the same bunch of riders had dismounted an' were going through the rubble, like. An' he swears he saw 'em pull a lady in a fine dress – like the gentry wear – out of the rubble. He shouldn've been hanging around on the wall of course, an' he got his lug clipped for it, and sent to fetch more arrows. An' he wasn't long down those steps when that whole curtain wall gave way an' took all the archers with it."

He paused and took another drink, looking around at his enraptured audience. "An' like, that was it. An' none of us believed him cos Barney's always been one for tall tales. An' there was nothing to say this was any different, 'specially with all the archers from that side dead an' all when the wall fell down. So no one believed him.

"But," and he paused for emphasis. "The other day I was

working with the master, sorting through the stone, an' I got to thinking about ol' Barney's story. Cos, y'see, we found a place where the rubble had been moved around, and there was like a hollow spot inside, an' I remembered what Barney said an' I got thinking: what if ol' Barney's tale was true, an' those folk had really dug a woman out of the rubble? An' what if that woman had been – well, someone important? Like, really important?

"Cos y'know I didn't believe Barney at all until we found that spot. An' while I was sortin' through the stone, well, can you guess?"

His audience variously shook their heads or chided him for not getting on with the tale.

"No, I thought not. When I was sorting through the stone, picking out the good stuff, I saw something shining. Really shining, like a new coin – I saw one once, at the market when a noble bought a horse off my da' – an' anyway, I poked around a bit, an' found there was something metal buried there. An' I dug around an' pulled it out an', what do you think?"

"It was a coin?"

"Nah." Shorty shook his head. "Better 'n that. It was real gold. It was broken, like, but I could tell it was the sort of thing a fine lady would wear. Round her neck, y'know?" He gestured. "Now what do you think of that?"

"I think ye're 'avin' us on." The thickset apprentice who'd questioned him before was unconvinced.

"I swear by the Goddess, may she strike me down if I tell a lie." Shorty spread his hands wide, grinning.

"So what'd you do with it? You got it now?"

"Course not. I couldn't carry a thing like that in here, wi' cutpurses and the like all over."

"You're lying." The thickset apprentice picked up his drink. "An' it's your round in case you've forgotten. If you're that wealthy you'll have no trouble buying it in."

Shorty tilted his head. "You think I'm lying? Go on then – I can prove it. An' if I do, you're buying the next round."

"Go on then, prove it. We all know you can't – just makin' shit up to make yoursel' sound important. Bet you don't even have a mate called Barney."

"He does." A skinny lad, who'd been listening intently without commenting, broke in. "I've met him an' all. 'Prenticed to the fletcher, he is."

"That proves nowt." Thickset apprentice was becoming belligerent.

Shorty laughed. "But this will. Here, see? He leaned over, fumbling with one hand in his scrip. The others leaned close and Peveril caught the glint of gold as he held something out for them to inspect. They seemed impressed, as he stowed the item safely back in his scrip.

All except the thickset one, who pulled a sour face. "That's nowt. You could've picked up a scrap like that anywhere. Lying on the street, most likely."

"Lay off, Rog, it looks right enough to me," the skinny youth butted in.

"No. He's a lying scrunt. You lay off." The mood of the lads changed as abruptly as weather on a March day and they erupted in a boiling mess of fists and shouts, brawling until the landlord ejected them from the premises.

But Peveril had seen enough. He got leisurely to his feet and followed the pack of apprentices out. Their day's carousing seemed to be at an end as they trailed off in ones and twos in various directions, mopping bloodied noses. He followed Shorty at a discreet distance. He wasn't about to let an opportunity like that go by.

Peveril waited until the lad turned away from his drinking companions to walk down an empty street. This was his chance. He straightened his uniform and slicked back his hair, thankful he hadn't bothered changing when he'd come off duty. He lengthened his stride so he could catch up with the lad's somewhat erratic progress.

"Evening, lad. You've got a slight stagger on there."

The lad was startled and sidestepped sharply, spinning round to face Peveril. Wary, this one.

Peveril spread his hands wide. "Hey, not what you think. Jus' bein' friendly, like." It wasn't often his broad Highkell accent was useful to him these days, but just now it was a blessing straight from the Goddess.

The apprentice set his jaw in a stubborn line. "Don't think you can mess with me. I'm stronger 'n I look."

He likely was, being a mason's apprentice. "I'm not lookin' to mess wi' you. Just got a word for the wise, is all. Heard you talkin' back at the *Miners'*, y'know. Couldn't help it, cos you were a bit loud, 'n all."

The lad was still poised for flight. Peveril could flatten him right now and take the fragment of jewellery, but there was bigger game to be had here. And Peveril was nothing if not ambitious. "That was an interesting tale you had."

The lad didn't relax his vigilance one iota. It would take a great deal of finesse to reel this one in. As a rule, Peveril thought such niceties a waste of time, but for once, this time, it might pay dividends. He smiled in what was meant to be a winning style but the lad took another step away from him, clenching his fists.

"No need to take on, lad. Don't you recognise the uniform of the palace guard when you see it?"

The lad's frown deepened, but he looked Peveril up and down and his stance relaxed ever so slightly. Peveril saw the line he must take. "There are those at the palace who'd be keen to hear that story you told tonight. Wealthy, like, an' keen enough to pay you well for it. An' if'n you've proof of it, they'll pay a deal for that, too."

"An' what's it to you if they would?"

Peveril gestured to his uniform once more. "I work at the palace, too. The way it is there, if'n a man serves well and is useful, he gets remembered, an' he gets rewarded. If'n I take your story to my master, I'll be rewarded, an' you'll be rewarded. But only if you can prove it."

The lad's chin jutted out again. "I can prove it."

"Well then. Come to the palace tomorrow mornin' and ask for Captain Peveril. Bring your proof an' we can do business. Mind you don't go blabbin' all over town about it though, or there's them as is low enough to take the tale to the palace themselves, an' help themselves to what you're carryin'. If'n I was you I wouldn't give them the chance. Jus' keep your lip shut and be there tomorrow mornin'. Me, I'll deal fair wi' you. Ask for Captain Peveril."

"Cap'n Peveril." The lad nodded. "I'll do it."

Peveril smiled. This was too easy. "An' watch your step on the way home. You're lucky it was only me overheard."

"Aye, I'll do that." The lad waited for Peveril to turn and walk away before he resumed his journey, the stagger a little less evident than it had been before.

CHAPTER TWO

"You are awake? Good." The bright-eyed woman moved over to Alwenna's side. "I have rarely seen such power as yours before – and I have seen a few in my time, believe me. Rogen fears it of course. I can understand if you do not have it in your heart to forgive him."

Forgive a man who had spoken so coldly of putting a knife between her ribs? When she was a guest at his campfire... Alwenna's head ached and her mouth was dry. But she could recall everything so clearly... There was none of the fog of waking from the sight. She pushed herself up to a sitting position. That was because that had been no vision of the sight. That had been a... what? A thing she had done. It had been real. She had torn a boulder from the cliff and brought it careering down the slope to their meeting place.

Goddess, was she running mad? She could remember every detail so clearly. The slow but inexorable descent of the boulder. And the glee in every fibre of her body as it sent showers of small stones cascading before it. For a moment that same glee coursed through her veins at the recollection of the ensuing chaos, but she damped it down ruthlessly. The bird-woman still watched her, eyes bright and curious, belying her years.

"You have a forgiving nature, I think, Lady Alwenna?"

"I believe I did, once."

"But no more?"

"I was brought up to believe forgiveness was a strength. But the more I see of the world, the more I am convinced it is a fatal weakness."

"And you have seen some things of the world that few others have, I think?" The woman watched her intently.

"You are referring to the grey brethren?" Alwenna knew the answer, but she asked anyway. Just how perceptive was the old woman?

"Yes." Shc nodded. "I am referring to the grey brethren. Once-dead men who walk among us again."

She knew – this woman understood. Suddenly Alwenna had the urge to unburden herself. "But they don't just walk. They talk and reason, and pursue their goals as if they had never died. Except..."

"Except, my lady?" The prompting was gentle.

She was revealing nothing the elder did not already know, Alwenna was convinced. "My husband, Tresilian. He was changed. His nature was altered, so deeply I could not at first believe it. Neither, I think, did Marten. Before, Tresilian was always kind. It was he who taught me so much about forgiving, before I learned to master my temper. He was loyal, and a true friend as we grew up. Even when he returned from battle he had matured, and perhaps hardened, but he was in essence the same steady character – kind to a fault."

"You think of kindness as a fault?"

"In a monarch, perhaps? It is better not to reveal too much of the kindness at your heart."

"Perhaps." The elder did not appear convinced. "Tell me more about Tresilian. It might help you, as well as the rest of us. Any detail, however tiny, might be key to understanding what should best be done."

Alwenna tucked her knees up beneath the blankets, wrapping her arms around them and leaning her chin on her knees. Her thickening midriff meant it was not quite as easy as it had once been. But she needed to talk about Tresilian now. She'd allowed herself no room to deal with what she'd witnessed at the summer palace, and she sensed this woman would not judge her as many might.

"Even the death of his father – which hit him so badly at the time – he dealt with that and he was still the same understanding man. I sometimes thought him old beyond his years, but I suppose he had little choice once his father had died."

"He was killed on campaign in the Marches?"

"That's right. Putting down a simple rebellion. After all he'd been through..." Alwenna recalled his disfigured face, last glimpsed through the smoke at the summer palace. She glanced at the woman.

"Go on."

"His father... He was one of the grey brethren. I– I saw him in a vision first, then... that last day, he was among those who burst into the throne room. We fled, Marten, Erin and I, leaving Weaver to hold them back." She'd almost forgotten someone else was listening to her words. "I thought he would turn and follow us in an instant, but he never did. To this day I don't know what happened to him."

"I have heard of this Weaver – a warrior of some repute."

"I knew none braver." Alwenna took a deep breath to gather herself. Some things she would not share with the inquisitive elder. It was more than possible she'd heard the rumours already, and guessed the rest. Or Marten may have told her. But he said he had not and Alwenna preferred to believe him. Doubting Marten had not thus far been helpful to her. That day in the king's chambers she'd sensed that Marten was crucial to her survival and she to his. She should ask the elder woman about that. But Jenna's next words drove all thought of Marten from her mind.

"There may be ways of finding out what happened to this soldier. There are certain rites. Not practised here, for they are frowned upon. But there are people who could help you find out. Freemerchants of a sort, who chose a different path many generations ago."

"Who are they? Could I send a message to them? Where might I find..." But she already knew the answer. "In the mountains to the north."

Jenna nodded. "In the mountains to the north. I think you've sensed their presence ever since you arrived here, have you not?"

Alwenna nodded, slowly. "Tell me more about them – please. I know this is important."

"You finish telling me about Tresilian – for that is equally important – then I shall tell you what you wish to know. You say you saw Tresilian's father among the grey brethren?"

Alwenna nodded, trying to recall the point she'd reached in her tale. "I only caught a glimpse. There were several of them, all wearing grey. And there was something in his expression – I just knew. It, he, was... wrong. Unnatural. When I first saw Tresilian he looked just as he had ever been. He was standing with the light behind him but I recognised him... No one had warned me he was alive. I'd seen his death in a vision, and until that moment I'd begun to believe the visions I saw were true. And of course, later, I discovered it had been true: I witnessed his death. I have no idea what they must have done to him, although I saw many times visions of him with that... priestess, and..."

"The healing."

"Why, yes. I was told it was called that."

"The rite they perform – it's a form of sacrifice. Every part of the process is in the nature of a sacrifice of one kind or another."

Alwenna, startled, looked at Jenna. "You know of the rites they perform?"

"It is an ancient magic. Not well understood today and, of course, forbidden in precincts throughout the Peninsula and beyond. For very good reason."

"Forbidden?"

"On pain of death. I imagine you can tell me why."

"Tresilian... He looked the same. At first, anyway. But his nature was changed. He was no longer the kind and patient man..."

"Might that have been your doing?"

"Who can be sure? I'm sure some will say so."

"But you would not agree with them?"

"No. I'd believed my husband dead for weeks." She did not need to justify her behaviour. She would not, not ever. "It ran deeper than that – everything about him was tainted, corrupted. When he had me touch the mortal wound, it had healed over, but it was... I can't explain it... Just wrong. Every instinct revolted."

Jenna nodded. "I understand. I, too, once lost someone dear to the grey brethren. When I discovered what had happened, I fled the place. I did not have the courage to stand and face him, as you did."

"Oh, I tried to run, but... Marten brought me back. As if he still believed Tresilian might honour his word."

Jenna nodded again. "Yes, he told me of that. You must appreciate how many years Marten spent working for that moment. He still hoped Tresilian might be convinced to keep his part of the bargain. Or he wanted to hope that. You can trust him, you know – you are his best chance of gaining what he has sought for his people all these years."

"I do not trust readily now."

"No. The things you have witnessed – it is, I suppose, possible that you might remain unchanged."

"Me? No. I've changed. I carry a block of lead where my heart once was."

"Then you will guard that heart with extreme care, I imagine. But I think you are not so cold a person as you would have the rest of us believe."

How to answer that? This was not Wynne she was speaking to, this was a stranger and Alwenna already felt she'd revealed too much. She'd balked against the lessons that outward appearances meant everything for royalty, but all those tutors at court had shaped her nonetheless.

"This is all by the by – what is done cannot be changed. Would you learn more of that soldier's fate?"

Of course Jenna had known the truth. She must have known it all along.

"I would. I owe him my life."

"Very well." The slightest raising of an eyebrow suggested the elder was not convinced by Alwenna's justification. "When the time is right, you will wish to seek out the outcasts who dwell in the mountains to the north. I am known to them: mention my name and they will receive you."

"When the time is right? What does that mean?"

Jenna smiled. "I cannot tell you. But you will know."

CHAPTER THREE

Myrna was nowhere to be found, either upstairs or in the kitchens or sculleries.

The cook was disparaging, expressing her disapproval with a loud sniff. "Sloped off again, that 'un has. No better'n she ought to be."

"One of the customers was asking for her."

"Well, that don't surprise me none. Like I said, no better'n she ought to be. Take this tray for the party in the dining room. Looks like we're near the end of the evening rush anyway. I'll have a word with himself, see if he'll put you front of house instead of yon flighty thing. She's done this once too often."

Lena hurried through with the tray of puddings. The merchants in the dining room had also been drinking all day, but they were quieter than the rowdy lot in the taproom, at least. Even so, she didn't want Myrna's job. The obscurity of the servants' areas suited her just fine. Dealing with the public meant a risk, however slight, that she might be recognised. A quick scan of the faces gathered around the table told her tonight she was safe enough. And hopefully in her changed situation, dressed in unfamiliar clothing, she would not be recognised by any but her closest acquaintances. They, for sure, would never be found in a downtrodden inn in Sylhaven.

She made her way back towards the kitchen, but was hailed

by Isaac Henty from the taproom doorway.

"Here, lass, come and deal wi' this bloke."

Not again. She quelled the urge to snap at the landlord. "Pardon?"

"Yon feller in the corner is asking after ye."

"He should make his mind up, you said he was asking for Myrna before."

"Aye, so he was. Just sweet talk him off the premises, he's been drowning his sorrows all afternoon."

"But, Isaac–"

"He's a wealthy man, go about it right and ye'll get a handsome tip, lass. He's harmless. There's others here I need to keep a close eye on tonight. See him safe home, then you can take the rest of the evening off." He vanished back inside the taproom and Lena trailed behind him. She was paid for kitchen work, not being polite to drunks. And she was paid precious little at that. Henty nodded towards the corner table as he resumed his place behind the bar. A man sat there, slumped over his empty tankard, hair falling over his face. He gave every appearance of remaining upright only by virtue of the substantial table on which his elbows and forearms rested. She sighed and threaded her way through the crowded room.

"Come on, sir, it's time for you to head home."

"What about Myrna?" He focused on her slightly unsteadily. "Isaac said he'd bring her."

"She's not here."

"She isn't?"

"No. She's finished for the night. And now it's time for you to go. Up you get, sir."

"The name's Nils. Darnell. You can call me Nils, if you want." He stood up, swaying slightly. She caught hold of his arm by the elbow just before he overbalanced.

"Watch your step." She steered him towards the taproom door.

"You haven't told me your name," he observed when they were alone in the hallway.

"There's no need to worry about that."

"I'd rather know your name, all the same, 's only polite."

"I'm Lena."

"Pleased to make your acquaintance, Lena." He executed a shaky bow. "You may call me Nils."

"Pleased to meet you." She supported him down the steps, hoping he'd find his sea legs in a minute, but he reeled sideways as they reached the street.

"Where do you live, Mr Darnell?"

"Call me Nils, I insist."

"Don't start that again. Where do you live?"

He raised his eyebrow.

"Where do you live, Nils?"

"Tha's better. Vine Street. It's the house with the biggest courtyard."

"That's nice." Lena hoped he wasn't going to lean any more heavily on her, she wasn't sure she could support his weight much longer. Thank the Goddess the walk to Vine Street wasn't far.

"I've done a lot of work on it, you know. It wasn't in the best order when I bought the place. Had to work hard to get where I am today. Damned hard."

Lena winced as he trod on her foot. He didn't seem to notice, however.

"Not good enough for the likes of Barrett, of course. Looks down his nose at a self-made man. Unless the money's generations old he's not impressed. Damn fool, I'll show him. Pardon my language, Lorna. Shouldn't have said that in the presence of a lady. Hope you can forgive me." He stopped and pulled himself up to his full height. "I must be making a poor impression on you this evening. Between you and me, Lorna, I've had a bit too much to drink. I don't normally drink to excess."

"That's a relief. Can you make your own way from here, Mr Darnell?"

He frowned. "Nils, please. We've been through all that. I can't call you Lorna if you don't call me Nils, wouldn't be right."

She sighed. "It's not right anyway. My name is Lena."

"Lena? That's much nicer than Lorna. Why'd you tell me it was Lorna?"

"I didn't. Is it much further to your house?"

"No. See the wide gate up ahead? That's it."

"Will you be all right the rest of the way by yourself?"

"I want to see what you think of the house. Can't do that if you don't come in."

She couldn't argue with his logic. "That's true, but it wouldn't be proper."

"I know how to treat a lady. Anyway you wouldn't be alone with me, there'll be servants about the place."

Nils pushed open the heavy courtyard gate, stepping back with a flourish for Lena to precede him. "After you, my lady."

"No, really, you don't need me from here. I'll bid you good night." She stepped back from the gateway, but Darnell followed her.

"Come now, the night's young."

"Not for me, sir. I have an early start in the morning. I wish you well in nursing your sore head tomorrow." A clunk from the top of the steps behind Darnell heralded the opening of the door. Light pooled out into the courtyard and a middle-aged manservant stepped forward, casting a wavering shadow across the cobbles.

"Sir, is there some trouble?"

"Evening, Rossiter. The lady seems to think I'm not to be trusted." The servant stepped closer, frowning as he studied Lena.

She was acutely conscious of her scruffy scullery maid's garb. Without thinking, she drew herself up to her full height.

"Isaac Henty of the *Royal Hart* bade me deliver your master safe home. I trust I can assure him I have left Mr Darnell in capable hands?"

The servant bowed slightly. "Of course, my lady." Lena knew a moment's satisfaction; she could still draw on the old ways when she needed to. But she ought not. It wasn't appropriate for her situation. But it was so, so satisfying to see the servant's manner change. She spent too much time at the inn taking the brunt of others' snobbery and the moment felt good. Maybe it was time she went back. Her grand adventure involved a whole lot more drudgery than she'd expected.

"Thank you, I shall inform Isaac Henty that Master Darnell has been left in safe hands. I bid you good night, Mr Darnell."

Darnell had straightened up in the presence of the servant, and perhaps regained some stronger sense of his surroundings. "Nils, I insist. At some more propitious occasion I shall hope to offer you my hospitality, my lady." He bowed, staggering only slightly as he straightened up. "But tell me now, who will see you safe back to the inn?"

"Have no fear on my account, sir, the troublemakers are all gathered in the taproom." She turned to leave.

"No, I protest, you can't go alone."

"Sir, a serving girl won't suffer ill at this time of night." The servant took his master by the arm and nodded towards Lena.

"Good night, then." She walked briskly down the street away from the gate, ignoring Darnell's protest that she could not leave so soon. She glanced back as she reached the corner; Darnell was watching from outside the gate. She walked on out of sight, shaking her head. Henty had been right, the fellow was good natured enough, an amiable drunkard. The world would be a better place if they were all like him.

Myrna was back in the kitchen when Lena returned, sitting at the table, pouting.

"I'd've seen to Master Darnell. You shouldn'a taken him,

Lena. You're nobbut a kitchen skivvy. I'll tell you what – you're gettin' ideas above your station."

"I was only doing what Isaac told me. Believe me, I'd rather have stayed warm in here than half carry a drunk up that hill in the cold."

"You'd no call to go stealin' my tips."

"Don't worry, I didn't get any tips." She hung her cloak on the peg behind the door. "He won't even remember my name tomorrow."

"More fool you." Myrna sniffed.

"There's a fool in all this, to be sure, but it isn't me."

Lena made her way up the back stairs to the attic room where she slept. It was tiny, scarcely large enough to hold a bed, but at least that meant she didn't have to share it with anyone else. She thought again of the manservant's instinctive reaction to her tone of voice. Just for a moment it had been good. Doubtless she'd pay for that moment's weakness somewhere along the way, that was how life seemed to work. And in the end, if her little deception was uncovered, what did it matter? It had been good to taste real life, but she had to admit the work was hard and the rewards were few. Really, she would be missing nothing if she were to return home now. Doubtless Myrna was already plotting against her, for her imagined usurpation as favourite of Nils Darnell. Not that she needed to. As Lena had said, he wouldn't even remember her name in the morning.

CHAPTER FOUR

All was decay: Drew was surrounded by it and it had consumed him, without and within. Every pore, every fibre stank of death, of corruption. Of something so wrong and so unnatural Drew couldn't bear to move, lest it sense him and somehow turn upon him. He lay there, stock still, a cold stone slab beneath his back. It pressed against the nape of his neck, it pressed against that point on his ribs where he'd fallen from a horse years ago and landed badly on hard ground, and it pressed against his tailbone. He felt as if his body was being torn asunder along a line connecting those three points. He had to move to ease the pressure, but he was frozen there. Immobile. He couldn't move so much as a single fingertip. His body refused to obey any of his commands. What was this? Death? Was death meant to be this painful? Surely...

He tried again, to lift one hand, to wriggle his weight on the stone slab to ease some of the terrible pressure through his ribs. But... nothing happened. How could he be here, aware, yet unable to respond? Where even was "here"? His eyelids refused to open, but somehow he knew it was dark. And dank, and chill. Yet he couldn't see, couldn't explore anything with his fingertips to confirm or deny his assumptions.

He was alone there in the dark, his will somehow set apart from the corruption that surrounded him. Did that corruption stir? Might it respond to his thoughts in the way his body ought to have done? Had it turned to gaze at him with sightless eyes and to examine him with un-scenting nose? A shudder ran the length of his body, involuntary; then another shudder, more powerful than the first, set his leg muscles cramping. Another shudder, even stronger and he felt his body twist and spasm. A dreadful half-grunt, half-moan issued from his mouth as his whole torso jerked upwards and new pain found him, firing every nerve end simultaneously and racking him until he cried out, even though he feared that terrible evil would hear him and turn upon him. And air crept into his lungs, every bit as fetid and dank as he'd expected. A rank taste swam into his mouth as he gasped on the slab like a dying fish. Except he was not dying, somehow he understood that. This pain, this torment – this was living. And if this now was living, what had he been before? Walking through some dream, some nightmare? And if he had, and living was new, where had the words come from to give form to the shapeless fears that flitted through his mind? Worst thought of all, had that unnatural corruption supplied him with the words, and the thoughts, and the pain? And if it had, why? And what evil would it visit upon him next?

A fresh spasm racked his body and Drew woke with a start, crying out, some inarticulate moan of fear. He was sitting up in bed, a soft mattress beneath him, the warmth of Jervin's body beside him. The air was fresh and sweet. The scent of jasmine carried in from Jervin's courtyard garden through unshuttered windows. That gentle breeze, benevolent though it was, was enough to raise goosebumps on Drew's flesh. He shuddered, trying to shake away the shadow of the nightmare, but the foul taste of corruption lingered in his mouth.

Jervin stirred next to him. "You've been restless these past nights. What ails you?" He sounded more peevish than concerned.

Drew ran his hands through his hair; it was down to his shoulders now, the tonsure of Vorrahan long since grown out. And it somehow felt wrong and alien at that moment. He shivered. "Just some nightmare."

"Then you've been having a lot of those lately." Jervin sat up, leaning over to study his face. "You sure you're not trying to keep some secret from me?" He ran a lazy fingertip over Drew's forehead, pushing back the unruly hair.

"No, I wouldn't. I couldn't, you know that."

Jarvin huffed with laughter. "Some wife and children hidden away in Highground that you've forgotten to tell me about? Inappropriate thoughts about those traders from Ellisquay?" The fingertip strayed down the side of Drew's face, down his neck. Drew's pulse quickened and he caught his breath with anticipation as Jervin's hand moved to his chest.

"Goddess, you're sweating like a horse."

Drew's face heated with embarrassment. "I– I'm sorry. Just let me go and wash–"

"Did I say I didn't like it?" Jervin reached beneath the tangled bedcovers, leaning over to kiss Drew hungrily, pressing against him, hard and eager and guaranteed to chase away any nightmare. Drew abandoned any attempt to think and lost himself in their lovemaking. There were moments when Jervin's sense of humour confused him, when Drew didn't trust him at all, but here, like this, in the bed they shared, Jervin became Drew's entire world. Whatever those dreams meant, they had no place here in the waking world. Jervin's eager body next to him was all that mattered.

CHAPTER FIVE

Alwenna woke. She was shaking from the horror of her nightmare. It was still dark, probably hours before dawn. On the cot at the other side of the chamber, Erin slept soundly, her breathing steady, untroubled by any night fears. Alwenna knew a moment's envy – at times the girl's outlook was so prosaic it bewildered her, but the former servant had weathered the same storms alongside her and come out of the experience apparently whole and unbowed. Alwenna knew a mixture of envy and respect.

She was tempted to wake her and ask her what she thought of the dream, but that would be unfair. All she wanted was to hear another voice to banish the terrible dread of that dank corruption. Instead Alwenna pulled a gown on over her shift and slipped quietly out of the cave and into the desert night. The sky was clear and the half-moon not far off setting, but it gave enough light for her to see by once her eyes had adjusted. She walked some distance along the foot of the escarpment, climbing the slope away from the other dwellings. The night air was still, and almost perfect. If only there'd been a whiff of jasmine to leaven the air, something softer than the scents of sand and rock and scrubby vegetation. Her skin prickled with a strange awareness – had there been a dream within her nightmare? Something kinder? She couldn't recall it if there had been. It had been that way of late, dreams crowding one another out. Some effect of her pregnancy, perhaps. The wisewoman Jenna had left Scarrow's Deep, saying she would return soon; Alwenna hoped she would, so she might ask–

"My Lady Alwenna. You, too, are abroad this fine night."

"Marten? You startled me."

"I beg your pardon, my lady. It was not my intention." Marten was perched on a boulder protruding from the cliff face some ten feet above where she stood, his long legs doubled up with his forearms resting about them. He must have been watching her walk up the slope since she emerged from her cave. She had to crane her neck to see his face, although it was lost in shadow so the effort yielded little information.

"I must suppose you are comfortable up there, surveying your domain?"

"Yes, I believe I am. It is a favourite place. Why don't you join me up here?"

The face of the boulder was undercut, and it butted up against a sheer blank rock wall. "I think you overestimate my agility."

"As you do mine – it's an easy scramble from the other side." He gestured with his left hand. Unsure whether to believe him, Alwenna moved round the foot of the boulder to see that it was indeed the case. This facet of the boulder sloped gently and, even hampered by skirts, it was an easy matter to clamber up the ramp where it adjoined the rock. Marten reached out a hand to assist her, but she declined, choosing a sitting place beyond arm's length. Marten shrugged.

"I am not yet forgiven?"

"There is nothing to forgive – the elders are not yours to command, after all."

"I had hoped they would be of more substantive use than proved to be the case, however."

There he was, speaking like a courtier again. Yet what

passed for court in these parts was several days' ride away – assuming it hadn't burned entirely to the ground. "You must know, Marten, when you don the guise of a courtier I cannot trust you."

"How so?"

"You need to ask? You sold me entirely to Tresilian at the summer palace, even though you claimed to be my friend. That is the cause of my anger towards you. It has nothing to do with the elders."

"Appearances can be deceptive, my lady."

"As can you, freemerchant." Whether it was the night's camouflage that made it easier to speak her mind, or the shadow of the nightmare that impelled her to seek the truth, she didn't know. "You have as many answers as there are days in the year. For once, tell me the simple truth."

"Truth – now we have discussed that before, have we not?"

"Have we, indeed? I cannot recall." Weaver had spoken of truth once, long ago on the road to Vorrahan. What was it he'd said? Something about death being the ultimate truth? His certainty then had been absolute. And she'd not doubted him, either. Those had been simpler times...

"The truth is what has happened, my lady, but it is so much more than a simple event. The way each of us sees the same events can differ. What matters to my eyes may not matter to yours, yet we both see the same thing."

Alwenna shrugged, scarcely listening to the freemerchant. He annoyed her when he went off on these flights of fancy. And that was all too often of late.

"Of course, right now, my lady, the truth I perceive is that you are troubled." He moved closer so he could set a hand on her forearm. "It is perhaps better to speak of such things. And for once there are none nearby to overhear."

Alwenna twisted her head to look at him. "Can you be so sure? I am not. And I believe some things are better not spoken." She glanced pointedly at the hand on her arm and he removed it with a self-deprecating gesture of apology.

"Does the sight still trouble you, my lady?"

Well, he didn't need the sight to guess that much, did he? Wandering alone beneath the night sky when most sensible souls were asleep was an easy enough portent to divine. "Yes, it does. It has been less of late, but..." What did one say? She had been dreaming of a dark place, where all was corruption and tainted. Where the whole world was pain, without remit. And there was something familiar about it all, yet she couldn't quite place it. Her dreams of the lovers... they had been sharper, clearer. These visions – if she chose to call them that – they were nebulous, shifting, as insubstantial as night fears became by daylight. "Do you have the sight, Marten? I've heard often enough that freemerchants do."

"A fair question. It deserves a fair answer." He paused.

"Am I to assume a fair answer is not forthcoming? Some freemerchant secret that you are forbidden to reveal, no doubt."

"Not at all, my lady, but I fear my answer may disappoint you. We do not have the sight as I believe you would understand it. I've been told our senses are somewhat sharper than the average but I cannot divine your thoughts. It would make my life a great deal easier if I could."

Ought she believe him? Not that it mattered. She'd cast herself upon his protection. And still she didn't fully understand why. She'd run to help him at the summer palace when it looked as if Tresilian would have overwhelmed him – that she couldn't explain, either. Only that it had seemed paramount that she should save the freemerchant. But how much of that had been driven by distaste for what Tresilian had become?

"You doubt me still, my lady?"

"I doubt you still."

Marten spread his hands wide. "I cannot blame you for that. As it is I remain in your debt for saving my life. Do not forget that. You may call on me when you have need."

"I shall, never doubt it." Yet she sensed that day would not come soon. "Marten, I fear I ought not remain here."

"You are safe here, my lady. Of course you should remain here."

She worried with her thumbnail at a patch of dry skin on the side of her finger. "It isn't a question of my safety, Marten, but of yours. And your people. If I remain, I fear they will no longer be safe."

"You are letting the elders colour your thinking, my lady."

"No, Marten. I've had this conviction for some time now. A great evil stirs in the east. I ought not remain here, for your sakes."

"And what about the child you carry? Here, you are both safe. What else can you do? You would not return to Vasic, I think?"

"I doubt he'd make me any more welcome than your wife has." Alwenna could picture the horror on Vasic's face if she should ever return to Highkell.

"No one from your world knows you are here. You are safe."

"But how long will that last? And I am useless here, I can do nothing to help and I do not belong here. The very earth tells me so."

"Come now, this is not what you believe; this is the prompting of nightmares, of the fears that haunt us all through the dark night. Let the daylight bring reason: you will feel differently then. I invited you here and you are welcome as long as you need to remain. I say so, and that is enough for my people."

"It will not always be so." Alwenna spread one hand over the rock on which they sat. It was nothing but an inert lump of rock, yet she knew that strange moment of stillness, of certainty. "It will not always be so. If I leave now it will be the better for you."

"If you leave now I will hold no advantage against Vasic."

His voice was low, suddenly intense.

"Honesty at last, Marten? Your friendship is far from selfless. I have always known that, even before you gave us such proof at the summer palace."

"I will never hand you over to him." Again that intensity.

"No? Before you even know what price he might offer? Don't make promises you can't keep, Marten. You would do anything for the sake of your people, and woe betide any landbound who get in your way."

"You cannot leave now. You have the child to think of."

The first light of the sun was creeping up the sky, casting a pink hue on the undersides of the clouds. He was right, of course. Right now there was nowhere else she could go. She set an uneasy hand on her belly, fuller and firmer than it had been. Her life had become like wading through deep water, every achievement seemed to require so much more effort than it ought.

"I will not sell you to Vasic. I will swear any oath you care to ask to prove my loyalty."

Alwenna shuddered, remembering the proof of loyalty Tresilian had demanded of Weaver. Marten's words had cast an uneasy shadow over the place where they sat. She'd once demanded an oath of loyalty from Weaver, and look where that had got him. "I will demand no oath of you. Such things seldom end well. Besides, I doubt Vasic would have me at any price now."

"Perhaps not." His voice was flat.

"You don't agree?"

"I don't agree." Marten hesitated. "The blood in your veins, and the child you carry – both could be used to further his own cause, just as Tresilian tried to use it. Don't waste time denying it – you know it is true."

Once again she had the sense Marten knew rather more about everything than he chose to tell her. But she also knew his words were true. "Some day, Marten, you will tell me all you know. And I pray to the Goddess that day will not arrive too late."

"My lady, I swear, you are safe here. No one knows you even survived the fire. Even now freemerchants are spreading word that you have not been seen since that day, and that we mourn our sister."

"Easily a dozen people saw us leave the palace."

"Did they have time to study your face? They were all busy carrying water, or recovering goods from buildings. They just saw two servant girls riding hell for leather away on stolen horses. And probably envied them their escape."

It might work.

"Ask yourself how many people there even knew for certain who you were in the first place, my lady."

That was easy: Marten, who sat next to her now; Erin, who slept safely in their cave further down the hill; Tresilian himself, dead at her and Marten's hands; Curtis, dead at Weaver's hands; Weaver, left behind to perish in the flames, may the Goddess watch over him; and Tresilian's pale priestess, with, perhaps, a few members of the vile priesthood.

"The priestess knew."

"She – and her kind – cannot touch you here. There are ancient wards about this place to prevent it being found by enemies. And for all they know you were grievously injured in the fire. You are safer here than you could be anywhere else on the Peninsula. Trust me."

"I trust you believe what you are saying." For all his protestations of loyalty, Marten would change his allegiance again. Of that she was certain. And she had no option, right now. She had to remain at Scarrow's Deep. But for how long?

CHAPTER SIX

Weaver could not have said how many days he'd lain in that room. It might have been forever. He lay there, conscious of air moving across his face, sometimes of sunlight that warmed his flesh, sometimes of shadow that sent a chill through his entire body. The pain was ever present: a sharp stabbing that lanced from beneath his arm and into his chest. He lay there, mute and obedient, because that was what was required of him. He saw no reason to question his understanding. It just was. Any kind of movement was too great an effort. He lay there, on his back, hands down by his sides. His limbs were too heavy to move at all. Even his eyelids seemed weighted with lead. Stolen from a roof, like as not... Although why that seemed to matter, he did not know. Thoughts like that made the pain worse. He had no business thinking for himself. Orders. He followed orders. Deep within, he knew that made sense. How he knew, he could not say. He drifted from moment to moment, untroubled by... Well, that was untrue. He was troubled: by the pain, by the sense that all here was not as it should be. But he was not so troubled he could stir himself to rouse from this lifelong sleep he seemed to have fallen into.

Voices intruded on his inertia. They were a jarring note against the silence. He wanted them to go away. To leave him to meld with the emptiness, the silence. It was all he required.

But instead they drew closer, louder. Two men.

"And how fares our patient?"

"Very well, sire. Very well indeed."

"His progress is slow."

"It is better this way, sire." The man's voice was hesitant. "We want him completely dependent on us, to lose all vestige of free will. This is the best way." The voices went on, but Weaver had no interest in them. He yearned for silence, for solitude. For the stillness that had been before. Before all this tumult of... What? Motion and commotion. The urge to move, to raise a hand. To tug at the source of the pain in his chest. The demands of life pulsing through his veins, insistent.

"Did his fingers move?"

"Yes, sire. That is to be expected at this stage. Soon he will be ready to wake."

"Very well, then. Keep me informed of progress. I want a full written account of the process..."

The voices drifted away then and Weaver relaxed. Except the silence was not absolute. Someone else moved around the room. Light footsteps hurried across the stone. There was a faint movement of air, the shush of fabric... Why would they not leave him alone? Had he not already done enough? How many times must he prove himself?

There was a stirring of air against the side of his face, then a voice whispered in his ear. "Can you hear me? You can, can't you?" There was a sharp intake of breath. "You can't trust any of them. But you should trust me." There was a girlish giggle. "You'll see soon enough."

The hair on the back of his neck rose in instinctive horror. Trust her? He'd as soon... but he had no words to express his revulsion.

There was a whisper of movement, then her voice sounded from further away. "They'll try to use you, just like they used me. But I'm going to help you, and then you can help me in return. That's how it works."

Another shifting of air and the padding of furtive footsteps across the floor, and then he was alone. Solitude and silence, blessed be the Goddess. Let the voices not return so they'd trouble him no more. Let him be alone with his pain. He'd earned that right.

CHAPTER SEVEN

This was getting repetitive. Bleaklow braced himself before stepping into yet another muggy tavern. The stale air was thick with spilled beer and cabbage, a particular favourite of the dockside. But, in a reversal of recent ill fortune, the very man he hoped to find was propping up the bar at the furthest end from the door. Or perhaps the bar was propping the man up – it was ever hard to tell. The man in question was a guard at the palace and, according to the roster, had been on duty the night of the wedding. Tonight he was very much off duty, and clearly had been for several hours. He studied his pint of ale with the fixed stare of one who no longer cared if he drank any more or not.

"Evening. You're Simmons, I take it?"

"Eh? Why? Who's asking?" The man was startled well and truly out of his beer-sodden reverie. It seemed reasonable to conclude he was indeed Simmons, sometime guard of the royal household and drunken ne'er do well.

"Simmons." Bleaklow smiled and set an urbane hand on the man's shoulder as the guard half stood, setting one foot on the ground. If he'd had any thoughts of making an abrupt departure he abandoned them, sinking back onto his bar stool.

Simmons took up his tankard, as if he feared Bleaklow was about to take it from him. "Now I'm not sure what people have been telling you, but I'm a peaceable, law-abiding man."

"Oh, I don't doubt it." Bleaklow bared his teeth in a cold smile. "But I'm pleased to hear it all the same, since I've some questions that need answers, and you are just the man to give me them."

Simmons didn't seem to find the smile or the words reassuring. His fingers tightened about the pint tankard. Good. Respectability had become something of a habit in the years Bleaklow had been working for the royal household and he'd been worried he might have lost his edge.

"Now then, Simmons. It's nothing too complicated. I gather you were on guard duty the night of the wedding. Yes?"

Simmons nodded slowly. "Yes."

Bleaklow nodded. "Excellent. Now think carefully: was there much coming and going to and from the palace after dark that night?"

Simmons' brow furrowed. He shook his head slowly, warily watching Bleaklow for any reaction. Reassured by his bland expression, he got up the courage to speak. "It were quiet. Right quiet."

"Again, excellent." Bleaklow smiled again. "In that case I'm sure you remember everyone who entered or left the palace bounds."

Simmons hesitated, his mouth dropping open for a moment. "Well, I don't know as–"

"How many people left the palace before morning?" Bleaklow didn't smile now.

Simmons licked his lips. "Well there were a couple of drays left with empty barrels."

"Who was driving them? Did they carry any passengers?"

"No passengers." Simmons scratched his head. "They were just the usual draymen – old Len from the harbourside, and that young chap from the top of the hill."

"Anyone else?"

Simmons scratched his head some more. "Well, there were

a few lads who'd been celebrating a bit much – got turfed out."

"Anyone else? Any women, perhaps?"

Simmons' jaw dropped again. "Well, now you come to mention it there was one. A laundry woman. Cheeky with it, gave me lip as she was waiting for me to open the gate."

Bleaklow doubted that. "How old would you say she was?"

"Young." Simmons nodded vigorously. "Definitely young."

"Tall, short? Fat, thin? What colour was her hair? Eyes?" Bleaklow leaned in closer to Simmons. "Make no mistake now, or it'll be the worse for you."

"She was... normal height for a woman? Maybe on the tall side. Shorter'n most men though. She wasn't fat. Was hard to tell cos she wore a thick cloak. Pretty. Long eyelashes, dark hair, I think. Tied back it was, but not fancy."

Bleaklow grilled the man until he'd extracted enough details of the laundry woman's appearance to be reasonably confident it was the Lady Drelena. A little more careful questioning elicited the information that she'd walked off in the direction of the harbour. But when he thought he'd pumped Simmons dry, the guard rallied.

"So why you lookin' for her? She done something wrong?"

The lie came easily now, he'd repeated it so often. "It's a matter of petty theft. Once the complaint was made I have to follow it up or I'll get no end of grief. Chances of finding her now are non-existent – but mind, if you see her again, there could be a reward in it for you. It's not so much what she stole, but who she stole it from. Important people don't like to be crossed."

Bleaklow left Simmons to enjoy the remains of his tepid pint. He doubted he'd have any need to speak to him again. She'd not be on the island any more, not if he understood her character right. They'd already searched the docks, after all. Although they hadn't been looking for a pert young washer woman with a sharp tongue and no manners. If Simmons could be believed; the man was just enough of a coward to have told him more or less the truth. He'd held something back, for sure. But that didn't concern Bleaklow right now: he had a runaway royal to find.

CHAPTER EIGHT

Peveril was waiting with a scribe in the guardroom when the apprentice turned up at the palace. He'd slicked down his hair and wore a clean smock, in an attempt to make himself look respectable. This was going to be too easy.

"I come, like you said. You said to ask for Captain Peveril." The youth enunciated every syllable with great care.

"An' you found him. Right then, lad, first we need to take your statement. This 'ere's a scribe an' he'll write down what you say. That way it's official. An' this statement is what my master'll read. Got that?"

The lad nodded, his expression sombre.

"We start wi' your full name an' address, so's it's all official an' above board."

"Address?"

"Where you live, like. That's what officials call it – the street, the house, the room you rent?"

"Oh, right." The lad took a deep breath.

It took half an hour to repeat his story, while the scribe laboured over the parchment, each stroke of the quill painstakingly slow. There were faster writers to be had, but this one was, frankly, cheaper. And Peveril had bought his silence years ago.

"And now, lad, I said to you to bring proof. You done that?"

"Aye, I have." The lad's jaw was set again. This was not a promising sign.

"Out with it, then."

The lad turned his eyes to the scribe. "You said be careful no one saw..."

"The scribe here will witness it. He's sound – like me he's in the pay of the palace."

The scribe looked up from his parchment and nodded sombrely.

The lad looked from scribe to Peveril then appeared to reach a decision. He fumbled open his scrip and drew out a tiny fabric-wrapped bundle. He unfolded the wrapping to reveal a piece of gold, formed in the shape of a leaf, detailed with intricate veining. Exquisite work. From one end of the leaf dangled a short length of gold chain, from the other a single gold loop that formed part of a clasp. He held the object out towards Peveril, but did not hand it over.

"That's a fine piece. But you said you had the rest of it."

"Aye. I do. An' if'n your master wants to see it, or buy it, an' names his price, I'll bring it then. An' not before."

Damn him, the lad was not as green as he was grass-looking. Not when sober, at any rate. "Very wise, Master Shott. Very wise."

The lad nodded tightly. "Aye. I'll keep it safe until then." He closed his hand about the leaf he held out.

"Understandable. But you see, my master will want to see for himself – he won't just take my word for it."

The lad's mouth tightened in a stubborn line. "I don't know much, but I know this is worth a deal of coin."

"Aye, lad, so it is." This wasn't quite as easy as he'd hoped. "That's why my master will pay ten coins for it, right here an' now. I'm authorised to buy it from you at that price. See, there's some as will take your statement at face value, but there's others won't believe it until they seen the glint of gold for themselves. And them's the kind my master has to deal with."

The lad licked his lips. "Ten coin, you say?" The hand holding out the bauble shook a little. That must be several months' work for a lowly apprentice.

"The whole piece would be worth a lot more, of course. Broken like it is, takes the value down. Can always see where these things have been mended. If'n you're not sure take a look down at the market an' see what you can buy from the goldsmith for that."

The lad straightened his shoulders. "Ten coin, then. I'll sell it to your master."

Peveril counted out the money onto the table, watching the lad carefully as he did so. He paused at eight, but the lad seemed to know that wasn't enough. Reluctantly he counted out nine, then ten before the youth nodded tightly again and finally handed over the leaf, scooping up the coins and adding them to his scrip.

Peveril wrapped the leaf in its fabric and likewise stowed it away safely, along with the scroll containing the youth's report. "It has been a pleasure doing business with you, Master Shott. Expect to hear from me soon about the rest of the necklace – I have no doubt my master will be keen to acquire it."

Peveril watched the lad cross the yard, looking far too perky for his liking. Arrogant young prick. This wasn't over yet. The lad strutted past old Marwick, who paused and glanced back at him before resuming his ponderous progress to the guardroom. It was time for the quarterly review of the accounts for the palace guard. The scribe was still scratching with his quill on a fresh sheet of parchment.

"Ol' Faceache's on his way – you done with that yet?"

"Very nearly." The scribe spoke without a trace of Highkell accent. It always surprised Peveril, perhaps because the scribe spoke so seldom. His face had been rearranged so many times Peveril always tended to think of the rogue as one of his own. And the truth was far from it. His best guess was the scribe had been a noble who'd fallen on hard times.

The scribe sprinkled sand over the sheet to dry the ink, then dusted it off and held out the sheet to Peveril. Peveril dropped a couple of coins into his hand, but the scribe didn't release the sheet.

"We agreed three, I believe."

Peveril had no time to argue, Marwick was approaching the door. He dropped another coin into the scribe's hand and the man released the sheet of parchment. Peveril pretended to study the sheet. He'd tried to learn his letters, but somehow never managed it. He recognised one or two, but they danced before his eyes and refused to line up one after another so he might decipher them. He wasn't about to let the scribe know that, however.

The door opened and Marwick stepped in, favouring his left hip. "Damned weather's on the turn. You have the accounts ready for inspection?"

Peveril nodded to the scribe. "Bring them out, Birtle."

The scribe jumped up from his stool and hurried to the shelves at the back of the room. He always moved a deal faster when the likes of Marwick were about. That was something else that vexed Peveril. Marwick didn't even know the half of what Peveril did – and Peveril knew enough to hang the skinny scribe twice over, ruined face and all. And one day–

"What was that young lad's business here? He appeared pleased with himself."

"The arrogant little tyke? Some tale of cutpurses hanging round after dark. I reckon he lost something he shouldn't have and wants to shift the blame off his shoulders." Peveril handed the parchment to Marwick, who took a cursory glance over it.

"I daresay you're right. His wasn't the face of one who'd lost a week's earnings. Have there been any similar reports lately?"

Peveril made show of considering. "Not that I recall."

"Strikes me anyone foolish enough to carry a full purse

abroad after dark deserves what's coming to them. We should never have lifted the curfew." Marwick dropped the sheet on the table next to the ledger which Birtle had helpfully opened on the most recent page. "There's enough to be done round here without running around on behalf of feckless citizens who haven't the sense to look after their own property."

CHAPTER NINE

Durstan pressed his hands to his temples and leaned back in his chair. He couldn't massage away the headache that had been gnawing at him all evening. This day had lasted far too long and he was no closer to a solution. He might as well sleep. He needed to be patient. It would take time to work on the soldier Weaver, to ensure he would offer them his full potential. The order had been given a golden opportunity, just when it looked as if they were finished.

Really the girl should have been rewarded for her loyalty to the order. There must be some suitable way of doing it that didn't give her undue status. A naming ceremony, perhaps. A name accorded to her by the order would be an honour indeed. He couldn't risk anything that would give her too much influence over the others because she was such a one as would abuse it without a second thought. Look how calmly she'd sold her brother's secret – and his life – to him. Even Durstan, in his position of honour, had to grudgingly admire her *sang froid*. And this was precisely why the order would be wise to keep her sweet. If she eluded their control she could cause no small amount of trouble for them. And until the child she carried was born... It irked him to admit it, but until her child was born, the order needed her. After that she could serve the order one last time, just as her brother had.

Durstan had little time for diplomacy but this situation called for the exercise of something close to it. The loss of Tresilian had been a bitter blow, indeed. The little priestess could have led him by the nose anywhere and she'd been happy enough with all the attention he gave her. Vain creature. Just like all her kind. And now she was unsettled and likely to cause far more trouble than she was worth. Setting her to tend to the soldier had gone some way to keeping her occupied. If she carried the late king's child, of course, her worth to the order increased beyond measure. And born out of the rites of rebirth, it would be a child like no other. The royal family had always carried the power in their blood, even though that power had long fallen out of use.

All their plans had been so close to fruition. Where the erstwhile queen had gone, no one seemed to know. But he would find out; oh yes, he would. He was seeking information from every one of his spies and contacts. Every favour he was owed he was calling in now, and if any dared to ignore his call for help – well, woe betide them.

The pounding of his forehead intensified and he finally reached for the bottle of willow water his physician had prepared. He tipped a few drops into a glass and added some wine to it.

The freemerchant was behind some of the mischief, that was for sure. That one had outlived his usefulness: Durstan wouldn't forgive his defection. It left him only one choice, although that might yet prove to be a lucrative association if he could but persuade Vasic of the value of the order to his plans. And who would not want an elite guard who were obedient without question? That's what would persuade Vasic. Unfortunately the usurper was notorious for his volatility. Doubly unfortunately, he was also their last best hope. And the only one of the royal line Durstan could lay his hands on at this point in time. On the plus side, he'd far sooner deal man-to-man with such as Vasic than be forced to deal with a woman. And by all accounts the Lady Alwenna had been as stubborn and intractable as he might have expected. Her blood made it inevitable, of course. Where a man had honour and nobility, and could be counted upon to deal with those around him accordingly, a woman had only wiles and fickleness. But, if the priestess's claims were true, then the same woman had also killed her own husband – her own kin, no less – with the ancient blade and that meant her blood now carried uncommon power as a result of the tangled family history.

He would do well to find the former queen before she discovered her own strength. That strength belonged to the order and she had stolen it out from under their noses. And he would have it back within their confines, harnessed once more so it would serve him and his people and lead them to eternal splendour in the favour of the one true Goddess.

CHAPTER TEN

"They'll just use you. Like they used me. You can't trust them." The same voice, repetitive and insistent, over and over. Why wouldn't she just go away? Let him sleep, just let him be. Even opening his eyes was too much effort. Let her just go away.

The small hand prodded Weaver's shoulder, insistent. "You can hear me, can't you?"

He tried to open his mouth, to speak, to tell her to stop. But it was as if he was fighting his way up from beneath deep water. The effort was so great, yet he couldn't seem to make progress. He sank back beneath the surface and drifted away into oblivion.

Was she too late? She leaned over Weaver, studying him closely. Breath stirred from his nostrils, his chest rose and fell slowly. He was lost in a deep sleep once more. There was nothing for it. She would have to stop him drinking the physic the order gave him. He was always drugged too deeply to respond to her at night, and that was the only time she could speak with him at any length. She had duties in the infirmary through the day – and she'd made sure she continued to be useful to the order in obvious, visible ways. It was the important people who got their way in this world, and if she hoped to topple a queen – even an exiled one – she would need to be very influential indeed.

The next day in the infirmary as she stowed clean linen in the cupboard she watched the priest preparing the last medication of the day for Weaver before he carried it through to the small chamber the soldier occupied. As she thought, it contained a great deal of poppy juice. No wonder she could never wake him or get any sense out of him. That would have to change. She would need to substitute it with something equally syrupy, so it didn't appear obviously different.

There was that voice again, disturbing his sleep. Weaver grimaced with annoyance. When the hand shook his shoulder, he raised his own hand to push it away. Weak muscles protested, unused to such abrupt movement. And in that instant he was wide awake.

What had happened? The weight that seemed to have been pressing his eyelids shut was gone. And his eyes were open. The room about him was unsteady, blurred. Shadows wavered and he could not see the far walls. For a moment he believed himself back in the cavern containing the holy well on Vorrahan. But the air here was not dank and chill, there was no whisper of slow-moving water, no echo from the stone walls of the cavern.

"Shush, now. Don't let them hear you." The young woman's voice whispered and the hand pressed his shoulder. It took a moment to bring her face into focus. She was a pale blur against the darkness, scarcely more than a ghostly presence. Perhaps he was imagining this – all of it. Yet the hand on his shoulder was very real, felt completely solid.

He shrugged his shoulder and this time she removed her hand. His tendons knotted up at the unexpected movement, tightening with a sharp pain. He flinched, despite himself. His whole body was similarly knotted up, every movement setting off spasms through unused muscles. What was wrong with him?

But his vision was clearing. The face before him resolved.

She was a young woman, slight but with pretty features. Her hair was palest blonde, her eyes a cool grey. Her features were pretty, but the expression in her eyes as she studied him chilled him to the core. And he remembered: the altar, the bowls, the blade. The king he'd sworn fealty to and his pale priestess standing before them. And there, facing them, the freemerchant and–

No.

Weaver's gut twisted with revulsion. In that instant he tried to spring to his feet, but succeeded only in knotting muscles that were weak from disuse with fresh spasms.

"Don't worry, you're in no danger from me." Her voice was saccharine again. "Because you're going to help me, and I'm going to help you. Right now, we need one another. Let me tell you how it will be."

CHAPTER ELEVEN

"An', if'n you can, get another sack of neeps from yon northerner. They cook well. He'll bring 'em round at the end of the day, maybe sooner if he's keen to get his money. Look lively, then."

Lena pulled her cloak on, before the cook could change her mind. She'd never been trusted to complete the errands alone. It was a sorry reflection of what her life had become that she was actually pleased to have an opportunity to look round the market. It would be a luxury to linger over the fine silks on the fabric stall, consider the leather purses – not that she had much to put in one – examine the boots on the cordwainer's stall, or dally with the notion of a new shawl. One last day of freedom before she brought this episode to an end, perhaps. Freedom involved a great deal of drudgery, it turned out. And she was feeling increasingly guilty over the anxiety her parents must be suffering. She had been away long enough to make her point, surely? Long enough to ensure the next time they talked marriage it would be on her terms, at the very least. If that had been her point – she was no longer sure. She'd wanted to see life, to taste it for herself. Mostly, she'd seen a succession of greasy pans in the scullery sink and tasted more mutton stew than she had in all the years of her life leading to that point.

The market square was set on flat ground just above the harbour. Sea freight had always been important to the harbour town of Sylhaven. Fishing was steady business, but the real wealth came in with the merchants' cargoes, traded across the oceans. That was what built the many stone houses on the sloping streets above the sea front; Sylhaven had been a prosperous port for many years. Henty had told her the larger ships now struggled to navigate the inlet, but it remained home to many wealthy tradesmen.

Herbs acquired, Lena paused to run her fingers over the bolts of silk on the fabric merchant's stall. It shimmered, even in the poor light of an overcast morning, but her fingers were so roughened from hard work they risked snagging the fine material. She lingered over a bolt of jade green fabric, just long enough for the stallholder to take notice.

"Now, my lady, you'd be fine indeed in that, 'twould match your eyes to perfection. There's not a man could resist you if he saw you clothed in that."

"Kind of you to say so, but I'm sure it would be beyond my means. How much for three ells?"

"To one such as yourself I could let you have it for fourteen coins, for I'm sure you'd tell everyone who admired it where you came by such fabric."

"That's a good price. If my employer were so generous with my wages I would not hesitate."

She moved on, scratching absentmindedly at the point where her rough woollen collar chafed her neck. It didn't take long to make her other purchases and she began to wend her way back down the other side of the market, determined to make the most of her few minutes of liberty.

The market was growing busier now as the first quiet of morning had passed. Someone bumped against Lena as she studied the haberdasher's threads.

"I beg your pardon." The man's voice was elusively familiar.

She looked up, to meet Nils Darnell's brown, if somewhat bloodshot, eyes. The pallor of his face suggested his head was giving him good reason to regret the previous night's imbibing.

"No harm done." She turned her attention back to finding the thread she needed to mend her blue gown – not that she'd have need of it if she returned home. Darnell clearly hadn't recognised her. The aisle was empty once she had negotiated her purchase. All just as she'd predicted. She only had the turnips to order, then her errands would be done.

She turned and made her way to the stall where the cook had bought the last lot of turnips. After spirited negotiation she bargained the stallholder down to a good price and set off back towards the inn.

"Excuse me, my lady." Nils Darnell stepped forward into her path, smiling tentatively. "We have met before, haven't we?"

"You bumped into me just now, certainly, if that's what you mean."

"But I thought at the time your face was familiar. Perhaps we have some acquaintance in common?"

"I very much doubt it, sir. I suspect we move in different circles."

"Surely not. This is not so large a town, after all."

"I work at the *Royal Hart*, perhaps–" She did not need to finish her sentence.

"That was you, last night, was it not?" His expression changed subtly to one of embarrassment. "I fear I must have left you with a poor impression. Small wonder you prefer not to acknowledge the acquaintance."

"I imagined on the whole you would prefer not to be reminded of the episode, sir."

His expression fell. "I had hoped my behaviour had not been so – at least permit me to thank you for your patient–"

A male voice, deep, broke in. "Step aside, Darnell. Let a man pass."

Darnell stepped aside, moving closer to Lena. "Master Barrett, and Miss Barrett. Good morning."

The young woman behind Master Barrett nodded distantly and her eyes flicked over Lena in rapid assessment.

The older man inclined his head with little attempt to be polite. "I see you haven't let the grass grow under your feet, Darnell. Good day to you and to your fair companion." He raised his hat in ironic salute and moved off while his daughter – as Lena surmised she must be – followed in his wake, keeping her eyes averted.

Darnell turned back to Lena. "Goddess, I'm so sorry. He's no right to speak of you like that. I should have introduced you, but I still don't, I think, know your name..."

"Can you truly not recall? It was the subject of much discussion last night."

"I was three sheets to the wind last night, as you well know." He glanced after Barrett. "Is there some less public place where we might continue this conversation?"

"I fear not, I must return to work. I've lingered here long enough already. Good day to you, Master Darnell."

"Permit me to carry your basket, at the very least. And I promise this time to remember your name if you'll be so tolerant as to tell me it again." He took hold of the basket handle, and she released it with good enough grace. It was heavy enough to be an inconvenience, although nothing like as heavy as he had been last night.

"Lena is my name."

"Delighted to make your acquaintance once again. If I'm to perform proper introductions, I'll be needing your surname."

"I cannot imagine the situation arising."

"It did just now. What's to say it won't again?"

"A great many things, I imagine. They must be more than obvious, even to you in the throes of your hangover."

"There are two things obvious to me this morning, Lena.

One is that I made a damned fool of myself last night."

They had reached the inn. Lena made to reclaim her basket, but he held onto it. "And the other, sir?"

"The other? That you are a highly unlikely inn servant. Everything about you speaks of high birth and a sound education."

"I was fortunate to be raised in a wealthy household where education was held in high regard. I have enjoyed opportunities denied to many women in similar circumstances."

"I enjoy solving a good mystery, Lena. I hope this will not be our last meeting." He released the basket and she hurried indoors, with a pang of regret. Solving mysteries with Nils Darnell was the most tempting prospect she'd encountered in her time at Sylhaven. Maybe she wouldn't leave just yet.

CHAPTER TWELVE

Marten and three slighter figures were hard at work on the flat floor of the valley beyond the old tree. His three sons each wielded a wooden training blade in turn as their father walked them through basic exercises. Alwenna was familiar enough with the forms from watching Tresilian training all those years ago. Sometimes – depending which fencing master had been teaching that day – she had been allowed to join in. She settled on one of the stones in the shade of the tree to watch. None of them had noticed her presence, and she was far off enough not to intrude. It was a peaceful scene, even though they were studying the art of war. And with Marten, as it had been with Weaver, it was indeed an art: the freemerchant moved with the same grace and precision. Of the three boys, the middle one, Brett, was closest to matching his father's style. He seemed to have a natural aptitude for the discipline, soon mastering the footwork of the various moves Marten showed him. The youngest, Pieten, didn't seem greatly interested in the finer points. His endeavours were mainly limited to brandishing the wooden sword and hacking wildly at his opponent and he laughed off Marten's attempts to improve his technique. Malcolm worked stolidly and seriously, as he did at everything, but he lacked the speed and agility shared by his father and Brett. At the end of the session he joined Pieten, who had long ago abandoned any pretence of training and, ruffling his younger brother's hair, they set off back towards the dwellings.

Brett clearly hadn't had enough, and he and his father engaged in another bout, working through the set routines Alwenna was so familiar with. Just how long ago had it been when she sat and watched Tresilian sparring with Weaver at Highkell? It felt like a lifetime and more... She knew a moment's dizziness, as if the sunlight had suddenly dazzled her, even though she sat there in the shade of the tree. She'd learned of late, somehow, to prevent the sight catching her unawares, if not being able to entirely stop it. This was just a reminder it was never far away, always watching her... Which was a foolish thought. The sight was a part of her, whether she welcomed it or not. As was her past. And it would always intrude on her notice when she thought she'd turned her back on it at last.

"My lady. Have we provided you with adequate entertainment this morning?" Marten saluted her with his wooden sword. He was looking more like the man she remembered from the summer palace, vital and alive. The man who'd sold her to her undead husband without turning so much as a hair. It didn't hurt to remind herself of that at frequent intervals.

"The finest display of swordsmanship I've seen this side of the Peninsula."

Brett grinned and blushed deep red.

Marten also grinned. "The only display of swordsmanship this side of the Peninsula." The likeness between them was very apparent at that moment.

Sundry other boys were hanging around watching from a distance, while pretending not to be at all interested.

Alwenna stood up, dusting the ever-present layer of sand off her gown. She was aware of the vigorous weight in her belly as she stooped. She'd lost track of the number of days that had passed, but it must be visible to the casual observer by now. She pushed the thought away. "Tell me, Marten, have you no other pupils keen to learn your skills?"

Marten glanced up the hill to where the others were watching. "Alas, no. Not as yet."

"I think they might be persuaded soon enough."

"Their parents are against it. It's difficult to..." Marten tucked the wooden sword under his arm and walked alongside Alwenna. "Freemerchant lore would have it the Hunter gave us weapons to be used as tools for catching and butchering our food, nothing more. I'm not only going against the old ways, but some of the basic tenets of our faith. Some say I've spent too much time in the towns of the Peninsula, drinking with soldiers and kings."

"Do you think you have?"

"Perhaps, for all the good it's done me."

"But you're still teaching your sons according to landbound philosophy?"

"I want to teach my sons to live in the wider world, because I fear one day it will come knocking at our door, whether we invite it or not."

Alwenna's gut knotted with apprehension. "So the elders have convinced you that I will bring disaster in my wake?"

Brett was tagging alongside them now, listening to their conversation.

"No such thing, my lady. Here, Brett, you take this sword back home for me. Let your Ma know we're done, in case she's been holding food back for us."

Brett took the wooden swords and dashed off up the hill.

"He is very like you – I imagine you must have been just like him at that age."

"I've been told that more than once." Marten stopped. "And I've told you more than once to disregard the rubbish old Rogen spouted. The years haven't been kind to him and he'll look to blame everyone and everything but himself for any imagined slight. Pay no heed to the old fool's words. He doesn't have the backing of a majority on the council."

"Don't you realise, Marten? I've been told everything he said before. Growing up at Highkell there were constant jibes from the other children: I was ill-omened. And do you know who told me it most recently, before Rogen? Father Garrad. Just seconds before he turned that blade upon himself." She paused to find the words. "I don't want to seem negative when I say this, but I am beginning to believe there may be some truth in it. I– I've grown up with the knowledge of it. Ever since my parents died. Every childhood taunt... Recent events have given me enough evidence to think it may be true."

"That's nonsense. I'm sorry, my lady, but that's the truth. You are no more a creature of ill-omen than anyone else here. I'll grant you there has been dark power at work, but that resides in the blade, not in you."

"Can you be so sure of that?"

"You are better since you have been parted from it, are you not? You don't suffer the same visions and night fears?"

"You've been talking to Erin, I suppose."

"It's my business to find out the things I need to know. Had you forgotten?"

"You need not resort to subterfuge: you might simply ask me."

"I believe I just did. You assumed I've been questioning Erin."

"I did. And you didn't deny it."

Marten smiled. "I didn't, did I?"

It was impossible to hold a reasonable conversation with him. "I've been thinking about it though. The visions... I think they're stronger when I'm near water. There's so little of it here, not like it was at Highkell. Even at the summer palace, there was a spring in the fountain courtyard. And by the well..." She'd been overwhelmed by a vision as they'd tried to escape. And Marten had come to their rescue, only to hand them over to Tresilian after all.

Marten twisted his mouth, unconvinced. She hoped he hadn't followed her train of thought.

"That could all be coincidence. It's the blade, I tell you. It's drawn the blood of your kin."

"We could at least put these theories to the test."

"How? Should we give you a bath?" Marten laughed.

"This is no time for levity. You should give me back the blade."

Marten's laughter died. "You're serious, aren't you?"

Alwenna spread her hands wide. "What else are we to do? We've learned nothing here and we're no further ahead than the day we arrived."

"No, Alwenna. I can't permit that."

"Why not? Do you want the blade for yourself?"

"Goddess, no. Of course I don't."

"Well then, why not? We might learn something, at least."

Marten shook his head. "It's too dangerous. We don't know how great the power of that thing is."

"In truth, Marten, I think what you're saying is you don't know how great the power of the blade is when it's held in my hand. Now tell me again where you believe that power resides."

"It's drawn the blood of your kin. I told you before."

"Then let me take hold of it again. That blade belongs to me."

"That blade would destroy you. Weaver told me what happened when you took hold of it. I saw for myself what happened at the summer palace. It would destroy you, and I will not let that happen."

Always the menfolk talking and settling everything between themselves. Don't let her do this or that, lest she hurt her silly self. "Maybe, Marten, I'm stronger than you think. Maybe I would rule the blade and not the other way around."

"Maybe, my lady, that thought has already crossed my mind." Marten's expression was sombre. "Maybe that is what I most fear."

CHAPTER THIRTEEN

There was a new routine to Weaver's days, as the priests worked on him through the day, then administered the syrup they believed would make him sleep at night. It was just as the priestess had warned him it would be, but thanks to her he knew the right answers to their incessant questions, knew what was expected of him. He had no wish to be beholden to her, but until he recovered his strength he had little option. The less he tried to resist, the sooner the priests would leave him in peace. But, Goddess, he wanted to resist them. With every fibre of his being. It was one of his few certainties in that bleak time, and he clung to it. Those priests were his enemies, and one day he'd see them brought down. Then they'd pay for every slight against him. He knew he could not trust the priestess either, but she had been right: they needed one another if they were to fight free of this situation.

And focusing on that taxed him enough. There were so many questions at the back of his mind, but he refused to allow them space during waking hours. It was the only way to get through this. Once they'd broken free, then he might dare to consider the half-buried thoughts and memories that ghosted through his sleep. They were there now, gnawing at the edge of his consciousness, but he dared not grant them attention. Let them stay away, leave him in peace. He knew he wasn't ready to deal with them. He may never be ready. The priestess had told him as much. It was usual, she said, for patients like him to need help after their recovery. Right now, his only certainty was relief that the pain was finally easing. In the night, when there was no one around to witness it, he rose from his bed to exercise. Somehow he had to reclaim his body from the pain and the weakness; somehow he had to rebuild his strength, ready for his escape.

Weaver stood now at the back of the altar chamber as the priest droned on. The prelate, highest on earth, he was supposed to call him. Old lopleg, the priestess called him. But there was a roomful of people standing in devout silence, listening to his words with rapt attention. Or perhaps, like Weaver, they chose to stand meekly and look as if they were paying attention while their minds wandered over more interesting terrain.

And Weaver was paying scant attention to the man's droning. He was largely absent from the moment, absent even from his own mind. He was surprised when a young woman stepped forward to the dais where the prelate was holding forth, acclaimed by the prelate in a booming voice.

"And this day, loyal brethren, I bring forward a new sister to join your ranks. She has served the order well and proven herself loyal to the faith."

Weaver had no difficulty recognising his night-time visitor: the pale priestess. She appeared startled, her tiny nostrils flared as if she was scenting for danger. A suspicious creature, that one. What she suspected of the world said much of what she was prepared to deal out herself. Much, and more. Weaver would never have chosen her as an ally, but the Goddess had seen fit to deliver her to him and he was not about to question the Goddess's choice. And where had that thought even come from? What Goddess? Had the brethren been feeding him poppy juice again for his mind to wander so?

The prelate was still extolling the virtues of the sharp-faced priestess. No, Weaver decided, the wary look on her face convinced him she had not expected this at all. But she kept her head bowed until the prelate ordered her to kneel before him.

"And now, daughter, I welcome you to our order." He anointed her forehead with wine. "And I commend you to your new brethren, and I commend your name to your new brethren: You are welcome as one of us, Sister Miria. Brethren, bid your sister welcome."

"Hail, sister Miria, you are welcome among us. And you are one with us. As one we will uphold the order. As one we will follow the faith." The priests assembled in the room murmured as with one voice.

The priestess stood to take the place the prelate indicated in the front row of the assembled priests. There was a telltale tension to be seen in the set of her head and shoulders, before she turned to face the prelate, clasping her hands and bowing her head in outward obedience to the rule.

After she had received the prelate's blessing he directed her to a chair where she sat stiffly while her new name was tattooed on her right forearm. The wary look never left her face throughout.

No, she had not expected that.

CHAPTER FOURTEEN

Peveril prided himself on keeping in shape. Sure he'd gained a bit of bulk over the years, but he'd lost none of the skills he'd acquired in the days of his youth. It hadn't been difficult to find the room over the cobbler's shop that the builder's apprentice, Shott, rented. It had been the work of a moment to scale the rubble stone wall leading to window, and to flick the catch open with a small knife he carried between his teeth. Almost too easy, even if he needed a pause to catch his breath once he'd squeezed through the window and stepped down from the sill, all without making the slightest noise to alert anyone to his presence. From what he'd seen the lad would be at the tavern an hour or two yet – although he'd been amused to notice the youth was staying tight-lipped about his sudden good fortune. Well he might, the young fool.

Finding the necklace, however, proved less easy. A rapid search had revealed it was in none of the more usual places. Years spent as a housebreaker – before he'd been pressed into the army and turned respectable – had taught him the most rewarding places to look. Now he went through them again, more thoroughly, groping around the underside of every piece of furniture, and lifting the mattress right off the bed as well as inspecting the mattress itself for hiding places. Nothing. He went over the room, checking for loose floorboards, but they were all sound and solid. He went through every item of clothing in the chest, though Goddess knew there was little enough of that.

He couldn't fight off the growing suspicion the lad had been lying to him all along. And if that was the case…

Peveril only heard the footsteps on the landing outside at the last minute. He pulled the kerchief back over his face and ducked behind the door. There was nowhere to hide in the tiny room, but all he needed was the element of surprise. A key rattled in the lock and the apprentice stumbled in, not entirely steady on his feet. But this meant he took a step sideways to recover his balance and that turned him to face the door, and the spot where Peveril had hoped to remain concealed for a few more seconds while he retrieved his cudgel from its hiding place.

Goddess, but his luck was out tonight.

The apprentice gaped at him, his mouth dropping open in shock. There was no time for anything subtle as the lad reached for the door. Peveril dived forward, smashing the lad's hand clear of the door handle. He ignored the crunching sound from the lad's finger bones and grabbed him around the throat, silencing his yelp of pain and shouldering the door shut as he did so. He dragged the lad to the floor by the throat and pressed him down, pinning him there with his knee while he shoved one hand over the lad's mouth. The youth whimpered and clawed at Peveril's face with one hand. Peveril tightened his grip on the lad's windpipe, slapping the youth's hand away from his face, but not before the kerchief covering his nose and mouth was wrenched free. Recognition dawned in the lad's eyes and some of the fight went out of him. He made a gagging sound as he struggled to draw breath.

"Tell me where it is, lad." Peveril pinned the lad's upper arm to the floor with his other knee. "If I find you've been lying to me, I won't be best pleased. An' right now I think you have been lying to me. Where's the necklace?"

Beneath him the lad trembled and gasped.

"Not happy? Then you'd best tell me where to find it, sharpish. I'm not a patient man." Peveril eased one hand off the lad's face.

The youth sucked in a shuddering breath, in sharp bursts, unable to speak. His hand flapped.

"No, you tell me now." Peveril tightened his fingers about the boy's windpipe again. The boy scrabbled his hand against Peveril's thigh. Peveril closed his fingers about the lad's throat.

"I'm all out of patience."

The boy, panicking, flapped his broken hand, not to strike at Peveril, but towards his own chest.

"Hurts, does it? You'll be sorrier still that you tried to cross me, you arrogant prick."

The boy's eyes widened and his head seemed to spasm as he attempted to shake it, but Peveril had no option now. The boy had recognised him. He closed his second hand about the boy's throat and clamped it in an unforgiving grip.

Eventually the boy fell still and the spasming of his limbs ceased. Peveril released him, easing the knots out of his fingers. He had the single leaf, after all. It was distinctive. It might be more than enough proof of the Lady Alwenna's survival.

He searched through the boy's scrip, pleased to find most of the coin he'd given him still in there. He added that to his own, leaving a few small coins so it wouldn't be obvious the lad had been robbed.

Dead eyes stared up at the ceiling as Peveril searched through the rest of the youth's clothing. And there, in a flat pouch on a leather loop about the boy's neck, hidden inside his smock, he found it. Wrapped in clean linen, a small bundle, unyielding inside the fabric. Suddenly the boy's flapping gestures made sense. He'd been trying to tell Peveril, all along. He'd probably even had it with him the day he'd sworn he'd never carry such a valuable thing with him. Peveril grinned as he untied the leather loop and placed it about his own neck, still warm from the youth's body heat. He stood up, easing the knot in his shoulders.

It wouldn't hurt to cover his tracks.

Peveril heaved the lad's shoulders up off the floor and dropped him face down on the bed. There was little enough weight to him. He unbuckled the lad's belt and pulled his leggings down to his ankles, then hitched up his smock, leaving his dead, bare arse exposed to the view of the world. Let it look like a rough game gone badly wrong.

He'd been here long enough, and he had what he'd come for. Peveril refastened the kerchief tighter over his face, leaned out of the window to check all was clear and clambered out the way he'd entered.

CHAPTER FIFTEEN

The sky was overcast. The sea beneath it churned sullenly. At some point on the horizon the two merged almost seamlessly. As an Outer Islander, Lena had been raised by the sea, knew its every mood, every timbre, yet today the familiar left her sombre. Despite herself, she shivered and leaned closer into Darnell's embrace. "What was it you wanted to show me?"

"The water level. You see the marker there for high tide?" He pointed down to a wooden pole fastened to the harbour wall. At some point in the past it had been painted white, but it was now faded and peeling.

"Yes, but I can't see any tide markings on it. Have they all worn off?" His arm about her shoulders was comforting. She didn't want to be standing out here with him. She wanted to be back in his bed, glorying in his body, glorying in the terrible hunger that overcame her whenever they were together. She didn't want to be standing here on this cold harbourside, watching the creeping sea with a sense of dread that spoke to her very bones.

"They haven't worn off – they're underwater already. There are three hours and more to go until high tide."

"But… It's not even a spring tide, surely?"

"No. It's not." Darnell stared out across the harbour. "It's been happening steadily over the years – ever since I settled here. Every year, the tides have climbed higher and higher up the harbour wall. But this is the worst I've seen it."

And three hours to go to high tide? Lena looked down at the rising waters. The lower level of the harbour was submerged already, along with several of the steps leading down to it. The water washed back and forth, revealing then concealing another step. Even as she watched the tide climbed higher so the surface of the step could no longer be seen, except through a shimmering layer of water. She slid her arm about Darnell's waist and they watched and waited together as another step was gradually overtaken by the sea.

"How high will it get? Will it stop?"

"I reckon it will top the harbourside this year, and flood these streets. And it won't even take a storm to do it." Darnell nodded over his shoulder.

Lena turned to look, trying to visualise the familiar scene overrun, submerged in sea water. All the goods that were stacked waiting for hauliers to take them away, the crowd of people waiting to board the ferry that had just arrived from the Outer Isles. The passengers were filing off it now, carrying bags and bundles, negotiating the gangplank with varying degrees of ease. And the very last passenger moved leisurely behind the others, his bundle rather smaller than theirs. There was something familiar about the way he carried himself, but it wasn't until he stepped onto the harbour wall that a shock of recognition ran through her. And, as if he sensed it, the newcomer looked directly at her.

Bleaklow.

Darnell must have felt her tense, for he was distracted from his contemplation of the sea. "What is it?"

She twisted round to put Darnell between her and Bleaklow. "This place, it chills me today. Let's go back to your house." She knew a sudden desperation. She had no idea if Bleaklow had recognised her in that instant: why should he have, after all, her hair cropped short, wearing a commoner's garments and entwined in the arms of another man. There had been no recognition in that instant his eyes had met hers. But why else would her father's servant be here, if not to search for her? She tightened her arm about Darnell.

"Let's go back right now. I want to feel alive. I want you to love me."

Darnell hesitated, troubled. "What is wrong? Not that I don't welcome your suggestion... But–"

"Wrong? Oh, don't ask me to explain. I just have this sense we may not have so very long together." She tugged at his hand. "Come with me now."

Darnell needed no further invitation as he caught her sense of urgency and they wasted no time returning to his house.

SIXTEEN

Rekhart shivered. He'd been standing out here in the cold a good hour or more already and the barge was late. If it didn't turn up soon he'd a good mind to tell Jervin just where he could shove his latest errand and go home to the warmth of his bed. A chill mist had crept up from the river, occluding the clear sky which promised frost before dawn. Goddess, he'd better not still be waiting here by then. Where was the accursed barge?

Rekhart stamped his feet and blew on his fingers in an attempt to warm them. He'd long ago finished the contents of the small flask he carried. He was tempted to slip away and replenish it at the nearest tavern, but the only money in his scrip right now belonged to Jervin. And every coin of it was destined for this contact of Jervin's who was travelling on this abominably late barge. Of all the things he might have been doing on his first night off duty in ten days – well, this was not what he would have chosen. There wasn't even a night watchman here tonight to keep him company. But he'd have cleared the last of his debt soon and there'd be no more hanging about on cold docks waiting for whichever shipment of goods Jervin had due in. No, by the Goddess, there wouldn't. He'd learned his lesson.

Rekhart shoved his hands deep inside the pockets of his

surcoat. Alongside the key to the warehouse he could feel the pouch containing his dice. He still carried them, fool that he was. They were what had led him into this in the first place. He'd had some vague idea of keeping them as a reminder, but instead they were a source of constant temptation. He drew the pouch out of his pocket and untied the loop that fastened it shut. He tipped the dice out, turning them over in his hands. They were a fine set, carved from quality bone, with no chips or blemishes. Absentmindedly he rolled them on the flat top of the harbour wall. All twos and ones.

No use to anyone. And what did he imagine he was doing with them now? As if rolling sevens would change anything.

Rekhart scooped the dice up and stuffed them back into the pouch, fastening it tight. The surface of the river was still, the current running deep and unseen. Moonlight spread over the water, calm and accepting. On an impulse Rekhart drew his arm back and hurled the dice pouch out over the water. The pouch sailed far beyond reach of the harbour lights, then dropped into the water with an unremarkable plop. Ripples spread from the point where it sank, setting the moonlight dancing.

It was as easy as that. He would turn his life around and close this sorry episode. Maybe three, four more nights to do and he'd have settled up with Jervin. And then... There was that merchant's daughter from the trade quarter. He'd spoken to her at the spring fair. He saw her sometimes, fetching and carrying from her father's market stall. She always had a shy smile for him. Perhaps–

From upriver Rekhart heard the unmistakable splashing of oars deployed by tired hands. This would be his barge, at long last. He'd be able to stow the goods in Jervin's warehouse and be tucked up warm in his own bed before another half hour was out.

He gave his hands a last rub to warm them through and paused to check his knife was snugly in position on his belt, ready to grab at a moment's notice. Many of Jervin's business associates were less than savoury.

The barge nudged up against the side of the dock with a gentle thud. Rekhart caught the line the captain threw over and secured it about the nearest bollard. A moment later a figure stepped up from inside the barge and leaped easily over to the dock.

"You're Jervin's man? Not seen you before." The voice was a woman's, of low timbre, but unmistakably a woman's.

"I'm Jervin's man." The words seemed to stick in Rekhart's throat. But not for much longer, he wanted to add.

The woman eyed him with curiosity. Her long hair was wild and unkempt, and she had a front tooth missing. "Aye, well. If you say so, you likely are." She grinned. "Best get this done then. You got my money?"

"I have. You can count it in the warehouse."

She shrugged, chewing on a mouthful of tobacco and spitting on the ground. "You're the cautious one. Makes no odds to me." She turned and shouted back to the barge. "Wait there, Tam. No unloading till I've counted up."

She walked with Rekhart to the warehouse, clearly knowing the way already. He unlocked the door and they stepped inside. He soon regretted his decision to conduct their business behind closed doors rather than out in the open – some time must have lapsed since any of the woman's garments had been washed, let alone her person. He didn't delay in handing over the fat purse Jervin had given him.

She opened it there on the spot and counted through it, taking her time. Then she counted out half a dozen coins and handed them back to him. "You give that back to Jervin, an' you tell 'im the load's not complete. I'll not charge him for goods I can't deliver. And you make your mark on this 'ere paper so's I've proof you took it from me. I'll not have Jervin chasin' me for short delivery."

The woman looked pointedly around the warehouse as Rekhart signed a receipt for her.

"We 'ad some trouble wi' this lot on the river. Be glad to unload 'em. You got the cellar key, too?"

"Yes, of course." Rekhart drew the key from his pocket, wishing the woman wouldn't stand so close. In truth he'd forgotten about it, but Jervin had instructed him this consignment must go in the cellar. A particularly expensive vintage, he guessed. He unlocked the solid door, to be greeted by a rush of rank air, fusty and damp. He hoped the wine barrels were well sealed.

The woman had already set off back to the barge and he followed her, grateful for the relatively fresh air outside, despite the usual dockside smells.

"Let's have 'em, Tam."

A stooped figure clambered up on deck of the barge, while the captain had set up a gangplank to allow them to unload the goods. Rekhart hoped it wouldn't take long. He was ready for his bed. And if they thought he was about to help with the fetching and carrying...

He stopped, one foot on the gangplank as one small figure after another emerged from the cabin behind the individual known as Tam. This was no trick of the moonlight: the stooped figure was leading a string of children from the cabin, their hands bound, each one tied to the child in front like so many mules. He stepped back as Tam tugged at the leader and they shuffled one by one along the gangplank, past Rekhart and onto the dock. For the most part they kept their eyes downcast. One gave Rekhart a wary glance, as if they would sooner not walk so close to him, lest he lash out.

"Wait. What's this?" Rekhart turned to the woman.

"Nine of 'em. I gev you back coin for the other, like I said. Get 'em inside, Tam. Cellar's open."

Tam grunted and tugged at the leader of the string of

children, who stumbled after him. The rest followed, their steps uncertain as if they'd spent a lot of time crammed into a tiny space. And from Rekhart's scanty knowledge of barges, they must have.

"But... they're children." The eldest couldn't have been more than ten or twelve.

The woman turned back from paying off the barge captain and walked off the gangplank. "Aye. An' all fit an' healthy. You'll not catch us passing off substandard goods, no–"

"Oy, wait!" The captain emerged from the cabin. "You've left one behind."

The woman rolled her eyes. "An' I told you, you gev 'em bad water. It's your problem."

"I did no such thing. The others would be ill, too, wouldn't they?" The captain gestured towards the line of children vanishing inside the warehouse. "They're fine, can see for yourself. You want me to run for you again, you'll take this 'un off, too. I can find plenty work without havin' to clear up after my cargo."

The woman shrugged. "'Ere, gie's a hand." She tugged on Rekhart's sleeve and he followed her numbly. She ducked inside the cabin and emerged backwards a moment later, stooped over as she dragged a limp form by the shoulders. "Grab 'is feet, then."

Rekhart stepped forward and picked up the child's feet which were trailing on the deck. He guessed this one to be nine or ten. The boy's eyes opened briefly and he stared at Rekhart with the unfocused gaze of the fevered patient. His head slumped back and he moaned as Rekhart lifted his feet in the air so they were no longer dragging over the ground. The boy's arms dangled free. At least they'd had the humanity to unbind his hands. The child needed a healer, there was no doubt of that. Who would be safest to consult? He was vaguely aware if the woman moved any further back she'd miss the gangplank at the end of the barge altogether, and get a long overdue washing.

"You ready?" The woman adjusted her grip, raising the boy slightly. Rekhart nodded, likewise raising the inert form so they could lift him onto the gangplank without injury. Then the woman swung the boy's head and shoulders bodily out over the edge of the boat and let go. Reflexively, Rekhart tried to hang onto the lad's ankles with the result the lad's upper body pivoted in mid-air, swinging round before he dropped out of sight and his head smashed against the side of the barge with a sickening, hollow thud. Rekhart couldn't have said quite when or how he lost his grip on the lad's ankles, but he was left clutching one worn old boot as the boy sank beneath the surface of the water without so much as a kick of his bare and grimy foot.

The ripples had almost stilled before Rekhart dropped the boy's boot in after him.

Behind Rekhart the woman guffawed with laughter.

PART III

CHAPTER ONE

"You want the truth, Marten? The truth is there's bad blood in that woman's line and you should sever all connections with her. Is that plain enough for you to understand?" The words were spoken in a low voice, brusque with anger, but Alwenna had no trouble hearing them; it was almost as if she had been intended to all along. She tried to turn away, to close her mind to them, but somehow she couldn't.

Marten's boot heels scuffed on the floor of the cave as he paced back and forth. "Damn it, Rogen, we can do better than that. We must. She is key to regaining everything we've lost these past weeks."

"I always knew you were stubborn to a fault, Marten, but blind as well? It's as well your father isn't alive to hear this."

"He may not be, but my children are. Keep your voice down."

Rogen laughed bitterly. "Why should I? They should know what manner of a man fathered them. By the Hunter, I swear if I'd known then what I know now I'd never have let my daughter be taken in by you."

"Stop now, old man. You go too far. Your daughter made her own choice and she's more than capable of telling me herself if she's had second thoughts."

"She never will. She thinks she owes you some kind of loyalty because she's given you no children. Truth is she should find a real man who can get them on her – one who will provide properly for his family and isn't always chasing around the Peninsula on mad schemes that'll be the ruin of us all."

For a moment there was silence. Alwenna could no more close her mind to it than she could have climbed out from beneath the rubble that had buried her at Highkell. And now she was suffocating under the weight of the two freemerchants' anger.

"It's as well for you, Rogen, I was raised to respect my elders. Because of that I'll only tell you how wrong you are. I brought the Lady Alwenna here because I believed the elders were best placed to advise her on how to proceed. And there's been nothing but backbiting and acrimony."

"You should have known better than to bring a landbound witch among us. Nothing good can come of it. Nothing."

"I've been working towards this for years. You know that. And with Tresilian gone, she's our only hope of gaining redress. You know that, too. Stop to think, just for a moment, Rogen. For the sake of our people: we can't go on scratching out a living here, not the way we have been. There are fewer and fewer children born among us. We need to act now, or there'll be no freemerchants left because the remnants will be scattered to the furthest corners of the Peninsular Kingdoms. And we will have no history, because no one will speak our names."

"And so be it, if the alternative is to become landbound breeding stock, fattened for some lordling's profit."

"Sometimes I forget how old you are, Rogen. But tonight I see it: your age has addled your wits. It's time you stepped down from the council, before you lead everyone down roads that aren't clear."

"I'll leave the council the day I go to roam with the Hunter and not a day sooner. So it was with my father, and his father, and his father before him."

And they were all inbred fools, the lot of them. Even though Marten didn't speak the words out loud they rang clear in Alwenna's mind. Hadn't she heard those words before, somewhere? She shivered, and became aware of her surroundings.

She was seated on the bench, slumped over the rough table that was one of the few furnishings in their home with the freemerchants. A few vegetables were scattered about the table. Before her was a bloodstained eating knife, while a small amount of blood had pooled and begun to congeal on the tabletop. She straightened up, pressing her hands on the table for support, and was rewarded with a twinge of pain from her finger. She'd cut it. Must have cut it while she was chopping vegetables. And... what? Had she fainted? The child twisted in her swollen belly. Was this what pregnancy did: made invalids of perfectly healthy women? Was she really such a weakling?

And then there was the dream... Marten and Rogen arguing.

Except she knew it was no dream. The sight had found its way to her despite all her determination to fight it. She had no control over her own body and even less over her own will.

But there was one thing she could do: she could leave this Goddess-forsaken place before her enemies closed in around her.

She pushed herself to her feet, stretched, and moved over to the clay basin to wash her blood from the knife. It was time for her to leave – she could ignore the troubled visions no longer. There were those outcast freemerchants in the mountains. She should have sought them out weeks ago, instead of tarrying here. She picked up the clay basin to tip out the fine layer of dust that had accumulated in it. She couldn't depend on Marten's protection, oughtn't remain here, not while her presence caused difficulties with–

Footsteps scuffled in the doorway behind her. Instinct told

her this was danger, and she spun round, basin in one hand, the knife in the other. Rogen stood there, clutching a cudgel, breathing heavily.

"Well, old man? What are you waiting for?"

Rogen took a step forward, flexing his fingers about the grip of the cudgel. "As the Hunter is my witness, witch, I'll put an end to you."

"Indeed? This is your legendary freemerchant hospitality?" She twisted the knife about in her hand so she was holding it as she'd seen Weaver and Tresilian do in their training bouts.

"This is how we deal with a threat against our own."

He had Alwenna cornered, blocking her route to the door, giving her no option. She hurled the clay basin at his face. It caught him a glancing blow, enough to make him duck and she dived forward, grabbing the cudgel and hacking at his right hand with the small knife. He bellowed in anger as more footsteps came running up outside. Goddess, let them not belong to supporters of Rogen.

An instant later Marten burst into the chamber, shouting. "Let her go!" He grabbed Rogen by the shoulders, pulling him away, and Alwenna stepped back, hands beginning to shake as she dropped the cudgel. It bounced on the stone floor, rolling over and over until it came to rest against the ever-present drift of dust by the doorway.

CHAPTER TWO

Durstan set the account books to one side. The tale they told was not a happy one. To think they had been so close to success, before Tresilian's queen had been brought into their midst.

"Curwen, put these ledgers away and fetch me parchment and ink."

The slightly built priest jumped as if startled. "At once, your holiness."

The summer palace had been a good place for the order, but without Tresilian's patronage they couldn't hope to continue there. They had few enough resources at their disposal now, never mind taking on repairs to the damaged portions of the palace. They needed tithes, a more populous region to draw their supplies from and to pay them their due. Land that could be turned to food and profit. They needed the support of a wealthy new royal patron: he had one such in mind. One who had the resources and the power to find the Lady Alwenna, wherever she may be.

"Thank you, Curwen." Durstan stirred the ink. It was a poor batch, too watery, but it was all they had at their disposal.

"I will need to undertake a journey of pilgrimage which I hope will secure the brethren's future. I will be leaving you in charge."

Curwen bowed his head. "Your holiness, you do me a great honour."

"I shall expect you to continue our work in my absence. There are, I believe, two soldiers still in the infirmary who are ready for the rebirth rites?"

"Yes, your holiness. I believe they will make good candidates. If you wish to inspect them for yourself–"

Durstan waved his hand and the monk fell silent. "All in good time. What progress have you made with the soldier, Pius?"

"He is always biddable, your holiness. He asks no questions, never speaks out of turn. His strength is returning – each day I see an improvement in him."

Durstan nodded. "Then he has passed the most critical stage. When will he be ready to travel?"

"To travel, your holiness? I do not understand."

"Pius will be accompanying me on my journey, Curwen. I need him as an example of our work, to show our king Vasic what benefits would accrue to him if he were to take the order under his kingly wing. Pius will be the proof I was unable to offer Tresilian or his father before him. What monarch would not welcome an elite guard, not only blessed by the Goddess, but loyal to the death?"

"Your holiness, this is an ambitious plan."

"It is time the order was brought back into the light. We will skulk no more at the edge of the kingdom, but take our place at the heart of all things, that the Goddess shall receive her dues once more as is her right. The whole of the Peninsular Kingdoms will return to the one true faith."

Curwen murmured, "Praise be to the Goddess. Bringer of life and bringer of death." He shuffled his feet. "Holiness, I have heard it said that many call this Vasic a usurper and would sooner bend the knee to the Queen Alwenna than swear loyalty to him."

"That is why we must find the Lady Alwenna before anyone else does, Curwen. And that is why Vasic might be persuaded to provide us with the funds to do so. As long as she lives she will be a thorn in his side. And as long as she lives she will carry the power that she has stolen from the grey brethren. We will have that power back, Curwen. And then none can hope to stand in our way as we re-establish the old order of the Goddess."

"But, your holiness, how can we hope to achieve that? We have not food to carry us through another–"

"The Goddess spoke to me in a vision, Curwen. She spoke to me, and told me we have her blessing. And she told me what we must do, every last detail. If we prepare our ground carefully and remain faithful we cannot fail."

Curwen bowed. "Praise be to the Goddess."

"Praise be to the Goddess," Durstan echoed. "And now, Curwen, we have much to do if I am to set off for Highkell in timely fashion. Show me these two soldiers. We will treat them as we did the man Weaver, and by the time I return they will be ready to serve the order."

Durstan strode over to the door, throwing it open and stepping out into the corridor. He'd set Curwen's doubts to rest, now a bold stratagem needed bold gestures to carry it through. The corridor was empty, but he could have sworn he heard the swish of skirts as someone hurried away.

The image of the priestess Miria sprang unbidden to his mind. This was becoming unsettling. He must repeat his devotions to the Goddess, and perform them nightly, to rid his mind of this spectre. He would not be turned from his purpose by any living woman, however much she preyed on his mind. He would remain true to the Goddess.

CHAPTER THREE

Jervin's library was a place of peace for Drew. He suspected Jervin hadn't the faintest notion of the true worth of half the volumes in his collection. There was a rare gazetteer listing the reports of a high seer and his clerics who had examined all the precincts in Highground, itemising the value of tithes and comparing the merits of their various buildings. This orderly, who hailed from Lynesreach, had taken a dim view of the provincials with whom he found himself breaking bread as he did his rounds.

Sometimes Drew turned to the listing for Vorrahan and read through it, comparing the pictures in his mind's eye to the rather basic description. *"A refectory building, of rudimentary structure but more commodious than the size of the community at Vorrahan currently warrants."* The prelate had been reprimanded for excess and a replacement sought as a matter of urgency. The refectory had been draughty enough, certainly. Always a chilly contrast to the heat of the kitchens where Drew had been given duties on first arriving at Vorrahan. The librarian had requested a likely young novice to help him sort and catalogue the collections and Drew had been only too glad to escape the bustle of the kitchens, not to mention Brother Irwyn's less than kindly attentions.

The librarian had never spoken of it, of course, but Drew

guessed he knew... Yes, the library had always been a place of peace.

"A curiosity on the lower slopes of Mt Vorrahan is the chamber whence the holy well springs forth from the ground, gathering in a capacious chamber wherein it forms a pool. This pool has a local reputation for promoting visions of the future. As such the Order of Seers has long had a presence allied to the precinct on Vorrahan. Once a popular site of pilgrimage, the spring chamber has fallen into disuse of recent years. The prelate has requested a suitable seer be sent to serve the precinct and instructions have been sent for a candidate to be chosen and prepared without delay."

This may well have been the process that led to Brother Gwydion's selection. Drew reckoned up the years – it would have made Gwydion seventy years old at the very least by the time Drew had come to Vorrahan. He had never imagined it would be such a mundane process to select a high seer – far from the spiritual journey he had imagined. The whole book seemed to be a record of imagined slights and petty grievances, with concessions demanded to appease the pride of those affronted by the high seer's findings. And yet Gwydion had truly been gifted with the sight – Drew had no doubt of it. Gwydion had told him of the Lady Alwenna's journey in the weeks before her arrival. No, Drew thought, Gwydion had been a true spiritual, dedicated to serving the Goddess. Had he foreseen the disasters that would overcome Alwenna if she had returned to Highkell? If he'd had some hint of it, that might cast the agitation of his final days in a different light.

Drew had the distance now to see that the precinct's treatment of Gwydion had been lacking. The seer had been given scant respect by Garrad and kept at arm's length from the main precinct. Even his dedicated servants had been looked at askance by their brethren. And he had even been sent to Vorrahan at what seemed little more than a whim by a higher authority. What might Gwydion have been if he had remained in the south and not been sent into effective exile on the grey, windswept island? Or was this how destiny worked – through such trivial chains of consequence? If Alwenna and Weaver had tarried even one day more on the road to Vorrahan, Gwydion might have died without passing on the knowledge of ages. Or Drew himself might have been the recipient.

A raucous burst of laughter intruded upon Drew's thoughts. The traders from Ellisquay were downstairs in Jervin's study, ostensibly discussing important business. They disturbed the evening calm of the house. Jervin had made it clear to Drew that he was not included. Sensitive matters were involved, he had said, that must go no further than the walls of the room in which they were discussed. Their business didn't sound sensitive. Not at all. It sounded drunk. It didn't sound anything like business at all. Drew tried to concentrate on his book again, but rather than distract him the subject matter served to vex him. He might go and select another from Jervin's library. It was far too early to think about going to bed and sleep was doubly unlikely with Jervin's noisy visitors in the house.

Mind made up, he hurried down the stairs. The hallway was empty, all the servants clearly having been banished as he had. He could listen at the door and there would be nobody to see him. He took a couple of steps past the library door before doubling back. What was he thinking? Ten to one he'd be caught peering through the keyhole as a servant brought more refreshments for the party. Jervin had impressed upon Drew the importance of providing generous hospitality for one's business associates. No matter how tight times might be, he had said, it was vital such connections should see only success: a man at the top of his game; a man they wished to be associated with; a man whose wealth couldn't help but rub off on them simply because of that association.

From the household accounts Drew had seen that wealth wasn't so much rubbing off on them as being poured straight down their gullets. And – going by those same accounts – those traders from Ellisquay had an appetite second to none. With a sigh he opened the library door and stepped inside. The voices were almost as distinct in here as they had been in the hallway. He set his book down on the table, considering. There were built-in cupboards flanking the fireplace that backed onto Jervin's study. Shelves in the top half housed Jervin's collection of ceramics from all corners of the Peninsula and beyond, the whole being protected by glazed doors. The bottom half contained cupboards, closed off by pairs of panelled doors.

The sound was far more distinct from the right side of the fireplace. Drew hesitated, then stooped down and gently opened the cupboard doors. The cupboard was more or less empty, containing a few folded cloths and nothing else. And when he peered through to the back he could see a tiny chink of light from the room beyond. On closer inspection he realised that side was closed off by a wooden panel that had split along the grain. It was through this crack that the sound of conversation was reaching him. He couldn't help himself now, and leaned closer.

The Ellisquay traders were doing most of the talking. Drew struggled to follow the thick Ellisquay accent at the best of times, but now, well lubricated, they were talking faster than ever, and talking over one another. He could make out odd words, but could not get the gist of what they were saying at all. Occasionally Jervin, seated at the far side of the room, interpolated a lazy comment in his low voice, but mostly he was letting them run on. Drew could picture him sitting there, glass in hand, smiling to himself as the drunken traders spilled their secrets. It was not the orgiastic scene he'd half expected to find – his initial flush of relief was rapidly followed by shame that he hadn't trusted Jervin in the first place. Goddess, what was wrong with him these days? How could he have doubted him? Jervin was simply sitting there, smiling to himself, with murder in his heart.

Drew shivered and pulled back out of the cupboard. Where had that thought come from? He had no idea, but he did know he ought not be eavesdropping like this. He closed the cupboard doors as softly as he could, fastening them with care and retreated to the bookshelves where he grabbed another book at random and hurried out of the room, mortified by his own behaviour.

CHAPTER FOUR

Kaith bowed low before Vasic. "I was unable to see the Lady Drelena at all, your highness, for she was indisposed throughout my visit. However, I have been reliably informed she is a great beauty, and I think you will agree this portrait bears that out." With a flourish, he gestured to the servant who followed in his wake, clutching a fabric-wrapped bundle. The servant hurried forward and offered up the bundle to Kaith, who loosened the ties holding it shut and unwrapped the covering. Leaving the fabric in the servant's hands he held up the portrait for Vasic's inspection.

The portrait showed a round-faced young woman with a bright smile, dark, curling hair and not an ounce of Alwenna's reserve. He couldn't have found someone who looked less like his previous bride-to-be if he'd drawn up a detailed specification. "She appears comely enough. I imagine if she had a squint the artist would not have portrayed that faithfully."

"I have never heard it said that she has a squint, highness. I think you need have no fears on that score."

"Nonetheless I would sooner have had the evidence of your own eyes at this point, Kaith. I might as well have sent a letter for all the good this does me. This was not well done on your part." He gestured to the portrait irritably.

"Highness, I did everything I could. The Lady Drelena's

rooms were kept well guarded and the servants could not be bought. Her parents were most apologetic to me. But she had contracted one of those tiresome childhood diseases, and did not wish to be seen while she was woefully spotty, or so I was given to understand by the servants."

"You managed to question the servants, at least?" Vasic studied the likeness. The artist had captured an enchanting smile. It would be disappointing indeed to find it was more the work of the artist's imagination than real life.

"Yes, sire. It was clear they all held the young lady in close affection, and were somewhat downcast by her illness. These diseases can be far worse once the age of adulthood is reached."

"It is all most dissatisfactory. We must hope her face is not disastrously pockmarked as a result." Vasic pushed himself up out of his chair and crossed over to the window, peering down at the main gate. Builders swarmed there, busy completing a temporary footbridge. They were a severe drain on the royal coffers. Pockmarked or not, he'd have to make his new bride welcome. Kaith may have failed to catch sight of the girl, but the terms he'd negotiated with the Lord Convenor Etrus were generous indeed. Vasic could not afford to prevaricate now.

"This matter must proceed with all possible speed. You will waste no time returning to the Outer Isles bearing my reply and suitable gifts." Vasic glowered out of the window at the construction work. He would have to take his chance with pockmarks.

CHAPTER FIVE

Peveril threaded his way through the market square. Market days were still deathly quiet, even though the footbridge had been opened for traders to bring in their produce. The once-fat purse used to carry payment from traders for their stalls was woefully slim today. Too slim for him to quietly take his usual cut before he carried it up to the counting-house. But that wasn't Peveril's chief concern today. More vexing was the ongoing absence of some of his more creative contacts. In particular, the goldsmith he'd hoped would pay a tidy sum for the necklace he'd acquired from the apprentice. That business was beginning to look like a deal of work for very little return.

Peveril opened the counting-house door to find Marwick waiting there with Birtle.

"You have the market takings?" Marwick looked... watchful. Did he suspect Peveril of creaming off the profit from the stall fees? Good luck to him proving it.

"Aye. They're down again. Still quiet." He dropped the purse on the table between them.

"So I see." Marwick picked up the purse, hefting it thoughtfully.

"You can go and count them for yourself if'n you don't want to take my word for it – it won't take more'n a minute or two, there are so few traders."

Marwick gravitated towards the door as if tempted to do precisely that. "I expected the footbridge would bring more people in."

Old fool. "The story going round is a bunch of traders have taken their goods to Ellisquay and chartered a ship to Lynesreach."

"But that would be prohibitively expensive."

"It's what I heard." Peveril shrugged. "Doesn't mean it'll be profitable. Folks still got to eat either way – there's not many can afford to wait for a new road bridge."

Marwick turned away from the door again. "You make a fair point there, Captain." He studied Peveril just too long for the soldier's comfort. "A fair point." He passed the purse over to Birtle. "Bring the ledgers up to date. The captain and I have a suspicious death to investigate."

Peveril followed Marwick up the side of the street. He'd already guessed where they were going, but the old man walked painfully slowly. Sure enough, he turned in at the lodging house where the young apprentice had lived.

The room smelled of decay, unrelieved by the air from the window which had been opened wide. Flies buzzed hopefully around the body. Marwick pressed a handkerchief over his face and gestured towards the bed.

"What do you make of it? Looks to me like that youth who was complaining of cutpurses the other day."

Peveril scratched his head and made a play of studying the lad. "Can't be sure. Was his hair not longer?" He could swear Marwick was watching him closer than usual.

"He gave this as his address."

"Did he, now?" Peveril leaned closer. "You may be right at that." The visible parts of the lad's face had taken on a bloodless pallor.

Behind the handkerchief it was hard to tell if Marwick was convinced by his response or otherwise. He looked from Peveril to the dead youth, then a fly buzzed against his face and, distracted, he swatted it. "He appears to have been strangled."

"If'n his pay was stolen like he said, it figures he might have been looking to earn summat to cover the rent."

"A bit drastic." Marwick's eyes were on Peveril again.

"Wouldn't be the first." Peveril shrugged. "It stinks in here."

"Now that's what I expect from you, Captain. Not concern at the ills of the oppressed in our fair land."

"Eh?"

"Young people who can't pay their rent; traders who can't feed their families. When did you develop a social conscience?"

"I grew up poor. I'm doing all right now, but that don't mean I forget how it was."

"I can imagine." It was Marwick's turn to shrug. "Meanwhile, someone strangled the lad. No one was seen about the place who shouldn't have been. I want you to find out where he was and who he spoke to since he lodged that complaint about cutpurses. He was up to something that day. I'm not altogether convinced he wasn't part of some gang – trying to set up their rivals with a false report, perhaps. As you say, people will do all sorts for a bit of extra money."

"Sounds more'n likely. An' him with good prospects, too." Peveril didn't need to assume a pious expression as Marwick was already headed for the door.

"Ask around, Captain. Find out what you can."

CHAPTER SIX

Bleaklow scanned the sizeable crowd on the harbourside. Where to begin searching in a town the size of Sylhaven? There must be a dozen taverns on the street leading up from the harbour alone. The ferry captain had been adamant she'd crossed on the ferry and not boarded another, so this was where his search must begin. Bleaklow fingered the miniature portrait stowed safely in his pocket. It had been removed from the expensive mount and set in a more modest locket: nothing said runaway royal like the elaborate gold filigree of the original. Her mother had been distraught when she'd seen the portrait – painted for Drelena's eighteenth birthday – set in its new, humbler frame. Bleaklow had tried to offer words of comfort, without, he hoped, revealing the depths of his own guilt in the whole business. Goddess, if he'd not given in to temptation and kissed her that night. Or, worse yet, turned his back on her when she would have had him wait. He'd failed the king he served, the mother who doted upon her daughter, and the daughter herself. He'd failed every one of them. And so he'd find her, to assuage his own guilt. And then, no doubt, she'd tell all about that stolen kiss and his worthless carcass would hang off the yardarm of the royal vessel until the gulls stripped his bones clean. It wouldn't take them long. Certainly less time than it was taking him to find the errant Drelena.

He didn't dwell on the possibility he might never find her. Until she was safely restored to her family, his life was worthless. And once she was, well, if his life was forfeit, so be it. It would be no more than he deserved.

He certainly hadn't expected the shock of recognition when he'd scanned the faces – almost without thinking – of the people on the harbour wall. His gut knotted when his eye fell on the fresh-faced young woman, wrapped in a long cloak as well as the arms of some man. When her eyes fell upon him and moved away immediately he was sure he had been mistaken. He had to be mistaken. Drelena would never have looked so coldly past him, would she? Goddess knew it had only been a kiss, but...

The woman in the cloak and the man with her had turned away from the harbour. The cloak obscured the way she moved. And the man's arm remained tight around her. Bleaklow couldn't be sure. And what were the odds of seeing Drelena the instant he set foot on land? He shouldered his bag and hurried after them, before they were entirely lost in the crowd.

For a heart-stopping moment he thought he'd lost them in the bustle of the market square, but he saw them again, hastening off down a side street that led slightly uphill. Why hurry like that? Did it mean it really was Drelena? Goddess, he hoped not. The way she clung to the man's embrace... It couldn't be Drelena. He had to have been mistaken. Much as he wanted to find her, he didn't want to find her in another man's arms.

The couple turned off to the right at the end of the street. He sped up, reaching the corner just in time to see them entering the forecourt of a well-to-do merchant's house. The man – a merchant, he presumed – leaned solicitously over the woman, casting an arm about her shoulders. She leaned into him, raising her face to his and they kissed with such urgency

Bleaklow felt awkward for intruding on a private moment.

An instant later and Bleaklow was left standing alone in the street, wishing the sea would rise up and swallow him. That would be the best end to him now. If he'd found Drelena, it was the hollowest of hollow victories.

He ought to knock on the door straight away. Announce himself and his business and tear her from the arms of her lover, then board the next ferry back to the Outer Isles. Between them they could swear none of this had ever happened – perhaps she'd keep secret the kiss he'd stolen from her, if he kept secret the kiss he'd just witnessed... And everything might be as it ever had been.

Bleaklow straightened his surcoat. He could do this. He must do this – he'd sworn to his liege lord that he would. He took a couple of steps towards the house, before he noticed movement at one of the upstairs windows. Drelena and her lover, caught in an urgent embrace, breaking apart to divest one another of their clothes before moving out of sight.

All his worst fears confirmed. Goddess, he couldn't.

CHAPTER SEVEN

"Hold out your arm." There it was again, that peremptory note in the priestess's voice. It didn't matter how many times she told him their fates were tied together, Weaver would never believe her. Each time she visited him, he weighed his options. His strength was returning, he had little doubt if he chose he could break her slender neck and put an end to her petty interference once and for all. Maybe he would rot here forever, like she said, but he didn't believe that any more than the other things she told him. She was not to be trusted, he knew that, he'd seen the proof of it for himself, when...

When what? Something prickled at the edge of his consciousness, tugging, insistent. But whenever he turned his mind towards it, there was nothing there. He ought... Had he forgotten? How could he have forgotten?

"Hold out your arm, Weaver." The priestess's voice was sharper this time. He could swat her away like nothing more than an annoying fly, but he had to be sure the time was right. He would get the element of surprise only once. Weaver raised his right arm slowly, holding it stretched out before him.

"That's better. Don't make me wait again, when I order you to do something."

She removed something from inside her tunic, fidgeting with the fastening. Weaver's skin prickled with apprehension.

He knew what it was she held: a blade, in an ornate leather sheath. He knew without having to look it was that same three-sided blade that had ended the young kitchen boy's life. The same blade that had drained his lifeblood.

He held his arm out straight, without so much as a tremor to betray his recognition. Was she about to end it for good this time? He wanted to live, he needed to live – somehow he knew that, above all else – but… if she did, if she were to plunge that blade into his heart, wouldn't that be so much easier? Easier than all this uncertainty. Easier than trying to hunt down the half memories that taunted him and fled laughing whenever he looked their way. Easier than forcing himself up off his mattress each morning. Easier than trying to appease this angry child-woman who seemed to at once blame him for every ill in her life, yet promise him untold rewards if he should help her.

She pressed the chill tip of the blade into the crook of his elbow and he reached up with his left hand to catch hold of her wrist. "Why are you doing this?"

"I told you a thousand times: we need to help one another." Her voice was icy. Her arm twisted beneath his grip but he held firm.

"How is this helping me?"

"You are helping me for once. Let go. We haven't much time."

"If I am helping you, then you will be in my debt."

"Don't you dare try to tell me my business. Let go of my arm."

Weaver tightened his grip about her wrist. "My blood is my business, not yours. And it's not yours to take."

"Let go." There was the first hint of uncertainty about her voice.

"If I do, then I'm giving you my blood, and you will be in my debt. Admit it, or I'll snap your arm in two."

"You don't know what you're meddling with here." Her words hissed between tightly clenched teeth.

He dug his fingertips into her wrist and could feel the pounding of her pulse. "Neither do you, for all your assurance. If you take my blood now, you will owe me." He released her arm abruptly. "The choice is yours."

She hesitated, the blade unsteady against his skin as her hand shook. "I will not let you stand in my way." She made her decision and the blade bit into the flesh of his arm, deep and hard, striking a chill of recognition to his very core. The world seemed to swim about him, to spin, as blood welled about the tip of it and trickled over the inside of his arm.

"You have made your choice. Let the Goddess be our witness." It was a victory of sorts.

"Keep quiet." She withdrew the blade from his flesh, pressing on the skin about the wound, twisting it as if she would wring his arm dry of blood. Weaver stood, impassive, as she pressed a small bowl to his arm, directing his blood into it. He'd seen her do this before. The bowl had been different then: larger, polished, glinting bronze and he… he had wielded the knife.

He hadn't wanted to.

"Be careful." The child-woman's voice was sharp. "I mustn't spill this here or they'll find out."

Weaver steadied his arm, watching the blood drip into the bowl with a curious detachment. He didn't care if his own blood spilled or not. But last time… then he'd cared. But he'd had no choice…

Finally the priestess was done and she bound up his arm with a strip of cloth. This was all familiar, and yet not as it had been before. If only he could recall clearly. It had been important to him at the time, but why, or where…

"Lower your arm." The priestess stepped back and studied him. "Were you always so slow, or did they break you after all?" She seemed to want an answer.

He lowered his arm. "I don't remember."

It was no answer at all, but she smiled, her face losing the pinched look and she suddenly looked much younger. "Do you want to remember?"

Weaver shrugged.

"Do right by me and I'll help you remember."

He doubted now she could do that. Whatever she was trying to achieve, she had strayed far out of her depth. "In payment of your debt?"

She scowled at him. "Don't underestimate me, Weaver. Or it'll be the last mistake you make."

She wiped the three-cornered blade clean on another scrap of cloth and slipped it carefully back inside the tooled leather sheath. Weaver's eyes slid to the place where she set it down on a side table.

"Don't think of trying to touch it yourself. It knows your blood and it knows you – your innermost thoughts, every lie you told, every secret you ever tried to keep. It knows them all. And you'll never be able to hide from it."

"It's only a knife." Even as the words left his mouth he knew he'd spoken them before. Or something so close it made little difference.

"You poor, simple fool." She stepped closer to him. "You don't understand anything at all, do you?" She pressed her fingers to his lips and trailed them down his chin to trace the line of his jaw. "Hush now, don't worry about it yet. I'll tell you everything you need to know when the time comes."

Her fingers carried the scent of blood – his blood – and beneath that something else. When she left him alone in his room he washed his face over and over until he could smell nothing but the pungent soap favoured by the brethren.

CHAPTER EIGHT

Alwenna heard a scuffling sound outside. Her first instinct was to reach for the knife that was never far from her hand since Rogen's... visit. The blanket over the door was flung aside. Marten stood there in the shadow, swaying uncertainly, his chin sunken to his chest. His attitude was that of a man defeated.

Alwenna half rose from her seat at the table. "What–?"

He stepped inside, half forwards, half sideways to catch his balance, moving with none of his usual deliberation. He bowed in a loose version of courtly style, wine sloshing in the open bottle he carried in one hand. "Your servant, my lady."

Something hadn't gone his way, for sure. As he stooped she saw the freemerchant's long braids had gone. His russet hair had been chopped off unevenly, leaving ragged tufts in some places, exposing his scalp in others.

"What's happened?" She subsided into her seat again. "Was this Rogen's doing?"

Marten straightened up, spreading his hands in a self-deprecating gesture. "That is a fair question, my queen. A fair question."

"I'm no more a queen. I've told you before."

"And I, my lady, am no more a freemerchant." He plucked at the ragged remnants of his hair. "My people have shamed me. We are both displaced now, you and I." He staggered over to the table and sat down opposite her. The table lurched, making the pots in the centre rattle. The wine bottle rocked perilously as he set it down.

Alwenna reached out and steadied it. The dark red contents sloshed back and forth, a storm-tossed sea in microcosm. The waves tried to draw her in, there was something they had to show her, something she should know. She shook her head and released the bottle, chasing the ghostly whispers from her mind. "What do you mean? Why would they shame you? The elders reprimanded Rogen for his actions, did they not?"

Marten spread his hands palm-down over the rough table and drew in his breath, leaning forward to stare into Alwenna's eyes. "Why indeed. They say I have broken with freemerchant ways. My ideas are too radical, too dangerous for them." He sat back, lowering his eyes to the table. "Some say I have fallen under the influence of a witch, and brought a curse down upon them when I brought you among them."

Alwenna's heart skipped a beat. For a moment her pulse thundered in her ears. The child twisted uneasily in her belly. This was not good news. Marten had always had influence. Rogen had his own particular reasons to dislike him, but if the rest of his own people were turning against him, what lay in store for her and her child? She'd been persuaded to remain after the incident with Rogen, against her better judgement. "Some, you say? What of the others?"

"The others sat silently by while my hair was cropped."

"Are you here to tell me I must leave?"

"No, my queen. I think none of this surprises you greatly, does it?" He looked closely at her.

It was Alwenna's turn to examine the rugosities of the rough-hewn timber from which the tabletop was fashioned. There was still a faint stain visible from her blood, where it had soaked into the woodgrain. No, it didn't surprise her. The sight had forewarned her – but she'd been too weak to act upon it.

She'd clung to the hope that it had been only one of many possibilities the sight had trailed before her, had been nothing more than a fleeting glimpse into a future that would never be. "I am sorry to hear this."

"It was not your doing, my queen. Although I have little doubt our friendship was seized on as excuse by some." He shifted on the bench seat and looked directly at her. "And I know you tried to warn me. I was so certain of my own invincibility I did not take your warnings as seriously as I ought to have done."

"And do you imagine it will help coming straight up here?"

Marten's mouth twisted. "I... thought you might have some kind of sympathy to offer me." His hand moved across the table to touch her fingertips.

She withdrew her hand and set it on her lap, out of reach. "No. I have nothing of the kind to offer you."

"I believed it might be otherwise, once. When last we spoke–"

"We both know it would be outright folly. And you have a wife, or do you forget that, too?"

"Oh, yes, I have a wife. And she it was who called the elders to sit in judgement over me for failing to provide for my family."

Had things slid so far? Alwenna should have left when she had first made up her mind. She would not be blamed for ruining another man's life.

"It grieves me to learn that – you and she have been together many years. I think you might deal better with one another if I were not here."

Marten shook his head. "No. It has gone too far." He hesitated. "And her suspicions are not without foundation. You have been in my thoughts more than she these past weeks."

Alwenna pushed herself to her feet, her distended belly brushing against the edge of the table as she stood up. "What? This jest is not a funny one, Marten. Dare I hope you have also discovered guilt at trying to sell me to Tresilian not once, but twice, even after you claimed to be a friend?"

Marten lowered his eyes, studying his fingernails. "I did that for the sake of my people – and for the sake of my family. I did not know you then…"

"Nor did I know your family. Now I do, I will do nothing to cause them further distress." Maiming Rogen by stabbing him in the hand weakened her argument somewhat, but Marten was too far down the bottle to contest that point.

Marten rubbed his forehead wearily. "I have managed that myself without any intervention from you." He ran his hand through what remained of his hair. "I deserve their ridicule." He picked up the wine bottle and swigged from it.

"It's not like you to admit defeat, Marten."

"I've spent over a decade working to secure rights for my people. I was so close…"

"And so you will be again." She spoke the words without thinking.

Marten looked up sharply, setting down the wine. "What do you mean? What do you know?"

"I…" She shrugged. This was not the time to start dealing in cheap prophecies. "I know if you give up now you will never succeed." She set a kettle over the fire in the grate that had been hollowed out from one side of the rock chamber. "Let me brew some kopamid. You'll think clearer."

"I'm thinking clearly enough now. Where's Erin? You have a servant to do tasks like that."

"She's out." Did he know about the servant girl's relationship with his eldest son? Erin had been very close-mouthed about it herself. It was not for Alwenna to interfere.

"Then this would be a good time to tell me just what you know – your sight has shown you something?"

Alwenna straightened up from the kettle, easing the persistent knot in her lower back. "You never expected it to be easy when you set off down this road."

Marten jerked his head sideways in disagreement. "You don't need the sight to know that."

"Marten, the sight raises more questions than it ever answers. I've seen you as a great man. You had everything in place before Tresilian betrayed us all. And you can again. You will. But you must stay true to your people."

"What, the people who made me a laughing stock today?"

"They are still your people. You risked everything for them once."

"Never again." Marten stood up slowly, his eyes on Alwenna. "I'll see you set back on your throne as queen of all the Peninsular Kingdoms before I'll treat with them." He pushed away from the table and the wine in the bottle was stirred by his movement, ripples spreading across the dark surface. Alwenna's attention was drawn into the darkness beneath the perturbed surface and she could no more resist her sight than she could convince Marten of what he must do.

She dived down and down, deeper into darkness, moving through the liquid as if it were nothing more than a breeze. Her hair trailed loose behind her, free and unfettered, and her heart pumped blood through her veins with a wicked glee. It was so good to be alive, so good. And revenge would be even better. Ahead of her lay a small cairn. As she drew closer she could see it was composed not of rocks as she had assumed, but of bones. Reposing on the very top of the cairn lay the jewelled dagger.

CHAPTER NINE

What impulse made Drew look out of the library door that evening when he heard voices in the hall he never knew, but he had a total conviction that he must not let the visitor go.

He crossed the library and poked his head out of the door, in time to see Rekhart in the hallway, speaking to a servant. The expression on Rekhart's face he could only describe as haunted.

"Why, Rekhart. I gather Hale has told you Jervin is away. Perhaps I can help?"

Hat in hands, Rekhart shook his head. "I cannot impose on you, I fear."

Whatever troubled him, Drew knew he could not let the commander of the watch just walk away. "Nonsense. I would be glad of some company – in truth you would be doing me a favour."

Rekhart hesitated.

"Hale, bring us refreshments." Drew turned his attention to Rekhart. "Please, join me in the library. The fire is already lit."

Rekhart twisted his hat in his hands, looking as if he might refuse the invitation, before apparently reaching a decision and stepping forward into the hall proper. Drew ushered him into the library.

Up close, there were heavy shadows under Rekhart's eyes and his face was grey and heavily lined. It only then occurred to Drew he might be bringing some kind of contagion into Jervin's house, although he suspected what ailed Rekhart was no physical malady, but an affliction of the spirit.

"Please, do have a seat."

They'd done no more than seat themselves and exchange commonplace remarks about the weather before a servant returned with kopamid, leaving the tray on the table for Drew to serve.

It was a routine Drew had grown fond of and he'd even developed a taste for the kopamid, after being reluctant to enjoy the local drink at first. Tea of one sort or another had been the norm in his family household, and the only hot drink available in the precinct refectory at Vorrahan. There was something calming about the ritual, the preparation, the pouring. Presenting one's guest with the small beaker. And the beakers Jervin used were remarkable things: embellished with an abstract enamelled design of vivid colours, jewel-bright. Exquisite.

"Thank you." Rekhart took his beaker and sipped at the hot liquid. He drew a deep breath and eased back in his chair rather than sitting ramrod straight. He was clearly troubled by something.

"I'm sorry Jervin wasn't here to speak to you, but perhaps I could pass word on to him for you?"

"I... In truth it's the sort of thing a man ought to say face to face or not at all." Rekhart seemed heartened by the kopamid as he took another mouthful. "I will be unable to continue working for him, and had hoped to be able to say this today, in person, rather than put it off again."

"Again? You are not happy with the arrangement you have with him?" It was a delicate subject, of that much Drew was certain.

"I'll be able to pay back the rest of the money I owe him at the end of this week." Rekhart twisted the ornate beaker in his hands.

"I can pass that simple message on to him if you wish – we expect him back tomorrow."

"I would not slight him, you must understand. He has been good to me, and helped me out of difficult times." Again the jewel-bright enamels in the beaker glinted as Rekhart turned it in the candlelight.

"And yet...?" Drew prompted. There was more to be told here.

Rekhart drained the last of his beaker. "It would be unseemly for me to speak disrespectfully of our host in his absence."

This was important. Drew had never been more certain of anything. "Is it a matter concerning his particular business that troubles you?"

Rekhart set his beaker down. "No, I ought to say no more. If I am to criticise him I will say it to his face. My apologies, I did not wish to trouble you. But I will say this: you are, I think, a decent young man, and I suspect you do not know the full nature of the company you keep. There are things going on that I am convinced you would sooner not be involved with."

"What things, Rekhart? You need not fear to speak plainly with me. I can be trusted with a confidence." Drew's unease grew. He'd sensed this all along: that something wasn't quite right here. And he'd been too happy with his new life, too besotted with Jervin, that he'd turned a blind eye when he ought to have looked all the closer.

"Of that I have no doubt. Forgive me, I ought not to speak of this at all in my host's absence. But I've seen such things. Goddess help me, I've even done such things..." Rekhart tailed off into silence.

"What things? What has the power to trouble you so?"

"What? Things that stop a man resting easy at night. Things that haunt him through the waking hours. None of them good things. You would be wise to leave this place before you are drawn into them as I have been."

"Those are harsh words. But you cannot convince me if you continue to speak in riddles."

"That is what shame does to a man. Pray you never find out for yourself." Rekhart stood up. "I'd be much obliged if you would be so kind as to tell Jervin I will call on him by the end of the week with the remainder of what I owe him. I thank you for your time today. And I apologise if my words have troubled you. I ought not have spoken so, when all you sought to do was help. Good evening." Rekhart had left the room before Drew could gather his wits and get to his feet. He heard the hall door opening and closing in swift succession and crossed to the window in time to see Rekhart cramming his hat onto his head and striding off down the street.

Drew's view of the street outside was distorted by tiny bubbles of air trapped in the glass. He ran a finger down the windowpane, every imperfection suddenly so apparent to the touch. All this luxury came at a price. And up close he could see it was flawed, however perfect it may appear at first glance.

CHAPTER TEN

Alwenna sat up in the dark, her forehead pounding. The mattress rustled beneath her. She was on her narrow bed in the cave. Barely a glow escaped from the embers of the fire, not enough to make out even the familiar furniture in the room. A faint snuffling sound, and an uneven inhalation told her someone else was in the room with her. As her eyes adjusted she could make out a shape huddled over the table.

"Erin? Is that you?"

The shape moved, unfolding and lifting as whoever it was straightened up. "You're awake?" It was Marten's voice, clouded by sleep and more harshly formed than usual as a result of the wine he'd drunk.

"Yes, I suppose so." Her head pounded with the effort of speaking. What had happened? All she could remember was... what? Ripples spreading across the surface of the wine... She'd put water on to boil... "Have I been asleep long?"

"You collapsed. Do you not remember?" Marten had moved to stand between her and the fire.

She sensed he was uncertain – he'd never witnessed the sight overcome her before. His hesitancy now suggested he found it every bit as repellent as Weaver once had. She swung her feet down to the floor and sat up straight. "I remember." The dryness of her mouth told her she must have spent some time in the grip of her sight. It hadn't seized her like that for a long time. She'd begun to hope–

"Did you have some kind of vision?" Marten's question was almost casual. And she had nothing to gain by lying. He knew what she was – he'd known even before she had herself. "I tried to wake you – but I couldn't. And yet you weren't asleep."

"It was a vision. But there was no clarity to it." There in the dark she could hope he might not see her lie for what it was.

Marten snorted. "That means, I take it, you will not trust me with what you saw."

"I– No." And yet didn't he speak the truth? "Sometimes visions are sharp and clear. This one was all confusion. I was swimming through dark water, free, swimming towards a cairn. And when I got closer I could see the cairn was made of bones – bones of all different sizes. Bones of men, and women... And children. And on the top rested the ornate dagger you still have in your possession."

She heard Marten snatch in his breath. "Why does that startle you? The dagger? You do still have it, don't you?"

"After a fashion. My wife tried to surrender it to the elders' care, but they refused to take it." His voice was tired. "There's still no sign of your servant."

"Erin? She's not my servant." Was Marten trying to change the subject? "Sometimes she stays out all night."

"So you're not expecting her back?"

"She'll be back at first light, if not before."

"You shouldn't be left here alone."

"I'm not a child that needs to be watched over lest it hurt itself."

"I know you're not a child." In the dark she knew the freemerchant took a step closer.

"Marten, go back to your wife and make amends."

"She threw me out." He spoke so quietly his words scarcely stirred the darkness.

"Oh, Goddess. Go back to her. Have you no sense?"

"Very little, it would seem. I who have fed kings from the palm of my hand."

Alwenna stood up sharply. There'd be no more sleep for her that night. She moved over to the fire and stirred the embers into life, adding some dry sticks which flared up obligingly. Now she could see Marten's expression. His face was drawn, shadows making him appear even gaunter than usual. She stepped past him and poured herself a beaker of tepid water, swallowing it down in a bid to calm her headache. Marten watched her, his attitude belligerent.

"Do you want to pick a fight with me, Marten?"

"Far from it, my queen."

"Go back to her. The pair of you have too many years together to throw it away like this."

"If I stood at your side I would not consider it thrown away."

Alwenna made a gesture of impatience. "At my side is a dangerous place for anyone to stand. Have you not noticed?"

"You'll find I'm no coward."

"Neither was Weaver. It didn't help him in the end." That was a better barrier to put between them than any other words she could have chosen. The names of dead lovers had such power…

Marten bowed, setting his hand against his shoulder. "When your grief is done, my queen, you will find me waiting."

"No, Marten. That is not so. Your people will welcome your return, but not with me on your arm."

"Have you seen this, my queen?"

"I know it. I do not need to see it."

Marten sat down again at the table, one long leg stretched out, the other bent at the knee. "Then tell me what I must do. Unless it be return to my wife with my tail tucked between my legs. That I do not wish to hear."

"Then we would never get on, Marten, for I am done with

telling people what they wish to hear – unless it should serve my own purposes. And I do believe you should go back to her – as soon as may be."

"You cannot mourn for ever."

"Can I not? I shall be the judge of that." She studied Marten. He was lean built, with the slight stoop at his shoulders common to the tall. Would he be all eager haste, or take his time? The latter, she guessed. But it would not do. "Your wife already hates me."

"Then what have we to lose?" He watched her closely.

"Everything." A flicker of heat deep within her began to build. She squashed it ruthlessly. "But most of all we will have the satisfaction one day of telling her how she has misjudged us both."

"No, my queen, she's judged me aright. But I'll hope to be present the day she apologises to you." He picked up the wine bottle.

"Leave it on the table. You'll go back to her sober and respectable, at the very least."

"Respectable? Like this?" He ran a hand through his uneven cropped hair. "I'll be the laughing stock for years."

"What? You'll take their punishment lying down? I never imagined you to be so biddable, Marten."

"I planned to be less docile, but you aren't willing, my queen."

"Well. Let me make amends. Why not shave it off? You would be the first freemerchant with no hair at all."

Marten grimaced. "The braids are at the very heart of what we are."

"So let them see you are not afraid to stand alone."

"By the Hunter, yes. You're right."

It took a few minutes to heat more water. Alwenna set to work with Marten's knife, carefully shaving the roughly chopped hair away. The remnants of the shorn locks dropped to the floor as she worked soap into a lather and cleared another patch of scalp. Marten sat preternaturally still as she worked, his neck muscles tense. Occasionally her swollen belly brushed against his shoulder. Her back was aching from stooping over him before the job was done. She stepped back, stretching. "Should I take off the beard as well?"

Marten ran his hand over his scalp. "We ought to do this thing right." His smile was tight, almost nervous, but he raised his chin so she could begin. First one pass up his throat to the tip of his chin, then another. It was rough and would need to be repeated. As she began the third pass he set one hand on her hip.

"Marten, I have a knife at your throat. Be very careful what you do."

He raised his chin further and lifted his free hand, gently drawing her wrist aside. "For pity's sake, kiss me. Just this once." The hand on her hip tightened.

After a moment's hesitation she stooped and pressed her lips to his forehead, then straightened up and pulled away. "Do you want me to leave you with half a beard?"

"I want a great many things, my queen, but for now I'll be content if you finish the task in hand." His eyes were filled with scarcely suppressed laughter.

She pushed away his hand and stooped again, cautiously scraping the blade over his skin. She could see the pulse point in his neck; one slip and his crimson lifeblood would spill over her fingers... She closed her eyes and willed away the image. When she opened them she was able to continue, feigning a brisk manner, until his face was clean-shaven, without any mishaps. She could remember Weaver, similarly clean-shaven as they left Highkell, after what felt like half a lifetime ago. He had borne a shaving cut on his chin – had that been a sign of things to come? There were no such ill omens here, in any event. She straightened up, stretching her back again as she stepped away from Marten.

He ran his hands over his head, exploring her workmanship. His face and scalp were pale where his skin had been guarded against the sunlight. "A fine job you have done. May I count on your services again in future?"

There was a flurry of footsteps outside and two voices, laughing. The door burst open and Erin stepped inside, her laughter dying as she saw Alwenna and Marten together at the table.

"My lady, beg pardon–"

Behind, a young man bumped into her, knocking her off balance so she staggered further into the room. Laughing, he caught his arms about her waist. Erin nudged him hard with her elbow, shushing him, and he stopped short, gaping at Alwenna and Marten.

The youth released Erin and bowed. "I bid you good morning, my- my lady. Pray forgive the intrusion."

With a scraping of the wooden bench across the sandy floor Marten pushed himself to his feet. "Malcolm, a very good morning to you. I need not ask how you have spent this night." Marten's eyes moved from Malcolm to Erin and back again. Malcolm stared in amazement as he recognised his own father, beardless for possibly the first time in his son's life.

Malcolm blushed even deeper. "Sire, I..." He looked up, as if realising for the first time the import of finding his own father seated at Alwenna's table. "I beg your pardon." He spun on his heel and left them there, his footsteps hurrying away down the slope outside as the first light of dawn spread over the hillside.

CHAPTER ELEVEN

It was risky. Too risky. But if she stayed here she would be buried in a shallow grave next to her brother before the year was out. And if they marked her grave at all, it would bear the name "Miria". And – may the Goddess be her witness – that was not and never would be her name. She must seize her chance, now.

Her hands shook momentarily as she daubed the blood on her bedlinen, and on her clothing. She could lose everything if her deception should be discovered now. But what did she have now that she could not easily bear to part with? Only her life. And that was hemmed about by the rules of the order. She would break free, and live to damn them all, hypocrites that they were. She smeared more of the blood between her legs. "Goddess, forgive me for this blasphemy. I do what I do now to protect the life of your loyal servant, blessed as I have been by your bounty. Grant me this boon, that I may avenge the death of my lord before his child is brought into this world. Grant me this, my Goddess, grant me my freedom, grant me my life, grant me my own name, Ilsa, and I shall serve you to the end of my days."

They were poor enough words, without the cant the priests used, but they were her words. And they were honest words. Perhaps the only honest words she'd uttered in her life.

She took a piece of clean linen and rubbed at the bloodstains on the sheet, as if she'd been trying to clean away the evidence of her supposed failure. Weaver's blood, it was smeared over her hands and was already drying black and dark beneath her fingernails. She could hear others stirring now, in the rooms on either side of hers. It was time.

Standing by the bed in her soiled shift, bloodied linen in one hand, she drew in a lungful of air and screamed.

Footsteps came running to her door and it was thrown open without ceremony.

She kept her back to the door, staring at the bed, willing tears to spill from her eyes.

"Goddess spare us, what is this?"

Whatever did the fool think it was? But, thank the Goddess, it was Curwen. The devout priest would not question her tale – if she guessed aright he would not dare so much as look at her, in her unclean state.

"The Goddess has... withdrawn her blessing." She punctuated her words with convincing sobs as the tears began to pour down her face. Now she'd started she would struggle to stop. Tears were useful things, granted the right audience. "She has turned away from me."

She turned her tear-stained face to the priest. "Please, take me to his holiness, that I may receive his blessing." She reached out an unsteady, bloodstained hand and the priest took a hasty step back. Other faces appeared at the door, curious to see the cause of the disturbance.

Moments later a gown had been thrown over her and she was being shepherded by a concerned group of priests through the palace to the prelate's rooms.

Outside his door they waited as he was roused from his devotions. Her head was beginning to ache from the effort of keeping the tears flowing. Goddess, she hoped she didn't have long to wait, she couldn't keep this up for much longer.

Finally the door was opened and she was admitted to the prelate's presence.

She dropped to her knees before him.

"Prelate, I have failed." She hung her head low, never for a moment raising her eyes to his, puffy and tearstained as they were she still feared he would divine the truth from her.

"You ungrateful wretch. After all the order has done for you."

"Please forgive me, prelate. Tell me how I may serve the order. I will do anything to prove my loyalty. Anything." She knelt before him, risking a quick glance up at his face before folding her head to the floor in obeisance. "Anything, I swear it."

"The order has no need of one with your taint." His sandalled foot turned away. Dark hairs sprouted from his toes, she noticed.

"If you must send me away, I will go because it is your order, sire. But at least send me where I may continue to serve our Goddess. I could not bear to live if she turned her face away from me now."

"How dare you make any claim to our Goddess's attention?" He turned away.

"Your holiness, she marked me with her favour once. I will devote my life to her in whatever way I may. I don't care how dangerous it is. I beg you permit me to continue to serve the Goddess. I cannot turn away from her now. I owe her everything."

"You would do anything, child?"

"Anything, I swear." She kept her forehead to the floor, tensed for a blow as he took several steps away, then returned to study her where she knelt.

"You will fast for nine days, and take nine lashes in silence at the dawn of each day, to prove your loyalty. If you prove yourself sound in that way, I shall find a way for you to serve the Goddess.

Nine lashes? Each day? Goddess, that was harsh. But she bit back the words of protest that sprang to her lips. "I thank you, sire, for the chance to prove myself worthy."

The prelate snorted. "We will see how worthy you truly are. Your fast begins at sunset tonight." He strode away, his sandals paf-paffing into the distance. She waited until she was sure he was out of sight and out of earshot before she straightened up. May the Goddess forgive her for the lies she had told. Nine lashes on nine days. Nine times nine. That was a great many. Punishment and more for her falsehoods. Might she not prefer to join her brother in a shallow grave after all? Was that not what she deserved?

CHAPTER TWELVE

This had to be the place the servant had told him about. Bleaklow stood in the street across from the *Royal Hart*. Now he was there he found himself strangely reluctant to step inside. Drelena wouldn't thank him for what he was about to do. She was far more likely to hate him, in fact.

As Bleaklow approached the bar the landlord assessed him with a glance. He ordered an ale, doing his best to summon a friendly smile as he did so.

"I've been told a girl going by the name of Lena works here."

The landlord set a brimming tankard down on the wooden bar. "Some folks'll tell a stranger anything."

So it was going to be like that, was it? "Stranger? We're all islanders in these parts, aren't we?"

"True enough." The landlord's expression was sceptical at best.

"I bring news from her family. If I might speak to her, I would be obliged."

"If such a girl did work here, why should I believe she'd want to speak to you?"

"I've known her since she was knee high. Worked for her family these past sixteen years. I probably know more about her than she's ever told you."

The landlord shrugged. "No offence, but I don't go questioning good workers about all the things they don't choose to tell me."

"She does work here then?"

The landlord shook his head. "Even if she did, I wouldn't be discussing it with customers, islanders or not."

"But there'd be no harm in telling her I was here and asking after her, would there?" Bleaklow set a couple of coins on the bar.

"And no point in asking me, either." The landlord folded his arms. "Why don't you finish up that drink and take your questions elsewhere. You'll get no answers from me – nor from any of the staff here, neither."

Bleaklow scooped the coins back into a pocket. "I daresay in your place I'd take the same line. I'm not looking for trouble, just–"

At that moment the door from the kitchen burst open. "Isaac, the cook says–"

Drelena.

She froze, staring at Bleaklow in something close to horror. "Bleaky. Then it was you after all."

"Drelena. It's taken some time to find you."

"I saw you at the harbour, didn't I? I'd begun to think I'd been mistaken." With a glance over her shoulder she shut the kitchen door and advanced into the room, drying her hands on a square of linen.

"Now, Lena, if this fellow's bothering you I can bring the lads out."

"No, Isaac. There's no need. I– I've been expecting him." She set the linen square down on the bar. "The cook said to tell you the butcher wants paying. He's through there now."

Bleaklow realised he still had one hand crammed in his pocket. He tugged it out hastily, dropping one of the coins on the floor. "Your parents have been worried." He stooped to pick up the coin. "We all have."

"There was no need. I've been – very happy."

Yes, he wanted to say. He saw.

The door from the kitchen burst open again, this time another servant girl. "Isaac, the butcher won't deliver until he's been paid for last week's." She stared in undisguised curiosity at Bleaklow and Drelena.

Isaac raised a warning finger towards Bleaklow. "Don't you try anything, understand?"

"Isaac. He's all right. Really."

"That'll be why you're overjoyed to see him."

"Go pay the butcher. I'll be fine."

Bleaklow slid the coin into his pocket as the landlord stamped over to the kitchen door.

"He seems to have taken a dislike to you." She bit her lip. He'd seen her do that a thousand times before, but this time his stomach curdled with guilt. "You could say you couldn't find me. Just–"

"You have to come back now, Drelena."

"I know. But… You could give me a few more days."

"You know that's not possible."

"Please, Bleaky. It would mean a lot to me."

Goddess, was she going to cry? "Who is he?" He knew, of course. It had been easy to find out about the wealthy merchant.

"He's a wonderful man. So kind, and…" Her voice caught and she fell silent.

"He's a merchant, Drelena. You know it won't do. Your parents–"

"I know. They have other plans." She folded her arms. "Bleaky, you can't make me go back."

"Drelena, I'll do whatever's necessary."

"Nonsense. I've known you for years. You wouldn't force me to go back with you. You'd never hurt me. You couldn't."

Bleaklow's gut twisted with guilt. "You're right. I couldn't. But Darnell has no such claims to my loyalty."

She looked at him sharply. "What are you saying?"

Must he spell it out? "You never told him you were daughter of the lord convenor, did you?"

"I..." That bite of her lip again, as she contemplated lying. "No, I haven't. Not yet."

Bleaklow tried to smile – a reassuring smile. Her expression told him it fell far short of target. "Then I need never tell your father whose bed you've been warming while you've been here. Come back with me today and all will be well. You'll see."

"Or?" There was a glint of anger in her eyes now.

Bleaklow's stomach curdled. "If you care about Darnell – and I know you do – you will come with me, without fuss and without causing trouble."

"And if I don't?" She raised her chin in defiance.

"Then Darnell will be clapped in irons and brought before the Lord Convenor to answer charges of abduction, indecent behaviour, assault against your person... I imagine your father will think of others to add to the list, given you're his only daughter."

"You wouldn't be so cruel." But there was doubt in her eyes now.

"I told you, Drelena. I will do whatever's necessary to bring you safely home to your parents."

"I see. And if I come with you willingly, he will be safe?"

"He will."

"Do you swear it?"

"I swear it."

She studied his face for a long time; it took all his resolution not to turn his eyes away. Finally, she spoke.

"Very well."

That was the moment the light in her eyes died. It would haunt him to the end of his days.

CHAPTER THIRTEEN

Alwenna sat on the flat-topped stone, leaning back against the cliff face. It was a relief to sit outside in the late afternoon shade, once the sun had moved round behind the escarpment. After the heat and stillness of noon, even the slightest drift of air along the escarpment was a blessing straight from the Goddess.

She was enjoying one such moment of perfect peace when Marten came walking up the slope, a bag slung over his shoulder. This was it, then.

"Marten."

"My lady." He hunkered down beside her, his back against the rock.

"You are leaving?"

"I am leaving. I have been waiting only for the heat of the day to die down."

"Then I wish you well." She need not tell him her own thoughts had been following similar lines.

"Thank you my lady, that is more than I deserve. And yet... I wish you would join me."

"Indeed?" She set one hand on her swollen belly. "I doubt I'll be going anywhere for a while." The unborn child twisted beneath her hand, as if it knew her words were untrue.

"I can delay no longer. I shall achieve nothing while I remain here."

The same could be said of all of them. A wave of weariness swept over her. The moment of peace was gone beyond recall.

"We must follow different paths this time, Marten. They will like as not lead to the same place in the end, anyway."

"Do you dabble in prophecy now?"

"I can think of few things more futile – I shall not make a habit of it."

"You will be careful, when I am gone?"

She pressed a hand to her bulging stomach. "Right now I have very little option."

"Even so – you are uneasy, my lady. Promise me you will do nothing rash."

Alwenna shook her head. "Such a promise would have seen you dead on the floor of the summer palace months ago. I will do whatever's necessary."

Marten pushed himself to his feet. "Then I must go without reassurance from you."

"You're a grown man, and you've managed well enough these past years."

"Indeed I have. Behold the proof of my success: destitute and cast out by my own people."

Alwenna smiled. "Free and unfettered. I wish you well, Marten, truly. You will find the courage to do what is right in the end."

He hesitated. "What do you know? Will you not tell me?"

"I know a thousand things, none of which may come to pass. Ask me what I don't know, that would be easier to answer."

"Then tell me what you do not know, my lady."

No need to lie this time. "We are stepping out into darkness, Marten. I do not know where our feet will land."

Marten bowed his head. "I cannot argue with that. It is not easy travelling by night, but it is sometimes safer to avoid the heat of the day."

"You will make a fine prophet one day. May your road be clear, Marten."

"And yours, my lady."

He made his way back down the slope, his pace unhurried. It was the gait of a man embarking on a long journey. As he passed the door that had been his own, his sons came out. The eldest stood off to one side, awkward in his new-found maturity, while the younger two hugged their father. His wife looked on, her arms folded. Alwenna couldn't see her expression from this distance, but she could picture it: the woman's lips pressed tight with disapproval, her brow creased.

The youngest boy returned to his mother's side as the eldest shook hands awkwardly with his father. The middle son, Brett, walked with him to where his horse waited, helping to saddle up, before watching by the meeting tree until his father had ridden out of sight.

She still had one ally at Scarrow's Deep, at least.

CHAPTER FOURTEEN

Market days in Brigholm were colourful. Drew wound his way between the stalls laden with goods – some familiar, some exotic – shipped from far off places. He couldn't be further removed from his provincial beginnings. If the Lady Alwenna hadn't come to Vorrahan he'd still be trapped there now, stifling under the dour gaze of the grey stone precinct. He wondered how she was faring. Word of a catastrophic fire at the old summer palace had reached Brigholm but there had been no details. But he'd have known if she'd been caught up in that – he was sure of it. Jervin had no time for freemerchants, so he'd heard little gossip. And he was convinced the freemerchants would have word of her. Drew didn't stop to question such instincts these days – dwelling on such things just led to lack of sleep.

Somewhere about there had to be a freemerchant trader. Drew scanned the marketplace. There were bolts of fine fabrics brought up from Ellisquay, jewellery and pottery from local craftsmen, bags and gloves produced with leather from the tanneries downriver. But there were quite a few empty stalls, too – produce from the south simply wasn't getting through to Highkell and existing stocks had finally been used up. The only flour to be had was the rough-ground local stuff and even that was scarce now. Prices had gone up at the bakers' stalls, too. And there weren't as many people about as he would have expected for that time of day.

Then he saw a familiar face approaching: Jaseph Rekhart. The commander of the city watch must be off duty for he was not wearing his usual livery. He was startled by Drew's greeting, but he stopped to talk. Drew saw then that Rekhart's face was deeply lined and carried several days' growth of stubble. The city watchman must still be haunted by recent events.

"Are you well, Rekhart?"

"Can't complain."

"Then join me awhile for a drink. I was about to stop here." He gestured towards a nearby kopamid house.

Rekhart appeared to fight some inner battle, but his mouth twisted in something approaching a smile. "That would be welcome, and I cannot pretend otherwise, but… I have no money."

"I invited you to join me, I don't expect you to pay. I would be glad of your company – I know few enough people in Brigholm and am always glad to catch up with a friend."

"I'm honoured to call any friend of Weaver's a friend of mine."

It was clear that whatever troubled the city watchman had not diminished in recent days. He was living under some kind of strain. Perhaps now Drew would learn what. It seemed important he should do so, although he was at a loss to explain why. Was it the promptings of his meagre sight, or simply a desire to speak to someone from outside Jervin's household?

Drew poured the kopamid. The beakers in this kopamid house were plainer than those at Jervin's home, but still brightly coloured. The blend of spices made up for any lack of ostentation, rich and aromatic. Drew had found himself taking to the ritual of drinking kopamid as one born to the habit. He passed Rekhart's drink to him and the watchman took it with unsteady hands, setting it down on the table sharply.

"My thanks."

"Let us drink to continued good health." Drew drank from his beaker first; some of the freemerchant ways had caught on in Brigholm.

"I'll gladly drink to your health." Rekhart raised his own beaker, sipping a small quantity of the dark fluid.

"But not your own?"

"I'm not a deserving case. Not right now."

"Surely not. Can I suggest you are being too hard on yourself?"

"I told you when last we met I'd seen and done such things as…" Rekhart clasped his fingers together, to steady them. "Even now I cannot bring myself to speak of them, I have found them so repellent. In truth, that's why I am glad to encounter you today."

He fell silent, as if he felt he'd suddenly said more than enough.

"If I can help in any way, then I shall. You can count on my friendship."

Rekhart shook his head. "You're a good man… and I hate to put upon you. But… I understand you took holy orders. I… have been thinking of late of joining the precinct, as a way to make amends." He looked up at Drew then, searching his face for… what? Approval?

This was all the wrong way round. What advice could he possibly offer when he'd fled the precinct under a shadow? "In truth, I do not know what to say. My time at the precinct was… well, I wouldn't be here now if I'd been successful in finding my true place there."

"But… to withdraw from all this. To spend my time in prayer and reflection, to make amends for my poor choices…"

"My friend, if you hope to discover spiritual peace at the precinct, I fear you would be disappointed. One of the reasons for my departure was the lack of any true spirituality. After Brother Gwydion's death, there were few there who were as devout as he had been. And Father Garrad, of course, betrayed a sacred trust for the sake of money when he handed over the Lady Alwenna to the new king. There were others there, too, who held high rank, but…" What to say about Brother Irwyn? There was every possibility he might be in charge now without Father Garrad to guide the precinct. "You were frank with me when last we spoke, and now I must return the favour. Vorrahan has a reputation for piety and spirituality, but as your friend I cannot urge you to go there. That is not at all what you want to hear, is it?"

Rekhart took another mouthful of kopamid. "I don't expect it to be easy… but I thought, if I could devote myself to service of the Goddess…"

"Can you not be content serving the Goddess through your work with the city watch? That is vital, after all. A great service to her people."

Rekhart ran a hand through his hair. "I no longer work for the city watch. I was dismissed several days ago."

Drew gaped at him. "Impossible! How can that be?"

"How? Very easily if a commander turns up drunk to work. Easier still if an influential businessman has already laid information against him, before plying him with drink."

Drew's heart sank. "And that businessman…" He didn't need to ask, but he needed to hear the answer spoken all the same. "It was Jervin?"

Rekhart nodded, then drained his beaker. "The very same."

"But… you and he had an understanding."

Rekhart ran his hand through his hair again. "We did indeed. I was foolish enough to think I could break with him."

Some of the sunlight had leached out of Drew's day. Jervin wouldn't have been so petty? Surely… He recalled the snippets of conversation he'd overheard when he'd eavesdropped on his meeting with the Ellisquay traders, the sense of Jervin's implacable resentment. He pushed the thought away. "There must have been some misunderstanding. Let me speak with Jervin and see what can be resolved." Did he have enough influence with him, when all was said and done?

"There's no need. I'm sorry to have mentioned it at all, Drew. None of it has been your doing and I ought not set you one against the other."

"But my friend, surely this can be resolved?"

"Jervin made it clear if I would not work for him I would work for no one in Brigholm. I fear he was as good as his word."

"But... that's unspeakable. I pray to the Goddess there has been some simple misunderstanding."

"I cannot ask you to intervene."

"Would you work for him now, if you were given the chance? If only until you could make other plans? I'm not convinced the precinct will be what you need."

Rekhart hesitated. "Goddess knows, I dislike going hungry. See, even my pride has left me. I would swallow all my principles to see a square meal on the table again, after only a matter of days."

"It need not be for ever. Only until you find something better."

Drew watched Rekhart's expression harden as he warred with himself again, and lost.

"Do you think you can persuade him?"

"I can't promise anything. But you have my word I will try, my friend."

Rekhart nodded and got to his feet. "Have a care for your own wellbeing. I will not think the less of you if you change your mind."

Drew watched Rekhart walk away. He'd found the courage to act on his doubts, and Jervin had broken him. Could he really be telling the truth? Drew couldn't believe Jervin would treat one of his own so harshly. He refused to believe it.

CHAPTER FIFTEEN

Peveril set the necklace on the table in his room and sat down, staring at it. It was a fine piece of work. For all he'd told the apprentice it couldn't be repaired, he had no doubt it could – by the right craftsman. But with the way old Marwick had been sniffing around lately he couldn't risk taking it to anyone in Highkell. And no one in the south, either, if his guess as to the origins of the necklace was right. That left east – Brigholm, or beyond. There were plenty of dealers there who'd give him a good price for it and ask no questions.

The real question was, would they give him more than Vasic might pay for the tale he'd overheard? He took a swig from the wine bottle at his elbow. It set his teeth on edge, but he could afford nothing better. And he suspected Vasic's generosity would do little to improve that situation. No, if he told the king his bride-to-be had been rescued from the rubble he doubted Vasic's generosity would even be expressed in anything as tangible as money. A promotion, perhaps. Most likely in the form of a succession of taxing duties that would prove far more onerous than his present work. And would Vasic welcome the news anyway? He'd more likely be relieved to learn for certain that his erstwhile bride-to-be was dead. And the more Peveril thought about it, the more he suspected Vasic was likely to pay generously the man who could make sure of Alwenna's death.

Now there were possibilities. But discovering she lived was one thing; scouring the country to find her was quite another matter. He'd recognise her again, for sure, but he couldn't hope to have the good luck of stumbling upon her during a routine patrol. She'd be far from Highkell anyway, if she had any sense.

No, Vasic would not be overjoyed to learn she may have lived. Peveril prided himself on understanding human nature. It would be a waste to offer the entire necklace to him: the single leaf would suffice to support Peveril's tale. The king need never learn about the rest of the necklace, unless his reaction was unexpectedly favourable.

Was there anyone who might pay him more generously for his information? Vasic had enemies – would they be able to make better use of the secret? There were all sorts of rumours flying about the city already. The Goddess had handed him a rare opportunity with this necklace: he must turn it to a profit on his own account somehow. Peveril scooped the necklace up and folded it away, tucking it inside the leather pouch that he slung around his neck. Truth was, he was slowing down. If a gift like this had come his way a year or two ago he'd not have hesitated the way he was now. But he'd learned caution. This was too big a matter to risk his hand being detected. Art Peveril was on the up, and he wouldn't waste this chance by acting hastily.

The scribe, Birtle, was already bent over the ledgers scratching away with his pen when Peveril walked into the counting house. He looked up as the door opened.

"Good morning."

Peveril grunted. There was little good about it. The leather pouch nestled against his chest, taunting him for his failure to find a way to turn it to profit.

"That's no way to greet a fellow who's just being sociable."

"Is that so?" Peveril turned a dead-eyed stare to Birtle, who remained unabashed.

“Not when you hear what I have to tell you.” Birtle set his pen down. “Your friend’s been asking a lot of questions about you lately.”

“Which friend would that be?” Peveril kept his voice non-committal.

“Of course, you have so many.” Was that the ghost of a smile that crossed the skinny cleric’s features? Birtle rested his hands on the desk in front of him, clasping his fingers together. “That would be the friend you usually refer to as Old Faceache.”

“Has he nowt better to do?”

“Apparently not.” The cleric fixed him with a steady gaze.

Peveril fought the urge to turn away. “Are you implying something, Birtle? It would save us both time if’n you just came right out and said it.”

“Not at all, old fellow, not at all. I just thought it fair to warn you.” Birtle unclasped his fingers and took up the quill again, dipping it in the pot of ink on his desk. “We go back a long way. Neither one of us is likely to benefit if the other were to fall foul of the authorities now.”

Peveril had no arguments on that score. “There at least we agree.”

“Be careful of Marwick. He’s under pressure from the king to deliver impossible demands. He’s looking for easier ways to keep face.”

“If he thinks taking me on would be easy, he’s a bigger fool ’n I ever thought.”

“Again, we are in complete agreement, my friend. But he has taken a great deal of interest in that business with the stonemason’s apprentice. Poor lad was found dead, face down on his own bed. Strangled, apparently.”

“Arrogant little prick likely asked for it.”

“Like as not. The honourable Lord Marwick is yet to be convinced of that, I fear.” The cleric bent over the ledgers once more.

Birtle knew too much. Far too much. But he was one of Peveril's more useful connections and he wasn't about to cut off his nose to spite his face. Marwick, on the other hand, was rapidly becoming a thorn in his side. Something might have to be done about that.

CHAPTER SIXTEEN

Durstan watched from the gallery above as the soldier now known as Pius applied the last of the day's nine strokes to the priestess's back. The soldier applied the whip mechanically, without any apparent force, but the girl flinched a little more with every stroke. There was a time Durstan would have ordered the soldier to apply the whip harder. He liked to think he'd learned compassion in recent years.

This was the ninth of the nine days. Durstan found himself clenching his fist about the holy sceptre he held before him. He could not speak out now – he had set the punishment, and he must be seen to be unyielding. At the seventh stroke, a tremor ran through the girl's slender frame and fresh blood sprang to the surface where her back had been repeatedly crossed by the lash. His orders had done this.

At the eighth, she shuddered and her head sank lower, but still she bore the punishment in silence. Few men had displayed her courage in the face of such an ordeal. At the ninth her knees gave way and she sagged where she stood, arms bound above her head else she'd have dropped to the floor.

The soldier took a single step back, impassive, coiling up the whip. He stood to attention as if the girl didn't exist at all. That was one of Durstan's doubts laid to rest, at least: he'd never quite believed they'd succeeded in bending the soldier to their will, but the man he'd once been would not have carried out those orders in so bloodless a fashion. If only he could allay his other doubts as easily…

Now it was for Durstan to bless the girl, and beseech the Goddess's forgiveness for her failure to carry the dead king's child to term. He raised his head, stretching his neck and clenching and unclenching his hands about the sceptre. May the Goddess give him strength to speak the words without stumbling over them. He proceeded to the narrow stairs, making his way down with all the dignity he could muster. Not an easy task with the way his lame leg was paining him in recent days. The girl was in no state to notice if his progress towards her was uneven, but… As one ordained in the service of the Goddess he must maintain his dignity.

Priests stood either side of the altar chamber, rigid and tense, awaiting Durstan's orders. Did they dare disapprove of the girl's punishment? If either of them thought it overly harsh, they did not betray it by so much as a look. The prelate nodded to Curwen.

"Release her hands."

At the sound of his voice she opened her eyes. There was no mistaking the pride in their startlingly pale depths. It had to be pride, for once her hands were freed there wasn't an ounce of defiance in her slight frame – she crumpled to the floor as her legs gave way beneath her.

Durstan raised his sceptre. "The Goddess has witnessed your devotion to her these nine days. May her blessing be upon you this day and every day henceforth."

The girl pressed her eyes shut again then pulled herself upright, holding the front of her backless shift to her chin. She rose unsteadily to a standing position, tremors running through her. She opened her eyes once more, meeting Durstan's gaze fully for the first time, as if she were his equal. Her effrontery was… magnificent.

"Do you accept the will of the Goddess?"

"In all things, your holiness." Her voice was unsteady, but the words were intelligible.

"Do you accept the law of the Goddess?"

"In all things, your holiness."

"And will you be obedient to the Goddess?"

"In all ways I will be her humble servant, your holiness." She met his gaze with fierce pride a moment longer before lowering her eyes with due deference. "I stand ready to do her bidding."

Only the rapid rise and fall of her chest spoke of the ordeal she had just undergone. Durstan turned his attention to Curwen. "Take her to the infirmary and see her wounds are tended. She will serve the Goddess as none other has before."

Curwen frowned. "Your holiness, I don't understand."

"The girl has done her penance and now the Goddess has work for her. See she receives the best healing care."

"Yes, your holiness." He gingerly reached out one hand to support her by the elbow.

Durstan nodded his head to the other priest. "You there, assist brother Curwen."

The priest hastened to do his bidding, leaving Durstan and the soldier alone before the altar. The soldier's expression remained utterly vacant.

"You, there. Pius. Hand me that whip."

The soldier turned blank eyes to Durstan. After a moment he held out the hand holding the whip. Durstan took it from him, and the soldier lowered his hand again.

"Return to your normal duties."

The soldier blinked, hesitated, then turned and made his way out of the chamber. Once in motion he moved steadily enough, as if he understood the instruction. He would do. He would have to: right now he was the best they had.

Durstan waited until he was alone in the room before

examining the whip. He ran a finger over the coiled lash; it came away reddened with blood. Her blood. Given so that she might appease the Goddess for her failure.

Durstan shivered.

He bowed his head in prayer and pressed the whip to his forehead. He would take the lash to his own back, and before another hour was out his own blood would mingle with the girl's. May his sacrifice please the Goddess twofold.

CHAPTER SEVENTEEN

Vasic studied the letter a second time. His new bride-to-be would be sailing for Lynesreach in a matter of days. The letter had a rather plaintive tone, as if the Lord Convenor Etrus felt slighted Vasic hadn't travelled to the Outer Isles in person. Had that been why they'd insisted the girl was too ill to be seen?

Kaith's voice intruded upon his thoughts. "She is their only daughter, your highness. A degree of concern on their part is understandable, I believe."

"This is not an expression of concern, Kaith. It is a demand that I trail down to Lynesreach to greet the girl. It is a gross piece of impertinence. The journey's tedious enough as it is, without having to undertake it without my own horses and carriage." Why the girl couldn't sail into a northern port and progress overland from there... Well, he knew that. Lynesreach had the deep water port. Lynesreach was the capital. They couldn't have the future queen of the realm arriving to take her place on a humble ferry along with the livestock and commoners. She would sail into Lynesreach on a vessel appropriate to the rank and wealth of the only daughter of the lord convenor of the Outer Isles.

"It is indeed unfortunate repairs to the bridge and road will take so long, but highness, it is important that it be seen you do not let such difficulties stand in your way." Kaith bobbed his head in obeisance.

Nearby, Marwick's jaw worked, but he remained silent. The two courtiers rarely agreed, but on this occasion they had both expressed the same opinion to Vasic. Both equally unsought and equally unwelcome. Both right, though it galled him to admit it. Taking Highkell had been a bold, decisive move on his part. His recent illness had done much to counteract the impact of that. He'd told no one of his conviction that the Lady Alwenna had cursed him, of course. The maid he'd set to spy on the queen might have guessed his suspicions, but she'd perished in the collapse of the tower. As had, he could have sworn, the Lady Alwenna – for how else could he explain the sudden lifting of his illness? It had to have had a supernatural cause. Vasic recalled the expression on Garrad's face before he turned the knife upon himself. No, he would take no chances.

"On the eve of my departure there will be a ceremony, laying to rest the victims of the collapse." He would bring his new bride back to a stronghold free of taint from past events. "I will not have it said devotions to the Goddess have been neglected. You will accompany me to Lynesreach, Kaith. Marwick, you will remain here to see all runs smoothly in my absence."

Marwick bowed. "As you wish, your highness. It will be a great joy to welcome my sister's child to Highkell in the fullness of time."

"I have no doubt. Since horses and carriages will be impossible, I expect you to have a pathway cleared through the gorge sufficient that the Lady Drelena may be carried in a litter, as befitting her station."

"It will be done, your highness." Marwick bowed. Evidently he felt he'd cavilled enough for one day.

"And one last thing – send a messenger ahead to alert the palace of our journey. And make sure the High Seer Yurgen will be present at Lynesreach, for I wish to consult him on certain spiritual matters."

Vasic retired to his private chambers, dismissing the various servants and hangers-on who littered the citadel these days. He poured himself a glass of wine and sat down at the table by the window. There he withdrew from his belt pouch the small bundle the sharp-faced captain had given him. He opened out the fabric and spread it flat upon the table. There, incongruously untarnished against the stained fabric, nestled the single leaf. It was still an exquisite artefact, even though it was bent out of shape and attached to a broken length of gold chain. He could remember the day he had given it to Alwenna. She'd stood as if carved from ice as he'd fastened it about her neck.

He picked up the leaf and turned it over, admiring the veining. She had worn it for the wedding ceremony as he'd requested. Why had the thing come into his possession now, when he had determined upon a new start? Was the Goddess trying to tell him something?

Vasic had been inclined to dismiss the captain's story out of hand. He still was: the fellow was an opportunist, nothing more. He'd happened upon the relic and concocted the tale in the hope of a generous reward from his king. There could be no more to it than that. If she lived still, wouldn't he have known?

CHAPTER EIGHTEEN

"Rekhart again? What is it with you and that fellow?" Jervin's irritation wasn't the good-humoured sort. Drew should have known better than to raise the subject at the breakfast table.

"I happened to meet him in town yesterday, that's all." Now Drew had started down this road he might as well push on. "Did you know he'd lost his job with the city watch?"

Jervin snorted. "The man's a whining fool who doesn't know when he's well off."

This was not a promising start. But he needed to push this issue. Why, he couldn't have said. He just knew it must be done. "I always thought him a man of principle. It troubles me... to think he may have lost his work because of something you might have said."

Jervin set down his bread and stared at Drew. "I've told you before not to trouble yourself with my business."

He should apologise, beg Jervin's forgiveness. "I'm sorry. I can't help but notice things sometimes." Drew set aside his plate, no longer hungry. "But Rekhart losing his job like that, all of a sudden – that is your business this time, isn't it?"

"Are you questioning my decision?"

Goddess, this was more difficult than he'd feared. "Then you did have him dismissed? He seemed to think so, but I confess, I couldn't believe it. You've always been so generous with me."

Jervin pushed slowly to his feet. "Of course I had him dismissed. He needed to see what happens to those who try to cross me."

Drew forced himself to remain still in his seat. He pressed his fingers against the fine table covering, as if that would somehow help him. "I think he has learned his lesson."

"And have you?"

"You let me see a side to you denied to others. I think… if you were to offer Rekhart work now he would be loyal."

"You think, do you? Does it occur to you I might not be interested in what you think?"

"Apparently not." Drew raised his chin slightly, keeping his hands on the table to stop them shaking. "Rekhart is a man of principle. If he is no longer torn by his duty to the city watch he will serve you well. Better than before."

"You think and talk a deal too much about Rekhart."

"I have few friends besides you in Brigholm, but he is one of them."

"And you think that is a recommendation?"

"No. It is the simple truth. I do not lie, Jervin. And I do not cheat. If that makes me foolish and naive, then so I am. And since I am it troubles me that a friend could be made destitute for one small mistake."

"Yes. It makes you very foolish and naive indeed." Jervin walked over to the glass-fronted cabinet, studying the exquisite ceramics displayed on the shelves. He steepled his fingers, bowing his head as though he was lost in thought. His shoulders were tense. "I won't have you thinking of Rekhart as a martyr. I'll offer him work." He turned to face Drew. "Whether he accepts or not is another matter. But I'll make the offer. And you won't repeat his name at this table again. Is that clear?"

Air crept into Drew's lungs again. Quite when he'd held his breath he couldn't be sure. "Thank you, Jervin."

"It's more consideration than he deserves, but he can be useful to me yet."

Drew nodded, willing his limbs to be steady once more. He hadn't felt this way since he'd fled the kitchens at Vorrahan.

Jervin paced across to the window. "I'll need to go away in a few days' time. Those traders from Ellisquay are proving more troublesome than ever and I intend to petition our new king for trade sanctions."

Was Drew's first reaction really relief?

"Have you nothing to say to that, in your naivety? Do you not think it ironic I intend to petition the king?"

"Well – it sounds like a bold move."

"I'm going to become a respectable businessman in this community, Drew. The most respected businessman in the Marches. I shall surround myself with fellows like your principled friend."

"I see. Do you want me to take care of things in your absence?"

"No. I have stewards for that. You will come with me and grace the royal court with your presence."

Drew's heart sank. "Jervin, I cannot. There is a price on my head in Highkell. I can't return there."

"Nonsense. My mind is made up. You will be travelling in my entourage – I am a successful businessman and you'll be untouchable. You'll see." Jervin laughed. "You're no longer the runaway novice from Vorrahan – take a look in the mirror and see for yourself."

Jervin bent over Drew, raising his chin with a finger and placing a languorous kiss on his lips. "Now I have much work to do, so I cannot stay here all day with you as I would prefer to."

"Can't it wait – just a while?"

Jervin shook his head. "No, not today. But we will settle this tonight, over a bottle or two of wine."

He straightened up and left the room, looking well pleased with himself. Drew sat at the table a moment longer. Jervin's changes of mood were as unpredictable as they were frequent. To go to Highkell would be madness. But… He knew a sudden moment of clarity: he should go. And not because Jervin said so. Highkell was the place he needed to be. He could not mark time forever here in Brigholm, living out his days in tangled sheets and uncertainty.

He got up from the table and crossed over to the cabinet Jervin had been studying. It contained some of his best enamelware: exquisite pieces, all of them perfect, all of them flawless, imprisoned in this glass case where dust could not touch them, sunlight could not fade them and no one could damage them. The back of this cabinet was mirrored glass and there stood his reflection, surrounded by row upon row of carefully hoarded treasures. His hair reached to his shoulders now, his chin bore a beard trimmed in the style Jervin favoured. His face was gaunter than when he'd left Vorrahan, his shoulders squarer. Yet there he stood in Jervin's house, just another piece in his exquisite collection.

Yes, he must go to Highkell.

CHAPTER NINETEEN

The nightmare was the same every time. And every time the thing that was pursuing her drew a little closer. Alwenna tried to push herself upright, flailing awkwardly as the ancient mattress sagged beneath her. The bulk of unborn child in her midriff made her movements ungainly at best, and things she had routinely done were now virtually impossible, but lifelong habits died hard. She tucked her knees up and twisted onto her side so she could swing her feet onto the floor. Now she was able to push her upper body clear of the bed until she was sitting upright, bulging midriff and all. Goddess, if only she could laugh at herself right now.

It was still dark and all was silent in the cave chamber. Erin must be out somewhere with Marten's eldest again. That was all to the good; it meant Alwenna would not disturb her as she made preparations. She should have done this days ago. Goddess knew why she hadn't: perhaps so she could not be accused of chasing Marten? As if it mattered now what anyone thought of her. She could scarcely lift her own royal carcass out of bed – she was a threat to no one.

She shivered. The night air was not cool, but some deeper apprehension gripped her. She was as close to helpless now as she had been at any time in her life. Why had she tarried here so long? It had been clear for months the elders could do nothing to help her, even had they been willing. The only exception had been the wisewoman, Jenna, and she had not been near Scarrow's Deep for weeks. Alwenna had pinned too many hopes on her returning, even though she'd been gone far longer than she'd said she would. Alwenna feared some mishap had overcome her. And now she dared not wait any longer, for the thing that stalked her during her sleep was drawing closer, night by night.

So she would run away, just as she had fled the summer palace, tail between her legs. But first she would take back what was hers.

She took up the wine glass, wiping it out with a cloth to be sure it was clean. Of all the ridiculous luxuries to have in an out-of-the-way place like this, wine glasses had been the most unexpected. She rummaged around in the storage niche cut from the stone of the cliff until she found the whetstone, then settled down to apply it to her eating knife. The sharper the better. Once she would have used water, or even wine, but instinct told her only blood would tell her what she needed to know this time. She lost track of time as she honed the blade, recalling one evening on the road to Vorrahan when Weaver had sat sharpening his knife. She'd watched him in silence then, but every movement came back to her now. She'd never imagined she would need to know how to do such a mundane task. That had been a fault of her imagination, she now realised, not of the events that had brought her here.

She tested the blade across the pad of her thumb absentmindedly. It was sharp enough, as the slice across her thumb testified. She pressed on her thumb and blood welled obligingly along the cut. How much would she need?

She'd thought to reopen the scar where blood had been drawn before, but now this slight damage was done... Murmuring an invocation to the Goddess for guidance she applied the blade a second time, then held her hand over the wine glass so the blood dripped into it. A smudge on the table had been enough before, after all, but she was asking deeper questions this time. She set the question firmly in her mind as she watched the blood drip. Where was the dagger: the blade that had twice ended Tresilian's life, once in Vasic's hand and once in her own?

She watched and waited until the cave blurred around her and she was sitting in some other darkness in some different enclosed space. The floor rose and fell beneath her – was it about to collapse and trap her all over again? She fought a moment's panic before she began to note other sensations: the creaking of timber and another sound, one she recognised as the slap of waves against a timber hull.

"Who's there? Is that you, Bleaky?" A young woman's voice, sharp with mistrust and weighted with loss. The sound of a mattress shifting and settling as she sat up in bed. A soft knock at the door.

"My lady, did you call me? Are you unwell?"

A silence followed the question before the mattress crunched and settled once more as the unseen woman lay down again.

"No. I thought I heard someone, that's all."

"Can I–?"

"No." The syllable was final. Dismissive. There was no more to learn here, in this darkness.

But there was another darkness, more absolute. Another young woman's voice. "They'll just use you. Like they used me. You can't trust them." The skin on the back of Alwenna's neck prickled with revulsion. She knew that voice. Within the darkness beyond the priestess something stirred, something tentative.

"My lady? Is it you?" A voice so familiar it spoke direct to her soul. A voice she'd not heard since they left Weaver in a burning room at the summer palace. She wanted to stay there, to answer, to listen a while to whatever he might have to say, but she found herself spinning away.

This time the darkness was pinpricked with pain. She heard the sound of leather striking flesh, heard the gasp as pain bit, felt it sear across her own back even as he raised the whip again and flourished it, just so. Nine times nine. He would break this obsession of the flesh, he would. The Goddess would see there were none so worthy, none so honourable. The lash bit again and Alwenna pulled away in revulsion.

The darkness was not so deep here. "How many days must I wait for the king's attention? I bring him news of the most particular kind." Marten, cast out by the freemerchants but determined to trade every last secret in his possession, however much his conscience protested. He still carried that bag slung over his shoulder. It drew her attention, this time, for it hung there so very rigid and straight. He kept one hand over it at all times. That bag didn't just contain spare clothing… A gift for Vasic, no doubt. A most generous gift, unless she missed her guess. But the king would not be so pleased when he arrived at Scarrow's Deep to find her already gone. She whispered as much in Marten's ear and he spun about, startled, as if he expected to find her standing there, but she had already moved on.

It was almost dawn now. Drew lay awake, Jervin breathing softly next to him. He didn't know how to leave him, didn't want to leave him. He didn't have to. He could stay, and close his eyes to all that was going on around him. He twisted round and set his arm over the sleeping man. Each day might be their last together. But not this day.

Pre-dawn light filtered through threadbare fabric. "Well, Jenna said she was powerful. Surely it's worth trying?" The woman's voice bore a heavy accent Alwenna could not place. There were hints of freemerchant and Brigholm, but something else, something more.

"We'll get no thanks if we do." A man's voice, surly, dismissive.

"It's not about getting thanks, it's about doing what's right – about helping one of our own. Jenna said she–"

"You know Jenna. She only sees what she wants to see."

Alwenna had nothing to learn here. She moved on.

The first rays of daylight had found the cliff face. Malcolm stepped in through the door, grinning.

Brett hastily closed the chest against the back wall of the cave.

"You up to no good again, young 'un?"

"I'm not so young."

"Maybe not. But if Rina catches you in there she'll still tan your hide."

"She won't. Not unless you tell." Brett locked the chest, then returned the key to its hiding place beneath Rina's pillow. "You been with her again?"

Malcolm raised an eyebrow. "She has a name. I've told you before you should use it."

Brett shrugged. "I'll go help Rina fetch the water."

It was full daylight now. Alwenna sat at the table, staring blankly at the broken wine glass. Blood had spilled over the table and was sinking into the grain of the wood as it congealed. Her thumb stung where she had cut it, the eating knife still held in her right hand.

The blanket over the door flapped open as Erin returned with a bucket of water.

"Goddess! My lady, what's happened now?"

Where to start? At the end. "Marten is trying to sell me, one last time – old habits die hard, it seems. It is time for me to leave Scarrow's Deep. Erin, if you please, tell Brett I need to speak to him."

Stepping out into darkness. Alwenna had told Marten how it would be. And she'd wished him well, the duplicitous bastard. A pebble twisted beneath her foot, tugging on her ankle. It was still weak after being crushed in the rockfall at Highkell. How long ago had that been? She couldn't measure the time in days or weeks, only by the weight of the child distending her belly. Even had it not been dark she'd not be able to see where she was setting her feet now.

"Be careful, my lady, or you'll not be travelling far at all." Erin supported her by the elbow as she slithered down the loose path.

Brett was waiting by the entrance to the valley, with a horse already saddled and bridled. "It's the same one you rode when you came here, my lady."

The horse was leaner than when they'd arrived – unlike Alwenna – a testimony to the poor grazing enjoyed by the livestock at Scarrow's Deep. But that was not the foremost thing on her mind right now. "Did you find my dagger?"

"No, my lady."

"Then it has indeed been taken by one who left Scarrow's Deep before me. I should believe myself well rid of it, yet somehow I cannot. I brought it among your people and I should have been the one to remove it." Alwenna withdrew a sheet of paper from the bag she carried. "I owe you my thanks, Brett, you have done well. As we agreed, the other horse is yours. And here is my letter to prove it."

Brett took the paper with a shy nod. "Thank you, my lady. I would still accompany you – it is not right that you should leave without a single outrider."

"Your offer is appreciated, but I cannot accept. Your mother will have need of you, Brett. I will not have her claim I took you from her."

"I'm old enough to make my own decisions."

"Then make them wisely. You have my thanks for your help, but I must ask nothing more of you."

Erin legged Alwenna up into the saddle, then vaulted up behind. Alwenna nudged the horse forward and they rode away towards the mountains. Alwenna twisted round to look back. Marten's son stood where they had left him, a lone figure outlined against the predawn sky.

PART IV

CHAPTER ONE

"Yes, I have heard of you." Vasic studied the priest. He was a scrawny, wrinkled individual who looked faintly ridiculous in the fine robes he affected to wear. But Marwick had insisted the man was worth hearing.

Durstan bowed so low his nose almost scraped the floor. "Sire, what I offer you is the ultimate in loyal soldiers. They feel neither fatigue nor remorse, and they will obey you without question. They do not fear, and they do not doubt. Once engaged with the enemy they will not stop until the last one has fallen."

"Indeed?" Vasic had never seen a less likely military commander.

Durstan straightened up, slowly. "As we all know, sire, appearances can be deceptive. Let me show you a sample of my work. Let the quality of that speak for me."

Had the fellow read Vasic's mind? Marwick had insisted it would be worth his while speaking to this... Well, until now he'd been convinced he was nothing more than a charlatan. And doubtless he was. He was letting Yurgen's maunderings get to him, that was the truth of it. It was as well he'd sent the old fool and his prophecies back to Lynesreach. He was tempted to abolish the position of high seer altogether. And yet... some of Yurgen's pronouncements had proved uncannily accurate.

"The morning advances. If you have a sample of your work, show it without further delay."

The prelate bowed again, a slighter affair this time, and turned to one of his underlings. The man in turn gestured to the guards waiting at the door, who opened the door with all due ceremony.

Vasic drummed his fingertips on the arm of his throne. "You have been less than precise as to the nature of your work, prelate."

"It is better, highness, for you to see the end result. It has taken us many years of study to perfect our method." Behind the prelate two priests appeared at the doorway, flanking a taller man who walked between them. "I think, sire, you will agree the results are remarkable."

The trio who approached the throne looked very unremarkable indeed. Two more scrawny priests wearing the robes of the order – did they never feed their adherents? – and a man clad in a simple commoner's smock and joined hose. The man was clean-shaven, his hair cropped close in a manner that stopped short of monastic. But his bearing was not that of a commoner. He carried himself erect, with a measure of deportment that suggested military training, looking neither to right nor to left. His eyes were fixed straight ahead and he seemed not to register his surroundings at all. When the three of them halted in front of Vasic, the man looked straight at Vasic, yet his eyes moved through him as if he wasn't there at all. It was the vacant stare of a halfwit. Did the accursed priest think this was some kind of joke?

"What is this, Durstan? I see nothing remarkable here."

"Highness, I offer you your future champion." Durstan gestured to the two priests and they stepped back, leaving the halfwit standing alone before Vasic, with Durstan at his side. "Behold; is he not a fine specimen? Truly a man fit to serve a king."

Durstan was too pleased with himself: he was enjoying some joke at Vasic's expense, Vasic was sure of it. Yet there was no guile in the man's face, more expectation.

Vasic looked again at the commoner standing before him. He was not bound or shackled in any way, and showed no signs of rough handling... And why would he, brought here as the prize specimen of Durstan's outlandish order? And yet...

Vasic studied the man's face. There was something familiar about this man. He'd seen that face before, with a swollen lip and blackened eye... To be fair that did not narrow things down a great deal: he'd dealt with many men in that condition. It was part of the king's lot to encounter those who were less fortunate, or were simply outright wrongdoers. But the last time he'd seen those eyes they had been full of defiance and resentment. Now they were utterly devoid of expression; they seemed not to recognise the king who stood before him at all.

"I know this man."

"Indeed, your highness." Durstan's voice was unctuous. Then he turned and barked at the man in a very different tone. "Brother Pius, remove your smock."

The man blinked. It may have been in recognition of the command, or it may have been nothing more than a coincidence. But he complied, tugging the hem of his shirt out from his joined hose and peeling it up over his ribs before pulling it off over his head. He lowered his arms to his sides once more, the garment trailing from one hand and onto the floor as the man stood there as vacant and passive as he had before.

He was in good shape: muscled as one would expect of a soldier, with no spare flesh hanging about his belly. But on his side a tight, white scar stood out across his ribs: a scar in the shape of a "V". Of course Vasic knew this man. He'd set his mark upon him... when? How many months was it since he'd applied that branding iron in the vaulted dungeons beneath Highkell? The dungeons that lay buried now under tons of rubble from the collapse of the tower. As if it mattered how long it had been: such trivia were beneath a king's notice. The man's name was one such trivial detail, but he knew him nonetheless: the commoner who'd dared besmirch Alwenna's good name, who'd signed a confession to the same. The commoner who'd once served his half-cousin Tresilian as king's man.

Durstan watched Vasic, an acquisitive expression on his face.

"Prelate, you have brought me a common criminal. He was, as I recall, remarkable for nothing but his stubbornness. There is a bounty on his head, and you will be rewarded accordingly." Vasic was prepared to dismiss the man. He wanted no reminders of the Lady Alwenna in this place. Not even the vacant stare of this upstart whom he'd bested months ago.

"Sire, I beg the indulgence of a few more moments of your time." Durstan spoke hastily. "Pray, examine the man's side more closely." He barked again at the soldier. "Raise your left arm. And turn to face the far wall."

Without hesitation the former king's man complied. There beneath his arm, some inches above Vasic's brand, was a livid, angry scar, surrounded by a criss-crossing of dark veins, as if poison had entered his blood. The centre of the scar bore the unmistakable imprint of a three-sided blade, which must have entered the flesh there at a precise right angle. Such a blow must surely have penetrated to the man's heart, yet he stood before him, plain as day. Unless the scar was something the charlatan had done for show. The man stood there, inert, his underarm exposed. This could all be some trick to make Vasic look foolish.

"His looks haven't improved any since I saw him last. What of it, prelate? He was ever a churlish fellow. What need would I have of men like him?"

"Sire. This man is no longer the man he once was. He has

been reborn, in the favour of the Goddess. He will obey your every order, without question. Where once he was stubborn, he will be unquestioning. Where once he was strong, he will be stronger. This soldier was found grievously injured after a fire. He was dying. We took him in and secured his rebirth in the favour of the Goddess. He knows nothing of his former life. He will be yours to command. He will be untiring in battle: unbeatable. And he will be obedient."

"And what generous impulse makes you bring such a rare find to me?" Vasic suspected his sarcasm was wasted on the prelate.

"Sire, this is only one man. Imagine what you could achieve with a whole detachment of such warriors. They would be invincible."

"I see one man who's acquired several holes in his hide over the years. He appears far from invincible." There were one or two knowing sniggers amongst the courtiers at his witticism. "Your claims are outrageous, prelate." Vasic snapped his fingers and two guards strode forward. "See this braggart off the premises, and his halfwit soldier along with him."

"But your highness..." Durstan fell silent when the two guards took him by the arms. The soldier stared at Vasic with that same vacant disinterest. Two more guards closed on him, taking hold of his arms as they had Durstan, but the soldier erupted into motion. He sprang from between the two men, bashing their heads together and seizing one of their spears, clubbing its owner about the head with the shaft, before circling around the fallen man to face his comrade, flourishing the spear about his head. Onlookers fell back in haste, while the two guards holding Durstan released him and spun about, readying their own spears. Neither seemed keen to engage, however, once the soldier poleaxed the already dazed guard with the butt end of the spear.

"Stand fast." Vasic raised a hand. To his surprise the soldier obeyed the order, assuming a military stance with the spear held upright at his side. "Prelate, tell your man to lay down his weapon."

Durstan nodded to the soldier. "Do as the king commands, Pius."

There was an infinitesimal pause, then the soldier stooped, setting down the spear on the floor. He straightened up and stood to attention as calmly as if nothing had happened. The prelate's claims no longer looked so far-fetched.

"I must travel on more pressing business, prelate, but I shall consider how to put your claims to a true test upon my return. You will await my convenience here."

CHAPTER TWO

The air was colder as Alwenna and Erin climbed into the foothills proper. They had found a faint track and, for want of any more specific instruction, they followed it as it wound its way between hills and over passes. The direction felt right, at least. And someone must have made the path, after all. If it was not those Alwenna sought, then it might be someone who could point her to where she might find them.

Boulders were strewn about the landscape; large and small, they were plentiful as trees in a forest. As they approached one such cluster of boulders their horse raised its head sharply, ears pricked.

"Halt right there!"

The man's voice startled Alwenna. She stopped the horse and looked all around, but could see no one. He must be hidden behind one of the many boulders. The horse sidled uneasily.

"I said halt." A man stepped out into the path ahead of them, sword in hand, and walked up to take hold of the horse's bridle. He glared up at them suspiciously. He had a weather-beaten face with high cheekbones and hollow cheeks. His clothing might once have been black but had long since faded to an uneven grey.

"You'd better step down from that saddle, nice and easy, and tell me what you're doing here."

She'd heard his voice somewhere before. But where? Alwenna spread her hands wide before setting one over her belly. "Forgive me, but that's a little difficult at present. I'm looking for friends of Jenna the freemerchant."

If he recognised Jenna's name, his face gave nothing away. "Step down anyway. Then we'll talk."

"Very well."

Erin slithered down from behind Alwenna and supported her as she dismounted in turn.

Alwenna's legs were tired and unresponsive from the days spent on the road. Now she was down on the ground she had to look up at the stranger. He was perhaps a head taller than her, with pale grey eyes in his deeply lined face. "Now move over there." He gestured to the centre of the path with his sword hand.

Alwenna obeyed, watching him warily. "I'm no threat to you. I've only–"

"Save it for later. Take those knives from your belts and drop them on the ground. Slowly."

This man seemed to be a stranger to laughter of any kind. Alwenna dropped her knife in the dust a foot or so in front of her feet and Erin followed suit.

"Now step back three paces."

Again they obeyed.

Keeping an eye on the women he stooped and picked up their knives, tucking them in his own belt. He straightened up and studied them, calculating. "You're no freemerchants."

"No. But we've been their guests these past weeks."

"Tired of their hospitality, did you?"

"I need to speak to some people Jenna told me about. She said I'd find them in these mountains. Dare I hope you're one of these people?"

Was that a ghost of a smile that crossed his face? "I can't think why you'd want to."

No, nor can I, Alwenna thought. She kept her peace.

He shrugged. "Since you've come this far, you'd best bring that horse and follow me. You won't be able to ride it down the track I'll be taking you. And if it slips, best to just let it go."

If it slips? What did that mean?

He sheathed his sword and turned his back on the two women, setting off along the faint path they'd been following. He put his fingers to his lips and gave out a sharp whistle, gesturing to someone concealed on the other side of the path.

So the path led to something worth guarding. Alwenna knew she ought to find that reassuring. As it was, she'd just recalled whose grey eyes the man reminded her of: Tresilian's pale priestess. Was it likely the girl should have kin out here in the mountains? Alwenna's skin prickled with unease. She hoped not.

The stranger paused beside a boulder that reached his shoulder height. "Take care here. The path twists sharply down to the right."

Alwenna followed him, but had to stop and set one hand on the boulder to gather herself. The path had brought them to the edge of a steep escarpment. The ground dropped away abruptly below her feet, a near-vertical cliff face rising from a steep slope, covered with loose stone. Now his comment about the horse made sense.

She navigated the step with caution. Her bulging stomach was enough to disturb her natural balance and she found the descent tiring. Erin followed on with the horse, accompanied by much slithering and scattering of loose stones as it disturbed the ground.

Alwenna's legs were weak and trembling from the effort by the time they reached easier ground below. Basking in the sunshine at Scarrow's Deep had not been the best preparation for this journey. A small stream wound its way across the flat valley floor which was littered, like this whole area, with an assortment of boulders. Across the far side of the valley was an equally steep shelving slope, bare rock in places, in others a jumble of loose stone and soil, cut through by runnels carved out by rainwater.

Alwenna paused and looked back. She could see the line of the path they'd descended sloping down the valley wall. From this angle it appeared almost civilised. It also appeared to be the only such approach to the valley floor. No one could enter the valley without being seen by anyone watching from below. Yet they clearly felt the need to place guards at the top. It occurred to her any intruders might be more readily dealt with from the top of that steep slope. A pragmatic solution...

"We still have some way to go." The stranger was waiting some yards ahead. "If you want to ride the horse again from here you may."

How many unwanted visitors had he pushed from that escarpment over the years?

"One or two. You are right, friend of Jenna. It is easier that way." He turned and walked on.

Alwenna and Erin exchanged looks.

"What does he mean, my lady?"

"I was thinking they must push anyone who was unwelcome off the top of that cliff."

"That means we are welcome? Goddess, I'd never have thought it. Will you ride the horse again, my lady?"

Alwenna hesitated before nodding. She didn't want to show weakness, but the climb down the steep path had exhausted her more than she'd imagined possible. Erin legged her up into the saddle, but elected to walk alongside.

"What are these people, my lady?"

How to tell the girl she had no real idea; that she'd brought her all this way on some vague sense she needed to learn what these people knew?

"Jenna spoke of them once. They were freemerchants, but

broke with them years ago."

"So that's why they know what we think without our having to speak it?"

"This man certainly seems to."

"I fear no good can come of this, my lady."

Landbound thinking... Alwenna caught the thought up short. Was she falling into freemerchant ways despite everything? "I fear you are right, Erin. But to deal with what lies ahead the thing I need most is not goodness."

CHAPTER THREE

"The king is well pleased with what I can offer him." Durstan nodded towards the high table where Vasic sat with his favoured courtiers. The prelate selected another piece of meat from the platter before them, gnawing every last scrap off the bone. The priestess could have sworn he'd put visible weight on since they'd arrived at Highkell.

The priestess continued to pick at the food on her plate. She'd never known such bounty before, but her appetite had all but deserted her. The food repelled her, but she needed to eat. She could remember Tresilian's queen's expression when she'd sat at table at the summer palace, and began to understand perhaps what she'd been experiencing then.

It was odd to know a moment of empathy for the woman she'd sworn deadly enmity against. But what was a little more oddness in her life? She'd turned her world upside down when she'd deceived the prelate – and, though she'd paid the price with scars across her back, she feared the Goddess was still displeased with her. If she'd really put an end to the child, she could understand it. But the child was safe. Had she been unwise to throw herself headlong into this adventure? She was free of the precinct, was she not? All she had to do now was secure that freedom, take her destiny in her own two hands and shape it for herself. Maybe she didn't even need the halfwit – he had no influence in this world, after all.

Sat further down the table he was watching her now, that vacant expression on his face. She frowned at him. After a moment he turned away, his expression never changing. Sometimes his blank scrutiny made her feel uneasy. And that was nonsense – she had done nothing to him. Nothing but help him recover his sense of self before the order eradicated it completely. How was it possible to feel that blank stare judged her?

She had eaten her fill, and pushed the plate away. Beside her, Durstan continued to gorge. He sickened her. She glanced up to the top table and found the king was watching her. Now there was a man with influence. How did one secure the interest of a monarch when surrounded by dozens of people going about the noisy business of eating and drinking? She held the eye contact for a moment, before lowering her eyes demurely.

She stood up and left the table, taking her time about it, with a quick glance to see if he was still watching her, then made her way down the side of the hall to the main door. Through there were the garderobes, as well as other sundry chambers. And far fewer people.

It was a relief to be free of the noisy, chewing crowd. In truth she cared little if the king chose to follow her or not. She had been so determined at the summer palace that she would go to Highkell with the others. And now she was here, all the fight seemed to have slipped away from her. She crossed some room or other to gaze out of the window. The ground dropped away beneath the sill, almost dizzyingly. By the moonlight she could see across the gorge. Trees grew along the ridge, above an ugly scar where the ground had slipped away. That was where, she had been told, the road to the south should be. Now it was little more than a goat trod, until the damage was repaired. She had also been told the king would soon be travelling south to meet his new bride and bring her back to her new home at Highkell. That didn't bode well for Durstan's plans.

She shrugged. Whatever happened, she could not deny the outlook was beautiful, if not entirely comfortable. There were no such dizzying heights where she had been raised.

Footsteps disturbed the stillness of the room behind her. She turned, taking care to move gracefully. Her heart skipped a beat when she saw it was indeed Vasic. She knew what Durstan required of her, and it suited her own purposes: if anyone had the power to find the missing queen, it was this man.

The king carried his wine glass, she noticed. She curtseyed low, grateful for the time she'd spent practising.

"Highness." Just the right amount of humility and breathlessness.

"You're Durstan's little priestess." He sipped thoughtfully at his wine as he regarded her.

He was not ill favoured. She could see a family resemblance to Tresilian, although Vasic's features were somewhat sharper.

"I am a priestess of the Goddess. I do not serve Durstan. I shall not serve any man, unless it be the will of the Goddess."

"Is that so?" His mouth twisted in distaste. Evidently he disliked her answer.

"That is so, your highness." She smoothed her skirts, not too hastily, almost too slowly. "But the Goddess has brought you to me tonight, and it shall be my pleasure to serve you." She glanced up at him, demurely. "If it would please you, your highness?"

He swallowed down the last of his wine and set the glass on a side table.

"It would please me."

CHAPTER FOUR

A week he'd been kicking his heels here at Highkell. A whole week. A week of mutton stew, served at the lowest table in the king's hall. Marten took another piece of dry bread and mopped the last of the stew from his bowl. How much longer would he have to wait? Not that he wasn't glad of the steady supply of food, however greasy...

He had the uncomfortable sense someone was watching him. It took a moment to find the cold grey eyes considering him from close to the top of the table. Tresilian's priestess. Had she recognised Marten? One of her companions spoke to her and she turned her attention to him with a pained expression. This man wore the robes of the priesthood, but embellished in such a way that suggested he was of some importance. Marten could not recollect seeing his face before. But when the man sat back, Marten saw a face he recognised immediately.

Weaver. Alive and kicking, by all appearances. Marten watched covertly for several minutes. No, not kicking, for the soldier appeared to be sunk into a depression of some kind, the same morose mood he'd had those last few days at the summer palace, perhaps. The priest leaned forward again and Marten could see no more. But a few minutes later Vasic rose from the top table, and gestured to the group. The grey-eyed priestess stood immediately and made her way over to the door where

Vasic waited, pausing only to usher her through, setting one hand on the small of her back. As if they had been waiting only for that, the priest and Weaver stood up and left the table. The priest moved stiffly down the room, his gait uneven. Perhaps Marten's original estimate of his age had been mistaken. Weaver followed behind the older man, looking neither to right nor to left, but kept his eyes fixed straight ahead. The soldier had ever been watchful in company. Had he received some injury during that last fight? Marten could not credit he'd have turned coat readily. Nor could he credit the order would keep one of the Lady Alwenna's staunchest supporters among their own. Not unless they had been able to make sure of him in some way... This was a mystery in need of solving. He was about to rise from the table and follow them, when a page boy ran up to him.

"Are you Marten, the freemerchant?"

"I may have been once."

The boy's mouth dropped open in uncertainty. "But... I have a message for Marten, the freemerchant."

"I am Marten, born a freemerchant of the Peninsular Kingdoms."

The boy drew in a deep breath. "Then I am to tell you the king will grant you an audience in his private chamber at noon tomorrow. You must present yourself in the antechamber with time to spare, for the king will not be kept waiting." He'd clearly memorised the words.

"Noon tomorrow?" This was progress.

The boy nodded, an expectant look on his face.

Marten dug in his scrip for the smallest coin he could find and handed it to the boy. It was not difficult finding a small coin, for he had precious few large ones at present. He held the coin out to the boy, then paused. "You, with your memory for messages and names... You might be able to tell me who the old priest is, and the soldier with him? They were sitting up there, with the priestess."

The boy's mouth dropped open again. "They're here on the king's business, so I'm not supposed to say."

"Ah, I understand that." Marten dug in his scrip and found a rather larger coin, exchanging it for the one in his hand. "Attending the king as you do, you must hear a great deal about his business. As will everyone else in his chamber at the time. I daresay if you don't tell me, one of those other people will."

The boy licked his lips. "It's true, sir. I hear a great deal."

Marten smiled. He who had once charmed kings so they fell in with his plans was reduced to working his wiles on page boys. "You'll go far at court if you please the right people." He twisted the coin between his fingers.

"The priest you spoke of is the prelate Durstan, come from the east to offer the king a mighty army. The soldier is named Pius. He is untiring in battle and impossible to defeat."

"Is that so? And this prelate makes these claims?"

"Yes, sir." The boy glanced at the coin anxiously. Marten handed it to him and he pocketed it with a mumbled word of thanks before hurrying away.

Marten took up his tankard and drank deeply. The ale was poor stuff, but probably more palatable than any wine that might find its way this far down the table. He set the tankard down, pondering the boy's words. Untiring in battle and impossible to defeat? It seemed Weaver could be suffering the effects of something far worse than a morose mood. Perhaps the Lady Alwenna had been right after all, in mourning his loss. And if the former king's man had gone beyond recall, Marten did not want to be the one to give her that news.

CHAPTER FIVE

Gatekeeping was a profitable business – far more so than soldiering. Peveril only wished he'd woken up to the possibilities years ago. No more night watches, or uncomfortable dawn patrols. Instead all he needed to do was sit in a comfortable guard room – by a warm fire if the weather was inclement – while a succession of hopeful citizens came to him and begged him to lighten their purses so they might gain an audience with the king. And he had Marwick to thank for this change in his circumstances. Birtle kept a creative record of the transactions, of course. He listed all the petitions they brought to the king and quietly pocketed a portion for himself. Their association continued to be a lucrative one, as people seemed to be coming round to the way of thinking Vasic was their monarch, for good or ill, so they might as well gain what they could from him. Peveril suspected any such gain would be minimal.

It was easy money, gained from gullible folks. Except for this one in front of him now: some merchant from Brigholm. He'd given his name as Jervin, although Peveril doubted it was genuine. The so-called merchant's eyes were cold and calculating; they spoke to Peveril of a childhood spent in the slums, scraping to get by, crossing whichever lines were necessary to survive with the only constant allegiance to himself. If eyes were mirrors to the soul, then Jervin faced an eternity in torment. All this Peveril could understand – and even empathise with.

Jervin refused to divulge details of his business with the king, although he had little difficulty parting with the usual amount of coin to smooth his way.

Peveril steepled his hands thoughtfully. "His highness is pressed for time at present. He is due to leave Highkell shortly and is able to consider only the most urgent cases. If you cannot give some indication of your concern then it makes it difficult for me to plead your case with the king."

"I have other business to transact while in Highkell." Jervin regarded him with a glacial stare. "How long will the king be away?"

"A matter of weeks, I believe. Perhaps a month or more. I will do what I can to bring it to the king's notice, but can make no promises – he has little time to spare at present." And little good humour, for all the time he spent with his new favourite. The skinny priestess must know some uncommon tricks.

"Then do what you can. If necessary this matter will keep until I speak to the king in person. I trust you will notify me upon the king's return, with an early appointment." Jervin's tone made it clear this was not an idle request. "I am lodging at the *Crown*."

Jervin was a man with expensive tastes. To contemplate spending a month or more there, he must be well heeled indeed – or supremely well connected. Both, in all probability.

"Very well, we will inform you of an appointment upon the king's return. Make a note of it, Birtle." He bowed politely as Jervin made ready to leave. "If you require anything from me in the meantime, just ask for me here by name: Captain Peveril. I will do whatever I can to assist you."

Jervin looked him up and down with that cold stare. "Captain Peveril. I will remember that."

Peveril exchanged glances with the scribe after the merchant had left. "Tread warily with that one. He's not a man to cross."

CHAPTER SIX

The king was late. Marten had been cooling his heels in the antechamber a good half hour before, finally, the king strolled in accompanied by his retinue. Marten studied them without being too obvious about it: he recognised only Marwick, who'd been prominent in Highkell society for many years. He'd seen the tall skinny fellow before, too, although he could not put a name to him.

It was he who approached Marten now. "You are Marten the freemerchant?"

"My name is Marten."

"Then the king will grant you his attention now. Be sure you use his time well, or he will not forget."

The tall man led Marten to the door of the chamber where the king now sat, waiting. The room was otherwise empty. The air struck chill as if the place had not been warmed through in days.

"Highness, this is the freemerchant, Marten."

"Very well, Kaith. You may leave us."

Marten bowed low, in best court style. Now he was playing courtly games once more he regretted having left all his finery behind. It belonged to his old life as a freemerchant and had no part to play in his new life, but in this place he had no doubt a man would be judged on the worth of his clothing.

"Highness. I am honoured to be granted an audience." He noted Vasic's finger tap impatiently on the arm of his throne. The king's rumoured impatience was true, then. If he'd had the forethought he might have questioned Alwenna about the king – she knew him better than most. She might also have wondered why he was taking such an interest in the upstart monarch...

"You spoke of a valuable artefact?"

"Indeed, I did, your highness. It is an item that I believe may hold some particular importance to you."

"Importance? That is a bold claim."

"But not ungrounded, your highness. This artefact was once in the possession of your late cousin, Tresilian. It is a dagger – a particularly fine one."

Vasic's brow creased, but Marten had his attention now. "Do you intend to talk all day, or to show me this dagger?"

Marten bowed, slipping the bag from his shoulder. "I have it here with me, your highness. If it might be of interest I shall be only too happy to show it to you. I would not have you misconstrue my producing it when in such close proximity to your person."

Vasic glanced to the door – it stood open allowing those in the antechamber to see the exchange, without being close enough to overhear. There were guards posted at either side of that door, alert for any command from the king. "You will find my understanding significantly stronger than my patience, freemerchant."

Any physical likeness to Tresilian was superficial at best. Yet there was something about his manner that reminded Marten of Tresilian's changed nature at the summer palace. That was something that deserved more thought... Vasic drummed his fingers on the chair arm.

"Well?"

Marten removed the cloth-wrapped bundle from the bag,

unwinding the cloth that hid the dagger. It had been opened since they'd tied it up securely by the stream the day they'd left the summer palace. Picked over by the freemerchant elders, and rejected...

Vasic was a more appreciative audience for the dagger. Yet it would be so easy to end this now. Vasic was the single largest obstacle between Alwenna and the throne. Marten could remove him, right now, and her way would be clear. She would be undisputed ruler of the Peninsular Kingdoms. And Marten would be unlikely to get as far as the doorway before the guards felled him. This was not the moment to act on impulse. He'd always played the long game... And yet, handing over the dagger to Vasic was difficult. Was it exerting influence over him the way it had over Alwenna? That was fanciful nonsense, surely?

Marten held out the dagger, as if the tattered cloth was some kind of presentation cushion. At least it meant he didn't need to touch the jewelled hilt. Vasic sat forward, eyes on the dagger.

"This was Tresilian's, you say?" He leaned closer, one hand reaching towards the hilt. "And you know this how, freemerchant?"

Whatever Marten might have said in the heat of the moment, he *was* a freemerchant – to the core. This was why he was doing this. He must not lose sight of his goal now. She would understand... hadn't she expected as much all along, and mocked him for his self-delusion while he was waiting for an audience? Or had that whisper been some effect of his guilty conscience? "It was identified to me by one who held it in her hand."

Vasic looked up sharply. "What mean you by that? Speak plainly."

"By the Lady Alwenna's account, your highness, you already know this blade well."

"What could you possibly know about that, freemerchant?"

"Sire, I know only what the Lady Alwenna told me herself. This blade fell with her when the tower collapsed, and was found nearby when she was dug free of the rubble."

Vasic studied the freemerchant for a moment, then reached out and picked up the dagger by the hilt. He seemed relieved as he turned it over in his hand, admiring the craftwork. The jewels glinted in the light from the window, but nothing more. Then it was true: Vasic may have wielded the blade before, but it did not know his hand. There had been no other way to discover this.

"So... The Lady Alwenna gave you an account, you say? She survived the collapse?"

"That is correct, sire."

Vasic studied his face. "How is it possible that none should know of this?"

"I imagine there must have been a great deal of confusion at the time, your highness."

Vasic turned his attention to the blade again, turning the dagger over in his hands, admiring the play of light on the jewels. There appeared to be nothing sinister about it. "There have been rumours, of course, but none from credible sources. Your tale, however, with the weight of this dagger behind the testimony... I find it more plausible."

Marten bowed. "Highness. I am your humble servant."

"Are you, indeed?" Vasic studied him, his brow creased in a frown. "How selfless an act on your part, to bring me this dagger."

"I hope, your highness, it will prove how useful I may be to you."

Vasic raised one eyebrow. "In what way, precisely?"

"In these changing times, your highness, a man must look to his future. Freemerchant ways are sliding into antiquity by failing to change with the times, yet I have learned much on my travels. I know languages and far-off places that few have seen for themselves. I have conversed with kings as well as commoners; I can conduct myself honourably in court or agreeably in a poor man's hovel. Doors, in short, are open to me where they would be closed to other men. Highness, I would serve you. I offer that dagger as evidence of my utility."

Vasic weighed his response. "And you seek no reward for this?"

"I am not a greedy man, your highness. It is worth a king's ransom, but I do not ask for that. I would however be grateful for a modest salary in recompense."

"Would you, indeed?" Vasic turned to studying the dagger again. "Precisely how did you come by this?"

"It was recovered from the rubble when the Lady Alwenna was dug free, highness."

"Yes, yes, you told me that before. Was it you who dug her free?"

"No, your highness. I was not present. At the time I was in the Marches, discussing the supply of provisions to the old summer palace there." He paused. "I believe you have here one priest who goes by the name of Durstan. His order have been based there in recent years."

"Is that so? And are you aware of their work?"

"Indirectly, your highness. My contact there was steward to the prelate Durstan, whom I never met in person. But I have seen the results of his work firsthand."

"And?"

"Their work is remarkable. They can make dead men walk, restore them to life as whole as if they had never fallen." Better not to bring Tresilian's name into this. "I understand that blade has been used in their rites. It is at once powerful and dark – and now we come to my reason for bringing it to you, your highness." He hesitated. Was he right to do this? "If that blade were to be turned against you its power would be multiplied threefold, because of its history with your kinsmen."

Vasic digested this revelation with suspicion. "And?"

"Highness, I thought you might seek to keep it safe, where none can touch it, to ensure it cannot be used against you."

"So you contend the dagger is inimical to me?"

"It may be, highness. And, knowing of the dagger as I do, I have also heard rumours that the high priest Durstan was seeking to recover the dagger. Given the power his order wield, I would fear the consequences if they were to gain possession of it. None could hope to keep it safer than you – you who are ruler of the combined Peninsular Kingdoms."

Vasic turned over the dagger, studying it closely. Marten had little doubt he recognised it as the one he had used to dispatch his own cousin: it was too distinctive.

Vasic pursed his lips. "And the Lady Alwenna? Have you news of her? You claim to have conversed with her."

"Not in recent days, your highness. But she was in good health when last I saw her."

"And how am I to know your bringing me this dagger is not some trick of hers? She turned it on the priest from Vorrahan when he held it in his hands – I saw it happen with my own eyes."

"I have heard others speak of that day, highness. Terrible though it was, I doubt she could achieve anything from so great a distance."

"So she is at a great distance now?"

"She was when I last saw her, your highness: she has left the Peninsular Kingdoms entirely, with no intention of returning."

"Has she, indeed? You are very careful not to commit yourself, freemerchant."

"I pass on only information I know to be true. It is safer for all that the Lady Alwenna remain a great distance removed from that dagger."

"And so you brought it to me?"

"You are her closest surviving kinsman, and so you have a

stake in this. It seemed only right that you should know."

"Indeed?" Vasic set down the dagger on a small side table and clapped his hands. A servant appeared at the door. "Summon Marwick to attend me." He looked over at Marten again. "I shall reward you for bringing the dagger to me."

Marwick hastened into the room. "Your highness?"

"The freemerchant here has brought me a valuable item. Reward him with a fat purse for his trouble. And put your mind to considering how we might find a use for a man with his skills upon my return from Lynesreach."

They had been dismissed. Marwick bowed low, and Marten followed suit before following the courtier from the room. He couldn't blame the king for being cautious: both of them knew what had happened last time the blade had crossed Vasic's path. But leaving the dagger there was harder than Marten had ever imagined possible. The dagger had been the focus of all his thoughts and plans on the journey to Highkell and he felt its loss as keenly as if it had been one of his own children. His only consolation was it could do no harm to Alwenna now, nor could she do any harm with it.

CHAPTER SEVEN

"Don't be a fool – no one will even recognise you, not when you're with me. I didn't bring you all the way here so you could hide in this room the whole time." Jervin dragged his shirt on over his head. "The king's not even here, now – do you imagine anyone will remember a single prisoner who escaped months ago? You don't even look like the same person any more." The mattress shifted as he got to his feet.

Drew gnawed on his thumbnail. Jervin was right – who would be likely to recognise him here? He'd been shut in the dungeon most of the time. And those he'd travelled east with were not here to be seen with him, so what had he to lose? Vasic might have known him, but Vasic was gone to Lynesreach to meet his new bride.

The king would know him, he was sure of it. There had been an unpleasant intimacy about the way Vasic had leant over him as he applied the branding iron… Drew had been so convinced he ought to come to Highkell, but now he was here the certainty had deserted him.

Jervin had pulled on his trousers and boots. "Do you plan to sit there all day?"

Drew shook his head. "No. I'll come out with you."

"Then you'll be needing these." Jervin scooped some trousers up off the floor and threw them at Drew.

•••

The market square would once have been teeming with people eager to examine the traders' wares, but today it was sparsely occupied. Drew wandered among the stalls trying to take a desultory interest in the goods, but there was little to catch his attention. Jervin had soon tired of the exercise, and had left Drew with Rekhart as he went to discuss what he had described as a small business matter. Rekhart was in subdued mood, contributing so little to the conversation Drew had given up and walked in silence. Jervin had made this trip out to be a bold adventure – sallying forth into the town where there was a price on Drew's head. But… No. It was a dull business. Drew should never have accompanied him here in the first place – his presence was a constant source of acrimony. Jervin was displeased that he'd been unable to see the king before his departure for Lynesreach, and that made it difficult for everyone about him.

There was nothing on the final row of market stalls but a couple of fabric merchants. A young woman stood at one, studying the bolts of fabric. The hair on the back of his neck rose with apprehension. He'd never seen her before, to his knowledge, but there was something about her that made him uneasy. Her hair was so fair it was almost colourless. Her face was equally pale; there was something bloodless about her. And that face was the one that had been haunting his sleep in recent weeks.

Abruptly Drew turned away and bumped straight into a tall man who was crossing the street.

"I beg your pardon." Drew was intent on putting as much distance between himself and the priestess as possible.

"Well, now. You're the last person I expected to find here."

Drew recognised the freemerchant by his voice rather than his appearance. It took a moment to recall his name. "Why, Marten. We met briefly on the road east."

"That's right, young Drew. And of course, I know commander Rekhart of Brigholm."

"Commander no more, but I never forget a face." Rekhart offered his hand to Marten, who shook it.

"Just as I am a freemerchant no more. Perhaps we will find a common cause here in Highkell."

"Perhaps." Rekhart's tone was non-committal.

"Our mutual friend, Weaver, is in town, too. You may already have seen him?"

"Weaver? No I haven't, but I would be glad to speak with him again."

"I've seen him at court, although I haven't yet had the chance to speak with him." Marten gestured towards a nearby kopamid house. "But we needn't stand around out here, will you join me for some kopamid?"

Rekhart shrugged, but Drew agreed with alacrity. The chance to speak with someone outside Jervin's immediate circle was more than welcome.

Marten poured the kopamid into the utilitarian beakers favoured by this particular kopamid house. It was situated on a side street just off the main town square, set up above the pavement by a short flight of steps. Patrons might watch passers-by from the window without themselves being observed. Marten had chosen the seat that gave him the clearest view of the town square, Drew noticed. Weaver had told him little about the freemerchant, so he was interested now to see the man for himself. It had been clear that Weaver did not trust the freemerchant, even though the former king's man had been working for him when they last met. Like everyone else, Drew had heard the many rumours about events surrounding the destruction of the summer palace. This could be his chance to learn more about what had happened.

"To your health, gentlemen." Marten raised his beaker and drank. "I've been told the blend they use here is the best in Highkell. Nothing brings clarity like a good, hot shot of kopamid."

Clarity. Yes, that was something Drew had been lacking in recent weeks. He sipped at his drink. Marten was right: it was a good blend. But now he had so many questions he didn't know where to begin – or how much he ought to reveal to the freemerchant of what he already knew – even though, or perhaps because, it was very little.

"You spoke of our friend, Weaver – at court, I believe you said. Does he work now for the new king?" Drew set down his beaker on the wooden table top. It bore ring marks from dozens of hot beakers that had been placed there over the years.

"Not for the king, no. But he is his guest, along with members of the order lately travelled here from the Marches."

"When last we met, he was working for you." Drew picked up his beaker again, keeping his eyes on the freemerchant.

"That is so. I have suffered some reverses since then." Marten met Drew's gaze levelly. "My royal sponsor of several years' standing proved in the end to be unworthy of the trust his most loyal servants had placed in him." There was no trace of bitterness in his voice, yet Drew guessed events had not unfolded as simply as the glib reply suggested.

"I beg your pardon, but I can be slow on the uptake. You speak of 'him', but I must assume you do not mean Vasic?"

"That is correct. I speak of Tresilian, late king of Highground and ruler of the Marches in his wife's stead."

Drew glanced at Rekhart, who appeared as much at a loss as he was to understand this. "But... Tresilian died when Highkell fell to Vasic's army, surely?"

"Yes and no, young Drew. Yes and no. You may have heard tales of the mystic arts studied in the Marches in the distant past. Mystic arts so dark they have been forbidden for many years and are practised now only in the utmost secrecy?"

"I have." Rekhart spoke up. "It was said some of the royal family were caught up in the rituals. From time to time the city watch would find... evidence that suggested the tales were not entirely fabricated. But no one asks many questions when a vagrant dies suddenly."

Drew didn't press for more detail – Rekhart's expression suggested he'd said all he was prepared to on that matter.

Marten stepped into the silence. "Then you may not need me to tell you this dark magic tampers with the very bounds of life and death. Tresilian did indeed die with the fall of Highkell, but he was reborn, through a ritual abhorrent to all right-thinking men. I myself was in his service at that time, but what I saw then convinced me the ritual is one that has been rightly forbidden."

So far so nebulous, thought Drew. "Reborn, you say?"

"Reborn through blood and pain. Reborn, the order would have it, stronger and indefatigable."

"But you would disagree?"

"He was strong, and he did not tire…"

"And yet, Marten, you remain reticent on certain matters. You must know your reputation as a talkative man precedes you."

The freemerchant smiled briefly, without humour, then took another mouthful of kopamid. "I am reticent, Drew, because I am not proud of the part I played in subsequent events. You must understand I had an agreement with the king. An agreement of long standing. And when the time came to deliver his part of the bargain, he cavilled and insisted I had not played my part to the full. Even though he stood there, alive and vital, strong as ever, he was somehow not the man he'd once been. His character was… much altered. His compassion, which had always been his strength, was gone. In its place… I only begin to understand it myself now. There was, I believe an even deeper magic at work." Marten's gaze flicked between Drew and Rekhart. "You remember the blade you dug from the rubble at Highkell?"

"I do. But how can you know of it?"

Marten lowered his voice. "The Lady Alwenna herself told me of it, when she handed the blade into my care."

"The Lady Alwenna?" Drew leaned forward. "Then you know where she is now? She escaped the fire?"

"You learned of that, then?"

"There have been a great many rumours, but none I've heard yet that had the ring of truth to them."

"Do you doubt me, then, young Drew?"

"I know Weaver did. I shall be guided by him until I learn otherwise."

Marten's mouth twisted. "Your choice is not unreasonable. I have not conducted myself with great honour these past weeks. The lady lives, and is in good health. More than that I shall not say in a public place, although I think I guess your question and I can only repeat: she is in good health. But I was telling you of the dagger: it was the same blade that was used to kill the king Tresilian, wielded by his own cousin, Vasic. This, I think, is not news to you?"

Drew frowned. "In part it is. The Lady Alwenna told me what she saw long ago, as we travelled from Vorrahan. But I did not realise that blade was the same one I found in the rubble. And that was the blade Garrad turned against himself?" Goddess, he'd been right to fear the dagger.

"That is correct. It is a powerful thing. I had hoped the elders would know some way to destroy it, to break its power–"

"It must not be destroyed!" Drew spoke up without thinking. "She will have need of it before the end."

Marten raised one eyebrow. "Is that so?"

Drew nodded, cheeks flushing in embarrassment at his outburst. "It is so. I saw it when I was in a fever."

"You may rest easy, little brother. The elders held it in such abhorrence they did not want it to remain within the bounds of our community."

"Then where is it now?"

Marten twisted his beaker on the table. "That I am not at liberty to tell you, other than to reassure you it is where it cannot damage any of your friends."

Drew knew there was more the freemerchant wasn't telling him. "Is that by your doing?"

The freemerchant nodded tightly. "My doing, albeit not entirely intentional on my part. While I had the blade in my possession… it was not good for me."

"She will have need of it, Marten."

"What is done is done. The blade's influence is baleful. I cannot yet see my way clearly…"

Drew would have said more, but he remembered his own unease when he came to from his fever in the room at Jervin's house and realised the blade that had haunted his fevered dreams was among his possessions. And the relief when Weaver and Alwenna had taken it away with them. "Are you able to take a message to the Lady Alwenna?"

Marten shook his head. "It is better that I do not. For many reasons, but most of all because messengers are too easily followed."

Truth. Drew was clear on that much, at least. Was this the reason he had been so certain he must come to Highkell? He had much to think over. "And our mutual friend, Weaver? A guest of the king who put a price on his head? How has this come about?"

"Precisely how I have not yet ascertained. But it seems to me Weaver is not entirely the man he used to be."

"In what way?"

"As it was with Tresilian. I believe Weaver has been remade to become Durstan's man."

Drew frowned. "Durstan?"

"The prelate of the order of who brought about Tresilian's rebirth at the summer palace."

Rebirth. Remade to become… "You mean Weaver has undergone the same ritual?"

Marten nodded. "I suspect so. I fear we must assume Weaver is now Durstan's man, just as Tresilian was before him. And Durstan, it would seem, is now Vasic's man."

Drew shivered. Again, Marten's words had the ring of truth about them. "I find that hard to believe. Weaver would never betray his friends."

"The man he once was would not." Marten downed the last of his kopamid. "We can have no such certainty about the man he has become."

CHAPTER EIGHT

Gulls shrieked outside the windows at Lynesreach. Vasic found the sound oddly uplifting, if only by contrast to the matter he was discussing with high seer Yurgen.

"Highness, the magic you speak of has long been forbidden throughout the Peninsula. I know little of it, save the consequences of its use were deemed so dreadful by our forebears, that every practitioner was put to sword and then flame, lest their work be carried on in secret. Their ashes were divided into three, each portion being buried in a separate kingdom."

"That is all very well, Yurgen, but I have learned that these dark rites are being practised even now. Their abhorrent creations walk among us. What have you to say to that?"

Yurgen clasped and unclasped his hands. "Highness, I can scarce credit it. The rites are..."

"Forbidden? You already told me." Vasic paced over to the window. The outlook from Lynesreach was fair. Today, sunlight glinted on the crests of the waves in the bay. Small fishing boats were moving about their business, hurrying in with their day's catch before the tide turned. Soon enough the lord convenor's yacht would arrive from the Outer Isles, bearing his new bride. He would see then if she could live up to the promise of the portrait.

Yurgen broke into his reverie cautiously. "Highness, if you would rather discuss this at a later date…?"

"No. This has become a matter of some urgency. Tell me what you know."

"Very well, your highness." Yurgen cleared his throat. "My research so far has informed me the rites for rebirth require the sacrifice of an innocent. And if this weren't enough to condemn the practice, blood rituals commonly take place following the rebirth. Again, if the blood of an innocent can be taken, this is preferred. The blood confers new strength on the reborn. The belief is that if the sacrifices please the Goddess then the one reborn will be blessed with untiring strength, greater than any mortal man. He will be impossible to defeat in combat."

"This sounds remarkably like an old wives' tale to me." But the seer's words were uncannily similar to those of the prelate, Durstan.

"I understand, your highness, that specially forged blades are used in the rites. The blades draw the strength of the sacrifice along with their blood and they create an unholy bond between the sacrifice and the reborn. The creation of these blades is a lost art, thanks be to the Goddess, and there are no smiths in the land now capable of creating such an abomination."

Vasic had not mentioned the blade to the seer; not at all. He turned away from the window, away from the sunlight and broad sky. "Do we know how many such blades are at large in the Peninsula? What appearance they have?"

Yurgen shook his head. "I fear not, sire. All I know is that the blades are attuned to an ancient force. I do not know if that is the force stirring in the east that I spoke of when last we met. My research continues. I understand there may be books in the library at Vorrahan concerning these dark practices. It is my understanding they were taken there as it was the furthest edge of the Peninsular Kingdoms from their origin in the east."

"Why would anyone keep such things? Why not destroy

them along with all the practitioners of such dark arts?"

"All this was long ago, highness. We have only incomplete records of decisions taken at that time. Perhaps they feared in the future we might have need to understand the forces we appear now to be dealing with. It is my understanding that, save these few sent to Vorrahan, all other works referring to the forbidden rites were destroyed so that none remain within the Peninsular Kingdoms."

Goddess, if the fellow's speech grew any more convoluted he'd trip over his own tongue. "Then you must continue to find out what you can. If you cannot present me with any further information before I must leave I shall expect your written report at Highkell as a matter of urgency."

Vasic turned to the window again. A new sail had appeared on the horizon. Could it be the lord convenor's vessel, bearing his bride-to-be? He remained oddly unmoved by the prospect: it was better to keep expectations low in such matters.

CHAPTER NINE

Peveril had learned that Jervin had spent some considerable time on the street where the goldsmiths had premises, browsing in each of the shops where Peveril might have hoped to sell the necklace, if only it hadn't been so distinctive. Discreet enquiries had revealed this Jervin was a wealthy collector. And Peveril was not one to waste an opportunity. The *Crown* was an establishment that had a very high opinion of itself, as did the staff, so Peveril had elected to wear his uniform for this visit. Sure enough, it had opened doors which might have been barred to him otherwise.

Peveril had little time or inclination for the niceties of small talk. "I understand you have an interest in antiquities."

Jervin's expression remained non-committal. "I have an interest in many things."

Did he think Peveril could not recognise quality when he saw it? "Certain pieces come my way in the course of my duties at the citadel. Quality pieces that might be of interest to the discerning collector."

"Am I to understand you have many such pieces?"

"At present I have one in particular – it is of rare quality, and believed to have had royal connections in the past."

"Royal connections?" Jervin's mouth twisted in a moue of disapproval. "Are they in such dire straits they're selling off their heirlooms now?"

"This was found abandoned in the ruins after the collapse of the tower. It has not been possible to trace the previous owner – indeed, many believe her to have perished right there in the rubble." Easy now, he mustn't push too hard.

"A piece with a tragic tale attached, then. A royal tragedy?"

Jervin worked on his level. Peveril had been sure of it all along. "That would be a fair description. It is exquisite: a necklace of the finest craftsmanship."

"And it is yours to sell?"

"Only, as I said, to a discerning collector."

Jervin's mouth tightened in a cold smile. "Do you have the piece with you?"

"Not today, no. But if you wish to see it, I could bring it to show you at a time convenient to yourself."

"I am curious enough to see it. Bring it this time tomorrow."

"Very good." Peveril bowed and turned to the door, just as it was opened and a young man entered the room. His hair flopped over his eyes, in contrast to his beard which was neatly trimmed. The youth stepped aside sharply as he took in Peveril's appearance, his eyes widening in something like alarm.

"I beg your pardon. I did not know you had a visitor."

"Captain Peveril was just leaving." Jervin looked pointedly to the door.

Peveril bowed again, with utmost politeness, glancing again at the youth. He never forgot a face; it was a point of pride. "Good day, gentlemen." He knew that face, but from where? Right now he couldn't recall, but it would come to him; it always did.

Drew watched the door as it closed behind Peveril, as if he could still see the man retreating through it. "Captain Peveril, you say?" Of all the questions he could have asked, that was the one for which he didn't need an answer. "What was he…?"

"He's an enterprising fellow. Seems to think he has some

piece of jewellery I'd be interested in."

How had that come about? Had Peveril recognised Drew already in town somehow, and was using that as a pretext to find where he was staying? "The thing is…"

"What?" Jervin looked up. "Are you about to tell me how to run my business again? Spit it out."

"No! Nothing like that." Drew fidgeted. "You remember when I told you how the Lady Alwenna and I were captured after we left Vorrahan?"

Jervin shrugged. "What of it?"

"Peveril was in charge of those soldiers. If he's recognised me…" Drew took a turn about the room. "I can't risk staying here any longer. Not now."

"Why would he recognise you? You look nothing like that novice."

"But what if he saw us in town and followed me here?"

Jervin considered. "I know his kind. He's ambitious, and that means he can be bought. Depend upon it."

"I can't go into town again. Not now."

"Don't be so foolish, Drew. Act as if you have something to hide and people will look all the more closely. Act as if you're above suspicion and they will believe it."

Drew clenched his fists. He was not being foolish. He knew all too well what it was not to be insulated by wealth, even if Jervin himself had forgotten. "My concerns are real, Jervin. I wish you would not dismiss them so lightly."

"I don't dismiss them lightly. Why do you think I insist Rekhart accompanies you everywhere you go?"

"I– I never thought."

"Never underestimate the importance of outward appearances. He's of an age to be a friend of yours and that makes him perfect to be your bodyguard. Don't ever doubt I shall look after my own."

It would have been churlish of Drew to object, but at that moment he found Jervin's words more chilling than reassuring.

CHAPTER TEN

Drelena glowered out of the window at the sun-drenched scene. Figures were hurrying about their business at the harbour, loading or unloading vessels, carrying bundles to and fro. Beyond them sunlight danced on a sea that had taken on a benevolent air of calm. The view was idyllic, and not so unlike home. Or rather, the place she had once called home. Her notion of home was now shaped by the bustling streets of Sylhaven, where there was nothing to be seen but streets and alleyways and rooftops unless one ventured out to the quay, where the sea waited, sometimes holding itself aloof, sometimes pressing close to the top of the harbour wall as it had been the day Bleaklow had come to reclaim her.

She twisted the latch and opened the casement. Cool air flooded in, laden with the scent of the sea and the sharp keening of gulls. Perhaps it would be better to be at Highkell, where there would be no sea to taunt her with reminders of her time at Sylhaven. Try as she might to put thoughts of that brief freedom behind her, she could not. Every sight and every sound brought it back to her with an intensity she could not have thought possible. Perhaps time would blunt the edge of her pain.

There was a knock at the door to her chamber.

"Enter."

"My lady."

Bleaklow's voice was apprehensive. When she turned to face him, his expression was even more so. Good. It was unfair of her to blame him for this situation, she knew it was. But he was the one who'd found her and brought her back.

"Bleaky. I'm glad you are able to spare me a few moments of your time."

A muscle in the side of his face twitched. He bowed hastily. "I was at the far side of the palace when your summons arrived, my lady. What is it you require of me?"

An apology, she thought. A grovelling, abject apology. Tears and begging forgiveness for ruining her life. That would do for a start. She turned her back on him, reached out and closed the window, shutting out the sound of the gulls.

"My lady?"

She took her time before turning to face him again. "It is simple enough. I have a letter here, which I wish to have conveyed to the merchant Nils Darnell in Sylhaven." Her voice held steady.

His mouth tightened. "My lady, I'm not sure I ought–"

"You damned well will, Bleaky. Or shall I tell my father how you manhandled me the night I left?"

"I– It was not my intention… I did not…" His face reddened.

"What? Did not mean it? That would reassure my father greatly, I have no doubt."

He licked his lips nervously. "My lady, I am sure we can–"

She silenced him with a sharp gesture of her hand. "It does not matter to me what you think, or what you have to say. I doubt I will ever forgive you for what you have done."

He lowered his head, fixing his gaze on a point on the floor.

For a moment she felt almost guilty. But only for a moment. "I wish this letter to be carried to Nils Darnell. You scarcely gave me time for more than a few words of explanation, and you owe me this much. You will ensure this letter reaches him. And if he replies, you will ensure likewise that his letter reaches me. I am not seeking to establish a permanent correspondence, but I feel he deserves a fuller explanation of what really happened that day."

He nodded tightly. "I understand, my lady."

"Do you? I wonder."

His shoulders tensed as if the barbed comment had torn his skin. "I do understand, my lady." He looked up then, his gaze suddenly intense. "More than you can ever guess."

"What? Must you also marry a stranger this afternoon?"

He lowered his eyes. "I will ensure your letter is delivered safely, my lady."

"Very well. It is on the table there."

He crossed to the table and picked it up, glancing her way. "I– I am sorry for the part I have played in this. It was my duty. I hope one day you will forgive me."

She raised an eyebrow in scorn. "Your duty, Bleaky, that I can understand. But threatening Nils Darnell to ensure I complied? That was no part of your duty and I doubt I shall ever forgive that."

"No, my lady. I can see that." He made for the door. "If I may be so bold, my lady, I wish you all that is good for your future." He looked up as he took the door handle in his hand.

Drelena said nothing. After a moment he lowered his head and left the room, closing the door softly behind him.

Drelena returned to the window, with its dancing sunlight and shrieking gulls. A dull pain had begun to nag at her temples. She opened the window once more, to breathe the outside air, to have one last taste of freedom. A bride ought not feel like this on her wedding day.

CHAPTER ELEVEN

Col had been unhelpful from the outset, and seemed determined to continue that way. "What do you want, my lady? There are no amulets I can give you, no incantations to ward off the evil that stalks you. That evil is as old as time itself. All I can do is teach you how to build your strength – and even then that is something you must do for yourself. That strength is what you need to keep the evil at bay."

"And what of my child?"

"It is for you to do whatever you are able to protect it."

Alwenna left the campfire then. A lifetime of other people telling her what she ought to do had in no way prepared her for this. If anyone understood what was going on they were not prepared to share that understanding with her. There may have been a perfectly good reason for that, of course.

She'd made a mistake coming here; Jenna's confidence these people might help had been misplaced. She herself, in her determination to leave Scarrow's Deep, had placed too much reliance on the hope they'd be able to help her.

She'd been convinced she'd find peace in these mountains, far removed from the places her various misadventures had taken place. She'd found no such thing.

Alwenna made her way over to the tiny misfit stream that wandered along the floor of the valley. If no one would advise her on what she should do for the best, she had to fall back on her own resources. She knelt by the water's edge, movements awkward with her increasing waist and not helped by the dull ache in her lower back. She sank her hands into the water. It was chill with the hint of ice from the higher mountains, more chill than the night air in this place. She wondered if it might have been better to wait for daylight, then she pitched forward into a stifling darkness. She was lying in bed, staring up at the canopy, or at the place where the canopy would be if it were not so dark she could not see it. At her side was the rhythmic breathing of her new husband, sunk in a deep sleep. Taking care to make no noise, she pushed back the covers and set her feet on the floor. The polished floorboards were cool against the soles of her feet. She pushed back the drapery surrounding the bed and found moonlight illuminating the room.

She padded across to the window and eased the casement open, drawing in a lungful of fresh air. This would be it, to the end of her days. She could count herself fortunate she'd known something better for a few precious weeks. But would that be enough to sustain her through the years ahead?

An owl screeched nearby. Not a seagull, but every bit as free and alive...

Alwenna pulled away. She was not here to intrude upon such personal pain. But in pulling away she became somehow dislocated, and drifted into a place of deeper darkness where she fell and fell, endlessly. Fell down a chasm a thousand times deeper than the gorge beneath Highkell citadel, towards a place no light could reach, a place where no light had shone since the beginning of time. Towards a place where her arrival was anticipated... This had been it all along: this was what she was meant to do.

"No, my lady, do not go further. You will find nothing but pain there, pain and sorrow." The voice was familiar, she ought to recognise it. "Return to us, for your own sake and your child's sake. And if that is not enough, return for me."

She knew that voice.

Alwenna dropped into awareness with a start, shaken loose from her vision of falling. Her hands were chilled, sunk beyond her wrists in the stream. She pushed herself upright, shaking the water from her hands and shivering, but whether that was from the chill of the water, or from the shock of her descent into darkness she did not know. She sat back on the rocky ground. Above the sheer sides of the valley the night sky was clear and the stars shone as brightly as ever. The Hunter was there, watching over their fire.

The Hunter was not the only one watching. She twisted round. Col leant against a boulder, arms folded, shoulders slouched.

"Well, my lady, what did you find?" He strolled over to where she sat. For all his unconcerned attitude, he was watchful.

"Do you not know already?"

Col shrugged.

"I found the king's new bride who is too far from home and her loved ones. And I found a place of darkness such as I have never known before."

"A place of darkness? You found it and returned?"

"I was called back." Should she tell him or could he already guess? "By one I believed dead."

Col nodded. "And what will you do now, my lady?"

She pushed herself to her feet, ungainly. Col didn't offer to help. Like as not he knew she'd have refused it. "That is a good question." She dusted dirt and grit from her hands. "I will do what I must."

CHAPTER TWELVE

At the top table Vasic sat next to his new bride. He was plying her with tasty morsels from the dishes set before them. She smiled prettily, and laughed at his jokes, but her eyes were empty. All this the priestess ascertained through lowered lids as she watched them covertly. Even so, for the time being the king seemed well enough pleased with the Lady Drelena.

Durstan, who had been watching the happy couple in a less discreet manner, drained his wine goblet, grimacing as he swallowed the coarse vintage. He stood up, rocking the bench seat. For a moment it seemed as if it must overbalance and the priestess had to catch hold of the table.

"You, see you stay here in case the king looks for you. Mind you don't go until he's left the table."

She nodded.

Durstan nudged Weaver's shoulder. "And you keep an eye on things. Your duty is to keep those favoured by the Goddess safe."

"Yes, sire."

The soldier was answering questions with less hesitation now. She eyed Weaver thoughtfully as Durstan hobbled away.

He glanced her way, one eyebrow raised in question.

She shrugged. "He still thinks I'll learn something important. The king isn't interested in talking to me."

"You should tell him."

"No. He won't listen." More to the point, it would be unwise: if Durstan once got the notion she could no longer be useful her prospects would be bleak.

The soldier looked up. "He watches you, you know. When he thinks no one's looking."

She glanced up at the top table. Vasic was still engrossed with his bride. "Who? The king?"

Weaver shook his head. "No. The prelate."

She curled her lip in scorn.

"Have a care. His kind don't forgive easily, and never forget."

"What have I done that he must forgive?"

"Nothing, yet. Just have a care."

"Why bother to tell me that? Would you play games with me?"

"We help one another, remember?"

"Durstan despises me since I… failed in my task." The lie came uneasily to her lips, she suspected the soldier was weighing her words carefully.

"If he despises you, it is because he blames you for his own weakness. I will not always be able to watch your back."

"You are bound to me."

"Only as long as Durstan wills it so." The soldier picked up his tankard and said no more. He seemed to slide back into the vacuous state of mind she had become accustomed to seeing. It was almost as if he assumed it like armour. Was it possible he could do that at will, to deflect suspicion? She would have to be more careful what she said in his presence in future.

Beyond the soldier, at the high table, Vasic continued to converse with his bride. She felt suddenly sick and pushed herself to her feet. "Wait here for me."

Weaver looked up, then nodded.

She hurried away to the garderobe.

•••

The girl had scarcely vanished from sight before a tall man came up and sat next to Weaver.

"Well met, my friend." The newcomer held out a hand in greeting.

Weaver knew the face, the aquiline nose, the expression at once curious and calculating. After a moment he reached out and they shook hands. The newcomer's grip was firm. He knew him, but summoning the recollection was almost too great an effort...

"When last we met you shook no one's hand, freemerchant." The name followed an instant later.

"You know me then?"

"I know you. Marten. Even shorn of your hair, I know you." The summer palace. Sunlight slanting in at the window where a moment before...

Marten grimaced. "That's a tale I might hope to tell you one day, but we do not have much time."

Weaver forced himself to concentrate on Marten's words. There had been smoke, so much smoke... Even the thought of it was enough to bring an insistent tickle to his lungs. Weaver cleared his throat. "No, we do not have much time." The freemerchant's clothing was far more restrained than Weaver was used to seeing him wear.

Marten picked up a morsel from one of the serving plates. "The grey brethren own you now?"

"They healed me, after a fashion. But first they killed me." He'd never found the words for it until now, but once he'd spoken them, he knew it was true. He pushed the awareness away; it was no help to him, not in this place.

"So they do own you?" The freemerchant studied him with that familiar look.

The man would spill his innards just to see what colour they were. This was not a new thought. "No man owns me."

Marten nodded. "That I can believe, my friend. But what of the priestess?"

Weaver shook his head. “I am not hers to command.”

“Unless someone else is looking on?”

Weaver nodded slowly. “You ask many questions, freemerchant, but I have one for you: where is the lady?” He could see her in his mind’s eye, as clearly as if she stood before him. Every detail of her face familiar, yet still her name eluded him.

Marten raised one eyebrow. “I could ask you to be more precise.”

“You know who I mean.” Her name was right there, at the edge of his consciousness.

“She is safe – far from Vasic’s reach.”

“And is she well?”

“She is indeed well.”

From the corner of his eye, Weaver saw the door open as the priestess returned. He inclined his head to Marten who stood, briefly setting one hand on Weaver’s shoulder.

“We will speak again, my friend. It will be like old times.”

The girl took her seat, glancing at Marten’s retreating back. “Who was that?”

Weaver shrugged. “Some drunk.”

“I’ve seen his face before.”

“He said he knew me of old.” Weaver shrugged again. “If that is so, I do not know him.”

The girl looked up to the top table, rubbing her forearm thoughtfully, even though the tattoo had healed over completely.

Vasic and the Lady Drelena were leaving. The king made much of taking his lady by the hand. She thanked him with a smile and they crossed the dais towards the door leading to their private chambers. She looked neither to right nor to left, nor at her husband.

The priestess turned her pale gaze to Weaver. “You would not lie to me, would you, Pius?”

"No, Lady Miria, I would not." He nodded his head towards the door where the king and his lady had now vanished. "Are we done here?"

"I told you not to call me that." Her mouth tightened with disapproval. "My name is Ilsa, and that is how you will address me. We are done here."

Weaver drained his tankard of ale. It was poor stuff... another memory stirred. Someone long ago had complained about the ale, and they'd argued over what it was to be a true soldier... The rest of the scene remained elusive. And, as ever, he was aware of the priestess's scrutiny, as if she sought to divine his thoughts. She should have a care: she'd learn nothing good about herself from him.

CHAPTER THIRTEEN

Rekhart was drunk even though it was barely past sunset. He was hunched over his tankard in the back room of the *Crown*, not senseless, but belligerent.

Jervin eyed him with distaste as he scraped his chair back from the table where they had been eating. "Let's leave him to it. I'll show you some of the new pieces I have for my collection."

Drew pushed back his chair. The barman glowered over at their table. "We can't do that. They'll throw him out on the street, like they did with that merchant the other night."

"Best place for him, if you ask me. He's no use to us like that."

"No, but... I'll get him a kopamid. I'll follow you up when he's sobered up a bit. He's not so far gone."

"You're too soft on him."

"He's my friend. If I won't help him, who will?"

Jervin shrugged. "He should have thought of that before he drank so much."

"He's troubled."

"No, Drew, he's trouble. I should never have taken him on again after he kicked up last time."

"You never did tell me what that was about."

"Nor shall I. Mop his fevered brow if you must. I can tell you now you're wasting your time."

"Why? What do you mean?"

"He's given up. You can see it in his eyes: got no respect for himself any more."

"He's a bit down, that's all."

"If you think you're such a good friend, why doesn't he confide in you?" Jervin leaned closer. "Because you're the reason, that's why. He knows he only got his job back because you begged a favour from me. There's few men can live with themselves knowing they're a charity case, and he's not one of them."

Drew was taken aback. He'd not seen it like that before, but Jervin's words rang true. "Then that's all the more reason for me to help now."

Jervin shook his head. "You'll see. He won't thank you for it." He strode off through the door that led to the guest rooms.

Drew ordered kopamid and sat down opposite Rekhart, pouring it into the beakers. "Here, drink some of this. You'll feel better." He slid the beaker over to Rekhart.

Rekhart looked up. "Gone, has he?"

"Jervin? Yes."

"Dunno why you put up with him."

Drew was taken aback by the morose remark. "He's always dealt fairly with me."

"Has he?" Rekhart shrugged. "Of course, you have something he wants."

Drew felt his face reddening. "He gave you your job back, didn't he?"

Rekhart swallowed a mouthful of kopamid. "And I was fool enough to take it." He studied Drew. "Don't get me wrong – I was grateful when you spoke up on my behalf. But if I'd had any backbone…"

Drew took a mouthful of his kopamid. It was not as good as the blend served at the place off the market square. "I think you're being too hard on yourself."

Rekhart shook his head. "But it isn't about me, don't you see?"

"Not really, no. You've lost me there."

"He's not a man to cross, I always knew that. And pretty much most of the city watch were in his pocket one way or the other. So I wasn't so much stepping out of line, as stepping into it." Rekhart's gaze focused on the middle distance, as if he'd forgotten Drew was listening. "And it wasn't big stuff; I'd check shipments through the city gates, if there were more barrels on a wagon than the paperwork said, well, as long as something was being paid to the city, there was no reason to bother." He drained his beaker and pushed his ale tankard aside. "Everyone was doing it and none of it was important. At least, that's what I thought."

Drew refilled their beakers from the pot of kopamid. "So what changed?"

Rekhart shook his head slowly. "It was still little things at first. One of Jervin's men was arrested – caught burgling a shop after he'd decided to do a little freelancing. And Jervin ordered me to bury the charges, lose the paperwork. That made me stop and think. But by then I was nearly clear of debt – I decided I'd settle up with him and that would be an end to it."

"And that's why I heard you arguing with him?"

"Probably." Rekhart shrugged. "Anyway, there was one of the regular night-time shipments due in from downriver. To go in the warehouse cellar. I was to make payment and lock the goods away. Just a few barrels of wine, I thought." He fell silent.

"What happened?"

Rekhart glanced over his shoulder, then leaned over to Drew. "I swore I wouldn't tell you this, but if I don't tell someone I'll go crazy. And I apologise, because you won't like what you hear."

"Go on."

"You'll judge me, and find me wanting. And it's deserved, because I stood by and did nothing." Rekhart picked up his beaker, then set it down again. "By the Goddess, I swear going in I didn't know what was happening. The barge arrived – it was running late and I wasn't too pleased at waiting about in the cold. But the woman running the shipment came onto the harbourside. She said the delivery was short, and gave some of the money back. Then they brought them above deck…" He grimaced. "They were only children, Drew. All tied together, hand and foot. Like a string of mules. They must have been sitting in their own filth the whole way from Ellisquay."

"Surely not." That was impossible. Rekhart had to have been mistaken.

"I swear I didn't know before that night what was going on."

"And this was one of the regular shipments?" Jervin was shipping children upriver from Ellisquay like so much produce? Just another commodity?

"That's right." Rekhart pushed his beaker away. "But you haven't heard the worst of it. There was one lad – maybe ten or so. He'd been taken ill on board. I had to help carry him off the boat. I thought we'd take him to a healer, but… The woman in charge slung him in the water. I had him by the ankles… His head hit the side of the barge… I just let go. I saw him go under the water. I could have dived in and tried to save him, but I just stood there. I did nothing, Drew. I just stood there."

Drew was lost for words.

"You see now, why I can't live with myself?"

"Why tell me this? I can't absolve your guilt."

Rekhart shook his head. "You've been a friend to me these past weeks. I… it's only fair to let you know what you've got into."

Drew pushed his seat back, jumping to his feet. He wanted to believe Rekhart was lying, had made up this tale for some twisted reason of his own. But he couldn't.

He hesitated at the foot of the stairs. Maybe he should walk around outside for a while, let the night air clear his head. And if he did, what then? Would he talk himself out of confronting Jervin? He should never have agreed to come back here…

Reluctantly, he climbed the stairs to the room they shared.

Jervin was busy wrapping some of his new treasures and stowing them carefully in a wooden trunk. He glanced at Drew. "Cheer up. It might never happen."

Drew didn't need to say anything. Rekhart might have been lying. Maybe he was testing him in some way. Maybe it was one of Jervin's games… But what sort of a man would make up something like that and think it a mere game? Drew felt bile rise in his throat. If that was the best excuse he could think up it was a pretty poor one. And there could be no doubting the self-disgust in Rekhart's expression as he related the tale.

"I was talking to Rekhart."

"Maybe now you'll agree with me there are better ways to spend your time." Jervin set the lid on the wooden box.

"Yes." The word was more forceful than Drew had intended.

Jervin looked up sharply. "What, no lectures about caring for my fellow man?"

"No. Not this time." There was no easy way to do this. No discreet way to enquire without damaging their friendship… Nor did that concern him, if what Rekhart told him was true.

"Here – is this not a fine piece? Fit for a queen would you not say?" Jervin held out a necklace fashioned in the shape of leaves, each one as delicate as nature itself.

It was exquisite: even in his mood of current discontent Drew couldn't help reaching out to touch it. Yet when he did, he had an overwhelming sense of stifling darkness. It pressed about him until he snatched his hand back. "The craftsmanship is remarkable. Fit for a queen? Do you mean anything by that?"

Jervin grinned. "It came with several tall tales attached. What do you think?"

Drew was in no mood for guessing games. "It's a great shame the clasp is broken."

Jervin's mouth tightened and he folded the necklace away in the cloth, adding it tenderly to the box. "You might try a little harder to take an interest."

This was his opening. "I do have a question for you, Jervin: how do you make your money?"

"You know, Drew. You handle the accounts."

"Some of them. But I don't know what it is the Ellisquay traders supply that you're prepared to spend so much entertaining them."

Jervin shrugged. "They supply many things. Wine. Spices. Carpets. But you know all this: why the sudden curiosity?"

"Oh, it's not sudden. I've been wondering for a while." It was Drew's turn to shrug, but his indifference was feigned. "Like the cargoes that come upriver at night; the ones that are locked away in the warehouse cellar. What about those?"

"What about them? Do you expect me to leave valuable wine out in the open?" Jervin moved the wooden box over to the corner of the room.

Drew's heart sank. Jervin could have owned up and told him the truth at that point. They could have made things all right. Somehow.

"But those cargoes aren't wine, are they?"

"I don't know what you mean." Jervin's mouth tightened to a thin line.

"Of course you do! Don't lie to me now, please." Surely Jervin would have a real answer, an explanation for it all...

"Whatever notion you've got hold of, I suggest you forget it now, Drew. I've given you a lot of leeway, but I won't tolerate accusations of lying."

"Then admit the truth! They're children, for Goddess's sake. Rekhart told me all about it. He told me how one child who was ill was thrown overboard rather than take him to a healer."

"Rekhart's a damned fool."

"Is he? Then deny it! Deny everything he told me."

"They come from the slums of Ellisquay. Their parents can't afford to feed or clothe them. I bring them here to be indentured, to learn a trade. They come here for a better life."

Drew could almost believe him. "A better life?"

"A better life. You've never been to Ellisquay, never seen real poverty. I grew up in those slums, Drew. Is it so wrong to offer them the advantages I couldn't enjoy?"

Jervin, the philanthropist. The collector of fine art. The connoisseur of fine food and wine. Drew wanted it to be true so much it hurt, physically. Rescuer of children from poverty. What was it Rekhart had said? All tied together, hand and foot?

"Tell me, Jervin, what advantages do they enjoy when they arrive bound like prisoners? When you've paid for them? I want to believe you, truly I do, but I'm not the naive novice fresh out of the precinct. Not now."

"Do you presume to judge me? You've enjoyed my wealth these past months – eaten my food, drunk my wine. Every thread on your back is of my providing. Why question it now? Where did you think it all came from?"

Jervin didn't deny it, then. Everything Rekhart had told him... "If this is true..." Drew leaned on the table for support. "If this is true, I can't stay with you. Not knowing this."

Jervin's face was ashen. "Did nobody tell you, Drew? No one leaves me. No one." Jervin closed the distance between them, reaching out as if for reassurance. Then something crashed against the side of Drew's head and he knew no more.

CHAPTER FOURTEEN

Alwenna woke, her head spinning, a sharp pain above her right ear. She sat up in the dark, taking a moment to return to her senses. The pain was not hers. She pressed her eyes shut, trying to recall the vision. A tall man stepping closer, his expression taut with anger... She had seen that face before, his expression carefully neutral, revealing nothing. The night they had returned Drew to Brigholm. Jervin.

"What is it, my lady?" Beside her Erin was sitting up, rubbing her eyes sleepily. "Not the baby?"

"No, not the baby." It was still far too soon, wasn't it? She'd lost track of the days since they'd left Scarrow's Deep, before that, even. She and Wynne had worked it out, long ago. But the year hadn't turned yet. Soon after the first frosts, Wynne had said. But did this Goddess-forsaken region even have frosts at the same time as Highkell?

Another burst of pain cut off her wandering thoughts. Jervin, angered... That could only mean the pain belonged to Drew.

"I think Drew's in trouble."

"He finds trouble everywhere, that one." Erin rolled over in her blankets once more.

"Most of it when he was travelling with me."

"But he's not now, is he?"

"No. That doesn't mean he doesn't need my help."

"My lady, get some rest. Not even Col would make the climb out of this valley in the dark. Big as you are now we'd have to haul you out."

Erin was right, of course.

"But I gave him my word..."

Erin sat up again. "My lady, are you seriously thinking of rushing off to help him? What do you imagine you could do? You need to put the child first."

"There must be something... I gave him my word. Whatever else I may have failed at, I can at least keep my promises."

"My lady, he's a good man. He would understand. And he would never ask you to put your child in danger for his sake."

"Without Drew I'd have died in the ruins of Highkell. I owe him my life."

"My lady, he would never reproach you if you didn't rush to his side. He knows your condition. I'm sure he would be devastated if you were to put yourself in danger on his behalf."

Erin was right, and they both knew it. Alwenna settled down in her own blankets once more. Whatever she might decide in the morning, she could hope to go nowhere before daylight. She had to rest: it was all she could do.

Uneasy visions haunted her sleep: of the dungeon at Highkell where Drew and Weaver had been held captive; the cell off the guardroom where she herself had been held; the vaulted chamber where Tresilian had been tortured by Vasic; the narrow culvert she'd escaped through the night she left Highkell, with Weaver and Wynne; the shadows in the depths of the gorge; and she knew something waited for her in the darkness there. The sense of that waiting shadow hung about her on waking, but she'd learned no more of what had happened to Drew.

Alwenna made her way over to the stream, knelt down and plunged her hands into the water. She gasped from the cold – it had surely not struck so chill the day before. Did that mean the first frosts would soon arrive? From the valley floor they could not see the higher mountains, but she guessed they might have had their first snowfall of the season.

She shut out the distractions, concentrating her thoughts on the water as it ran against her hands and numbed her wrists. It took longer than usual to slide out of her surroundings. She was annoyed with herself; she knew better than to let that happen. She tried to damp down the unhelpful emotion, but the annoyance stayed with her, clung to her like a burr to a dog's shoulder, caught in a place from which she could not hope to dislodge it.

She forced herself to concentrate once more. She became aware of a heartbeat: rapid, tiny. It took her a moment to realise it was her own child's. Such a small, determined thing... She could have lingered all day, marvelling at the tiny miracle, but she dragged herself away. A young woman rising from her bath, servants wrapping her in towels. The stone of the wall behind her was familiar, and Alwenna recognised with a start the bedchamber at Highkell that had once been hers. This had to be Vasic's new bride: she sat impassively as the servants brushed her long hair and fastened it up in an elaborate fashion. There was none of the despair there had been on the boat on the way over to Lynesreach; but there was no joy, either. The young woman was simply going through the motions. Alwenna moved on.

Vasic was seated in the throne room, doing little to hide his boredom. Various scribes were scribbling busily as one petitioner after another stated their case, then withdrew, pending the king's judgement. A few courtiers stood about the edges of the room. Her attention was caught by a tall man who stood close to the window. Only when he turned his face towards her, as if he sensed her scrutiny, did she recognise Marten. Was this king feeding from the palm of his hand? She very much doubted it.

There was a stir as the doors to the throne room opened and an equally tall figure strode in. Behind him followed two soldiers, holding a prisoner between them. The prisoner's head sagged, as if he was impossibly weary. She felt the first prickle of apprehension down her spine. The prisoner's face was hidden by his hair, but he was of slight build. It was then she noticed the soldier to one side wore the captain's uniform of the palace guard. She looked more closely and recognised Peveril on the instant: Peveril, looking well pleased with himself. The man in front was Jervin, dressed in court finery. She did not need to see the prisoner's face to know it was Drew, but she needed the proof. As if he'd heard her thoughts the prisoner looked up and met her gaze unsteadily. But that was enough: she had to try to help him. This was an obligation.

The visions faded and scattered, and Alwenna found herself staring down at her hands in the stream water. She pulled her hands out and they were white with cold, with barely any feeling left. She dabbed them dry on her skirts and stood up, tucking her hands into her armpits to warm them.

Erin waited nearby, her expression closed. "Well, my lady?"

"Vasic has Drew."

"I see, my lady." As ever, Erin didn't question Alwenna's sight. "That's bad news for Drew, but you can't hope to do anything to help. Not against Vasic."

"Nor can I stay here pretending it hasn't happened." Alwenna rubbed new life into her numb hands. They began to burn with the hot-aches.

"My lady, you can't be serious."

"I must do what I can. It will be little enough, but at least I'll have tried."

She thought the girl was about to argue with her, but instead Erin smiled. "Very well, my lady. Our bags are already packed."

"You know me better than I know myself."

"I won't be sorry to leave this place – it gives me the chills. But I feel bad for Drew, if we're his best hope of help."

The child in Alwenna's womb wriggled and twisted, as if it agreed.

CHAPTER FIFTEEN

Marten couldn't shake off the uneasy sense of being watched. He was in a roomful of people at court, of course someone would be looking his way at any given moment. Of course there could be no one behind him – he was standing at the edge of the room, after all – but he glanced over his shoulder nonetheless.

He was distracted by the throne room door opening.

A group of men entered, Jervin leading the way, far from his usual haunts in Brigholm. Behind him followed two soldiers, holding a prisoner between them. Marten knew it was Drew before he looked up, eyes moving towards that same place over Marten's shoulder. Someone had beaten the lad, who had a fat lip and a swollen eye. Dried blood clung to the corner of his mouth. One of the two soldiers wore the household guards' livery. A burly man, Marten had noticed him from time to time: in the market place, at the citadel gatehouse, about town.

The new arrivals approached the throne, escorted by Marwick.

"Highness, may I present Master Jervin, a merchant of Brigholm. His business today is twofold."

Vasic turned his gaze to the merchant, barely glancing at the group behind. The merchant bowed in courtly manner. He was stiff-backed, that one, whether through pride or infirmity Marten couldn't yet hazard a guess.

"Well, sir, state your business."

Jervin straightened up, stately and in no haste. "Highness, I thank you for the favour of your time. I bring you a token of my gratitude." He turned slightly to indicate the prisoner. "Your captain here informs me this young man is a known felon, who escaped from your custody some months ago."

The expression on Drew's face was one of hurt, but it changed subtly to one of anger as Jervin continued to speak.

"I have been employing him as a clerk, unaware of his background. When I announced we would be travelling to Highkell on business he was strangely reluctant to accompany me, but now I fully understand why. Your captain is to be commended for his alertness in recognising him. Rarely have I been so taken in."

Vasic took a closer look at Drew. "Well, well. It is my friend the young novice. You are indeed to be commended, Captain…?" He glanced at the soldier.

"Peveril, your highness."

"Captain Peveril." Vasic's gaze slid away from the soldier to the prisoner. "You've not improved the lad's looks any since I last saw him." He smiled.

One or two courtiers tittered at his witticism. Seated at Vasic's side, his new queen's mouth tightened. She raised her head and turned her eyes towards Vasic as if she would speak out, but something caused her to pause and instead she clasped her hands in her lap and fell to studying a point in the middle distance once more.

Now that was interesting. Marten made a note to speak with her at the first opportunity. He understood from court gossip that the marriage had secured Vasic's hold over the region by virtue of a more than generous settlement. Wealth always brought with it influence. But more importantly for Marten, the Lady Drelena seemed inclined to look favourably upon the underdog and his cause was never in greater need of a new royal patron. His original plan to ingratiate himself with Vasic seemed doomed to failure: Vasic was a very different creature to Tresilian. Or at least, to the man Tresilian had once been. Marten had sworn he'd court no more monarchs, sworn he'd drop his crusade for equal rights for the freemerchants, but it was a habit of long standing and was proving harder to break than he'd ever believed possible.

Vasic had ordered the soldiers to bring the prisoner forward. "Well, lad, have you anything to say for yourself?"

"In my defence, highness? Only that the charges levelled against me remain as false as the day they were first made."

"Consistent, if not particularly original." Again Vasic smiled, looking about the assembled courtiers. Again, a few obliged with restrained affectations of laughter. "Not entirely unexpected. Have you learned anything since we last met, lad?"

Drew glanced sideways at Jervin, whose expression remained cold and dispassionate. "Only a very little, your highness."

"Indeed. Dare I hope you have learned to fight yet? You might hope to earn yourself a pardon."

"No, your highness. I have mostly learned bookkeeping."

"Bookkeeping? That would not prove entertaining." Vasic seemed to lose interest in Drew. "Return the lad to the cells until I decide what is to be done with him." He turned to Jervin as Drew was led away by the two soldiers. "Your diligence will not go unrewarded. There is a purse due to anyone capturing the novice."

"Highness, rather than the purse, I beg you would consider my petition. There is a group of merchants operating out of Ellisquay who do not honour the trading laws. They trade outside the market places and shirk their duty to pay taxes, while stealing custom from honest men. I have here a record of several transactions that have been brought to my notice by other concerned tradesmen in Brigholm. I beg that the strength of the law be brought to bear against these criminals." Jervin bowed and handed Vasic a parchment scroll.

Vasic snapped the seal open and perused the document. "I shall look further into this. Those who flout the trade laws are robbing their fellow citizens as well as the state. We must make it clear what consequences such dishonesty entails. Marwick, you will oversee this matter." He handed the parchment to his steward.

Jervin bowed again, uttering words of thanks as Vasic stood and held out an imperious hand to the Lady Drelena. She rose from her seat and took his hand, letting him lead her down from the dais and through the throne room to the chamber where their meal awaited them.

Marten fell in with the gaggle of courtiers following the royal couple through. The new queen ate sparingly while Vasic conversed and drank with his current favourites, the lean ambassador Kaith among them. Marten suspected Kaith would not meet much favour with the Lady Drelena.

Further up the table, Marten spotted the unlikely trio of Durstan, the priestess and Weaver. At another table Jervin sat, with two soldiers. It took him a few moments, but Marten recognised Rekhart. He appeared ill at ease, perhaps having witnessed his friend's fall from grace, although Marten could have sworn he'd not been present when Drew had been brought before Vasic. This was certainly the first time the trader and his people had enjoyed the king's hospitality.

It crossed Marten's mind that he might have similarly bought the king's favour by divulging Alwenna's whereabouts and had doubtless incurred the king's displeasure instead. It appeared the dagger had not impressed Vasic half as much as it ought to have. But he hadn't been dismissed from court, not yet. He must learn what he could while he could.

Meanwhile the Lady Drelena watched Vasic with distaste as he continued to drink. She took care to conceal her emotions, but her feelings were apparent nonetheless. She must stand in need of friends at this new court. Vasic, glass in hand, looked about the room. He spotted Durstan.

"Ah, prelate. Just the fellow. I've a fancy to test out this champion of yours."

He brandished his glass to include the whole room. "Who among our number is swordsman enough to test his fighting ability? You there, Weaver, Pius, whatever you call yourself. Stand up. Let our challengers get your measure."

Weaver glanced at the prelate, who nodded. Weaver clambered out over the bench and stepped into the empty space that ran between the two long tables. He bowed slightly before Vasic. "Highness, I await your command."

"Who thinks they can best this man? Come now, don't be shy, gentlemen. Great honour and glory await the victor. And a fat purse."

Weaver waited impassively in the centre of the room. Marten saw the priestess lean over and whisper something to the prelate, who glanced over to where Jervin sat. He asked her some question and she nodded. Durstan pushed himself to his feet.

"What, prelate, would you take on your own challenger?"

Laughter ran around the room. The Lady Drelena had pushed away her wine glass and watched the proceedings with her mouth drawn into a tight line.

Durstan laughed, the awkward laughter of a man determined to please, whatever the cost. "No, highness, I fear my fighting days are long gone. But there is one noted warrior here who is in his prime and furthermore is known to brother Pius. He would make an excellent test of the brother's loyalty."

Weaver turned his head to look at Durstan for a moment before setting his eyes straight ahead once more. His expression remained unreadable.

"Who is this paragon? Show him to me at once." Vasic flourished his glass.

"I understand he goes by the name of Rekhart, your highness." Durstan glanced over to where Jervin sat. At his side Rekhart looked exceedingly unwilling to step into the fray. "And there he is, your highness." Durstan gestured in welcome to Rekhart. There was a burst of shouts which rapidly became jeers as Rekhart hesitated.

Jervin smiled. "Come now, Rekhart, you have caught the king's attention. This is your chance to prove yourself."

Rekhart eased to his feet, and a burst of raucous applause broke out.

Drelena leaned over to say something to Vasic. Whatever his reply it clearly displeased her and she watched stony-faced as Rekhart walked round the end of the table, to join Weaver in the centre of the room, rolling his shoulders and stretching his arms. Rekhart's jaw was clenched. He acknowledged Weaver with a tight nod. Marten had never seen a man more ready to embrace his fate.

Vasic watched the scene with ill-concealed anticipation. His queen glanced at him once, then looked away in disgust. And Marten hoped to further his cause by serving this man? Perhaps it was time he found a new cause.

CHAPTER SIXTEEN

They were still in the foothills of the mountains when the first birthing pain hit Alwenna. She doubled over in the saddle, gasping to catch her breath. No, this could not be; she must have strained something on the tortuous climb out of the valley. She'd ignored the tightening sensations in her abdomen, assuming it was from the sudden effort required. Surely that had to be it. It was too soon for the baby to come, wasn't it?

"Goddess, my lady! What is it?" Erin slid down from behind her, and ran round to take the horse's head, bringing it to a halt.

"Just a twinge–" Another pain racked through Alwenna.

"We need to get you down off that horse." They achieved it somehow when the pain had subsided. Erin guided Alwenna to a sheltered spot between several boulders. "It looks like that baby's on its way."

"But... it's too soon. Wynne said to expect it when–" Another spasm cut short Alwenna's words, resulting in a sharp pain and a gushing of fluid down her legs.

"They come when they're ready, my lady, and it looks like this one's ready now, whether we like it or not."

Alwenna nodded, trying to catch her breath as her womb contracted. And then there was more pain.

She lost track of time after that. At some point Erin's

encouragement faded out and gave way to worried silence. It could have been minutes, or it could have been hours. Alwenna had never been so exhausted in her life.

"The baby's wrong way round, my lady. If we had a proper midwife here we might turn it, but I can't get it out that way, not without damaging you both. The only way I can see is to cut it from your belly."

"Do what you must." Alwenna didn't care at that stage. Anything for the pain to stop. She was so tired… impossibly tired.

She barely registered the added pain as the knife sliced through her flesh, was barely aware of a thin wail that could have been her child's or could have been her own.

It was still some time before dawn when Brett woke. His sleep had been uneasy, run through by a sense that something was terribly wrong with the Lady Alwenna. His dreams had been all confusion, but the last of them had had a terrible clarity: a dark hand reaching out for her as he looked on, helpless. He sat up, pushing back the bed covers and the sweat on his skin cooled rapidly in the night air. Next to him his younger brother snored, oblivious to Brett's tossing and turning. Brett eased out of the bed. On the far side his elder brother stirred, mumbled, then slid off into a deeper sleep.

Brett pulled on his clothes and tiptoed out. The sky to the east glowed with predawn light, but true daylight wouldn't be upon them for another hour yet. It was a good time to travel.

He'd meant to walk around a bit in the fresh air, ease the tension in his mind and body, but suddenly he knew he had to act: he had to seek out the Lady Alwenna. She'd told him not to, but… this was something he could not ignore.

Mind made up, he crept back inside, grabbed some dried meat and a costrel to carry water. He would fill it at the stream on his way out of the valley. Balancing saddle and bridle over one arm he stepped outside again, closed the door carefully behind him and set off to the horse pasture. He'd not gone more than a dozen paces when a voice behind him interrupted.

"Brett, wait. What are you up to?" His elder brother Malcolm had followed him.

"I couldn't sleep. I thought I'd go for a ride, go hunting, you know."

"You left your bow behind. You won't catch much without that."

Brett shrugged. "I was going to check the snares."

"No you weren't." Malcolm studied him severely. "I'm not bothered what you get up to, but Ma'll worry. You know how she is."

None knew better. "She might worry less if I'm gone."

"What, seriously? You can't just sneak off like this."

"I've a good reason."

Sometimes his brother was more perceptive than Brett liked to admit. This proved to be one of those times.

"It's the landbound queen, isn't it? You're going after her."

Brett shrugged. "It's not like you make it sound. She's in danger. I've had such nightmares..."

Malcolm's expression changed subtly, from accusation to understanding. "You, too?"

"You've had them as well?"

"Whenever I slept last night, it was as if something was stalking me. I couldn't see what or where it was, but... It was enough to stop me sleeping."

Brett nodded. "Then you can see I've got to try and find them?"

Malcolm nodded reluctantly. "We don't even know where they went."

"I followed their tracks the day after they left. They went up into the mountains. I'll find them."

"I'm coming, too. Erin's with her, remember?"

"You have no horse, Mal. I think I need to travel fast. You

keep Ma at bay – someone should know where I've gone."

Malcolm grimaced. "I'd sooner come with you."

Brett grinned suddenly, an echo of his father's irrepressible humour. "I'm going, before you suggest swapping places."

A few minutes later, Brett was riding his horse out along the trail towards the mountains, thanking the Goddess he'd followed their trail all those days ago. It was a relief to be doing something at last, after all the days spent at Scarrow's Deep treading on eggshells, trying not to mention his father or the Lady Alwenna in his mother's presence when they'd been the two people most on his mind. The shadow of his nightmare still clung about him, but it had lost its strength out in the open as the sun rose. In its place was the certainty he was doing the right thing.

CHAPTER SEVENTEEN

Vasic had decreed the challengers should fight outside in the courtyard, where there was more room. They were surrounded now by an eager crowd. Vasic and his bride watched from a vantage point on the steps. The first thing Weaver noticed was how uneven the cobbles were underfoot. That would give Rekhart the advantage: he was young, strong, in his prime. Weaver was far from his best game. He'd not done anything like enough training to recover his fitness since the fire – the only advantage he could claim over his opponent was he'd been sober these past weeks and was sober now. But he'd taught Rekhart well, more years ago than he cared to think about, and that advantage would be of little use to him.

The sky was overcast, so there was no advantage to be gained from sunlight. They circled cautiously, neither willing to engage. The crowd began to jeer. This was helping no one. Weaver adopted fool's guard, placing his right foot forward and, holding his sword at waist height, lowered the point. Rekhart took the bait and lunged for his head: Weaver brought his point up, responding in kind and they'd broken the impasse.

The younger man fought with the desperation of one who was cornered and had only one way out: that way led through Weaver. Every campfire they'd shared, every tense wait for battle, the years of their friendship – all had come down to this. Rekhart's every movement was steeled with desperation, and, may the Goddess be merciful, he had the edge on Weaver now. His technique was ragged – always had been – but he was moving more easily on the uneven ground and his reactions were swifter than Weaver's.

Weaver slipped on the cobbles. His right foot shot out from under him and he overbalanced, dropping to one knee which hit the ground with a painful crunch, sending shockwaves jarring through his upper body. Weaver dropped his sword, hand slapping on the ground to keep himself upright.

Rekhart stared at Weaver, lowering his sword point and backing away. "Damn it, I never thought it would end like this."

"The time for thinking's long past, Jaseph. Just get it over with." The pain through his knee was incredible.

"No. Not this way. Take up your sword." Rekhart waited, his chest rising and falling rapidly. The crowd jeered again, louder than before.

Weaver gritted his teeth and took hold of his sword before pushing himself up to stand on his own two feet once more. Weaver tested his weight on his knee: the result wasn't good, but it held him. He had a vague recollection of the grey brother he had fought at the summer palace. The man had been unstoppable: he'd never blinked, never showed any sign of fatigue… It was an effort for Weaver simply to pull the air in and out of his lungs. He was no more one of the grey brethren than Rekhart here. Well, Goddess willing, here would be an end to it all. He was almost glad: his death would make a poor spectacle for Vasic.

"Come on, what are you waiting for?" Rekhart glared at him, his eyes wild. Once a man looked at life like that, there was no standing in his way. But old habits died hard.

Weaver readied his guard. "I've slowed down, Rekhart. A bit like you."

"What are you implying?" They began to circle again.

"A few years have passed since we last sparred in the training grounds. You've changed." The longer he kept Rekhart talking, the better his chance of recovering his breath.

"Everyone changes. What of it?"

"It can't just be the drink. Something must have driven you to it."

Rekhart shook his head. "You don't know what it was like."

"But selling yourself to the likes of Jervin? A far cry from the city watch. No wonder you turned to drink."

"Do you dare to judge me? I lost everything." The crowd were jeering and booing now, so no one was likely to overhear their words.

"That's too bad." Weaver shrugged. "I lost my wife and child, Rekhart, but I never lost my honour."

Rekhart grimaced. "Damn you, you've not always been so pure."

Weaver could guess what was coming next.

"Like when you were shagging your king's wife – not so honourable then, were you?"

Weaver saw red then. He'd had no appetite for this fight – not until that moment.

Weaver waded in with an overhand blow, feinting at the last minute. Rekhart sidestepped, too late to avoid Weaver's blade slicing through his ear. Blood spurted over Rekhart's shoulder as he hurled himself at Weaver. He displayed no science, no technique in his fury, keeping up the onslaught until, finally, Weaver had no answer. Weaver made a half-hearted attempt to parry the blow, but he was tired, so tired. And Rekhart found the precise point between his ribs with heart-stopping certainty.

The pain was every bit as excruciating as it had been the day Weaver had died on the stone slab in the cellar beneath the summer palace. Here was an end to it. He would have muttered a word of thanks, but his vision was already dimming, and his voice wouldn't respond to the commands his brain sent it.

Rekhart withdrew his sword from Weaver's chest, the blade stinging every inch of the way. Blood spilled from the wound, dark and thick and sluggish, congealing on the hand Weaver pressed to the gash in his chest. Not that he could hope to staunch that wound. He dropped his hand, realising it was useless, but the blood spilled no more. Weaver stared stupidly at his fingers. The blood there was dark brown, as if old and spent long ago. Yet he still stood. The pain in his chest had subsided. He still held his sword in his right hand, just as it should be. There was a rightness about it all.

Rekhart stared at him in open-mouthed dismay.

"What's the matter, Jaseph? Cat got your tongue?"

Rekhart staggered back. "Impossible. That was a fatal blow. I killed you."

Weaver smiled, a lazy smile that Rekhart seemed to find worse than anything he'd said before that moment.

"I killed you! I know it!" Rekhart lunged forwards again, swinging his sword wildly at Weaver, slicing his shoulder open. Weaver shrugged off the blow and Rekhart drew his dagger, plunging it into Weaver's chest where the sword had pierced him before. "I struck you through the heart, I know I did." He staggered back, leaving his dagger protruding from Weaver's rib cage.

Weaver pulled the blade out and tossed it away.

"Well, that much was thoughtful, I suppose. A clean kill. Do you expect me to thank you?"

If the Goddess had spared him, she'd done it for a reason. And Weaver had not far to look to find that reason: it glared at him through Rekhart's eyes, resentful and unthinking, like some feral creature. He'd been a good man once, but had lost his way beyond recall. Weaver knew what the Goddess required of him.

As if he sensed Weaver's new resolve, Rekhart charged

at him, launching an overhead blow, with the clear intent of decapitating him. Weaver raised his hands and deflected Rekhart's blade with his own. He stepped forward, capturing both Rekhart's arms with his left arm, so they were locked face to face. Rekhart's elbows were pinned, leaving his sword useless behind Weaver, with Weaver's blade between them at head height. Rekhart's anger turned to horror an instant before Weaver punched the cross guard of his sword through the younger man's eye socket, cleansing the fear from his face with a burst of gore.

Weaver released Rekhart. His lifeless body twisted as he fell to the cobbles and landed with his injured eye to the ground. His remaining good eye stared toward Weaver, devoid of any expression, but devoid, too, of any pain. The corpse that lay there was recognisable as his erstwhile friend, but Weaver could find no regret for him in his heart – or whatever it was that now impelled his body forward, day after day. Rekhart had fallen long ago, dragged down by evil deeds that should never have been his lot. All Weaver had done was tidy away the messy remainder of the man he'd once been. Now he methodically cleaned his sword and sheathed it once more.

Vasic clapped his hands and the rest of the onlookers followed with their applause. Weaver acknowledged it with a single nod as he fought to recover his breath. Durstan stood at the edge of the crowd, watching with an expression of unholy pleasure on his face.

PART V

CHAPTER ONE

From where he stood, Marten could see the soldiers lifting Rekhart's body from the cobbles. Vasic continued to applaud. Weaver was still catching his breath, acknowledging the applause with nothing more than a sour nod. The king had a new champion.

The Lady Drelena turned away from the scene, her expression stricken. A solitary maidservant scurried to keep up with her as she made her way back to the keep. She would pass close by the place where Marten stood. This was his moment.

He stepped forward, bowing with all the grace he could muster, once again regretting the absence of his court finery. "Your highness, I can see this scene has distressed you. May I offer you my arm for support?"

She eyed him with something close to suspicion. "I have seen you at court; my husband called you freemerchant, did he not?"

"He has done so, my lady, on many occasions. But I trust you will not think the worse of me for that?"

"I do not even know your name, sir. I doubt I shall think of you at all."

"My name is Marten, my lady."

"What, simply Marten? You must have the shortest name at court."

Marten bowed. "I may safely lay claim to that distinction. As a former freemerchant – for I can claim to be one no longer – I have no estates to my name and no title to brandish about."

"Well, there must be something to recommend you, or you would not be here. Dare I hope it is your wit? Lend me your arm, sir. I am, as you rightly observed, sickened by what has taken place here today – divert me and you shall have my gratitude."

"Shall I be your jester, my lady, and fill your ears with empty witticisms?"

"No. Nothing would annoy me more greatly. Tell me about yourself – of your homeland."

"My homeland? Alas, I was born a freemerchant and I have none. The road is my home."

"None at all?" They had reached the edge of the courtyard. Onlookers were still milling around, craning their necks to catch a glimpse of the carnage.

"Nothing that you would call home, my lady. There is a place where those who are too old or infirm to travel stay, where we have scraped shelter from unforgiving ground."

"Is it near the sea? That is what I call home."

"No, my lady, it is as far from the sea as it is possible to be."

"Further even than Highkell? I cannot imagine that. I am almost curious to see such a place."

"There is little enough to see. It is a barren place which offers little comfort save what we carry in our own hearts."

"And is that not enough?"

Marten smiled ruefully. "If it were, my lady, I would not be here."

"So you are a man with a purpose. Yes, I can see that. Does this place of yours have a name?"

"We call it Scarrow's Deep. But you will not find it on any map of the Peninsular Kingdoms." Marten stepped aside so she could precede him into the building. The silence within the stone walls was an eerie contrast to the activity outside.

"Is that a challenge, freemerchant?" Her voice rang out, startling in the silence, and she lowered it as she continued to speak. "Goddess, how this place broods. At home we were never free of the cry of seagulls. I miss them more than I ever imagined possible."

"Perhaps you would feel more at home at Lynesreach, my lady."

"Perhaps. But the sun sets over the land there, instead of over the sea. Everything is turned about. And Vasic was keen that I should return to Highkell with him. I thought..."

After a moment's silence Marten pressed her to continue. "You thought, my lady?"

"It does not matter what I thought, Marten. I was mistaken. I shall make it my business to return to the sea as soon as is practicable." They had reached the staircase to her private chambers. "I thank you for your company, Marten. You are my first freemerchant."

Marten bowed. "It has been a privilege, my lady."

Drelena sent the servant ahead to prepare refreshments and paused at the foot of the stairs. "Perhaps you will know: Vasic's previous bride. I was told she died in the collapse of the tower. I feel her presence acutely here, as if her soul has been taken into the very stones of the place."

"She is of an ancient line, my lady. They all of them had an affinity with this place, I cannot deny it. But if you fear she haunts you..." He hesitated. She must have heard the rumours, otherwise why would she be asking? "You have spoken of this to your husband, I imagine?"

"I did. He was... less than helpful."

It seemed his surmise was right: the Lady Drelena was in need of friendship. "I'm sure you have heard the rumours, my lady."

She nodded. "I have. Many, many rumours. Do you have

more to add to them?"

"It is said in these parts, my lady, if you want to know the truth you must ask a freemerchant."

"But you claim to be no longer a freemerchant."

"That is true. I may have been too hasty in accepting the judgement of others. But that is by the by. Whatever rumours you may have heard, I can assure you the Lady Alwenna lives. I have spoken with her myself."

"Truly? So the sense she is sometimes watching me is no more than foolish superstition?"

"I can assure you she would wish you only well, my lady."

"They say she cursed Vasic and all in his household. He himself told me the curse only lifted when she died – that was his proof."

"It is usually easiest to believe what we most want to believe."

"That is no answer, freemerchant."

Marten smiled. "There were no freemerchants present at the wedding ceremony, so I have only the word of the Lady Alwenna herself and her servant as to what happened that day. I know her nature enough to be confident she would offer you only support."

"Why should I believe you?"

"My lady, I will let you be the judge of that. I think your husband the king chooses to disbelieve me. Weigh what you have been told and, perhaps, ask yourself who stands to gain most by lying to you."

She tilted her head to one side. "I shall do just that. We will speak again, freemerchant."

CHAPTER TWO

The priestess stepped back into the cover of the crowd as the freemerchant turned to usher the Lady Drelena through the door. She wanted to hear more of that conversation, but it would have been too obvious to follow them inside. What was the meddling freemerchant up to now?

A hand caught hold of her arm and she twisted round, startled. Durstan dropped her arm as if stung. "What are you about, Miria? With the queen gone this is your chance to speak with Vasic."

No, she would not suffer the indignity of being rebuffed by the king again. "Prelate, he has no need of me at present, not with his fresh-faced bride to keep him company."

Durstan frowned. "You swore to serve the Goddess, did you not? This is what she requires of you."

"But..." Why waste her breath? "Very well." The Goddess would sooner have her tell him what she'd overheard the freemerchant saying to the new queen, but she bowed her head and said nothing more.

The king was surrounded by a press of courtiers who were placing bets on an impromptu fistfight inspired by the encounter between the champions. She made her way round to the far side of the crowd, out of Durstan's line of sight. Let him think she was following his instructions. She doubted very much the king had given her as much as a moment's thought in recent days. In all honesty, she preferred it that way. He was a poor replacement for his late cousin. And for all his pawing she'd learned nothing of use, and was not even half a step closer to exacting vengeance for Tresilian's death.

She drifted away from the crowd, to the edge of the yard. A small section of the parapet had collapsed – presumably during the earthquake that had accompanied the wedding. Some said a powerful curse by the Lady Alwenna had been the cause of it. She wasn't sure she believed that: surely if the Lady Alwenna had been possessed of such great power she'd have brought the entire summer palace down around their ears. She had no doubt the exiled queen had the sight, but...

She noticed old Marwick at the edge of the courtyard, speaking with that captain. What was his name? Peveril? Yes, that was him. The king had been pleased with the captain's service of late. She'd caught the man eyeing her with speculation more than once, when she had still been favoured by the king. As well, then, to move no closer to them. Peveril laughed at something, and clapped one hand on Marwick's shoulder – they had to be sharing a great joke.

A shout went up from the crowd and she glanced that way. The fight had seemingly begun. Goddess knew how any of them could see what was going on. A clatter and a sudden movement caught from the corner of her eye pulled her attention back to the two men. Marwick was toppling backwards, off balance, the wooden barrier over the collapsed section of wall tumbled behind his legs, tripping him. His arms flailed in an attempt to regain his balance, and he clutched wildly at the broken edge of stonework before dropping from sight.

Peveril leaned forward over the yawning gap, one hand resting on the edge of the stonework. He pulled back, turning slowly, his features composed. For a moment his eyes met hers. She recognised what she saw there. It was as if she'd held up a mirror to her own soul: an obstacle had been removed from his path. In that split second of recognition, she had no doubt what had transpired in the instant she had looked away from the two men.

Knowledge like that could get a person killed, where a man like Peveril was concerned. He looked to the crowd and shouted out. "Goddess! The old man just lost his balance and fell." One or two at the edge of the crowd glanced his way idly. A soldier ambled over to see what the fuss was about. Peveril's eyes met the priestess's once more. They both knew, and they both understood. This secret could prove to be her undoing. Or she might turn it to her advantage.

She slipped away into the crowd.

CHAPTER THREE

The moon hadn't risen yet. Brett unsaddled his horse by the last of the daylight and settled down to rest. He felt uneasy, as if stopping here was the last thing he should be doing. But his horse needed to rest, even if he didn't.

He settled down with his back to a boulder. He might as well doze himself, rather than fret about problems he'd not yet encountered.

He was walking over a vast, empty landscape. Every so often rocks twisted beneath his feet, tugging at his ankle. He knew he had to go on: if he did not, the thing that was pursuing him would catch up with him. And it must not happen here, for there were too many people who would be harmed as a result. The sand beneath his feet grew deeper and deeper, until every step became a struggle. The land was no longer flat and he was climbing a steep hill, sliding back half a step every time he took one foot off the ground to place it ahead of the other. The air about him grew colder and colder, and the last traces of light faded from the sky as one by one the stars were obliterated by a huge shadow that crept overhead.

Brett woke with a jolt as the shadow fell over him and he sat up, shivering. It was a huge relief to see the constellations above him in the night sky, just as they always had been; the Hunter rising to the south and already watching over his meagre camp, while the moon was cresting the eastern horizon.

But his relief was short-lived. For all the reassurance the night sky offered him he could not shake the sense something was terribly wrong. He could not stop here any longer; he had to ride on. He saddled his horse again and mounted up, pushing it on towards the mountains with a growing sense of urgency.

He'd been riding for an hour or so before his horse pricked up its ears and raised its head, snorting. The animal tensed beneath him, reluctant to move forward. Ought he dismount and lead it? But if there was danger ahead, he could lose precious time vaulting back into the saddle when he should be fleeing. His horse halted, planting its feet stubbornly, then off to one side another horse whinnied. Brett slid down from the saddle, keeping his horse between himself and the unknown traveller. He'd heard too many tales about savage folk who lived in these hills; if the Goddess willed that he had to walk straight into their camp, then so be it, but he need not make an easy target of himself.

He approached quietly, his horse settling now he was on the ground next to it. He could make out a bulky shadow that must be the horse he'd heard, its head raised, following his progress. He was perhaps half a dozen steps away from the animal when a figure sprang out from behind a boulder, startling his horse, which spun away. As he struggled to regain control of the animal he was grabbed by the neck and a cold blade pressed against his throat. The scent of blood enveloped him.

"No closer, friend, or it'll be the last step you take." A hand pressed against his windpipe. But he knew the voice.

He coughed. "Have you run mad, Erin? It's me, Brett."

The hand about his throat loosened, then he was released altogether.

"Oh, thank the Goddess. You're here just in time. I didn't know what to do."

"In time for what?" He could see her now, could see her hands were covered in blood. "What's happened?"

"I couldn't stop the bleeding for ages–"

From the cluster of boulders beyond the horse came a thin infant wail. Brett knew then whose blood it was on the girl's hands.

CHAPTER FOUR

Weaver couldn't have told how he found himself in the throne room that morning. But he was standing there, with the priestess and Durstan to his right. He was becoming resigned to these lapses of memory – to coming to an awareness of his surroundings with no recollection of how he'd got there, or of his purpose in being there. He scarcely troubled to question his orders from the prelate and the priestess any more, even though he harboured resentment against every word they spoke. He was forced to throw in his lot with them for now. Had he been given a choice he knew he would have chosen otherwise but the fog that obscured his mind hid the reasons from him. Yesterday...

Yesterday...

Or it may have been the day before. But he knew he had held a sword in his hand.

The great doors to the throne room swung open and the assembled courtiers made their obeisance as the king, followed by his entourage, entered the room. Once again, the new queen was among them. As Weaver straightened up she caught his eye for the briefest of moments. Her expression was cold as stone. Yesterday she had left the arena after he and Rekhart had fought. The name sprang to his mind as abruptly as the fog receded. He and Rekhart had fought. Every step and every parry of that dread fight came to his mind, and suddenly the pain in his side was explained. He and his friend of how many years' standing? At least a decade. He and his friend had done their utmost to kill one another. And Rekhart ought to have won – by all the laws of nature, that blow to his chest should have killed Weaver. He should not be the one standing here now. The moment of clarity was unsettling; perhaps the fog that so frequently occluded his mind was to be preferred.

Vasic had seated himself on his throne and was speaking. "... Lord Marwick's untimely death it is meet that I expand my personal guard. With immediate effect I shall appoint the soldier known as Pius to their ranks." He looked over at Durstan. "We will discuss the further terms of our agreement in private at the end of this court session."

The priestess glanced over at Weaver. Something had displeased her – and not Weaver's appointment to the king's personal guard. Marwick's death, then. Had she had some dealings with the old man behind Durstan's back? It seemed unlikely. More likely, perhaps, that measuring her success against Weaver's would jeopardise her position in Durstan's eyes. Whatever the truth of it, they must have reached the parting of the ways. Thank the Goddess. The priestess's presence abraded his soul, a constant reminder of things he ought to recall but could not. There were moments when he felt close to grasping the missing pieces, but... She'd told him she'd help him remember, but she'd done no such thing. She'd used him as her personal servant and treated him like...

The kitchen boy. Lying strapped to a heavy stone bench, arms tied down so he couldn't move. His eyes fixed on Weaver, as if he expected him to help. As if he trusted him. That three-sided blade, efficient but ruthless. And when he'd turned away she'd been there watching, Tresilian's priestess...

Tresilian. An awareness of failure washed over him. He'd betrayed his king, in thought, in word and in the flesh...

"You will take your orders only from me, or from Sir Kaith." Vasic's voice intruded, sharp and hectoring as if he was repeating his words. "Is that understood?"

An answer was required. "Yes, your highness." Weaver bowed.

"My steward will see you are furnished with suitable accommodation and livery then you will return here within the hour to take up your duties."

A man Weaver presumed was Vasic's steward appeared before him and led him away down the length of the throne room. Vasic was addressing Durstan.

"How many more such men can you bring me?"

Durstan's reply was lost to Weaver as they stepped out through the double doors.

CHAPTER FIVE

Alwenna's recollections of the journey were hazy at best, but the pain tearing through her abdomen was very real. She had the vaguest memory of the stitching process, Brett helping hold her still as Erin stitched the wound across her abdomen with linen thread teased from her own garments. They'd given her some kind of herbal infusion that had rendered her thoughts sluggish, and had the effect of shoring her up in a dim place where there was nothing but her pain.

The sun was high in the sky when they drew near to Scarrow's Deep, riding through sweltering heat. Dust caked Alwenna's lips. It was Erin's turn to carry the baby – they'd wrapped her in linen torn from their undergarments to protect her from the sun – while Brett rode his horse alongside. They'd all agreed Alwenna had enough to do just staying in the saddle. Even that simple task was almost beyond her. She was startled from a half doze by the shout of a watchman at the entrance to the valley; another instant and she'd have slipped from the saddle. As it was, pulling herself upright jerked the stitches across her belly. She pressed her hand to her newly slack stomach. She wasn't really about to spill her innards over the ground, it just felt that way. Or so she hoped.

Ahead of them, Rina had stepped out of her doorway, peering down at them with one hand shielding her eyes from the glare of the sunlight. Pieten came running down the slope to hold the horse's head as Alwenna dismounted, with Erin's and Brett's assistance. She waited, hunched over, for the biting pain across her abdomen to subside before she could begin to walk up the slope to where Rina waited, arms folded.

"You didn't stay away long, then." Rina's eyes moved to the bundle Erin carried.

"No." Alwenna's voice was hoarse. Speaking felt like too great an effort. "We have need of freemerchant hospitality once more. I trust you will not turn us away, if only for the sake of the child."

Rina's mouth twisted. "The child is blameless. You will have whatever you need."

Because of the child, and only because of the child. Her expression made that clear.

"I thank you for your generosity." Alwenna raised her hand to her shoulder in the freemerchant gesture and Rina responded in kind.

"The healer Jenna has returned. I will send her to you."

The cave chamber was much as they had left it, albeit with a deeper drift of dust across the floor. Erin shook the faded blankets outside before Alwenna lay down on the bed, trying to ignore the spasm of pain as her stomach muscles tugged the stitches.

Brett appeared a few moments later, clutching a wooden box. "Ma says you can have use of this."

Alwenna stared at him blankly.

"It's a cradle. She's looking out some bedding for it, too."

"That's kind of her." It was certainly unexpected.

"She's soft for children, and babies especially." Brett grinned. "You'll see."

CHAPTER SIX

Vasic's new queen was not content. She wandered from room to room in the private quarters in a restless fashion, examining everything, but, Weaver suspected, in reality seeing nothing. Marten accompanied her, keeping up a flow of idle chatter in an attempt to divert her from her melancholy. She paused at a glazed cabinet where various items were displayed, many of them gifts that it was diplomatic to keep in a prominent place.

"What about these? Such lovely pieces of jewellery and pottery, and right there in among them a dagger. It seems terribly out of place. It's not even sheathed."

"It is a particularly fine dagger, is it not?" Marten stepped alongside her to study it.

Weaver kept his eyes straight ahead. If the freemerchant was playing foolish games with the new queen, it was none of his business.

"It looks a particularly deadly dagger, if you ask me." She stooped to study it closer. "Why, I think I can see dried blood on it – right there in the engraving."

Marten inclined his head. "It is true, it has proved deadly in the past. There are those who say it will bring ill luck on the bearer."

"Why on earth would Vasic keep such a thing? Was it a gift from some important diplomat?"

"It was a gift."

She looked up. "That's the shortest sentence I've ever heard from you, freemerchant. Now I'm convinced there's a story behind it. How do you know?"

"How, my lady?" Marten glanced over his shoulder at Weaver, the only guard in the room. "The answer is simple enough: I brought it to him."

"You did? But why?"

"I could not throw myself upon the king's charity empty-handed. I had to prove I could be useful to him."

"And so you brought him an ill-fated dagger?"

Marten spread his hands apologetically. "I had to work with what was at hand, my lady. And you will admit it is a most beautiful thing."

She peered into the case. "It is, at first glance. But when I look more closely it makes me uneasy."

"You have good instincts, my lady. You would not, I think, venture to handle such a thing."

"No, I would not."

"Then you are wise beyond your years."

"Do you think so?" She looked up at Marten again. "If I were wise I would ask you to explain why you gifted such a fell thing to my husband."

Marten smiled. "But, my lady – it is because you are so wise that you do not ask such a question."

"Because you would not tell me the truth?"

"Because you already know the answer, in your heart. And you know if you were told a dangerous truth, you would feel honour-bound to warn your husband. As long as your answer is no more than surmise and guesswork, the blade is no more than a riddle to divert you in idle moments, and your doubts about it can be dismissed as irrational. And certainly nothing to concern anyone else here at Highkell."

She glanced once more at the dagger. "Do not speak so

lightly of such things, freemerchant. I have this uneasy feeling in recent days–"

The door opened and a man strode in, wearing travel-stained clothing. He approached Drelena then dropped to one knee. "My queen, I have done as you asked, and I bring you this reply." His accent carried more than a hint of the Outer Isles. He kept his eyes lowered and offered up a sealed parchment scroll to her.

Her hand trembled as she reached to take it from him. "I must thank you, Bleaky. I had thought the task quite beyond you." She spoke with cold detachment.

The newcomer kept his head lowered, but the fingers of the hand that rested over his knee clenched. "Whatever you ask of me, I will do, your highness."

Marten watched the exchange with undisguised curiosity.

Drelena frowned at the newcomer. "Well, you had better not grovel there any longer, Bleaky. At your age it cannot be good for your knees." She turned to Marten with a bright smile. "I do not know if you have met my father's loyal servant? Marten, may I introduce to you Bleaky. He has served my father's household since I was a child. Of course, I should call him Master Bleaklow really, but it has been our little joke these past years. He is not prone to laughter. Do see if you can cheer him up."

She smiled too brightly, then turned away to the stairs. "I beg you will excuse me, gentlemen. This matter requires my immediate attention."

Bleaklow stood up from where he knelt, his colour high and his movements ungainly, a profound contrast to his courtly demeanour of moments ago. He nodded to Marten. "Sir."

Marten bowed. "It is a pleasure to meet you."

"Likewise, I'm sure." Bleaklow studied the freemerchant with undisguised mistrust.

Marten smiled blandly. "It is good that the Lady Drelena

should have some familiar faces about her here at Highkell. She is far from home, and, dare I suggest, far from happy."

Bleaklow grimaced. "That is not my doing, and I'm the last person to make amends."

Marten spread his hands wide with a slow smile. "My friend, I would never suggest such a thing. I merely sought to alert you to possible changes in the Lady Drelena's circumstances. I am sure as a longtime servant of her family such things would be important to you."

"Of course. But the Lady Drelena holds me in dislike since I was the one to bring her here."

"She does not strike me as a resentful person – quite the opposite. It seems to me she cares deeply for the people about her."

"What are you implying?" Bleaklow raised his chin.

"Goddess, nothing. Nothing at all. It is an admirable quality in one of her rank – the Lady Drelena will never disdain her inferiors."

"Well, no, that is true. She has always been..." Bleaklow fell silent, seeming to decide he'd already said more than he ought.

Marten smiled. "The warmth of her personality is infectious, is it not? We are blessed to have her among us at Highkell."

"Indeed." Bleaklow bowed stiffly. "Pray excuse me. I have other business to attend to." Bleaklow hurried from the room.

Marten studied the dagger in the cabinet for a few moments before turning casually to Weaver. "That Bleaklow seems a pleasant fellow. He reminds me very much of you, Weaver. So very determined to do his duty, whatever it may cost him."

The freemerchant hadn't changed, then. Still determined to probe until he'd learned a man's innermost secrets.

"I do not criticise, Weaver. Quite the opposite: I am reminded of myself, too, although I was never so wedded to duty. Not to the extent that you were. Some people – dare I say some ladies? – inspire our loyalty so that we give up our hearts even though our minds tell us we should not."

Maybe if the freemerchant got some kind of answer he'd leave him in peace. "Yet you still can't help playing your games, freemerchant?"

"Freemerchant no more, my friend. But in other respects, yes, it is very like old times. Have you changed so very much?"

How to answer such a question? The truth was, Weaver didn't know. He didn't know his own mind. Sometimes, when he first woke, he didn't even know his own name. But in the end he didn't need to reply – Marten seemed to have found the answer in his silence.

"No, I thought not." Marten took a step towards the door, then paused. "You were ever particular about who employed you, Weaver. I might have a task for you soon – something more to your liking than your duties here. Would that interest you?"

"You were ever fond of dangerous games, freemerchant. It could be I'm ready to live a quiet life."

"But you do not refuse."

"No, I do not refuse. Not yet."

"We will talk again, my friend. You may count upon it." The freemerchant strolled out of the room.

After a moment, Weaver walked over to the cabinet Drelena had been examining. He had to lean down to see the dagger clearly, but he knew it on first sight. The hair on the back of his neck prickled with foreboding. He'd held that blade in his own hand once, and drawn the blood of one he'd sworn to protect. May the Goddess forgive him.

CHAPTER SEVEN

The priestess shuffled the food around on her plate, but she had no appetite. That soldier was there again, watching her from the far side of the table. The one she'd seen with Marwick the day of the champions' fight. Peveril they called him. Let him try pushing her off the citadel walls the way he had the old man. Just let him try. And he hadn't even benefitted from Marwick's death – that skinny Kaith had smoothly taken his place, and the freemerchant had been there to step into his place just as readily. But the soldier didn't seem unduly dismayed that the recent spate of promotions hadn't included him. He grinned across the table at her and winked.

At her side the prelate continued working his way through his meal, oblivious to his surroundings. Weaver would have noticed the soldier, but now he was officially attached to the king's household he no longer joined them at table. Weaver had not been exactly talkative, but at least he had been there, between them often as not. And, bar the one time, Weaver hadn't been in the habit of calling her "Miria". And Weaver hadn't constantly been urging her to put herself in the king's way. The prelate really had no idea. He was due to return to the summer palace shortly to prepare the order to transfer to new premises Vasic had gifted them. He still seemed to nurture the illusion she could remain at Highkell to discover all Vasic's innermost secrets. There was little chance of that now.

People had trod more warily around her once she had become Vasic's favourite – at least for a while. Now she caught those same people looking sideways at her, as if wondering why she was still at court since her fall from favour. Her hope was Vasic might soon tire of his new queen; there could be no doubting the Lady Drelena held him in no great affection. The queen had been unable to hide her disgust at the fight between Rekhart and Weaver. Vasic was not the sort of man to heed such subtleties. A quiet word at the right moment might open his eyes to his bride's distaste. But it would need to be done with care...

"You were Vasic's piece, right?" The bench upon which she sat lurched as Peveril sat down beside her, grinning. "You're likely at a loose end now he's got himself a new bride."

She clasped her hands in her lap. "I have many duties in service of the Goddess."

"What, Vasic wasn't the only one? That wouldn't please him..."

The man must be drunk. At her other side Durstan continued to eat, oblivious.

"It's no concern of yours."

"You say that now. I'm a man that's going places: you could do a lot worse."

That was one way of putting it. Seemed to her he was a man likely to die an early and violent death. But he'd made it this far and he'd let nothing get in his way... She glanced at him. His appearance had nothing to recommend him, but they had been raised in the same school of life.

He leaned closer. "What do you say? There's not much goes on round here without me hearing about it."

"I am sworn to serve the Goddess."

"So I saw." His grin was more of a leer. "I see a lot of things. Things like our new queen meeting with that advisor of her father's in private – he doesn't know I've been watching him, but he's sweet on her. An' that freemerchant's been hanging about, too."

She studied him dispassionately. "And why should I believe what you tell me?"

"I scratch your back an' you scratch mine, see? Could be there's an opportunity for us both, given a nudge to help things along. Vasic wouldn't hear out the likes of me, but you... well... you might have a better chance."

"Not while he has eyes for no one else but his new bride."

"He'll tire of her soon enough."

"And you'd have me spread lies about her? Why would I do that?"

"What's to say I'm not tellin' you the truth? He sets her aside, you'll be his favourite again."

"And?"

"Then we can be useful to one another, see?"

"You mean I'd be beholden to you."

"Think of it as a partnership." Peveril grinned and stood up. "Keep your eyes open for a day or two – see if I'm not right."

Durstan finally set down his eating knife. "What did that fellow want?"

"Nothing honourable. Your man, Weav– Pius, kept his kind away."

Durstan frowned. Whether at her mistake or Peveril's insolence she could not tell. "Once we have the new chapter house you won't need to eat here."

That was months away. In the meantime she would indeed keep her eyes open. There might be some way to turn the new queen's discontent to her own advantage, with or without Peveril's assistance.

CHAPTER EIGHT

Drew had lost track of how many days he'd been held captive in the bowels of the citadel. He could no longer gauge the time by the condition of the open wound on the side of his head since it had begun to heal over. By the blessing of the Goddess this room was not as dark or as rank as the dungeon he'd once shared with Weaver and his friends – it at least boasted some light and fresh air from slots set high in the wall. He guessed it was a cellar intended for storage and brought into duty as cells following the collapse of the main tower. But the guards were surly and prone to beating any prisoners who dared so much as raise their eyes to their faces when they brought in their meagre rations of bread and water.

The atmosphere in the place was such that no one spoke for fear of bringing the guards' wrath down upon them. Thus it was when the guards came for him he sat with his head down and eyes focused on the floor until a swift kick of his shins told him he was being addressed.

"You there, get up. You have a visitor." Drew was convinced he could hear the clink of coin from the man's pocket.

No one had visitors in these places. It must mean torture: he'd be racked for another confession, to Goddess knew what this time. The guards dragged him through to another, smaller storeroom, which smelled of smoke from a torchère mounted on one wall. The smoke made his eyes water so much he didn't notice the figure standing across the room at first glance.

The guards shoved him back against the wall before leaving the room. "Five minutes, right? No longer." The door clunked shut.

"Well, Drew."

He recognised the voice in a heartbeat. "Jervin?" This was it: he was to be freed. This had all been a terrible misunderstanding – perhaps Rekhart, in his melancholy, had lied about Drew, perhaps–

"You don't imagine anyone else would trail through this squalor to see you, do you?"

Drew raised his eyes so he could see Jervin. The light of the torchère flickered over his face, making his expression appear to shift between compassion and monstrous glee.

"I... No." He was right. No one else in the world would be bothered.

"Aren't you pleased to see me?"

"Of course." Drew stayed where he was, against the wall at the opposite side of the chamber from Jervin. The manacles on his wrists dragged downwards, biting into his skin. "I didn't expect it, that's all."

"No." Jervin's voice was thoughtful. "Neither did I. But you were keen for me to give people second chances, and..."

Was he planning to free him? Could he even do that? Fool, of course he could. Jervin had a habit of getting his own way, no matter what the law stated. Drew's eyes were watering from the smoke. Goddess knew what the torchères were made of, the smoke was acrid.

Jervin took a couple of steps closer. "Right now I see nothing much to recommend the practice."

"You hit me round the head."

"You asked for it." Jervin shrugged. "But if we're to talk second chances we can forget all that happened. Put it behind us."

"Can we?" Was he really going to set him free, or was this some sick joke on Jervin's part?

"We can go back to Brigholm and forget any of this happened."

Drew's heart leaped. They could. They could start over and it could all be like before. Could they? Could he, knowing what he knew now? And if he did, ignored all his misgivings over Jervin's business deals, how long before Jervin lost his temper again? Drew looked up, blinking. The light flickered and Jervin's face shifted: benign, monstrous. Benign, monstrous. Rekhart's tale of the ailing child thrown in the water... Jervin was a monster with many faces, and only one of those was the honest one.

Drew shook his head slowly. "No."

"What? I've come all the way down here and you refuse me?"

"Apparently. No one could be more surprised than I am myself." Drew managed to speak perfectly evenly.

Jervin took a step towards him, then halted. "You fool. I give you a second chance and you throw it back in my face. Well, this time I wash my hands of you."

"I'm sorry. I just–"

"You will be. I'll make sure of it if you ever set foot in Brigholm again."

Drew raised his eyes: the face he saw was monstrous. How could he ever have been fooled? He lowered his eyes again. "I won't. I doubt I'll ever get out of here."

"And you'll be well served. Like your friend Rekhart – did you hear your other friend, that soldier, killed him? Except Rekhart died quickly. You'll probably linger here for months and months, until you're finally too weak to draw another breath. Then – if they haven't started already – the rats will chew your face off. You fool." Jervin turned away.

"Rekhart? You're making that up."

"No. He'd served his purpose. Just like you." Jervin stepped out through the door and was gone.

The guards came back into the room, dragging Drew away from the wall and back to the ad hoc dungeon. He dropped down once more in his corner, wishing the place was a true dungeon, so the darkness would hide his pain from prying eyes.

CHAPTER NINE

The priestess was wishing she'd chosen some more comfortable place to wait. The draught from the window casement struck chill against the back of her neck, leaving her shivering. A pair of tallow candles gave out more odour than light, and precious little warmth. There was no danger of a guard posted here dozing off while on duty – freezing to death, more like. Goddess knew what it would be like in winter. Of one thing she was certain: she had no wish to find out. Unfortunately right now, Highkell was her best hope of a secure future. She rubbed her arms. She would freeze entirely if she had to wait here much longer.

Just as she was convinced the Lady Drelena must have chosen another way this evening, she heard footsteps on the stairs above. She straightened up, rehearsing her lines again under her breath.

A moment later the queen appeared, two servants in her wake.

"Your highness... my lady. If I may beg a word in private with you?"

Drelena frowned. "In private? Can it not wait until after we have dined?"

The priestess glanced meaningfully at the two servants. "It will only take a few moments of your time, my lady." She lowered her voice, while making sure the two servants could still hear. "I have a message for you, from the freemerchant. He wishes to speak with you – he says it is a most urgent matter."

"Indeed? Could he not tell me himself?"

"It concerns your father's loyal servant, my lady. The freemerchant says it is urgent."

As she had hoped, that caught Drelena's attention. "Has he brought more news from home?"

"I believe he may have, my lady." This was what the queen wanted to hear. "He mentioned a letter – that is all I know."

Drelena drew in her breath sharply. "He might have come to me himself with this news. Where is he?"

"He said he would wait for you in the deserted tower, my lady, in the old throne room. He said it might attract notice if you were seen together in the main palace. And… he told me to say if you do not wish to meet him he will understand."

"This is all nonsensical." Drelena glanced to where her two maidservants were waiting.

The priestess folded her hands in her lap. "Shall I tell him you will not meet him, my lady?"

"No. I shall tell him myself what I think of this nonsense. It is close enough by, after all. You two, go ahead. I shall join you in the great hall in a few minutes." She turned to the younger woman. "I know the way. Vasic showed me where they have begun the repair work. You do not need to guide me."

"Are you sure, my lady? I do not mind."

"It is not for you to mind. It is for me to decide."

"I beg your pardon, my lady." The priestess curtseyed, then followed after the two servants. She would sooner be in the warmth of the great hall than trailing about after a pampered queen anyway.

Drelena watched the priestess hurry away. She knew well enough the girl had been something to Vasic before her arrival at Highkell. And she would sooner not follow her alone through dark hallways. She could not pinpoint any one thing, but something about the girl's grey eyes left her uneasy. And why the freemerchant chose to use her for his message was anyone's guess. But none of that mattered: if there was another letter from home – or, more particularly, from Darnell – she would sooner read it far from watchful eyes.

And if this piece of nonsense turned out to be some fancy of the freemerchant, then she would tell him in no uncertain terms what she thought of him for dragging her all the way out here on a cold night. The anteroom to the former king's tower was unlit. Deciding she couldn't trust her eyes to adjust to the darkness Drelena went back to the room before and prised one of the tallow candles loose from its holder. Hot tallow splashed on the back of her hand, stinging. This was a piece of foolishness and no mistake. But of course Marten couldn't have illuminated the path for her, for then their meeting might be noticed. And if he had another letter from Darnell… Bleaky probably wouldn't have wanted to approach her himself, not after their last meeting. She had been overly harsh towards a loyal servant. She ought to set things right. And so she would, the very next morning if she did not see him at table tonight.

Drelena crossed the anteroom in silence, shielding the candle flame with her hand. It guttered as she stepped into the draught from the door to the old throne room. She paused, waiting for the flame to steady before stepping through the doorway. There was no sign of anyone else in the room: no light, no scent of smoke. She took a couple of steps forward, wondering if Marten might not have arrived yet. At the far side of the room, the ragged edge of the collapsed wall was silhouetted against the moonlight.

The skin on the back of her neck prickled with unease. This was foolish beyond belief. That priestess was playing some trick on her. Then she heard the softest of footsteps. Was someone there in the room after all? She would not wait to find out.

Drelena turned back to the door, and had taken a step towards it when a heavy blow crashed against the side of her head. She staggered forwards, dropping the noxious candle. The flame went out, plunging her into a dizzying darkness, clouded by a thousand swarming pinpricks of light. She lost her balance and would have fallen, but for the hands that caught hold of her and dragged her upright.

"Be careful now, your highness. You need to mind your step up here."

Not Marten's voice.

Not Bleaky.

A hand clamped over her mouth and nose. She clawed at the hand, kicking and flailing in an attempt to break free. Her assailant spun her about and dragged her across the floor.

"Steady on, my lady, you don't want to hurt yourself."

Still dizzy, she felt cold air whisper against her face and struggled harder. She had been so foolish. Abruptly the hands released her.

Off balance, Drelena stumbled sideways. She found nothing but empty air beneath her foot.

CHAPTER TEN

Two soldiers led Marten to the throne where Vasic waited. The king's expression suggested scarce-suppressed rage. Before Vasic, hands bound, knelt the priestess. At her side was the messenger boy Marten had been using for errands since his arrival at court, similarly bound while his face bore the marks of rough handling. Marten knew a moment's gratitude that he had at least been treated as befitting an officer of the court. He'd been dragged from his bed with little ceremony, but no ill treatment. The soldiers released him and stepped back, although they remained within arm's reach.

Marten bowed. "Highness, I am your humble servant."

"Indeed?" Vasic glared at him. "Then you must humbly explain this sorry tale I've been told."

"I will if I am able, your highness. Has there been some misunderstanding?"

Kaith was standing off to one side of the throne, his expression grim.

"One might say that." Vasic drummed his fingers on the arm of his throne. "You were not present at table last night, Marten."

"No, your highness. I dined in my rooms last night." His head ached dully from the wine he'd drunk to drown his sorrows.

"Is that so? Might one enquire why?"

Had Vasic learned of the planned meeting? "I was not in a sociable mood last night, your highness." Was this why Drelena hadn't turned up? Her seat beside Vasic's was empty. This was unusual – she always made a point of attending the morning court sessions alongside her husband.

"And not because you conspired to meet my wife that evening?" Vasic's glare was stony.

"Conspired, your highness? No." This was not good. "I was handed a note requesting that I meet her urgently, but no one was there. I guessed it must have been some courtier's trick and I was annoyed with myself for being taken in."

Kaith spoke up. "And can anyone vouch for your story?"

"It is no story, sir, but the truth. I threw the note on the fire. I don't think I spoke to anyone yesterday evening. But there were servants at work who saw me as I made my way to the herb garden." The situation was going from bad to worse. "The boy there handed me the note." He indicated the boy kneeling before the throne.

Kaith moved forwards to study the prisoners. "The same boy who took the message to priestess Miria?"

"That boy, right there. He's often run errands for me. I didn't think to question it when he brought me the note."

The boy straightened up. "It's true, I took him a note, your highness."

Vasic glared at him. "And did the queen give you the note?"

He shook his head. "No, your highness. It was her." He pointed to the priestess.

"I did no such thing, your highness. The poor boy is easily confused – he must have mistaken me for one of the queen's servants."

"But it was her!"

"Silence, boy." Vasic glowered at the boy until he lowered his head once more.

The priestess spoke up again. "Pray forgive him, your

highness. His wits are lacking and he often misremembers. This boy told me–"

"I did not! She lies! I–"

A soldier cuffed the lad round the ear. The boy hunched over in miserable silence.

"This boy told me," the priestess repeated in a calm voice. "He brought me the message and when I saw the queen on the way to dine I passed it on to her, word for word as I told you, your highness."

"And then what happened?"

"She sent her servants on ahead and said she would deal with this nonsense. I offered to go with her, but she said she would go alone. If I had only disobeyed her…" Her voice broke as if her throat was constricted. Her shoulders heaved and she drew a gulping breath then fell silent, head lowered.

Marten spoke up. "Your highness, the boy is slow of understanding, but I have found him reliable on the whole. Surely the Lady Drelena can tell us if she did indeed send the note?"

A gasp from behind told him he'd said something terribly wrong.

Vasic's fingers closed over the arms of his throne, knuckles white. "Do you think to jest at a time like this?"

Kaith leaned closer to the throne, keeping his eyes on Marten. "I believe he speaks the truth, your highness."

"You think so?" Vasic turned his gaze away from Marten.

"I'm sure of it, sire. We will question the servants who would have been in that part of the building – it will be easy enough to prove the truth of what he says."

Someone nearby cleared their throat. "Your highness, if I may be so bold. I saw the freemerchant going out into the herb garden, just as he said." Bleaklow stepped forward. "I was on the way from my quarters to the great hall."

Bleaklow was ashen-faced and his expression even more

sombre than usual. Only then did the reason for Drelena's absence dawn on Marten.

Kaith straightened up. "There we have it, your highness."

Vasic's eyes narrowed, but he nodded slowly. "Freemerchant, you may go about your duties." He turned to Kaith. "But we will have the truth of this. Have the boy questioned properly – I will know who brought him that note."

"What of the girl, your highness?" He nodded towards the priestess.

"Release her. She has told us all she knows."

Vasic withdrew and the courtiers drifted into little knots of people, discussing the news in subdued voices. Marten took Bleaklow by the arm. "I thank you for your intervention – I had not numbered you among my friends."

"Nor should you, if you caused her so much as a moment's trouble."

"Never would I. But by the Goddess, what was all that about?"

Bleaklow studied his face in silence. "It is true, then. You really do not know. Come with me, we cannot speak here." He led the way out of the throne room at a brisk walk. Only when they had reached the courtyard did he slow down. Bleaklow checked no one was nearby to overhear before he spoke.

"Last night..." He paused to clear his throat. "Last night, the Lady Drelena fell to her death from the old throne room."

Marten's gut churned in shock. "Goddess, no. How could such a thing happen?"

Bleaklow shook his head. "It was suggested... she had rebuffed your advances, and you pushed her. Had I not seen you myself at the far side of the palace, I might believe that still." He spoke in haste, as if he forced the words out before he could change his mind.

"You do not know me well enough to see that such a thing is not in my character, but I offer you my deepest condolences, nonetheless."

Bleaklow didn't speak for the best part of a minute. "That priestess had them all convinced for a while: it seems to me she wishes you ill."

"Someone must, to have sent me that letter. Unless it was the Lady Drelena herself – and that I cannot believe."

"Nor can I." Bleaklow's voice was sharp.

The fire had been almost out last night when Marten dropped the note in it. He recalled one edge curling and blackening in the embers before he'd dropped down on his bed in a wine-fogged stupor.

"Would you know her writing if you saw it?"

Bleaklow nodded. "I would."

Back at Marten's room, they found a portion of parchment remained in the grate. It was blackened and discoloured, but the handwriting remained legible.

Bleaklow studied it with a frown. "It looks much like her hand, and yet… I cannot imagine her forming her sentences in such a way. She was ever direct."

The Lady Drelena's body lay in state in the great chapel. Marten went down there alone that evening, expecting to find the place deserted, but Bleaklow was sitting there, keeping vigil. Marten would have turned away and left him in solitude, but Bleaklow looked around. Even by the candlelight it was possible to see his eyes were swollen and red-rimmed.

"Forgive my intrusion. I wished to pay my respects when it was quiet."

Bleaklow nodded, but that was all his reply.

Marten approached the stone slab where her body rested. From this angle, her face appeared near-perfect, marred only by a large bruise on her temple. Only now was it possible for him to believe her life had truly been cut short. He knelt, murmuring words to commend her to the care of the Goddess and the Hunter. He doubted she would have minded a freemerchant blessing –

her confidences on her unease at being so far from home told him they had at least that in common. Marten stood, leaning over to set a hand on her forehead in farewell, and he froze. The one side of her face was as perfect as in life, but the other… It had been bound up with care, but it was impossible to hide the fact one side of her skull had been smashed beyond recognition, the right eye socket clearly empty beneath closed lids.

He turned away, bile rising in his throat, and fought to master himself.

"They say now she must have taken her own life." Bleaklow's voice was hoarse. "Suffering homesickness, and shame at her feelings for a common freemerchant." There was a note of accusation in his voice.

"Then they are fools. She would never have done such a thing." Marten turned back to the open coffin and looked closer at that great bruise. It extended back beneath her hairline, across the side of her head. He steeled himself to look again at the crushed wreckage of the other side of her face.

"Forgive me, Bleaklow… I know this must distress you, but can you tell me, if she fell on her right side, how did the left side of her face come to be bruised?"

Bleaklow stood up unsteadily. "Why… I… I don't know." He winced as he looked on her face and his hand trembled as he reached out to examine the bruise. "This, here? It… appears someone struck her before she fell. But, who would do such a thing? She could have had no enemies."

"It is unthinkable." Marten had difficulty speaking. "Yet, someone did. Whoever it was, they sought to implicate me every step of the way."

"You were conveniently attentive to her." Bleaklow's words weren't an accusation.

"She stood in need of friendship. The entire court should have been at her feet in adoration."

Bleaklow turned away.

Marten looked one last time on Drelena's broken features. It was abhorrent to think someone had been prepared to extinguish so vital a being simply to damage his reputation. Whoever it was, he had to move quickly.

CHAPTER ELEVEN

Weaver was pretty sure Vasic was drunk again, even though it was still early in the day. But this time the king was not slumped in his seat maudlin drunk, as he had been the past few days, but resentful, angry drunk. Spoiling for a fight drunk. Weaver knew the signs: the set of Vasic's jaw, the tic in his cheek, the steel in his eyes. Whether the king had the mettle to act on the impulse was another matter: he was the kind who avoided damaging his own hide whenever possible. He'd sooner beat a man who was shackled down than take one on as an equal. Weaver knew this from personal experience.

Today, Kaith had persuaded the king to hear some of the more urgent petitions. A week of strict mourning was enough, he'd insisted: long enough to hold matters of state in abeyance; long enough to demonstrate a proper regard for the deceased; long enough for a king to display proof of weakness. Any longer would be to invite trouble.

And so Vasic had sat through a succession of petitioning citizens. The last had been Jervin, again seeking action against the group of rival merchants who were undercutting the prices of those who paid their full dues.

Weaver studied Jervin's face: his portrayal of an outraged taxpayer was convincing. His outrage may indeed be real, if he'd failed to bring these traders to heel by other means. If

Weaver hadn't known Drew was languishing in a cell thanks to information laid by Jervin he might have been fooled entirely. Even the fog in Weaver's brain couldn't obscure the certainty that Drew had been a loyal friend, both to Weaver, and to the lady whose name he could not – or dared not – recall.

Vasic was likewise studying Jervin. "Marwick looked into this before his untimely demise. He concluded it is a matter for the local tax collectors and the city watch – and not worthy of royal intervention."

Jervin bowed. "Highness, in the Marches the people have been too far from the influence of the throne for too long. If I may be so bold, it requires the oversight of one with greater authority to bring them into line."

"Are you suggesting I must collect my own taxes now?"

"Never, your highness. But I would suggest you appoint a representative to oversee the matter who knows the Marches and who understands how best to deal with the people there."

"And where would you suggest I might find such a person?"

"Sire, if I may again be so bold, I stand in readiness to prove myself a loyal servant to the crown." Jervin bowed again. "I grew up in the Marches and I would not be resented by the local people as one from Highground or Meallgard might be."

Vasic steepled his fingers, studying Jervin. "You have never set foot in court before this month; why should I trust you to carry out this work?"

"Highness, let the results speak for me. If I do not bring in greater revenue from the Marches over the next year you may deal with me as you wish."

"Well, you're bold, I'll grant you that." Vasic glanced to where Kaith waited. "What say you, Kaith?"

Kaith stepped forward. "Jervin has already proven himself loyal in the matter of the renegade novice from Vorrahan. I believe his suggestion has much to commend it."

"Then you may see to the details of his appointment to the

crown's service. The Marches will be brought into line."

"As your highness wishes." Kaith bowed.

Jervin withdrew, bowing and uttering words of gratitude. Weaver watched uneasily. If anyone could wring money from the Marches, it would be Jervin. Across the room the pale-eyed priestess followed the scene, her expression impassive. It had not taken her long to insinuate herself into the king's good graces once more. Not that there was much of grace or goodness about this particular king. The priestess raised an eyebrow, as if she'd divined his thoughts.

"With that we can declare the business of today's court closed." Vasic would have stood up at that point but Kaith intervened.

"I beg your pardon, your highness, but there are two more petitioners. They have been waiting some considerable time already for the favour of your attention."

Vasic sat back, making no attempt to hide his annoyance. "Then let them waste no further time in speaking."

The first was a landowner who complained of the depredations of brigands destroying crops and stealing livestock. Marwick had promised a detachment of soldiers to help restore order.

Vasic pressed his fingertips to his forehead. "Kaith, see Marwick's orders are carried out. And someone bring me more wine." The final petitioner had to wait as Vasic's glass was refilled by a servant.

His business was more complex, a matter of a disputed title to land. Marwick had been due to preside over a hearing, but his sudden death had prevented that taking place.

Vasic had had enough. "Kaith, take the details, we will make a decision in due course." He glared around the room. "You are all dismissed."

The priestess hesitated at the edge of the chamber but Vasic gestured her away. "All of you. Leave me in peace. And close the doors. Not you, Weaver. You keep your sour face here."

Weaver resumed the rigid stance he'd held throughout the morning.

When the room had emptied, Vasic stood up from the throne, swaying for a moment, wine slopping over the edge of his glass. He made his way across the dais to where Weaver stood to attention.

"You've not got much to say for yourself, have you, soldier?"

"No, your highness."

"You were stubborn enough back in the day."

"Yes, your highness." Goddess knew where this was leading; nowhere good.

"That weasel-faced prelate claims you'll obey my every command without question."

"Yes, your highness."

"And he claims you're indestructible." Vasic took another mouthful of wine. "Have you nothing to say to that?"

Saying nothing would be safer. He could still picture the disbelief on Rekhart's face after he'd plunged his blade into Weaver's heart, yet Weaver had not fallen. The pain Weaver could hope to forget, but Rekhart's expression… "I find it hard to believe, your highness."

Vasic nodded. "You always were more astute than you appear. Even now." He swallowed the last of his wine and tossed the glass aside. It smashed, scattering a myriad fragments across the wooden dais. "But do you know what, Weaver? I, too, find it hard to believe." He took a couple of steps across the dais. Glass crunched beneath his boots. "Durstan's services are expensive. And I have learned of late to take nothing at face value: did I see what truly happened during that fight, or did I see what Durstan wanted me to see?"

"There were no illusions, your highness." Now Weaver understood.

"Is that so? Do you imagine I'll take your word for it, turncoat?"

"No, your highness."

"Indeed." Vasic drew his sword from its scabbard, studying Weaver's face for a reaction. "Let us put Durstan's handiwork to another test, shall we? A test of my own devising. You will stand there, and remain perfectly still while I run this sword through you. You will not move, or shout out, or protest in any way. Is that understood?"

If Weaver was accepting, if he didn't fight back, could this be the end to it? To think he might not wake another day to the aching sense of loss, to the crushing certainty of his own failure. If all it took in the end was obedience... "Yes, your highness."

Vasic smiled. "Very well then. Before I begin, you will remove your sword belt."

Weaver undid the buckle and pulled the belt from about his waist, dropping it and the scabbard on the floor nearby.

"And now you will remove that brigandine. I will not risk blunting my blade on it."

Weaver untied the fastenings one by one. Would Vasic require him to be bound, too, just to ensure his own safety? He guessed he would. Although the king would require a servant for that; he could hardly ask Weaver to bind his own hands. Weaver shrugged off the brigandine and padded jacket and dropped it on the floor next to his sword belt.

"The shirt, too. There's no point putting a hole in good linen."

Weaver tugged the neck loose and peeled the garment off over his head, dropping it with the rest.

Vasic studied him for a moment. "With the number of scars on you, one or two more should make little difference."

"No, your highness." Goddess, why wouldn't he get on with it? "Would you have me kneel, sire?"

Vasic tilted his head to one side, considering. "No. I want to see you fall."

"Very well, your highness. I believe I am ready."

For a moment Weaver thought Vasic's nerve would fail him,

but the king licked his lips and raised his sword, elbow high, smiling an odd, tight smile. "I believe you are."

Vasic drew in a breath, then plunged the sword between Weaver's ribs.

The pain was immense, as if Weaver's chest had been torn in two and the separated parts set on fire. Vasic withdrew the blade and Weaver sucked in a shuddering breath, waiting for the dread sensation of blood filling the cavities in his lungs. But he drew in only air, and though he swayed on his feet, he remained standing. Vasic lunged at him again and Weaver staggered back as the sword sliced into his belly, dropping to one knee as Vasic twisted the blade and withdrew it. He remained there, seemingly held up by the magnitude of his own pain, as Vasic stepped back to admire his handiwork.

"Well, now, soldier. I thought you would have fallen by now." With a high laugh, Vasic spun round and smashed the pommel of his sword into Weaver's face. It missed his left eye by a hair's breadth. Weaver was forced to set one hand on the ground to maintain his balance. He heard, rather than saw, Vasic take several steps away from him, boots crunching once more on the broken glass.

"How long should it take, soldier?"

What, death? Days, like as not. It had last time, in the cellar of the summer palace... What a time for his memories to regain focus. "I do not know, your highness."

"Stand up, then. Let us see what you are made of."

Weaver pushed himself to his feet and straightened up, fully expecting his body to fail under the effort, but it did not. The pain from his injuries should have brought him low, but he managed to stand without assistance. He had to press one hand to the wound in his belly to prevent his entrails spilling out.

Vasic stared at him a long while in silence, then went over to his throne and sat down, sword still in hand, pressing the fingertips of his left hand to his forehead.

"Leave me. Take your clothes with you, and leave me. Now."

"Very well, your highness." Weaver stooped to gather up his garments and sword belt with his free hand, stepping in his own congealing blood as he did so. He made his way stiffly down the steps of the dais, the pain so great he doubted he'd manage as much as half a dozen steps further, but somehow he held together. It was a long walk to the doors of the throne room.

Weaver paused at the end, one hand on the door handle. Vasic still sprawled in the throne, watching his progress. He didn't appear pleased with his morning's work. A trail of dark blood stretched from the pool on the dais, marking Weaver's progress along the throne room. He hadn't kept to an entirely straight line after all. Weaver found that oddly reassuring: some tiny part of him must still be fallible – and human.

"Go on, then, I dismissed you. Find a healer to clean you up. And send Durstan's bitch of a priestess to me."

Weaver tugged the door open and stepped out into the antechamber. A crowd had assembled there and they recoiled in horror as he approached them, stripped to the waist, blood-covered, clothes and sword clutched to his belly. Only the priestess stepped forward, eyes wide.

Weaver gestured towards the throne room. "The king wants you in there."

She nodded and slipped through the door.

Weaver made his way through the anteroom expecting with every step that the pain would overwhelm his body, but that moment never came. He ignored Vasic's order to see a healer and instead limped back to his quarters and dropped down on his bed. If he didn't wake in the morning it would be no great hardship.

CHAPTER TWELVE

The prisoners were sleeping when Marten had the guard unlock the cell door. Drew sat up hastily as he recognised the noise of the keys, blinking in the unaccustomed light of a lantern.

"You're to come with me, Drew."

Drew stood up slowly, easing his limbs. He asked no questions, but followed in silence behind Marten as he led the way up the stairs. Behind them the door banged shut and keys grated in the lock. Marten heard a low exhalation from Drew.

Marten opened the door to an unoccupied guardroom and ushered him inside. A bundle of clothing sat on the wooden bench. "We haven't much time." He reached down and unlocked Drew's manacles. The flesh of his wrists was rubbed raw beneath them. "The clothing there is for you, as is this royal pardon. All charges have been dropped and it has been noted in the official records." Drew gaped at him, but took the sheet of parchment he offered, examining it in disbelief.

"Is this real? Not... some kind of trick?"

"It is real. As of this moment, you are a free man."

Drew set the parchment down on the bench. "But...?"

This wasn't the naive novice who'd sailed from Vorrahan with the Lady Alwenna. "I understand you would not be welcome in Brigholm."

"No." The wonder on Drew's face clouded for a moment. "In the end I was not sufficiently grateful."

"Well, you'll find I'm not looking for gratitude."

"But my freedom has a price, nonetheless."

Marten inclined his head. "I have work for you, if you care to take it on."

"What sort of work? Is it legal?"

"It is legal. It is the sort of work you would be well suited to, if you are prepared to enter the precinct once again."

"That is a high price to ask." Drew shrugged off his filthy shirt and dropped it on the floor before donning the freshly laundered one.

"I realise that, but you are uniquely suited to the role."

"I'm listening." Drew removed his leggings and pulled on the clean ones. A leather pouch fell to the floor from the bench.

"It concerns the Lady Alwenna. I have learned the precincts in the Outer Isles boast extensive libraries. They have recorded many of the old ways, and hold extensive records of the royal family history and the seers' lore."

"I see. Is this to satisfy your curiosity in some way?" Drew picked up the leather pouch, twisting the fastening between his fingers.

"Not at all. This is to repay a debt to her. I understand from what little Vasic and his advisors have let slip that the seers are uneasy some great evil has awoken. That blade you recovered from the rubble is tied into it in some–"

"She needs that blade. Have you found some way to return it to her?" The youth's expression had become intense.

Marten nodded. "I believe I have – and that is why we do not have much time."

"You have it with you now, don't you?"

Again, Marten nodded. "And that is why I would charge you with this research. You understand enough of this business to grasp the import of what you read."

Drew flexed his fingers. "I understand next to nothing – but I have witnessed much that I do not understand."

"And that is more than the rest of us can say."

"You could hand me the dagger and I could take it to her." Drew made the suggestion sound almost casual.

"There is one better suited to that mission – one who will be less susceptible to the dagger's wiles."

Drew smiled ruefully. "If you knew the nightmares it gave me… even here since I've been under the same roof… I do not understand why it can still tempt me the way it does. Are you proof against it, Marten?"

"I gave it up once, and I shall again. Within the hour if we can settle your business now. Will you take on this task?"

"I never thought to return to the precinct," Drew said slowly. "But any journey that takes me further from the blade can only be a good thing."

Marten nodded. "So you'll do it?"

"I'll do it."

"Then I have letters of introduction for you, to go with that pardon. One recommends you to the lord convenor of the Outer Isles, the other to the prelate of the main precinct. They have been written by Master Bleaklow, trusted servant of the lord convenor. He is a good man. You will no doubt meet him there in the fullness of time."

Drew glanced at the letters before stowing them in the leather pouch. "He is here at court?"

"For the time being. There has…" The boy needed to know what he was getting into. "You should know the lord convenor's daughter, recently married to Vasic, died in a tragic accident last week."

Drew stilled. "Then it was she who… who fell? I dreamed of it. Goddess rest her. It was no accident, that much I can tell you."

"No, it was not, although is not yet common knowledge.

But... she will be avenged. In the meantime, you must learn what you can from the Outer Isles libraries. I could not have hoped to find a better man for this task."

CHAPTER THIRTEEN

The commotion at the entrance to the valley caught Alwenna's attention immediately. She squinted into the morning sunlight: a rider on a common, cobby horse. Not a freemerchant, she guessed, as the guards held him back from entering the valley proper. She set down the bucket she had been carrying and raised one hand to shield her eyes from the sun, ignoring the twinge of protest from her newly healed scar.

The man carried himself like Weaver. He climbed down from his horse and moved aside with one of the guards. They spoke, their attitudes calm. Then she saw the guard nod. Both men turned her way and the guard raised his hand, pointing. Her stomach knotted, before realising he pointed towards Marten's home. The newcomer did not remount, but led his horse across the canyon floor in the wake of the guard. The newcomer moved in every way like Weaver. Her heart quickened. But it couldn't be, could it? Not after all this time? If it was him, wouldn't she have known beforehand?

Then again, her acuity had waned in recent weeks. She had believed she had learned to control it. Perhaps the dark power was fading now – it might have been linked with Tresilian in some way... Her marriage to her cousin might after all have been instrumental in bringing the whole thing about.

As if he sensed her scrutiny the newcomer paused and she

saw his shoulders twist as he raised his head and scanned the sloping ground where she stood. Again that knotting of her stomach. But how could it possibly be Weaver? A voice hailed the newcomer from a doorway further down the hill and Rogen strode out to meet them.

Alwenna could not help herself. She watched as Rogen approached the newcomers, then raised his ruined hand to his shoulder. The newcomer responded in freemerchant fashion. Voices carried to her on the breeze, the words indistinguishable, but the challenge in Rogen's voice evident. They vanished inside Rogen's quarters while a boy took charge of the horse.

She was tempted to go down to see what was happening, but the baby was due to wake soon.

Alwenna had finished feeding the baby and set her down to rest again when she heard footsteps outside. She moved over to the doorway and drew back the blanket covering the opening.

Weaver. Alwenna stared. Every contour of his face was familiar. The fine white scar on his chin still showed through the stubble. The set of his shoulders as he waited for her response was unmistakable. It was him, there could be no doubt. Yet, he was somehow subtly changed. He wouldn't hold her gaze, as if he feared – what? What could he fear from her? She owed him everything.

"Weaver." Her voice wasn't as steady as she would have liked. He looked sharply at her then. Goddess, could he ever forgive her for fleeing with Marten, leaving him behind in the burning building? How had he escaped? How had he found her – was he here now for revenge on Alwenna for leaving him? For killing his liege lord? For finally, at the very end, failing to trust him enough? Could she ever hope to make amends?

Weaver bowed, a creditable court-style effort.

"Your servant, my lady."

She shivered. They had so much to say, so many questions to ask, and to answer, but she had no idea where to start.

"You survived."

"After a fashion."

"I thought…" She sat down on the boulder outside the door. "Forgive me, this is a shock."

"It was a shock to me, too, my lady."

Was he attempting humour? She squinted up at him, but his expression was as hard to read as ever. "How so?"

"Death, my lady. It is not comfortable."

"Then you are… You were…"

"I am the newest member of the grey brethren. Although Durstan has plans to change that soon enough."

"Durstan?"

"Prelate of the order at the summer palace. He has joined forces with Vasic now. Much has changed these past weeks."

"Then why are you here?"

"Presently? I am Marten's messenger boy. After that… it rather depends on you."

"You have seen Marten?"

"He is at Highkell, delighting the courtiers with his wit."

"Then you all now serve Vasic?"

"No, my lady. It was expedient for a time, that is all."

"Are you telling me you have turned coat?"

"After a fashion, my lady."

"Then how do I know I can trust you?"

"Alwenna, I died for you. What more can I do to prove my loyalty?"

Was he speaking the truth? Of course he was. Now he met her gaze unflinchingly. This was the man she'd mourned all these months. Returned to her. She stood up and reached out one hand towards him then halted. Her fingertips trembled. She had touched Tresilian all those months ago at the summer palace, and every fibre of her being had been revolted at the corruption she found there. The moment was etched on her mind forever, the sense of decay, of mould, of everything

that had once been good now bro
goodness had been sloughed away
Would Weaver now be similarly tain

There was only one way to find ou

Inside the rock chamber the baby cr
back inside the doorway, hurrying t
baby slept on, disturbed for a moment l

Weaver waited at the doorway. "The ealthy?"

Alwenna nodded, and gestured to Weaver to see for himself. "She is healthy."

"A girl then?" Weaver crossed the floor softly to look down at the sleeping baby. The curtain fell over the doorway behind him, muting the daylight, enfolding the three of them in some separate place, far from the intruding eyes of the rest of the world. "She is perfect. I see your likeness in her. And her father's."

It didn't seem to occur to him invoking Tresilian in that room was a bad idea. At first. Until he looked directly at Alwenna. "Those were better days. It is good that she is born from them. Do you not think so?"

"I suppose... I hadn't given it much thought. She is what she is." She moved over to stand next to Weaver. The baby shifted slightly in her sleep, flung one arm out sideways then settled again.

"You have done well, my lady." Weaver took her hand in his. She started at the unexpected contact, but she didn't pull her hand away. Beneath the calluses his hand was warm. She closed her fingers about his, letting his need for contact fuel her own. Goddess, how long had it been since they were last together? She'd believed this moment impossible.

And he was holding himself so carefully in check, she sensed. The sight told her it was so. She could sense the pulsing of blood through his veins, the beating of his heart, strong and true, pulsing away the memory of the moment it had stopped.

ving, turning away from the darkness, death, from ...ure, from disgust–

Goddess, Weaver. What did they do to you?"

His fingers tightened about hers. "For a long time I couldn't remember. Now I have… I have no wish to speak of it. My business now is living." He raised her hand to his lips and drew her closer. He was whole. She knew it. He had not been corrupted by the rites as Tresilian had been. Had Tresilian always been the weaker man? Weaver bent and kissed her. Why was she thinking of her dead husband? Perhaps at heart she was convinced Weaver would betray her the same way Tresilian had. Perhaps she would betray him.

She ran her hands up his chest, tugging at the drawstring of his shirt as he kissed her, slow and lingering. Then he drew her close and she turned her attention to unfastening the rest of his clothing, kissing him ever more hungrily.

As Weaver unlaced her gown Alwenna knew a moment's doubt.

"I have battle scars of my own, now."

Weaver slid a hand over her stomach. "Honourably won, my lady."

Since they had last lain together her body had been changed by the passage of the baby. Her stomach was still soft and flaccid where once it had been flat and firm. But he didn't seem to find her wanting. She thought no more of the past as they lost themselves in a present neither had believed possible.

CHAPTER FOURTEEN

The funeral procession stretched from Highkell right down the gorge. The Lady Drelena's body had to be carried out on a litter, just as she had arrived so few weeks ago. An abrupt communication from the Lord Convenor Etrus had made it plain it was not acceptable for his daughter to be interred so far beyond the sound of the sea. Inexplicably, Vasic had not argued with Etrus' demands. She was to be returned home to the Outer Isles, to rest there with her ancestors, a stone's throw from the shore.

Vasic walked now behind the litter, head bowed. To Marten's surprise, the king's grief for his queen seemed genuine. After the initial shock he had become sullen and withdrawn. No awkward questions had been asked about Drew's pardon, and Weaver's disappearance had not been remarked upon, if it had even been noted. A replica dagger rested undetected in the cabinet from which Marten had removed the ornate blade. He guessed both men should have reached their destinations safely by now. And he was glad to be on the way himself.

He would accompany the funeral cortège to the Outer Isles, as ambassador from Vasic's court. Once there... He might be wise to disappear, and never show his face again at Highkell, but he and wisdom no longer travelled together. Marten still had work to do there: that throne was the Lady Alwenna's by right. And the Lady Drelena's death would not go unavenged. Her killer would be brought to justice, unless Bleaklow got to him – or her – first.

The errand boy had died under questioning in the first frenzy to learn the truth about Drelena's death. Marten and Bleaklow had been unable to learn any more. Drew's nightmare had been too imprecise to tell them more than they had already guessed. The priestess was keeping herself to herself and appeared to be as subdued by the tragedy as everyone else at court. Durstan had delayed his journey to the summer palace to officiate over today's ceremony, intoning invocations to the Goddess as what seemed like the entire populace of Highkell had shuffled past the coffin, now mercifully closed, to pay their respects.

Bleaklow walked ahead of Marten in the procession, just behind Vasic. They had established a strange friendship. Marten could understand the intensity of Bleaklow's loyalty to the Lord Convenor and his family, although he suspected Bleaklow had felt rather more for the Lady Drelena than loyalty. Marten himself had admired her, but scarcely known her long to enough to form anything more than favourable first impressions, whatever the rumours said. The conviction someone had contrived her death to strike against him, however, that weighed heavily on his conscience. Even if he had not sworn to Bleaklow he would do everything in his power to bring the guilty party to justice he would still have felt honour-bound to do so. No, however little Marten relished the prospect, he must return to Highkell. And if he wished to return to Vasic's court and wield any influence at all, he must cover himself in glory in the Outer Isles. He had no illusions that would be easy.

And he had no business pondering such worldly considerations at a time like this. Disgusted with himself, he bowed his head and muttered a prayer to the Hunter for the Lady Drelena. Whatever else he might have to do when he reached the Outer Isles, he would have no need to feign grief.

CHAPTER FIFTEEN

It was still dark when Alwenna picked her way down the slope from the cave. Erin was still off somewhere with Malcolm, as Alwenna had expected. The baby in her arms stirred in her sleep and snuffled, wriggled a moment then drifted back into a deeper sleep.

She didn't have to do this.

She could turn around right now, set the baby back in the makeshift cot, lie down on the straw mattress next to Weaver, pretend none of this had happened. No one had seen her. She hesitated. There was nothing to say the elders had been right, after all. None of them wanted her here. She'd always been aware of that. The sleeping baby made a little sighing murmur.

Alwenna raised her chin, stiffened her shoulders and ignored the tug of pain from her scar. She had to do this for her child's sake. As long as there was a chance the elders were right – and she'd seen enough visions of her own not to question their judgement – as long as there was a chance she could protect her child, as long as she had breath to try to make a difference, she must act. She continued down the steep path. A small stone twisted beneath her foot and her ankle tightened, an echo of the old injury. A sharp reminder of Highkell. And the threat she would protect her child from, no matter what the cost.

She knocked softly at the door to the place that had once been Marten's home. There was no response so she knocked again a little louder, then rattled the handle. There was a mumble, then a scuffling sound as someone crossed the floor. With a scraping sound the bolt was drawn back.

Brett blinked at her in the moonlight. He was already tall enough to need to stoop beneath the lintel over the door.

"What–?"

"Wake your mother. I need to speak to her."

He frowned. "But – it's the middle of the night."

"She won't mind." Not this time.

The youth turned away from the door, but was taken up short by his mother's voice, low so as not to waken his brother.

"What is it, Brett? Is it your father after all?" She appeared at his side, drawing a shawl up round her thin shoulders. Her mouth tightened to a thin line as she recognised Alwenna. "Oh. What do you want?"

The carefully prepared speech fell away from Alwenna. She wound the fringe of the baby's shawl about her fingers. "I need to ask a favour of you."

"A favour? Of me? Have you run entirely mad?"

"Ma, there's no need for that."

"I can think of no one better fitted to care for a child." Alwenna rushed the words out before she could change her mind.

"To care for a child? Why?" The woman's eyes flicked to the sleeping baby's face again, her expression softening as she did so. Alwenna fought the urge to turn away, to run back up the hillside to her cave with the precious bundle.

Instead she held out her arms, offering the sleeping baby to Marten's wife. "Because I can't take her with me to the place I need to go." Her voice caught in her throat for a moment. "She'll be safer here with you. She'll be safe. I know it."

The woman reached out slowly, her eyes suspicious as they

rested on Alwenna's face, softening again as she focused on the child. She took the bundle gently, drawing her close, her expression suddenly hungry. "I can take care of her. How long will you be away?"

Alwenna drew a breath. "I won't be coming back." Her voice came out tiny, breathless.

The woman looked up sharply. "What do you mean?"

"I'm leaving. I have to, for all your sakes." She needn't tell them what visions she had seen. "I have enemies who… I mustn't let them find me here. And I mustn't let them find my child. That's… That's why I want you to care for her. I know you will keep her safe. I want you to raise her as one of your own. Let her call you mother, let her never know I exist."

"But–"

"That's the only way I can be sure she'll be safe."

The child stirred and the woman soothed her, cradling her in her arms with a new intensity. "How could anyone harm such an innocent?"

"They never will if I leave her here with you."

"But how can you possibly leave her?"

Alwenna drew a tight breath. "I must. If I stay with her it will destroy her. I would have her live and be free."

"I don't know how you can leave her."

"That's because you haven't seen what I've seen. There's one more thing. Marten sent the dagger back with Weaver: I must take it with me."

"So that's it. You would trade your own child for a worthless dagger."

Goddess, this was harder than she'd ever imagined. "It's the only way to ensure her safety. I will take the dagger – and its ill luck – far away and bother you no more."

The woman nodded. "What will I tell Marten if he returns?"

"Tell him what I have told you."

"He won't like it."

"All the more reason for me to go now. While he is far away."

"He'll blame me."

"Erin will back my word."

"She's not going with you?"

"No. Where I'm going, no one must follow. She will stay here and help you. She has already sworn to do so, although she doesn't realise the full extent of it yet."

Alwenna took a step back. The baby stirred again, as if she sensed her mother's intentions. "Raise her as your own. Name her as your own. Let her never know her true father's name. Will you do that?"

The woman nodded again, her eyes suddenly full in the moonlight. "You're serious, aren't you?"

It was Alwenna's turn to nod. She bit her lip to keep it from trembling. The sky was already beginning to lighten in the east. "I must go, before Erin returns."

The woman frowned. "And just like that, you would walk out on her?"

Still suspicious, even now. "Think what you will of me, Rina, but know this – you have misjudged me all along. Whatever you think of me, I know you will not judge the child because of it. I know my presence here has brought you grief. I hope now my daughter will bring you comfort."

"So you would sell her to me to ease your conscience? Do you tire of her as quickly as you tired of my husband?"

"Ma..." Brett, who'd listened in silence up to that point, stepped forward.

"Oh, think what you will. I haven't time to argue with you now." The sky was perceptibly lighter in the east.

"I may have wronged you, although I still cannot understand you." Rina nodded towards the chest on the floor. "Brett, get the key from under my pillow and give her the dagger."

Brett hurried to obey, handing Alwenna the cloth-wrapped bundle. She didn't need to open it to be certain what it contained. She stuffed it down inside one of the saddlebags and slung them over her shoulder once more.

"Let me accompany you, my lady." Brett glanced guiltily at his mother.

Alwenna shook her head. "It is better that you remain here."

Brett's mouth tightened, but he didn't argue.

Alwenna stepped outside and hurried down to the valley floor, turning back for an instant. The door was already closed. She rode out of Scarrow's Deep on the same stolen horse she had arrived on all those months ago. Behind her lay nothing but regret, and ahead of her nothing but danger. And in her saddlebag nestled the blade that had cut her family asunder. A chill wind carried distant voices to her but whether they cried out to her to turn back or to take a different road, she didn't know, as she refused to listen. She had no choice now, never had except in one thing – in leaving her firstborn with the bitter woman in her cliffside home.

CHAPTER SIXTEEN

Weaver stumbled through a fogbound landscape. She was always there, just out of sight. He could hear her voice, her laughter, the catch of her breath as he moved deep inside her. But when he reached for her she was not there. Beside him the place where she'd lain on the narrow bed was cold and empty. His head was thumping and he had the leaden feeling of one who'd overslept. He sat up, rubbing his eyes. The ropes supporting the scantily stuffed mattress beneath him dug into his buttocks. He swung his feet off the bed, setting them on the stone floor. His clothes lay there where they'd been abandoned the night before. Of Alwenna, there was no sign.

He didn't need to cross the room to the cradle to know it was empty. He was alone in there now. He picked up his travel-stained garments, shaking sand out of the leggings before he pulled them on and tied the drawstring waist. He pulled his shirt over his head, grimacing at the unwashed state of it. The floor of the cave was gritty beneath his feet as he picked up his boots and crossed over to the doorway.

Weaver pushed the curtain aside. The sun was still low in the sky but it must have been clear of the horizon a good hour or more already. The cool of the night was dissipating fast and already the air was warm against his face. Further down the slope children played, voices bright and sharp as they disputed the rules of their game. He envied their absorption. Thoughts and memories crowded in on him – things he'd believed lost beyond recall. Every moment of his life had been restored to him, as sharp and clear as the wine glasses Vasic used at Highkell. Had Alwenna done that? If so, it was a bittersweet parting gift.

He sat down on a boulder to work his feet into his boots. She'd gone; he knew it. He should have guessed it last night. That hadn't been an eager reunion, but a desperate leave-taking. He laced his boots with deliberation, before picking his way down the hill to the place Marten's wife had emerged from the day before. As he approached the doorway he heard the thin wail of a hungry baby but, again, he knew: Alwenna would not be there.

ACKNOWLEDGMENTS

In a perfect world, there would be grateful thanks here to my beta readers who were standing by ready to road test this manuscript. As it is, at a time where it seemed as if almost everything that could go wrong did go wrong, my thanks go to Phil Jourdan and Marc Gascoigne at Angry Robot, for their infinite patience.

ABOUT THE AUTHOR

After spending her formative years falling off ponies, Susan Murray moved on to rock climbing, mountains proving marginally less unpredictable than horses. Along the way she acquired a rugby-playing husband, soon followed by two daughters and a succession of rundown houses. Cumulative wear and tear prompted her to return to study, settling unfinished business with an Open University Humanities degree. She lives with her family in rural Cumbria, England, where she writes fantasy and science fiction with occasional forays into other genres.

twitter.com/pulpthorn

Join us.

twitter.com/angryrobotbooks